MESSY PERFECT

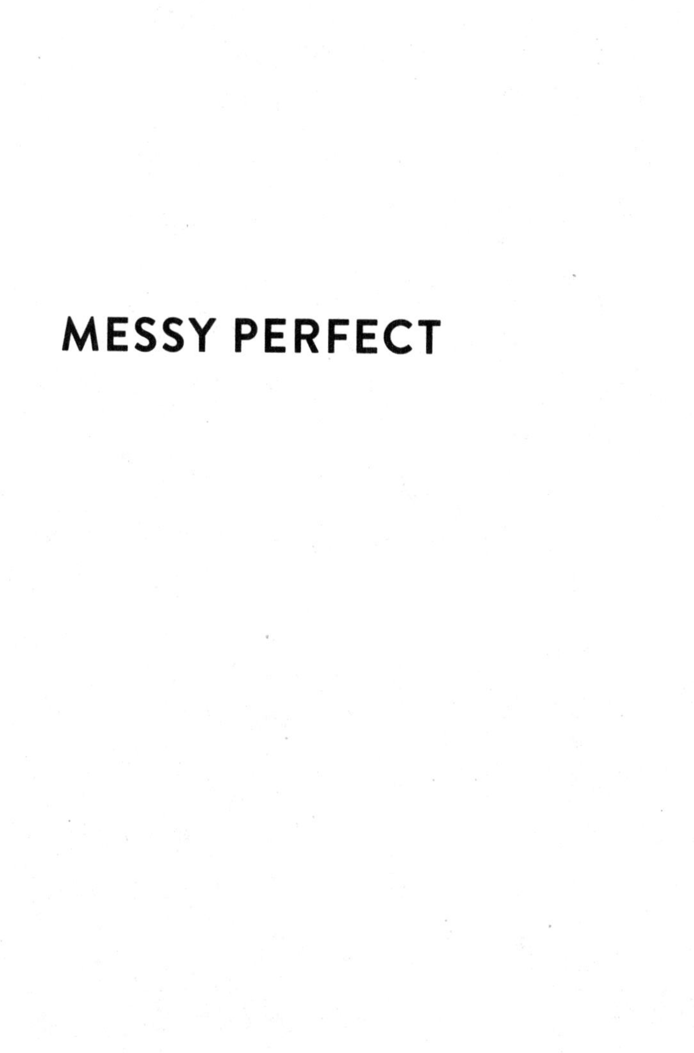

Also by Tanya Boteju

Kings, Queens, and In-Betweens

Bruised

MESSY PERFECT

TANYA BOTEJU

Quill Tree Books
An Imprint of HarperCollinsPublishers

Quill Tree Books is an imprint of HarperCollins Publishers.

Messy Perfect

For information, address HarperCollins Children's Books, a division of HarperCollins Publishers, 195 Broadway, New York, NY 10007.

Library of Congress Cataloging-in-Publication Data

Names: Boteju, Tanya, author.
Title: Messy perfect / Tanya Boteju.
Description: First edition. | New York, NY : Quill Tree Books, an imprint of HarperCollins Publishers, 2025. | Audience term: Teenagers | Audience: Ages 13 up. | Audience: Grades 10-12. | Summary: When a former friend reenrolls at their Catholic high school a few years after a homophobic bullying incident, Cassie decides to start an underground Gender and Sexuality Alliance, exploring her own sexuality in the process.
Identifiers: LCCN 2024012195 | ISBN 9780063358492 (hardcover)
Subjects: CYAC: Friendship—Fiction. | LGBTQ+ people—Fiction. | Catholic high schools—Fiction. | Schools—Fiction. | LCGFT: Queer fiction. | Novels.
Classification: LCC PZ7.1.B6755 Me 2025 | DDC [Fic]—dc23
LC record available at https://lccn.loc.gov/2024012195

Typography by David DeWitt
25 26 27 28 29 LBC 5 4 3 2 1

First Edition

To all educators and students making our schools safer for everyone. Inclusivity is a minimum. Abundance is the goal.

PROLOGUE

Ben rearranged my world from the moment he walked into it.

When he sat down next to me in the fourth grade and said, "Hi, I'm Ben," with the biggest smile on his face, I didn't know you could just do that—sit next to someone of the opposite gender and introduce yourself like it was nothing. Like you *weren't* going to look like a weirdo or start rumors that you liked that boy or girl.

Before I'd even had a chance to say hi back, he took out his multicolored stationery and started to describe a drawing he'd made, a circle of cartoonish birds in tutus twirling between jagged-looking trees. He explained—in one long breath—how he danced ballet and how one of the dances he was learning made him feel like a bird sometimes. A lisp presented itself at the end of certain words, but he didn't seem to care.

At nine, I'd never met a boy who danced ballet and had a lisp and seemed beyond comfortable talking to girls like this. It didn't feel quite right, and my brain told me this boy was odd. Between Catholic church and Catholic school and Catholic immigrant parents, I'd already learned a very specific set of rules and expectations for how to carry myself, and Ben seemed to have a completely different set of rules.

But I couldn't pull myself away from his drawing or his chatter, even if I was a little embarrassed by it all at first. Once he'd handed me a lime-green pencil from his polka-dotted pencil case, that was it. We were instantly friends, and by fifth and sixth grades, we were even closer friends. We both hung out with other kids, too—Ben was athletic enough that the boys tolerated what set him apart from them. And I forced myself to hang on to a small group of girls who gossiped and giggled over boys at lunch when I'd rather be playing ball hockey with those boys in the parking lot. Some rules were difficult to break at that age, I guess—at least when we were around other people.

When we weren't at school, though, we managed to carve out a world separate from all of that. The creek that ran right behind my house and through the school grounds became the center of that world. We used to play there constantly, exploring its waterways and grassy banks, searching for new paths and openings.

The water was shallow and slow enough that we could cross on rocks that rose above the stream or simply slap through it with bare feet or boots. On one side of the creek was the school playground. On the other side were dense bushes and tall, soft grass.

Early on, Ben and I were two spies, arranged in the thicket like crouching tigers, accompanied by notebooks and pencils.

We would hunker down in our favorite hollowed-out space in the brush, the grass cushioning us as we added to our notes. Ben would take out his bright journal and write his sentences in elegant cursive he'd learned from his mom. Not like me, who scribbled in fat, bubbly lettering—so different from the perfect print I used in class—and filled entire pages of my notebook with just one or two sentences, not caring about how big and ugly it was because no one would see it but me and Ben.

And Ben didn't care about my messy writing or the nonsense I wrote, because we both reveled in nonsense back then, making ridiculous observations like "Pecky the duck hates to get his butt wet" and "Pirates have left their rum bottles here and the rum tastes like feet."

But as time wore on, our imaginary observations became more tangible.

I'd fling a sentence across the page. "The rocks are greener today, slicker and sad," I'd read out loud, feeling fancy.

Ben started to take a little longer to write down his thoughts. I would watch him press his pencil into the paper, his tongue poking through his lips as he wrote with care and assurance.

"What did you write?" I'd ask.

"I wrote, 'Sometimes, I wish I could live right here.'"

I think we were both starting to feel that way by then—like we were building a little home for ourselves, away from the rules and expectations that just seemed to grow stronger and more rigid around us.

Midway through the sixth grade, our notations shifted to

questions and contemplations. At times, we'd abandon our notebooks altogether.

"It's annoying that I have to wear a kilt when you get to wear pants, right?" I asked once, examining the smudges of dirt on my knees.

We weren't supposed to wear our uniforms after school, especially if we were playing outside. We weren't even supposed to be *in* the creek by then, since my parents had decided it was too mucky and maybe even a little dangerous, despite the fact that the creek felt *safer* to us than most places.

Nonetheless, even though the school and creek were just behind my house, my parents wanted me to come home right after school with my younger sister, Kendra. Ben could come, too, but we were to stay put until one of my parents arrived home from work. And we weren't to roam around in the creek anymore.

We'd shunned the rule, however, swearing my sister to secrecy and setting her up with reruns of *Saved by the Bell* as we escaped to the creek, not even changing out of our school clothes in our urgency. It was like we needed to be there, at the water, in the bushes, to be these other people we were becoming. People who didn't want to wear uniforms, who questioned things we'd accepted to that point, who wanted to explore more than just the water and grass.

Ben shrugged at my kilt question and said, "Yeah. Dumb rules for girls, I guess."

"Dumb rules for girls *and* boys," I said. "Why shouldn't *you* get to wear a kilt, too?"

I giggled like it was a joke, but it wasn't really. Ben had already broken so many of those kinds of rules. He'd been dancing ballet since he was four. He still had a lisp and didn't say the gross things other boys his age said. He didn't show much interest in girls, except me. He was soft and sweet. He was periodically teased for these things, but I loved those parts of him—his softness and self-assurance had made me feel safe right from the start, like I could break some rules, too.

And I wanted to. I didn't want to wear dresses to church anymore. I wanted to go to the sixth-grade parties my parents said were too unsupervised and too late. And when the girls in my grade sent little bits of paper to a boy to ask him if he liked this girl or that, I wished I could send a note to the *girls* asking if they liked *me.*

"I can do whatever I want," Ben said, with a mixture of defiance and sass. After a moment, he added, "You can, too."

I scrunched up my nose and looked at the closed journal in my hands. "Maybe." Talking about these things here, with him, felt okay. But the rules seemed so much heftier beyond this space.

"I might not go to church anymore." I remember he said this like it was the most ordinary thing. Like he and I hadn't been going to church all our lives, hadn't been baptized and received first Communion and now sat near each other in the pews each Sunday.

We were crouching in our favorite spot by the creek, and it was March.

"Really?" I asked, a twinge of jealousy in me. Not because I didn't want to go to church anymore—I liked church, even if I was starting to question some aspects of it—but because he'd be defying his parents, and because I'd miss him sitting in the pew in front of me if he stopped coming.

He shrugged again. "Maybe. I'm not sure it's for me."

"Oh" was all I said. I guess I was trying to get my head around that kind of choice—the making of it and the repercussions that might come.

It went on like this, Ben and me, hidden away from prying eyes, becoming emboldened to share the bits of ourselves we weren't sure we could share with anyone else—the questions about God and Jesus and Mary we couldn't ask in our Catholic school, the wonderings we had about the two women who lived together in the house at the end of my street, the desire to be close to other girls and boys in ways that no one else seemed to want. With Ben, there in the creek, I was discovering new ways of being and was thrilled by the possibilities.

But we should have known our private world would crack open at some point.

When it finally did, it was May and we were nearing the end of the sixth grade.

After an annoying episode in school that morning where several girls were made to kneel on desks so our teacher could measure the distance between their kilts and knees, Ben and I had stolen away at lunch to a new spot we'd created along the creek bank—one with a bit more room to move around but that was still well hidden, or so we thought.

The school didn't allow us to go in the creek, but we went

anyway—when the most distracted teachers were on duty, and when the other kids were too absorbed in themselves to notice. But maybe we were a little careless that day. Maybe we were just annoyed and needed an escape. How else to explain the risk we took?

We'd decided to switch uniforms. We wanted to see what it felt like. We wanted to break these dumb rules others had set for us. I'd hinted to him by then that I might like girls. I already knew he liked boys—not just because of all the things that set him apart from other boys, but because of how easy it felt to talk about my own secret longings with him. Like he knew exactly how I felt.

As I climbed into his too-long school pants and he buttoned my kilt around his waist, we couldn't help our quiet giggles. We stood across from each other for a second before his face grew very serious and he said, "Oh, hold on." He rolled the waistline of the kilt a few times so the kilt rose up his thighs several inches. We looked each other up and down. We burst out laughing again, forgetting where we were. But eventually, our laughter died down.

I guess it wasn't that big a deal for me to wear pants. And maybe it wasn't even a huge deal for Ben to put on my kilt. But this wasn't something I would do with anyone else. And I knew he wouldn't, either.

The moment was over the instant we heard "Oh my God, what are you guys *doing*?"

We turned toward the voice, which was coming through the thicket to my left. We heard thrashing next, laughter, more exclamations of disbelief and disgust.

Panic invaded my chest. My heartbeat thumped into my throat. In a nonsensical decision, I started to unbutton the pants, but I saw Ben was just standing still, making no attempt at all to switch our clothing. My hands froze, but my next impulse was to escape back along the path we'd created to our spot.

I didn't have a chance, though. Four boys from our grade tumbled into the space with us, pushing at each other and snickering. Pointing at us, our clothes, and gasping with that exaggerated laughter people make when they're less amused and more intent on making other people feel bad.

My entire body tensed. I wasn't ready for whatever this was. I knew it the moment I heard the boys' voices breaking through the brush.

"Why are you guys wearing each other's clothes?"

"'Cause Ben wants to be a girl!"

"And Cassie wants to be Ben's boyfriend!"

"Are you guys gay or what?"

"Ha ha, yeah, they're *lesbians*!"

"Only homos cross-dress, freaks!"

I'd witnessed the taunts our classmates had leveled at Ben before. A jab about his lisp, a side comment about his ballet. It was bullying, of course, but we hadn't named it that yet—so convinced that this was just normal schoolyard behavior at that age. It's not like both of us hadn't put up with teasing about our ethnicities, too—Ben for being Chinese with his "ching chong" eyes and me for my "poo brown" skin. Ben just ignored these things, so I did, too. We had our space to retreat to and be safe and together.

But now we didn't. And this attention felt different. More targeted and cruel. Maybe that was just because it was also aimed at me now. Fear rose through me, right from the bottoms of my feet, into my legs and gut and chest. The words they were using were words I'd yet to use myself, but they pierced through me with their truth. *Gay. Lesbian. Homo.* The possibility of those things had felt okay here, with Ben. But those possibilities made public felt like a threat. A judgment. *Freaks.* They came with so many things I couldn't imagine fitting with the rest of my life beyond this place.

What could I do? In the face of so many loud boys and a secret, terrified self?

The words were out before I could stop them.

"It was Ben's idea, not mine! I'm *not* gay."

I could feel Ben looking at me, but he didn't say anything, and I avoided his eyes as the boys jeered and laughed at my accusation and insinuation.

"Gross!" one of them called out. "Let's get out of here before we get infected with *sin*!"

"Wait'll we tell everybody about this!"

They pushed and shoved their way out of the space and crashed through the bushes away from us.

I stripped off the pants quickly and held them out for Ben to take, staring at the ground the entire time. He did the same with the kilt. We exchanged the clothing and re-dressed in silence. My stomach lurched with fear.

The creek gurgled below us, and my body moved toward it like instinct. I worked my way through the bushes and back down the path. I didn't bother trying to find elevated rocks to step across the creek—I just plunged my school shoes right into the water and splashed to the other side. I blinked away the tears that kept trying to escape and hauled myself up the other embankment, then away toward the school entrance—fear and shame entwining around one another and into my bones.

CHAPTER ONE

I'm barely able to close the gate from my backyard before Manika, my lab-retriever mix, yanks me down the path to the playground of my old elementary school, Our Lady of Mercy. She's always eager to sniff around the monkey bars and bark at the ducks in the creek.

When we enter the playground, a few kids are hanging out on the new abstract structures made of metal instead of the giant wood-beamed pirate ship we used to play on. It's barely September and the air is already a little cooler. The sun is just starting to lower behind the school, sending the playground into shadow.

I'm not expecting to see Ben sitting there, on the swings. When I do, my footsteps falter, and I have to brace myself. His back is to me. Manika is still pulling, dying to sniff. My chest grows tight.

The last time I saw Ben was four years ago. It was the final day of sixth grade, and we'd barely spoken since the incident with the boys, despite a few pathetic attempts on my part to regain his friendship. I'd watched him walk across the small bridge that crossed the creek and then disappear behind the school. He never came back to Our Lady of Mercy after that. He left for the National Ballet School in Toronto that summer.

Since then, I'd only heard a few vague things about how he was doing. His family and mine still went to the same church. My mom still spoke with his mom from time to time, even after what happened. He was doing well. Wouldn't be home for Christmas. Too busy.

I always wanted to know more—if he was happy, if he missed home at all. If he thought about me. But I had no right to ask, so I didn't.

I watch him now, from a distance. He's leaning back and forth into his swings, and I can hear the chains clink as his swing shifts from one direction to the next. His bright yellow T-shirt billows around him as he moves. Though he's a little far from me, I can see he's grown tall—much too long for these elementary-school swings.

I tug on the leash and turn back toward my house. I didn't know he was back. I'm not prepared to see him, especially here, where we'd spent so much of our childhood together and where I'd made a mess of things. Maybe it's just Manika yanking on the leash, but I feel like I'm tilting sideways, off-balance—barely able to find a firm piece of ground to step onto. Moments from those last few weeks after he and I stopped being friends push at me, trying to break past the careful boundaries I've set up for myself.

I remember sitting in my sixth-grade classroom after lunch that day, curling and uncurling my toes inside soaking-wet shoes to keep them from freezing. I remember shivering in my chair, from cold feet but also from unease.

Giggles and whispers and pointing fingers made their way around the room quickly—the boys who'd found me and Ben had wasted no time in telling the story with as many elaborations as possible. Not just the facts: Ben was wearing a kilt. Cassie was wearing pants. But so much more: "They were acting so *gay*. Ben *loved* it. He was acting like a *girl*. Cassie said it was *his* idea!" The consequences for Ben were so much worse than for me—because he was a feminine boy in a kilt, and because I had put the blame squarely on his shoulders.

By the time the teacher started the afternoon lesson, I was just a girl in wet shoes who'd gotten mixed up with the weird gay boy. Ben sat in front of me, his body rigid, as though staying perfectly still would keep the whispers and blame from reaching him. I stared at the back of his head, frozen in my own way.

Eventually, the story made its way to the teacher, and then, because what Ben and I were doing was apparently so incompatible with the expectations set for us, the teacher made sure the principal and our parents knew.

That night my parents were very clear about how "not normal" it was for a boy to wear a kilt and for Ben and me to spend so much time together, alone like we had been—never mind how mad they were that I'd broken their trust by traipsing around the creek, and then come home with wet, ruined school shoes.

They even had the school chaplain at the time, Father Baird, speak with me. He sat me down to tell me that this kind of exploration—the kind Ben and I were doing—showed an impurity that would require the need for "reestablishing a firmer foundation of goodness."

I remember feeling at the time that the worst part wasn't what Ben and I had done—although I'd come to understand that as wrong, too—but more what *I'd* done. How quickly I'd turned on Ben when others had witnessed the smallest portion of our private world. How easy it was for me to allow my fear of anyone seeing certain parts of myself to outweigh our friendship. What kind of person does that?

Father Baird had asked me, "How will you recenter your goodness and faith, Cassie? What will you do?"

I've spent the past four years answering those questions. Making sure that whatever parts of me that caused all of this messiness—the terror in me, the weakness, the disappointment of others—remained packaged up and stored away. Those parts couldn't help me recenter goodness, so I abandoned them for what would. I focused on being a good student, a good daughter, a good Catholic. I didn't include friendship in my new focus—at least not the kind that would tempt out the messy parts of me.

But with Ben back, I'm not sure what my focus should be.

I find out from my mom that night that Ben is back for good and starting at my high school, St. Luke's. She tells me she spoke to his mom, Marianne, after their recent Catholic Women's League meeting. Marianne said Ben wanted to come home.

"Apparently he's been doing very well at ballet," Amma says, "but he wanted to have a normal high school experience." She shoves the dog food dish at me in her usual subtle way. My sister, Kendra, smirks and sticks her tongue out at me. This is *supposed* to be *her* job, but she skips out of the kitchen before I can shove the dish at her instead. Brat.

I take the dish and head to the kitchen cupboard where we keep the gigantic bag of dog food for Manika, who is stepping on my heels and already drooling.

As I scoop two mounds of food into Manika's dish, I glance at my mom to see if she's showing any signs of the concern she and my dad felt about me back then, when they found out what Ben and I had been doing, how other people were interpreting it. I can't tell, though. She's cutting up an onion for curry and just frowning in her usual way.

I shift to wondering if what Amma is telling me is the truth. Whether Ben really wants a "normal high school experience," given what he'd gone through in elementary school. After those boys told everyone what they saw, the teasing got worse. Girls offering him their kilts, boys lisping whenever he was around, more whispers of "gay" and "gross" and "weird."

I'd been mostly left alone. I'd only been wearing pants, after all. I'd made it sound like the whole thing was his idea. And I'd made sure any hints or whispers of my own transgressions were neatly packed away. Ben couldn't—wouldn't—hide his own differences, and it just made things worse.

Did he really think our high school would be any better? Or had he learned to adapt the way I had?

My careful adaptations feel fragile right now, though. Hearing this added info from my mom, seeing Ben at the park . . . All of the feelings I'd managed to layer over—with stellar grades, volunteering, church commitments, a solid social schedule, attention to rules and expectations—rise back up.

My chest seizes, and I start to cough as though I've swallowed too much water. I put the food dish down, and Manika butts her way in front of me to get at it. I continue to cough so hard that Amma leaves the cutting board to rub my back, which only makes it worse. When I finally stop, she looks at me, concerned.

"What's the matter with you?"

"I'm fine—just have something caught in my throat."

She frowns and looks at me, dubious. "Drink some water."

"I'm *fine*," I say.

But I know I'm not. These feelings—they can't be here. They'll make a mess of everything . . . unless I can prove to Ben that I'm not that person anymore, the one who can't control herself and her fears. The one who let him fend for himself.

CHAPTER TWO

"Cassie! You are an absolute angel."

Dr. Ida appears from her office as I'm tacking up a "Welcome back, St. Luke's Saints!" poster to the bulletin board beside it. I smile my biggest smile, even though I pricked my finger with one of the tacks just moments before. Even though my stomach is roiling from first-day-of-school nerves and now from all of the other feelings infiltrating my body.

But eleventh grade is no joke, and I have to be ready. I can do this. I press my thumb against the hole in my finger to stop it from bleeding all over the poster. "Good morning, Dr. Ida! Happy to help."

Any approval from Dr. Ida is more than welcome. She's a giant in our community. I mean, not in stature (she can't be over five four—my height), but in regard. She's been the principal at St. Luke's for twelve years and has belonged to our affiliated parish for more than that. She has a reputation for being fair, assertive, and brilliant. On top of all that, she's the only Black principal—of a public or private school—in the city, which feels both momentous and ridiculous all at once.

"And we're happy you're *willing* to help. Especially"—she checks her watch—"a full hour before school starts. I hope you didn't spend your last few days of summer just working on these signs, though." She places her hands on her hips and tilts her head, a small smile on her lips.

"Oh, not at all. I had a great summer! Prolific, even!" I answer with an SAT word—for practice and to impress Dr. Ida—and also with a brightness that the St. Luke's teachers have always noted on my report card comments. *Cassie's bright attitude brings energy to our classroom. Cassie shows a light and cheerful demeanor.* My parents have always stressed the importance of good manners and positive contributions, so these accolades are almost as important to them as the good grades that follow. Almost.

"Prolific! Wow. What have you been getting up to?" Dr. Ida asks, straightening out a photo I'd just pinned to the board.

In reality, I *did* spend the past few days making decor to help spruce up the school for the first week of classes. I like to take initiative like this—I feel it gives me a special kind of status among the staff at St. Luke's. But immersing myself in poster paints and cheerful signs also helped to distract me from the waves of imbalance and nausea that kept rolling through me.

I quickly glance at the rest of the photos to make sure they're all straight before replying, "I finished AP Chem, volunteered with the church—"

"And went to the beach and watched some good movies and hung out with your lovely sister and played with puppies, I hope?" She folds her arms and has an amused look on her face.

I falter, but only for a moment. *Right. All work and no play doesn't please the masses, Cassie.* I tighten my ponytail out of habit and reply, "Oh, yes, of course! Lots of beach time." Truly, I only went to the beach twice this summer, and only then to show my face to other St. Luke's kids and pop a few photos onto social media. Balancing work ethic with social practices is very tricky business, but I'd spent years perfecting my balance of "school-life Cassie" with "church-life Cassie," "social-life Cassie," and "family-life Cassie."

I grin and really try to sell it. "I love Spanish Banks best. Such gorgeous sunsets. What about you? How was your summer?" Adults *love* it when teenagers ask about them.

"Oh! It was lovely, thank you. I finally made a dent in my book stack."

"I'm glad to hear it," I say. "You deserve it!"

Some of my classmates probably see me as a suck-up, but that's fine with me. I'd rather be seen as *too* good than not good enough.

Dr. Ida smiles at me. Even with her hair in its customary tight bun, her expressions are almost always warm and friendly. "Well, thank you—I *do* deserve it, don't I?"

We both laugh more than we need to and then stand awkwardly for a few moments, staring at my display.

Thankfully, Dr. Ida says, "I'm off to a meeting. Try to enjoy your first day, okay? And have a great year!"

"I will!" I say as she moves past me with purpose. *I'm determined to.*

And then, it's minutes before the first bell, and I am laser focused. I get to my AP English Lit classroom before everyone else to make sure I have time to say hi to Ms. Miller. I'm going to get 5s on all my AP exams this year, no matter what.

Though my anticipation at seeing Ben is simmering just below the surface, I've become very good at compartmentalizing. It's a necessity for success, I've learned. As Ms. Miller begins the first class of the year, I force the unease invading me into the back of my brain and try to bring AP English and eleventh grade to the front. I sit up in my chair and focus. I smile at my returning peers. I raise my hand and answer questions and talk about the summer reading with confidence. I win my first class of the year!

Unfortunately, compartmentalizing can only take you so far, especially when what you're trying to keep at bay is right in front of your face.

At break, I say a quick hello to our amazing receptionist, Ms. Sylvia (because school receptionists should never be ignored), but bypass the twelfth-grade class presidents handing out welcome-back cookies in the foyer, because I need to get to the bio classroom and stake out one of the tables at the front. Mr. Asmaro, the bio teacher, likes to mutter and write in tiny lettering on the board, so having the best seat in the house is not only preferable, but essential in this case.

When I walk in, though, I freeze at the door. I see Ben's lanky body facing away from me. He's standing near the back of the room, peering into the aquarium that houses our axolotl, Sal.

I wonder if I should turn around and leave, but my feet won't move.

I notice his hair—it's so much longer than it used to be. Black waves reaching almost to the bottom of his neck and tucked behind his ear. The profile of his face is set, strong. He's biting down, engrossed in the watery scene in front of him.

I think, *He was your friend.*

My body feels . . . blurry. I can see him clearly, though, and he's just looking into the tank, one finger pressed against the glass.

I'm about to turn to leave—I can forgo the best seat to save myself from completely blurring into an abyss right now—but three girls in my grade stream into the classroom around me, their voices loud and obvious as they talk about some party they went to the previous night.

Their party talk pauses long enough for Nana to say to me, "Cassie! What's up?" as she passes me, and for Sara to nudge me playfully with her shoulder and add, "Yeah, why're you just standing here, Cassie?"

I will myself into clarity and grin as big as I can. "Oh, hey, you guys. I was just"—I quickly glance around me—"checking out Mr. A's meme wall." In reality, I think Mr. Asmaro's meme wall is tepid humor at best.

Nana takes a quick glance at the wall and says, "He really needs to update those."

They move as a unit to a table at the back of the classroom. I can tell they're eyeing up Ben, who's a new, tall, good-looking boy and therefore of great interest.

Wrong tree, folks.

Ben's gone back to observing Sal, but I know he's seen me, and I'm a mess of thoughts.

What's my game plan here? I don't know how I wanted it to be—the first time Ben and I met after all this time—but this is not it. I wish there were more people around. I wish there was no one around. I wish I'd prepared more for this moment. I wish he didn't remind me so much of his sixth-grade self standing there in his St. Luke's uniform, which is only slightly different from his elementary-school uniform.

I know that whatever I do now, I can't leave, so I make my way to the spot I wanted, front row and center, and heave my backpack onto the chair. I try to regain some balance and move my feet to the end of the row. I turn and continue walking toward Ben.

I can do this. I *have* to do this. So much depends on me doing this.

The axolotl is wagging its body back and forth behind the glass, suspended in the water. Ben has the smallest smile on his face, and for a moment, I think, *This might be okay.* It's been four years. He's gone off on an exciting adventure in another city and had a whole other life. Maybe sixth grade and the creek and my mistakes are just distant blips on his radar.

"Uh, hey," I say, because it's all my mouth can do.

He glances at me. The tiny smile disappears. My brief bump of hope fades with it.

Without standing up straight, without looking away from the tank, he says, "Hey."

I stare at Sal for a moment, glad that at least he's here, too. "So . . . you're back," I say, because I like to state the obvious.

"Yup."

"How—"

"Hi!"

Suddenly, Sara, Nana, and Roxy are around us, eagerness on their faces, their eyes bright and on Ben.

"You two know each other?" Sara asks, glancing at me, then back at Ben.

I wait for Ben to say something, wondering what it will be, but he just unbends his long body and turns toward the others. He shifts the backpack hanging off his shoulders. Stuffs his hands into his pockets.

It's getting awkward, so I finally answer. "Yes! Yeah. From elementary school."

"Oh! Which one? All three of us went to Bishop's," Nana says.

"Um, Our Lady of Mercy," I say. When I invoke our elementary school, my stomach tightens. I don't really want Ben to think about that time or place. At least not the bad parts.

"How come you're just coming to St. Luke's now?" Roxy asks. "Where were you before?"

Ben replies, "A school in Toronto."

He still has a lisp, I notice. He doesn't mention it was the National Ballet School, and I wonder if he's shy, modest, or embarrassed to share that part. Or scared.

"That's cool," Sara says. She's looking at me now, her eyes widening and flicking to Ben. I realize this is some teenage code for something I'm probably not very good at. She wants me to keep the conversation going or connect her with Ben somehow, but I don't even know how to connect *me* with Ben.

When I don't say anything, Sara gets exasperated (it only takes about five seconds) and says, "So, like, did you two keep in touch all this time?"

"Yeah, were you, like, pen pals?" Roxy adds, with a friendly smile.

It's light conversation, but it feels heavy to me. I can feel Ben looking at me, and that feels heavy, too. Because we didn't keep in touch. Because how could we? Because I ruined our friendship and couldn't possibly reach out to him after that.

"Ha . . . no" is all I say.

More awkward seconds.

Then Ben's shoulders are suddenly straight and his hands are out of his pockets and his thumbs are hooked into his backpack straps. "We weren't really friends," he says.

The others' faces are an array of surprise, embarrassment (likely for me), and uncertainty. The tightness in my stomach twists into something more painful. My eyes start to sting, and I blink to keep them from tearing up here, in the middle of this classroom, in front of these people. In front of Ben, who isn't my friend. Who never was, apparently.

"Oh, well, we can't all be friends, right?" Nana says, following with forced laughter, which the others quickly copy. Even Ben offers a smirk.

I want to just turn to leave, but my legs don't feel solid enough. I should just laugh along with the others. I should just act like this is all totally normal—it is, in some ways. Ben could just be stating a fact. People from elementary schools *aren't* always friends.

But we were.

We were.

I take too long to respond. Sara says, "Uh, cool, well—if you're looking for friend options . . ." She indicates herself and the other two. They all laugh again. Ben lifts his chin in acknowledgment.

Mr. Asmaro enters the room with a steaming mug of coffee and yells, "Hey, keeners!" He sees Ben and adds, "And who do we have here?"

As Mr. A makes his way over to Ben to introduce himself, Sara and the others disperse back to their seats. I do the same, but not before trying to make one last moment of eye contact with Ben. He's not looking at me, though. Why would he? He thinks who I was at the creek that day is who I always was. And who I am now.

I have to show him it's not.

CHAPTER THREE

The rest of the school day is a haze of absorbing an absurd amount of information during classes while also trying not to fall apart after my interaction with Ben. I don't want his words to impact me this much, but they do. It's the first time since being at St. Luke's that I feel like I don't have a handle on a situation. And it's the first time I've had confirmation of what I've been scared of—Ben hates me. Because he knows who I am at my worst. And with him here, I'm scared I won't be able to keep those terrible parts boxed up anymore.

His presence makes me yearn—against my will—for some of those moments we had when we were together, in private. When it felt easy and natural to talk about complicated things and flout the rules we'd been taught. But how can I have that without all the threats that come along with it? The way people would see us? The way I would act when they do?

At the end of the day, despite these worries clouding my brain, I have to put my head down and plod my way through an after-school meeting with the student government. The group of ten class presidents was voted in at the end of the previous school year—one girl and one boy from each grade (because things are still very gendered like that around here, but what can you expect?).

Today's meeting is a brief one to "touch base," as Natasha and James, the twelfth-grade class presidents, like to say every chance they get. We play three different icebreaker games, and I'm usually exceptional at these, but today they feel like a special kind of hell. All I want to do is get home and set my mind to figuring out what to do about Ben and this messiness I feel.

But I suck it up as always and push through.

We're brainstorming ideas for fall events—making a wish list of possibilities—and James says, "Sky's the limit, my dudes," from the front of the room, where he's ready to record all of our ideas on the whiteboard.

"I'm not a dude," one of the ninth-grade class presidents says. I think her name is Yumi, but I was too distracted during icebreakers to remember. I notice that the eighth grader next to her—who has the most boisterous head of curly black hair—smiles at her comment like he's just heard the greatest thing of his life. Honestly, I'm impressed that a ninth grader is bold enough to say anything right now, too.

James looks at her for a few seconds, then sighs. "Think of it as a term of endearment. It's basically gender-neutral at this point anyway, like 'guys.'" He looks away from her and searches for someone with an idea to contribute. I notice that Yumi rolls her eyes, and I kind of love it.

We make a long list of ideas—I contribute only one because I'm already starting to compile a mental list of ideas for sorting things out with Ben. Unfortunately, that list has exactly zero viable items on it so far.

When I finally get home that night, I volunteer to take Manika out for her evening walk, even though it's my sister's night to walk her and even though I already have a ton of homework, like I knew I would. But I need to move. I need a little air. I need to clear my brain so I can figure out what to do next.

I have a few routes I take when I'm out walking with Manika, but tonight I'm drawn back to the creek. Maybe being there will motivate my brain to get to work.

Or maybe I just want to be close to my good memories of Ben and me, because even though the creek was where our friendship ended, there was so much before that moment that was good. I know there was. After what Ben said today, I need to remind myself of those things, to remind myself that we *were* friends and we can be again. I just need to figure out how to make that happen without also ruining everything else good I've built.

When Manika and I reach the playground, no one else is there, so I secure her leash to a pole and extend it so she can sniff to her heart's content. She's prone to running away, so we can't really let her loose. By the time I reach the bridge, she's already rolling in something I'll have to wash off her later.

I took for granted the little bridge that crosses the creek when I went to school here, but standing on it now, I realize how quaint it is. Only about ten to twelve slats of wood lie side by side and extend across the creek. My footsteps make a hollow thunking sound as I move across it. Iron railings guard the sides, low enough that I can fold my arms on top of them. It is definitely the kind of bridge a troll could live under if this were a fairy tale.

I watch the water gurgle and splash beneath me for a while, disappearing beneath the bridge and my feet. It seems darker now—harder to see the rocks and mud past the surface. Ben and I used to play "Pooh Sticks" here. We would each drop a stick into the water from one side of the bridge and then rush across to the other side to see whose stick reappeared first downstream.

I find a stick now and drop it into the creek. I hurry to the other side of the bridge, but the stick doesn't reappear. Or maybe it flowed away so quickly I missed it? I wait for a few more seconds, but all that appears are leaves and small bits of trash, tumbling across the surface of the water.

The creek moves so much faster than before—I'm not sure I could get a proper footing if I tried to walk through it the way we used to. I stay there for a long time, leaning over the railing and letting my eyes get lost in the twists and turns of the water. It's not until I hear Manika's impatient whimpers cut across the schoolyard that I realize it's getting dark, and I still have no idea how I'm going to fix any of this.

CHAPTER FOUR

The next time I see Ben, it's in biology class on Friday. I show up early, as always—he walks in just at the bell. I sit at the front; he sits at the back.

That's okay, though, because as I looked through my course syllabi last night, noting down project due dates and tests in my agenda, I finally had an idea for how to make things better with Ben.

I saw that Mr. Asmaro is assigning a paired project today (even though it's only our second class). Mr. A (he likes us to call him "Mr. A" because I think he thinks it sounds cooler or something) believes in project-based learning almost entirely. I don't mind this, but it's easier to just study for a test and get my As that way. He also believes in paired and group projects. I almost always hate this. I don't love depending on others for my grades.

But, as much as it freaks me out to place myself in this situation,

I realize that if I'm going to fix anything with Ben, I need to be able to spend time with him. And he is clearly not going to pursue time alone with me, so I have to make it happen myself.

I make sure to get to class before anyone else and am thankful to find Mr. A alone, smiling at something on his laptop. He's obviously checking Facebook or whatever older people do, so I don't feel bad about interrupting.

"Mr. A?"

He looks up, sees me, and slowly turns his laptop a little away from me, which just proves he's looking at weird memes or something.

He grins and says, "What's up, Cass-o-lass?"

Ugh. I hate this nickname. He's the only one who uses it, and I have no idea where he got it from.

But I grin back and say, "How are you?" I learned early on that teachers do *not* like it when students just launch into their requests and questions without at least *pretending* to be interested in their teacher's well-being.

"Super! Thanks for asking. You? Busy as ever, I guess?"

"Yeah, pretty much," I say, and then move on to what I really came here for. "I was just wondering if you were choosing pairs for the project today, or if we could choose our own pairs?"

"Ever the eager beaver!" He winks at me. "I'm assigning pairs randomly, as usual. Why?"

"Well, I was hoping you might pair me with Ben—the new guy? He's a friend from elementary school, and I've been wanting to connect with him a bit and help him settle in." None of this is a lie. My only worry is that Mr. A is going to think I'm crushing on Ben or something.

Luckily, most teachers here know that romance is definitely not my focus.

"Oh! That's nice of you. Yeah, I think I can swing that."

"Awesome—thank you so much." I'm about to ask him to keep this conversation between us, but then decide it might look suspicious. I'll just have to hope he makes things look casual.

Once class begins, Mr. A reviews some of the stuff from last class and then launches into the project, which is meant to introduce us to protists and then turn into a whole thing about changes in environments due to pollution.

I think Mr. A's going to keep things pretty cool as he reads the assigned partners from a list, but then he says, "And by special request, Ben, you're with Cassie," and my stomach instantly tightens. *Shit.* I can't bring myself to look back at Ben. I don't want to see what his face is doing.

Once Mr. A reads off all the names, he says, "Okay, follow me!"

In addition to project-based learning and group work, Mr. A *also* believes in what he calls "field trips," which are mostly walks around the neighborhood to look at nature. I *can* enjoy these, unless we have work due and could really use the class time to do it.

We follow him out of the classroom, down the stairs to the first floor, and out through the front entrance to the courtyard.

We stop by the maple trees that border the school parking lot. Ben is on the other side of the group, probably trying to limit the time he has to spend with me now that he thinks I'm stalking him, which is only partially true.

"All right, gang, since it's early in the year, and this project is *very* important, we're going to spend some time getting to know our partners first. Learning how to work with another person will be as important as the content, you get me?"

Everyone nods or mumbles a droning "Yes, Mr. A." I nod my head with enthusiasm, though. Teachers love it when you nod like you're the best active listener in the universe.

"Okay, see all these big, beautiful leaves starting to fall? Pick one you like and then find a spot close by to sit or stand with your partner. We're going to gift the leaves to our partners, but we have to give them a story *with* the leaf. And the story has to be about a time you either 'fell' or a time you 'rose'—however you want to interpret that. Get it?"

What the hell, Mr. A? This is some English-teacher-level, touchy-feely nonsense. It does *not* belong in science class.

Nonetheless, everyone disperses to find their leaves.

As I search for a leaf, I glance over at Ben and see that he's already got a leaf in his hand and is leaning against a tree. He must've just picked up the first one he saw. I don't want to keep him waiting, so I grab one that's a couple of feet away and walk over to him, my body vibrating.

"Hey," I say, stopping a few feet from him.

He's twirling the leaf by its stem between his thumb and pointer finger. He says "Hey" back without looking up.

"I guess you're stuck with me," I say, hoping to say something true but also light.

"Sounds like you stuck me with you."

A nervous laugh emits itself from my mouth. "Um . . . yeah. I just . . ." What the hell do I say now? I decide bypassing this part of the conversation is the best option.

"Do you want to just do this here, or go sit somewhere?" I ask.

"Here's fine."

"Do you want to go first? Or should I?" I ask, not wanting to go at all.

"You go."

I have zero idea what I'm about to say, which is not my forte (SAT word). "Oh, okay. Um." I take a step closer, partly because I don't want anyone else to hear whatever I'm about to say, and partly because I want Ben to look up. He doesn't.

A time I fell or a time I rose? There's one obvious fall I could talk about, but that's the last thing I want in Ben's mind. I try to use this opportunity to start convincing him I've "risen" from that time.

"Okay . . . okay. Um . . . a time I rose was when . . . I won the community service award in ninth grade? I'd never really volunteered anywhere but church before, but I signed up to do a bunch of stuff like organizing food at a shelter and playing board games with elderly people, and ended up getting the award."

When I hear the words, they sound like something my sister, Kendra, would kick me for saying. She'd probably say I was humblebragging and roll her eyes. But I just hope Ben will see something in them.

From the look on his face, though, he couldn't care less about my volunteer award.

Fail, Cassie.

"Anyway," I say, and shake my head. "Here." I hand him the leaf.

He takes a second before plucking it out of my hand.

"What about you?" I ask.

He pushes his lips around a little, and I realize he could easily talk about the same fall that immediately came to my mind, but thankfully he doesn't. Instead, he says, "Fell on my ass in the middle of a performance once. Only person to mess up that bad all season."

I'm surprised he's said this much, and I wait for him to say more, but he just holds out the leaf he picked up, still not looking at me. I take it.

"That sucks," I say. Because it does.

He shrugs. "Is what it is."

I'm about to step closer and say more, but Mr. A does one of those sharp finger-to-lips whistles. Like dogs, we all stop what we're doing and gravitate toward him. I try to stay near Ben as we do, though.

"All right, team, hopefully you learned a new tidbit about your partner. Interesting to see who talks about their 'falls' and who chooses to talk about their 'risings.' Nothing good or bad about either—just something to notice."

I really don't remember Mr. A being so into social-emotional learning before. Must've done some expensive professional development over the summer or whatever.

As we walk back to class, I make myself continue our conversation, if it can be called that.

"How were your first couple of days?" I ask, trying to keep up with his longer strides.

He shrugs. Again.

"What other classes are you—"

"Let's just do this project, all right?" he says, hands in his pockets, voice curt.

I flinch and take a quick look around to make sure no one heard him, but my eyes start to sting and I aim them at the ground.

I'm not that person anymore. Please don't act like I am.

I shake off the sting and pick up my pace so I'm even with him. I try to focus on the project, like he said. "Okay, but I should warn you—Mr. A likes to assign loooong projects, just to torture us."

He finally glances over—but it's just a glance.

We continue to follow the others in silence toward our classroom. I'm overwhelmed with the need to say so much more, but also with so much doubt about what to say. So I say nothing and soon we're back in the classroom, and he's back at his desk and I'm back at mine.

Mr. A explains that we'll be gathering samples, running experiments, and preparing a presentation. It's a project that will extend well into next month, apparently. He says he'll give us some class time, but most of the work will need to be completed outside of class, which makes me equal parts excited and nervous, given that I'll be spending so much time with Ben, whether he likes it or not. So far, it seems like "not," and I realize I need a new plan.

"This doesn't mean I forgive you, you know."

Ben was twisted in his seat, looking back at me from the desk in front of mine. I remember thinking that he sounded so mature, talking about forgiveness at age eleven. Most of what we'd learned had focused on sin.

"I know." Because I did know. I knew that lending someone an eraser couldn't actually erase all the crappy things you'd done to them. And that even though he was willing to use the eraser, he could still hate you for all of those things.

He turned back to face the front of the classroom. It was only a couple of days after the incident at the creek. We hadn't spoken at all since then, but others in the class were still talking about it any chance they could get.

I don't remember who my teacher was, or what she (they were almost all women) was trying to teach us, or who else was around. All I remember is offering my eraser to Ben and feeling a lift in my chest when he accepted it. But I also remember him keeping his forgiveness to himself, and I remember staring at the back of his head and understanding perfectly why he would.

CHAPTER FIVE

At lunch, I'm eating at my usual spot just outside the admin offices. I like to study there so that any admin walking by sees me working my butt off.

My course load this year is as heavy as our academic counselor would allow. I took AP Chemistry over the summer, and now I'm taking biology, physics, history, AP Macroeconomics, AP English, and AP French. Plus a religion course that all students take every year. I allow myself one spare to make more room for studying during the day.

I'm evening out my sciences and humanities to keep my options open. I'm leaning toward something in law or business, but am unsure exactly what yet. I hate that I'm not sure—everything about this school makes it seem like we *should* be sure by tenth grade. Luckily, my parents don't pressure me to figure it all out now, though whatever courses I *am* taking better be practical and my grades better be excellent.

I also have one slightly frivolous extracurricular: volleyball.

I started playing because everyone was playing *something* in eighth grade, and I was determined to fit in at this new school. I'd already spent my last year at Our Lady of Mercy taking on as many extracurriculars as possible, shedding anyone's thoughts about me as a freak—someone who spent all their extra time in a creek with a guy everyone thought had been too different from them.

I keep playing volleyball now because it feels like a bit of balance alongside my academics, volunteering, etc. The sweat feels good. And it doesn't hurt that a team-oriented athletics activity will help round out my university applications.

I finish my sandwich and get up to pee. On my way out of the bathroom, I hear, "We just wanted to let you know this was happening and maybe invite any St. Luke's students who are interested to join in the fun? We'll be decorating after school today."

I don't recognize the voice, but then, I don't know everyone in the school, either. It's definitely someone around my age. Something about their tone reminds me of when I'm being polite to adults but don't really want to be. It's Mrs. Keenan's voice I hear next. She's our vice principal.

"I don't think there's anyone here who will want to help with that, no."

Mrs. Keenan's voice is curt and maybe even a little annoyed. This isn't completely unusual. Mrs. Keenan is known at St. Luke's to be way harsher than Dr. Ida.

"Oh? You don't have a GSA? A Gay-Straight Alliance? Or we call ours a Gender and Sexuality Alliance, because, you know, everyone has a gender and sexuality, right?"

My body stills at the open entrance to the bathroom, hidden from whoever's talking. This is a different voice than the first, and this person is barely trying to cover up their impudence (SAT word). And what they're saying is sending ripples of nervous energy through me. A girl in the grade below me enters the bathroom, and I quickly pretend I'm checking my phone but keep listening.

The person's last comment must have thrown Mrs. Keenan for a loop, because she takes a few seconds to respond. "Thank you for coming by," she finally says, her voice less than thankful. "The road is public property. If Pinetree wishes to draw a rainbow across it, that's up to you. St. Luke's will not be participating in your display. Now, please—I have another meeting."

Pinetree is the public high school across the street, and the three people who appear in my view—all dressed in regular clothes, not uniforms—must be Pinetree students. They head toward the stairs leading down to the main entrance. I can only see them from the back, but then one—a white girl with a mix of shaggy and shaved hair—turns and waves. I guess she's waving at Mrs. Keenan, and she has a grin on her face. "Thanks! Hope your students enjoy Pinetree's Solidarity Week display!"

Her words are clearly meant to needle Mrs. Keenan, which gives me a small thrill, even as my belly still wavers with tension. Mrs. Keenan doesn't say anything. I wait a few more seconds until the three disappear down the stairs and I'm sure Mrs. Keenan has retreated to her office, too, then I head back to my table.

I sit down and try to refocus on my textbooks, but it's virtually impossible. There's not a lot of talk at St. Luke's about "gender and sexuality." Our health classes basically ignore it in all its forms, and we even have teachers who still hype up abstinence. And from the little I understand about GSAs, I can't imagine one here. I know it's not like this at all Catholic schools, but I guess St. Luke's is just firmly grasping on to tradition or whatever.

I'm not that mad about it, though. I don't really need any reminders or opportunities to talk about that stuff. I used to insinuate I liked this boy or that in eighth and ninth grades, just to be part of the conversation when others were going on about their crushes. But as school got harder, I realized I didn't really have to put much effort into that sort of thing. I could focus on academics and extracurriculars. This is less complicated on so many levels anyway.

But for the rest of the day, I can't get the three Pinetree students out of my head. All through history class, I wonder what those three students are like, given that they walked into the Catholic school across the street to talk to the admin about creating a Solidarity Week display outside their school, which apparently includes rainbows and their Gender and Sexuality Alliance. I wonder what exactly their display will look like.

By the time the final bell goes, my curiosity nudges ahead of my nerves and prompts me to find answers to my wonderings.

CHAPTER SIX

Usually on Fridays I'd head straight home to make a dent in my homework so that my weekend is less stressful. But today I find myself loitering in the library for a while, then heading outside once most people have left for the day so I can loiter outside the gym.

The immediate neighborhood around St. Luke's has three other schools in it. Pinetree is right across the street and is about three times the size of St. Luke's. Their size means their campus is much bigger than ours, and that they offer more programs and initiatives than we do.

They also seem to offer more when it comes to diversity and inclusion, as evidenced by the abundance of color that meets my eyes now.

Across the street, rainbow floodlights beam up into the long windows at the front of the school. Pride flags hang from the front gate. A glittering rainbow banner announces that it's Solidarity Week.

What the hell. The only rainbow signage I've ever seen at St. Luke's is on the office door of our librarian, Mr. Reyes, but I'm pretty sure that's just a splash of color, not any kind of signal to the gays.

My mouth falls open a little, taking in the sight. It's so bright and colorful. I try to imagine a rainbow over the entryway of St. Luke's or . . . a feather boa around the statue of Mary? I let myself smile at the thought, but then remind myself that none of those images are appropriate or possible.

I don't know why I do it, given that my rapid heartbeat is telling me to keep myself safely next to the gym, but I wander a little closer to the road, staying on the St. Luke's side of the street. I surreptitiously (SAT word) snap a couple of photos of Pinetree on my phone—not that I'll do anything with them.

As I put my phone away, a girl walks out of the front entrance of Pinetree carrying two white plastic buckets in each hand. It's the girl with the cool haircut who got sassy with Mrs. Keenan earlier. I tuck my phone away and watch her walk—or march—to the road like she's on a mission. She's wearing a blue hoodie, acid-wash jeans that end at her lower calves, and burgundy Doc Martens. She drops the buckets on the sidewalk, pries one open, and takes out a big purple piece of chalk. She's about to crouch down and start drawing on the street when she sees me.

"Hello? Can I help you?" she asks, eyebrows raised.

I look around me like a nerd. My mouth stops working for a second before I can get out "Pardon?"

"I'm about to draw a rainbow crosswalk from here"—she points to the road at her feet—"to there." She points at the curb

I'm standing on across the street from her. "You're not going to call the pope police or something while I draw, are you?"

"Oh, um . . . no, I . . ." My hands fidget with my kilt like I'm prone to do when I'm nervous.

Her eyes travel to my hands and kilt. Her eyebrows lower a little, and she tilts her head. I imagine she thinks I'm a little pathetic and feels sorry for me. "You go to St. Luke's, right?" she asks.

"Yes . . . yeah."

"Well, your vice principal didn't seem so keen on us doing all this." She waves one arm behind her at the rainbow decor.

"Oh" is all I can get out at first. Part of me is dying to cross the street and continue talking to this girl. I want to know more about what she's doing—why she's doing it. But a larger part of me is rigid with apprehension. What if someone sees me talking to her in front of all these rainbows?

She cocks an eyebrow at me. "Yeah, 'Oh.' Must suck going to a school that can't even embrace a rainbow crosswalk." She crouches down and begins scraping the chalk across the road, leaving a purple streak, and I guess she must be done with me.

But I can't seem to get my feet to walk away. I can't seem to stop my mouth from speaking, either, because it's suddenly moving and saying, "It doesn't suck."

The girl looks up from her purple and frowns. "No?"

I look both ways and start to cross the street. I can't believe I'm crossing the street, but I am. I step up onto the sidewalk beside her, and she cranes her neck to look at me. Her face is full of skepticism. She has a few light freckles across her cheeks.

"I mean, it's a good school," I say, and I know I sound timid. I clear my throat and try to sound a bit more sure. "Just because we're a Catholic school doesn't mean everyone is going to hate all of this." I indicate the colorful entrance.

She stands and narrows her eyes at me. Her hands land on her hips. "Really? Do you have any queer stuff at your school at all? 'Cause I sure didn't see any when I was there today. Do you ever get to talk about it or anything?"

"Uh . . ."

"I can't imagine it's fun to be gay at your school, is it? Is anyone even out?"

"Well, there are people who are . . . questioning?" I say in a questioning tone that I wish was more convincing.

"And out?"

"Well, no, but we definitely have, um, LGBTQ+ folks at the school." *I assume.* Just saying that acronym out loud makes me nauseous. I worry this rainbow-spreading girl will see right through me.

"And . . . ?" she says.

"And . . . ?" I should have just kept my mouth shut. This girl is supremely confident.

"And is your school a safe space for them to be out or not?"

I hate the uncertainty that flashes through my body right now. I can't get my head around her questions fast enough, and everything she's saying is striking something deep inside of me. I'm in it now, though, so I try to force these feelings away.

"I mean . . . people are kind to each other—just as much as any other school," I say. "No one is running around condemning any one lifestyle . . ."

She visibly flinches when I say "lifestyle," and then her expression grows hard. "Being queer isn't a lifestyle. And being 'kind' isn't the same as creating safety or justice."

She lowers herself back down to the pavement and starts to draw again. I can see her jaw clenched from where I'm now standing, completely dismissed.

I mutter, "Sorry," and start to walk back across the road, but as I do, someone shouts, "Yo!" When I turn back to look, two other people are exiting Pinetree's front doors.

"You started already?" yells a kid wearing what looks like red velour jogging pants, an oversize T-shirt with hamburgers all over it, and a purple backward ball cap. He's pale and skinny and swimming in his clothes. He jogs over to the girl with the chalk.

He's followed by another girl with light brown skin who's dressed with a little less flair—baggy beige cargo pants, black crop top. She doesn't seem to be in a rush—just saunters after the boy.

"Y'all were taking forever!" Judgy Girl says in response.

I pause for a moment. Even with my body still trembling from my interaction with the girl, I guess I'm still curious about what will ensue with this trio of public-school kids creating a rainbow bridge to our side of the street. I continue on to the St. Luke's side, though, so I'm not standing in the middle of the road like a fool. I start scrolling on my phone just to have something to do, but can't help watching the others.

When Pale Kid gets to Judgy Girl, he says, "We were *coming*."

Then he rolls his eyes and grabs a piece of red chalk. He looks both ways and walks to my side. When he sees me standing there, watching him like a creep, he pauses a couple feet away from the curb.

"Hi," he says, and smiles.

I swallow because my mouth has become so, so dry but quickly get out a "Hi" back, since his greeting is much more friendly than what's-her-name with the purple chalk. I also *really* love his pants. They look so soft and red and cozy. In my fixation, I add, "Your chalk matches your pants."

The boy looks at the chalk in his hand and then at his pants. He shrugs and says, "I guess I like this end of the rainbow." Then he grins at me again.

His features are sharp but his warmth is soft, and I grin back. I can feel my nerves and discomfort over the previous conversation with Judgy Girl start to dissolve.

"Wanna help?" he asks.

"Me?" I say, my eyes involuntarily flicking to my uniform.

"Yeah, why not?"

Maybe it's the boy's red pants, maybe it's what Judgy Girl said about creating safety and how it makes me think of Ben, or maybe it's something else . . . something that I hate thinking about—but whatever it is, it makes me say, "Okay."

He grins again and introduces himself. "I'm Sam. They/them. Cohead of the Pinetree High GSA." They do this nerdy little bow and hand flick that makes me laugh.

I introduce myself back, even though I'm already replaying

how many times I called them "he" in my head. I pray to God I can remember to use their proper pronouns.

"Go grab some chalk—there's more red. We can do this end together first." I look to the other side, where the buckets of chalk are next to Judgy Girl and where the other girl in the crop top is now using a ruler to space out the stripes for the rainbow. I hesitate. It's only a few feet, but the thought of crossing it to Judgy Girl makes it seem like miles of eternal damnation.

Sam sees my hesitation and appears to know what I'm thinking. "Halle can be a bit harsh, I know. But she's harmless . . . mostly. Come on." They wave me forward and cross back to the other side. I follow . . . slowly.

"Halle, this lovely human is going to help us. We'll be finished in no time! More red, please."

Halle looks up, the furrows in her brow so deep, I think she might lose her eyebrows in them. "*You're* going to help?"

"Um, yes . . . yeah. If that's okay?" I say, focusing on Sam and not Halle's piercing eyes.

Crop Top smiles and says, "Of course it's okay! I'm Naisha, but call me Nai. She/her. That's Halle. Also she/her. We're the GSA heads . . . which really just means we get stuck with all the grunt work while everyone else in the GSA gets to enjoy the spoils of glitter and jelly beans and rainbows."

I smile back at Nai and manage to get out "I'm Cassie. Um . . . she and her." I can't believe I'm doing this. My stomach can't believe I'm doing this.

Nai says, "We were at your school earlier today."

"Oh, yeah . . . I think I saw you, actually."

Halle pipes up, still scratching the chalk against the road like she's mad at it. "Well, then, I guess you saw your admin basically tell us she doesn't want anything to do with rainbows or our GSA."

"Well, that's not exactly how things went down," Sam says, "but yeah, I guess y'all don't have a Gender and Sexuality Alliance at your school?"

"Uh, no . . . it's a Catholic school—"

"So?" Now Halle's glaring up at me again, and I wish we could just move on to creating rainbows already.

Thankfully, Nai steps in and says, "I guess it *would* be harder to start a GSA at a Catholic school . . . but not impossible!"

"Ever thought about it?" Sam asks me.

I think about it now. And I think about Ben. I think about how I have to convince him that I'm someone he can depend on. That I'm better than I was back then. A *good* friend. The kind who will make him feel safe instead of leaving him to fend for himself.

"Um, well . . . I hadn't, but . . ."

A GSA might be a way to fix things with him. But the thought of aligning myself with one and everything it might involve is terrifying and causes a clenching in my chest. I want to support him, but I don't want anyone to get the wrong idea about me. There's no room for that with who I am now.

I can compartmentalize, though, right? Just like with other stuff. I can support him and still maintain everything I've created for myself. I totally can.

I've been hesitating for too long, and Sam steps in. "OMG . . . you guys, I have an idea!"

"Sam! Ten push-ups or bubble tea, please!" Nai says, to my confusion.

"Ugh. Well, I'm broke, so get ready to be amazed." Sam gets down in the middle of the street on their hands and toes and starts to do what can only be described as a cross between the Worm and a push-up, their slim body undulating like a wave.

The others laugh—even Halle—so I join in. I have no idea what's happening right now, but it takes the clenching in my chest away, and I'm thankful for it.

When Sam is done, Halle says, "Well, those were the grossest push-ups I've ever seen . . . and I loved each one." Her smile is so warm, and she looks a lot more welcoming than she did a few minutes ago.

I ask, "I don't get it. Why'd he—" I stop, horrified at using "he" instead of "they." "I'm so sorry—"

Halle is about to say something, but Sam jumps in, puffing a bit from the push-ups. "All good—just apologize and keep trying!"

I swallow and nod, feeling more out of my depth than I have in a long time. "Okay. Right. Sorry," I say to Sam. "But why did you have to do push-ups?"

"We have this thing," Nai explains, "that if one of us says 'guys' to address a mixed-gender group, we either have to do ten push-ups, or—for anyone who might not be able to do that—get a beverage for their friend."

"Oh, that's cool. I'd probably be broke or really jacked if I hung out with you all," I say, surprising myself with something like actual humor.

Sam and Nai laugh. Halle scratches her nose.

"It's all about effort and practice," Nai says. "Anyway, Sam, what were you about to say?"

"OH! So what I was going to say was what if—and just hear me out before kiboshing the idea, *Halle*—what if we opened *our* GSA to kids from St. Luke's who want to come? Like, join forces? Create a rainbow pathway"—they do a jig across the street and back again like Charlie Chaplin but in color—"from our school to theirs?"

We all just kind of look at each other for a beat, and I can practically *smell* Halle's cynicism, but I can also feel a stirring of excitement in my belly at this possible means to an end in my quest to make things right with Ben.

Of course, Halle is the first one to speak, and it's precisely to kibosh the idea. "You're kidding, right, Sam? How would that work? We'd need to get all kinds of permission from our school. She'd need to get permission from *hers*, which, clearly, she's not going to get. And I bet there'd be all kinds of annoying forms or whatever to fill out, too."

Everything she's saying is true—Sam's idea seems complicated and unlikely. Not to mention the idea of hanging around with all of these people who are so comfortable with themselves makes me supremely nervous. But mixed in with those nerves are also a thrill and some curiosity. What if St. Luke's kids—*Ben*—could join the

Pinetree GSA somehow? This might show Ben how out of my way I'm willing to go to create some space for him. It's a risk. But one a *good* friend would be willing to take.

"What if it was, like . . . an underground thing?" I blurt out, before I can second-guess myself.

One of Halle's eyebrows rises into a peak, I think out of interest, but I can't be sure.

"Ooh! Yuss, yuss, yusssssss!" Sam practically sings. "An underground rainbow for your queers to our GSA!"

"An underground rainbow . . . I like the contradiction," Nai says.

I like it, too. I picture a sparkly portal beneath the road we're standing on, and I can't help but smile.

"Wait, wait, wait," Halle says. "You know I like a little guerrilla-style diversity action—not to mention the chance to say eff you to the Catholic Church—but can someone please explain to me how that would work?"

Her Catholic Church comment irks me a little, but I let it slide, for now.

"You know what this calls for, right?" Nai says.

I stare at her, because clearly I have no idea what it calls for.

"It calls for gaz and toot in Little Persia!" She sees my continued confusion and adds, "Persian treats at my house!"

The thought of spending time alone with these three at Nai's house sustains the mix of excitement and fear that has been moving through me this whole time.

"Ooooh! Good idea—we can bring you on as an honorary

GSA head and figure this all out together. And I freaking *love* gaz!" Sam says.

Leaving explanations of gaz and toot for later, I say, "Wow. Are you guys—I mean—you *all* serious?" I did *not* need to do push-ups in front of these people right now.

"Good catch!" Nai says, grinning at me.

"HOLD ON," Halle yells. She finally rises from where she's been kneeling on the road all this time. "Are you losing it? We all just met and you're already forming a coalition? May I remind you that she goes to a *Catholic private school*?"

Sam pipes up. "And may I remind *you*, Mizzzz Diversity and Inclusion, that one of the mandates of our GSA is, and I quote, because I am *astonishing*, 'We exist to increase acceptance and celebration of all identities, across an intersection of gender, sexuality, race, ability, age, and religion.' Am I right, or am I right?"

I'm definitely impressed. And Halle looks sheepish, which I didn't believe she was capable of until this moment. But she just crouches back down to the road and says, "Whatever. I'm just saying, it goes both ways. So if you're a practicing Catholic, I don't want any of the bullshit that comes along with that in our GSA. We have some folks in the group who've been scarred enough by their parents' religions."

There's too much to say to that, so I don't say anything, but I file this conversation away for later to think about more. I'd need to organize my brain before addressing Halle's concerns in an effective way.

Echoing my thoughts, Nai says, "To be discussed further," and sends me a warm smile. Then, looking around at the three of us, she adds, "So? This weekend? My place? Gaz and toot?"

We agree to a time and exchange our contact info, then get back to work. Being out here, painting rainbows with quite likely not-straight people, makes my stomach a mess of nervous squiggles the entire time. But my determination to make things right with Ben—plus something else in my chest that I can't quite name—keeps me crouched on the pavement, scraping chalk against it. By dinnertime, a rainbow bridges their school to ours—and the tiniest glimmer of hope has bubbled up inside of me.

CHAPTER SEVEN

In front of me is a spread of desserts I've never seen before, and even though my belly is woozy with nerves again, I can't wait to dig into them. Sticky orange spirals, what look like mini golden churros, and some kind of nougat, maybe? With bright green pistachios in it like jewels. A pretty tin next to these holds chunks of brittle, laden with nuts. And a giant bowl towering with fruit sits alongside all the sugar.

We're in Nai's living room, the coffee table adorned with these treats, the four of us arranged around the table like panthers about to pounce. We're only waiting because Nai's dad is placing a silver tray down with a teapot, cups, milk, and sugar cubes on it.

When he's done, he says, "Eat all of it!" and glides out of the living room with a flourish. He's already performed a series of dance steps for us as he and Nai brought in the desserts. He is a revelation.

I look at Nai and say, "Was your dad ever in the circus? I mean that in a good way. I could see him with a top hat and coattails, creating all kinds of magic in a giant tent, is all." I'm rambling, but I'm nervous, and I guess it's better than being completely silent.

Nai laughs and says, "Not a circus, but he *does* claim to have been in a traveling theater troupe in his wayward youth. We have yet to see evidence, though."

Halle is watching our interactions so far with a mix of boredom and skepticism. "Okay, are we hashing this out, or what?" she says now. When I arrived, Nai and Sam gave me big hugs. Halle only gave me a head nod and a "Hi," but at least she wasn't frowning or rolling her eyes at me . . . yet.

"Yes! Let's bring this gaz and toot meeting to order!" Sam squeals.

I've learned, through the beguiling (SAT word) introductions by Nai and her dad, that gaz and toot are the names of two of the treats and that these GSA planning meetings are a common occurrence at Nai's house.

I'm blown away when Nai talks about the GSA in front of her dad, and he acts like it's no big deal. Just the thought of my parents knowing I'm anything other than straight sends panic through me. I can't imagine them acting like this—as though it's just another day in the household. They've made it clear over the years that certain ideas and expressions aren't okay—everything from kilts on boys to Pride parades to "all that gender confusion on TV shows these days"—and they barely acknowledge the existence of gay people in general, just like St. Luke's.

Fortunately, they won't be needing to associate me with anything like that.

"Okay, we need to figure some shit out to decide if this is even possible," Halle declares.

"Just a suggestion," Nai begins, and I can tell she's choosing her words carefully, "but why don't we start from an assumption that it *is* possible, and go from there?"

Halle rolls her eyes (not at me, though!), and I'm already seeing a well-worn dynamic play out between them—idealistic visionary maneuvers around cynical realist.

And Sam is the mediator. They add in now, "Totally. We can absolutely make it happen, but Halle's right. There are some things to figure out."

"Like . . . ?" I say.

I already planned before coming here that I would mostly defer to this group, since they obviously have a lot more experience running a GSA than I do (since I have none . . . at all).

I'd also done some research last night (when I should have been studying) about how LGBTQ+ people navigate religion. I found a few memes about Catholic guilt, and a lot of angry videos about the church from younger people, and a few references to books and documentaries that I'd need to check out at some point. I read a few blogs, but all of them were written by adults—and their experiences felt so distant from my own . . . so unreachable as a kid in a Catholic school with the parents I have and the kind of messiness all of that brings up.

After reading a few items and getting overwhelmed, I gave up and decided that if religion came up again with Halle and the others, I'd just agree to keep things separate for now. I couldn't really see any other way.

"Like," Halle begins, "where will we have these meetings and when? Are *all* our meetings going to be together? What about when we're planning bigger events—will your GSA be involved in that, too? And what happens if your school finds out? What's the risk for us? And budget. Who's paying for snacks and materials for a bigger group? And—"

"Wow, okay. Lots of great points, Halle," Sam says.

Halle takes a violent bite of brittle, clearly having worked herself up. I'm sure my face publicizes my bewilderment and I try to rearrange it, but I do wonder how we'll navigate around some of the things she mentioned.

Nai picks up the teapot and adds, "Those are all fair logistical questions, Halle. Let's just take one at a time. But before all of that, maybe we should ask you"—she glances at me as she pours our tea, and my stomach dips—"what you're hoping for from a GSA."

Though I'd come across some good points last night in my research about why a GSA is necessary at any school—including statistics about how schools with GSAs lessen bullying based on sexual orientation and gender identity and such—I didn't really have an answer prepared for Nai's question, beyond my hope of getting Ben to the GSA. I *hope* he'd see how hard I was trying to make a place for him. I *hope* he'd see I cared. I *hope* he'd forgive me and forget about everything that happened.

I hope these rotten, mucky feelings inside of me would disappear.

But I couldn't really share any of these hopes here, now.

I think about some of the blogs and testimonials I read, though, and manage to say, "Um . . . well, I hope people will feel *seen*, right? Like, there'll be a place for them . . ." *Or something like that.*

Sam adds, "Oh, totally—when my older sister started the GSA a few years ago, she knew there were queer and questioning folks at Pinetree, but there was nothing at the school *for* them. None of the teachers were out, there wasn't any safe-space signage anywhere—"

As Sam talks, something inside of me boils up, and my hesitation disappears. In its place are a whole bunch of absences I didn't even realize I'd noticed.

"Yeah, we don't have any of that, either," I blurt. "Or any LGBTQ+ books in the library, barely any sex ed as it is, never mind inclusive sex ed. No one ever talks about it—teachers, students, no one. Probably because they're too scared to. And even though there's no 'homosexuality is bad' messaging, there's nothing to *affirm* homosexuality, either, you know?"

My heart is beating so fast, like I've had too much sugar, but I haven't even finished one treat yet. I take a gulp of my tea now, self-conscious and worried about going off like that, about the moments of silence that follow and the gaze Halle sets on me. Scared that I might have revealed something I didn't want to. I add, in a calmer, slower voice, "I just want everyone who isn't straight at the school to feel like they belong, is all." I'm thinking of Ben, of course.

I'm surprised when it's Halle who speaks first. "Those are really good reasons to want a GSA." Her voice is actually gentle. Probably because she thinks I've lost it.

"Can I ask," Sam follows, "and you can totally say 'no comment' and we won't assume anything, we promise, but—are you queer? I mean, we all are, but you definitely don't have to identify . . . only if you're comfortable—"

A "no" is out of my mouth before Sam is even finished talking.

"So you're an ally!" Nai proclaims.

"That's cool," Sam says.

Halle frowns at me for a second. Her eyes are piercing and send a ripple through my stomach that makes me look down at my lap. After a few seconds, she says, "I guess it makes sense that anyone starting a GSA for your school would be straight, since no one feels safe enough to come out." I can't tell if her tone is disdainful or sympathetic. Maybe a mix of the two.

When I don't say anything in response, because my throat suddenly feels tight, Nai asks, "Okay, so you basically want to start a GSA so that the queer and questioning students at your school feel like there's a place for them?"

I nod.

"Awesome. That's totally in line with our purpose, too," Nai says, and smiles.

"*So*," Halle jumps in, licking her fingers from what I now know is zoolbia. "Back to logistics, then?"

I catch an eye roll from Sam, but Halle doesn't seem to see it.

"Yes!" Sam says. "We should decide on some of the who, what, when, where, and how. I'll take notes. Ready?"

When I get home that night, I'm exhausted but also filled with determination. I'm known at school for following through on things—it's one of the reasons why I'm able to get so much done, why teachers love me, and why my peers trust me with important things like organizing grade events. Once you become known for doing things well, people expect that of you all the time, and I'm not going to let those people down. Now that I've taken on this GSA situation and a team of people is involved, my resolve is as thick and solid as cement.

We planned and chatted well past dinnertime. I hadn't intended to stay so long, but I couldn't resist when Nai's dad brought in savory snacks to add to the sweets, complemented the snacks with a series of twirls, and blessed our "gay agenda" with an air kiss.

The snacks kept us going as we decided on the following (Sam started a Google Doc and shared it with all of us):

Joint GSA (TRIAL BASIS):

WHO:

- us, obvs 🤘
- people from St. Luke's (via word of mouth)
- regular GSA crew from Pinetree

WHAT:

- hangouts, movie nights, discussions, "outings"?

WHEN:

- evening meetings every Thursday night

WHERE:

- the "broom closet" at Pinetree

OTHER STUFF:

- must have a confidentiality agreement of some sort from all members!
- first meeting should be an opportunity to give input about additional guidelines/ideas
- Pinetree GSA will still meet in school on its own too, joint GSA is optional
- NEED A NAME!!!

Sam was very excited about "outings" that in their mind actually meant going to "the club," and I found their overall exuberance encouraging, even if their ideas were a little over-the-top.

Halle, of course, insisted that this was very much a *trial basis* and should be optional for all Pinetree members so they don't feel "forced to engage with religion."

And this sparse list doesn't reflect the sometimes long, circular conversations that accompanied almost every point, most of which could be summarized as follows: Someone suggests something, Halle shows vexation (SAT word) and doubt, lengthy discussion ensues (mostly among Sam, Nai, and Halle), religion is often maligned, more discussion ensues, some kind of agreement is made—and I nod along, just trying not to look incompetent.

The location prompted the most discussion. First we debated whether the club should meet on or off campus, but eventually decided that none of the off-campus places we came up with would be consistently available or safe enough (from prying eyes).

Then Sam suggested the "broom closet," which is not actually a closet, thankfully—because that would be a little "too on the nose," Nai pointed out. Rather, it was some room in the basement of Pinetree that only the maintenance staff uses. It has a separate entrance from the outside, and Halle somehow has a key to it, so we could use it after hours.

Sounded a bit sketch to me, and Nai seemed a little hesitant at first, too.

"I know it's an underground GSA, but this feels like we're pushing ourselves into the darkest recesses of the earth or something, maybe?" she'd said, a small frown on her face.

It took some very impressive knowledge on Halle's part about the history of underground countermovements in the name of civil rights to convince Nai that the broom closet was, in fact, the *perfect* place to meet.

I had my own concerns about liability, but I wasn't about to bring that up and look like a nerd.

I can honestly say, I learned a lot just from listening to the three of them talk. I found Halle's ongoing criticisms of the church irritating at times, but she made some fair points that I couldn't argue with. The Catholic Church *has* systematically persecuted homosexuality, and many people *have* suffered because of that. The Bible *has* been used as a weapon by people who interpret it to suit their own purposes, and the church *does* need to apologize, take responsibility, and move forward.

I can't argue with any of that.

But I guess I have some faith that we *can* smarten up and move forward? I mean, even the latest pope is changing things up a little. And I guess so much of the good stuff—like the way my mother takes so much comfort in prayer, or how the congregation at my church comes together to help each other in times of crisis, or even just our regular church barbecues and fundraisers and potlucks—has made me feel like the church and religion aren't *all* bad. That the people make up the church, and there are a lot of really good people around me.

I imagine Halle would set that fierce look of hers on me and say none of those things matter given all the bad stuff. Maybe she's right. I don't know. Not knowing isn't really my jam.

But right now, I have about four hours of homework ahead of me, and it's already eight o'clock. I sit down at my desk and try to focus on macroeconomics and English instead of on religion and queerness, or on Ben, or on the uncomfortable ripples that invade my stomach whenever Halle sets her gaze on me.

CHAPTER EIGHT

"Peace be with you."

"And with you," I reply, shaking hands with Mr. Fitzpatrick in the pew behind us.

I repeat this exchange with at least eight more people, including my own family. This is one of my favorite parts of Mass. You get to take a break from listening and guided response, and instead interact with the people around you. And I like the idea of passing peace back and forth, too. Maybe that's a weird way to think about it, though.

For me, there's something humbling and reassuring about sitting in these pews. The familiarity of the wood, the smell of incense, the act of genuflecting all transport me somehow into something like grace—it's not a state I'm able to achieve in many places. Expectations still surround me—I'm expected to be on my best behavior, participate in the rituals. But I guess I find the rituals of church therapeutic . . . grounding when everything around me is bigger and faster and more complicated.

Ben's family used to sit in front of my family in church. My sister and I dressed in almost-matching fancy dresses, my dad in a suit, my mom in a sari. Ben's family—six in total—took up half the pew in their mix of corduroy and polyester.

When we were still friends, Ben would always try to sit directly in front of me (my family was always one of the earliest families there) so he could do weird things that only I would notice—like pretend to send me secret messages with random hand signals behind his back or pinch his own butt. He was trying to make me laugh—partly to see if he could get me in trouble with my parents, but also just to make me laugh.

When it was time to shake hands with the people around us and say, "Peace be with you," he'd always pretend not to see me for a few seconds and shake hands with everyone around us except me. Then he'd startle like I'd appeared out of nowhere, stick his hand out, and cross his eyes as we shook hands and pronounced the expected words. We'd end the whole exchange with huge grins.

It was like his version of church was more playful, and that playfulness within these serious walls just drew me further to him.

We'd get caught sometimes, and then I'd get a severe look from my mom or dad, and Ben and I would have to quickly sort ourselves out. Church wasn't a place for messing around, after all, even if it made us both feel *more* at home there to do so.

Maybe those moments were what made me miss him most after things fell apart and we were no longer friends. Until he left for

Toronto, his family sat in a different pew altogether, clearly avoiding me. No more nonsense hand signals, no more hand-shaking. I took this avoidance as a sign that I shouldn't try to "atone" directly with Ben anymore. He clearly didn't want to interact with me, and I couldn't blame him. I could only blame myself. And so I did—I blamed myself, diligently tucked away the worst parts of me, and tried my best to be better than I'd been.

Now, I still find comfort in many of the regular rituals of church. But I miss some of that playfulness, too. I wonder if Ben and I will be able to get some of that lightness back if we spend more time together, but I can't be sure. Everything seems so murky and uncertain with him.

When my mom leans in to give me a hug and kiss on the cheek instead of a handshake, like she always does, I hold on to her just a little longer, grateful for this moment when the firmness of her arms and the steadiness of her embrace feel more like security than restraint.

CHAPTER NINE

Later that afternoon, Sam starts a thread about what to name the GSA.

Sam: How bout the velvet underground? Pretty queer, right?

Cassie: Velvet underground?

Sam: SUPER cool band but also an edgy novel from the 60s . . . about UNDERGROUND SEX STUFF

Halle: Nice!

My eyes widen at this, but I can't possibly say anything now that Halle has expressed her approval. Thankfully, Nai responds.

Nai: Might be a bit too edgy?

Halle: too edgy for catholic school girls, u mean?

Sam: Halle . . .

Halle: 🪁

I roll my eyes.

Nai: What about SOLID? As in SOLIDARITY? With others, with each other?

Sam: i like!

Cassie: Me too ☺

Halle: SOLID makes me think of mass and liquid. no chem terms pls

Sam: wtf Halle

Sam: do u have any ideas Halle

Nai: 👀

Halle: actually ya. Crosswalk.

Halle: cuz of where we came up w the idea

A few dots pulse on the screen. I'm surprised by how cute this idea is, but also want Halle to know I love it, so I text:

Cassie: That's a really great name.

Nai: I agree!

Sam: 👏👏👏

Halle: really?

Sam: ya, totally

Nai: It has symbolism, personal significance . . .

Cassie: And it sounds like cross talk which is accurate.

Sam: haha true like Halle cross talks over everyone?

Halle: 😡

Cassie: No no no not what I meant!

Halle: right

Cassie: For real!

Cassie: Like we're talking across the street, across schools!

Halle: uh huh

Ugh. This is why I try not to spontaneously say things. Or text things.

Nai: I knew what you meant, Cassie.

That's only somewhat comforting.

Nai: So Crosswalk it is?

Sam: 👍

Cassie: 👍

Nai: Halle for the win!

Halle: 🙈

Sam: see y'all next thursday at 7!!! so stoked!

Nai: Basic agenda—just intros and going over guidelines?

Halle: 👌

Cassie: Sounds good. I'll try to find others to come. Might just be me, though.

Nai: Just you is a good start. 😉

Halle: but like try 2 find other people at least

Sam: 🙄

Sam: just do your best cassie

The thread devolves into a series of back-and-forths between Sam and Halle about season 3 of something called *Dragula*, and I use a waving hand emoji to slip away from the conversation. I place my phone next to me on my bed and lean my head back against the headboard.

I have four days to try to get people to the first meeting, and now that I actually need to involve others from St. Luke's, my growing excitement shifts back into fear. It's not like I've ever tried to have a conversation with anyone at St. Luke's about anything to do with gay stuff—I'd been actively avoiding it.

My logical brain—the one that knows I've done a good-enough job of pushing back the parts of myself that need to stay hidden—is overcome by a pounding heart. My desire to start the GSA for Ben is momentarily blindsided by rising panic over possibly being seen as gay just for doing this. Nai, Sam, and Halle might not make assumptions, but what about everyone else?

That piece of me just doesn't feel like it fits—not with who I want to be and how I want others to see me. I'm a better Cassie without it. A tidier Cassie. It just makes sense.

My hands feel stiff, and I realize both have gathered up handfuls of my bedspread and are gripping the quilt so tightly, my knuckles are pale. I blink hard and release the material. I try to ignore my stomach ripples and rapid heartbeat, and bring my brain back into play.

I'd need to make myself out to be a clear *ally* for this Crosswalk group. Maybe talk about a few vague "people I know" who need this group (i.e., Ben). Or make up a family member? Anyway, I'd think about it more and prepare something that will *ensure* people know I'm straight.

I also decide that I'll wait a while before inviting Ben to a meeting. I'll see how it goes and then take it from there. The last thing I want is for him to come and for the meeting to be a hot mess because we don't really know what we're doing yet. Besides, I can't ask him to a GSA meeting when he barely acknowledges my existence. I'll need to make some headway with him first *and* make sure this GSA is awesome before he comes. I want him to be blown away by it . . . and by me and my efforts.

My phone pings.

Halle: so do u know who ur gonna ask?

I am beyond surprised that Halle is messaging me separately from the group, and seeing her name sends that uninvited ripple through me. I tell myself the ripples are likely just embarrassment and fear, and that she can barely stand me, it seems. So why is she messaging? Maybe she thinks I'm inept and can't figure this out on my own? I don't want to *look* inept, so I scrunch up my lips and think a moment before typing:

Cassie: Just making a list now.

Even though I'm not.

Halle: try the artsy types

Halle: there's always some queers in there

This is actually a helpful suggestion.

Cassie: Good idea.

Halle: or like people who are into social justice stuff . . . but not fakers. Peopel who actually DO stuff

It always amazes me that people can ignore their spelling errors enough to send a message with one in it. But her suggestions do spark something—a girl in my grade, Nicky, who posted photos of her and her friends at the Pride parade last year. I very clearly remember coming across the pictures and my stomach flipping at seeing someone from my school so openly supporting gay stuff. Nicky's also a theater kid. So, even though she may or may not be queer, she at least supports queer stuff *and* she's artsy.

Cassie: Right. You've already given me some ideas. Thanks!

Halle: np

She doesn't message anything else, so I guess the conversation is over. But that's okay, because I have things to do.

Okay. Priorities for the rest of my Sunday: (1) English essay outline; (2) study for AP French quiz; (3) study for history test; (4) read three chapters for AP Macro; (5) write out ideas for talking to Nicky about the GSA.

I try to focus on #1, but after ten minutes, I end up spending the next hour on #5 instead.

"A GSA? For real?"

"Yeah. It's just, St. Luke's is so conservative, but we definitely have queer kids at the school, you know?" I've practiced saying "queer," but it still feels foreign and a little scary coming out of my mouth. "And we're starting by asking people we thought might be more open-minded. I thought of you because of your Pride parade posts last summer. I hope that's okay." I'd also practiced not making it sound like I thought *she* was gay or anything. Just in case.

I tracked Nicky down after battling my nerves all day. Nicky started at St. Luke's in ninth grade. I am fairly sure she is a non-believer, given the Pride posts and other things she's posted on social media—stuff about the Bible being shitty fan fiction and the pope being an evil version of Elf on the Shelf.

When I see things like this, I sometimes wonder if the only way to critique Catholicism as a teenager is to hate on it with memes and GIFs. I feel judgy as soon as I think it, but I'm still waiting for someone my age to offer up something else. Then I think of Halle, who's been doing exactly that, and a mixture of annoyance and respect blooms in me.

"Oh, yeah, it's totally cool. I'm super open," Nicky says.

There's a moment when it's like we're both thinking the same thing—*Are* you *queer?*—but it passes quickly, and I charge forward before she can ask.

"Okay, cool. Would you be into checking out our first meeting? It's this Thursday at seven. At a 'secret location' at Pinetree."

"A secret location, huh? Nice."

"Yeah, it's kind of on the down-low, because we can't let admin know."

The smile on her lips grows. I knew this secrecy aspect would appeal to her counterculture nature, like it did with Halle.

I grin back. I can barely contain my excitement over how well this is going. "I'll text you the details?"

"Yeah, okay. I can probably come by for a bit, check it out."

Noncommittal like basically everyone my age, but I'll take it. "Awesome!"

We say our goodbyes, and I take out my phone to message the group with this success. I still feel like I'm not quite carrying my weight with the GSA—like that annoying group project member who does absolutely nothing but still gets the same mark as everyone else—so I hope this makes up for it a little.

Cassie: Think I might have found someone for the GSA!

After about a minute, Sam replies, and then the others.

Sam: sweet!! ✨

Nai: Good work, Cassie!

Halle: nice

The bit of approval sends some much-needed serotonin through my body, and I head to my afternoon class feeling a little less stressed about school and the upcoming Crosswalk meeting, and a bit more excited about what it might mean if this actually works.

CHAPTER TEN

In bio on Tuesday morning, Mr. A reviews the guidelines for our project and gives us ten minutes to touch base with our partners—to brainstorm and set up times to meet.

I'm surprised when Ben gets up from his seat at the back and makes his way to me. He pulls a stool over and sits on the other side of the desk.

I make myself busy by opening up a Google Doc and the project outline Mr. A sent us, and placing them side by side on my laptop screen.

When he's settled on his stool, I say, "Hi."

"Hey."

His one-word responses make me feel like he can't stand talking to me, so I try to just focus on the task at hand.

"So, maybe we should start by setting up some meetings? Just to make sure we have some before we run out of time today?" I say.

He thumps his elbows onto the desk and drops his chin into his hands. "Sure." He's staring into the back of my laptop, where I have a Model UN sticker from the conference last year.

"Do you have any after-school stuff?"

"Nope."

I'm desperate to break down this barrier between us, but I don't know how. I fall back on planning and logistics because that's what I know best. This project is also worth a lot of our grade, so I have to make sure we do well. It's all about balance.

"Okay. I have volleyball most days after school, but we should definitely meet at least once or twice this week. How about after I'm done? Like around five thirty?"

He shrugs. Looks at the door. Says, "Sure."

Is he depressed? I wonder. Or just bored and disinterested in me? Or . . . *Get real, Cassie—he just thinks you suck.*

Focus, Cassie. Get a damn grip. I crack my knuckles and stare hard at my online calendar.

"Great. So can we meet today?"

"Today?"

"Yeah, I mean, we should get going on this, don't you think?"

"Isn't this project supposed to take, like, weeks?" he says. He's looking at me now, but he's also frowning.

"Well, yeah, but I don't like to leave things until the last minute. Mr. A can be a really hard marker, and if we don't get started now, before our other classes get too busy, it might be harder to find times to meet. I'm going to have volleyball, student government, clubs, and a ton of other homework, so—"

Ben leans farther onto the desk and pushes the heels of his hands into his eyes. "Can you just relax for a second? You're stressing me out."

I'm speechless for a moment. I was definitely not trying to stress him out, but I can see that I am. His body has gone from lethargic (SAT word) and loose to rigid and tense. His face is flushed. *Nice work, Cassie. You're making great headway.*

"Oh. Sorry," I finally utter. "I'm just trying to get ahead of everything."

He's still rubbing his eyes. "Yeah, well maybe just stay where you are for a hot minute."

Okay. I mean, I don't want to make things hard for him, but being on top of things has worked well for me so far, and I'm not about to change my whole approach just because he throws some two-bit wisdom at me.

"Stay where I am? How does anyone get anywhere by staying where they are?"

He sighs and pushes his hair back. St. Luke's has a weird rule for hair where boys can't have it reach their collar. If Ben lets his grow out any more, he'll be breaking the rule. I kind of want him to.

"I *mean*, chill out," he says. "Quit worrying about the next thing."

"Wow. Thanks for the advice. Do I owe you for this therapy session?" I mean it to sound jokey, but his face doesn't register anything like amusement.

"Maybe an actual therapy session wouldn't hurt," he says, staring me dead in the eyes.

Ouch. That feels like a direct hit.

His eyes flick to the clock now, like he can't wait to get away from me.

This is not what I wanted at all. Desperate to make it better, I blurt, "There's cookies!" *What am I even saying?*

He looks at me like I've just turned into a human-size axolotl. "What?"

"I . . . We have homemade cookies at my house. We could meet there today after school and just, like, go over the project together or something? Like, low-key? And with cookies?"

His face doesn't change much, but at least he's looking at me and not the clock. "What kind of cookies?"

The fact that he doesn't respond with outright rejection is a win in my book. "Chocolate chip."

He eyes me up. "Same place as before?"

I have to try to keep the excitement from my voice when I say, "Yeah. At five thirty? After my practice?"

The bell goes, and he slips off his stool. "Fine. But I can't stay long."

"Fine," I repeat, still feeling unbalanced, but also like I've made a tiny bit of progress.

After my volleyball practice, I walk home, apprehensive about spending time with Ben outside of school, at my house. I wonder what it will feel like—to be there with him again after so much time has passed.

It's a little before 5:30, so I'm not expecting him to be here already, but there he is, leaning with his back against the fence running alongside our driveway. And he's smoking—*not* a cigarette. I thank the Lord my parents won't be home for a while and Kendra is at her friend's house. Neither of my parents even drink, and my mom would lose her mind if she ever caught me consuming alcohol or weed.

I slow my pace, but my heart beats faster. He sees me and doesn't bat an eye, just shifts toward me and blows out a long stream of smoke. "Hey," he says.

"Hey." This seems to be our standard greeting. I'm about three feet away from him now. I don't really know what else to say, so I ask, "You smoke pot?"

"Yup. You?"

"No! But . . . you're a ballet dancer." *Great job, Cassie. Head straight into judgment.*

"Ballet dancers smoke."

"But isn't it bad for you? Your lungs?" *Ugh. Stop.*

He shrugs. "Sure. But it's good for my anxiety and stress."

Oh. I don't know what to say to that. There are so many things to take in right now. Him, here, at my house. Him, smoking. Him, telling me about his anxiety and stress so openly. I wonder if this is what happened to him in bio today—if I triggered his anxiety. I pull at the drawstring on my sweats and twist it around my fingers.

"Looks like you could use some, too," he says, eyeing my hands.

I stop twisting and fiddling. "No, thanks. I'm good."

"Are you?"

My head is swirling right now. I feel so flustered with him. Like the air around me is moving in waves and I can barely keep my feet planted to the ground.

Pull it together, Cassie. This is your chance to fix things.

I blink away the blurriness and pull my shoulders back. "Want to come in?"

"As opposed to . . . working out here?" He indicates the driveway.

Right. "I meant . . ."

I meant do you really *want* to come in? Are you *ready*? Because I'm not sure I am.

"I don't know what I meant. Sorry." I also don't know why I just stand there, looking at him.

He puts out his joint and tucks it into a pocket of his backpack, which hangs off one arm. I finally turn and open the gate we have across the driveway to keep Manika from escaping. She bounds toward me now, all loose skin and fur. When she sees Ben, though, she bypasses me entirely for this new person and spends a good thirty seconds wiggling into his pats.

Once we get inside, I pour us some water and plate some cookies, as promised, and then we go sit out on the deck, overlooking the big grassy field behind our house.

I've lived here my whole life. The field has always just been a field. Always dry and never green. Neither of us mentions the school that is just out of sight, beyond the field, or the creek that runs along it. I wonder again how he feels being here, so close to our childhood and to me.

I ask him a parent question because I still don't really know what to say to him. "How are you liking St. Luke's?"

He leans back in his lounge chair and shields his eyes from the sun. He swallows the entire cookie he just shoved in his mouth and gives me a kid answer: "It's fine."

I slip out of my knockoff Adidas slides and lean back as well. Manika is lying on her side, panting softly in between our chairs. The weather is warmer today, and the late afternoon heat hangs, windless and heavy, over the backyard. I'm still sweaty from practice and the walk home, and I'd kill for a shower.

"Are you glad you came back?" I ask.

He's silent for a moment, then says, "I'm not sure yet. I'm glad to have a break from dancing."

"Were you not enjoying it anymore?"

"I just needed a break."

Hmm. Okay. I try something different. "Your parents must be happy to have you home."

"I guess."

I turn my head toward him to see what his face is saying, but I can't really tell. He's squinting. I want to ask him more, but he doesn't seem intent on talking much.

Ben had been so chatty and energetic before. "Rambunctious," my mom had called him. He'd tell jokes he made up and talk about his older brothers all the time. About the books he read and the hikes his family went on. About ballet, even though he sometimes got teased for it. He didn't care as much about what others thought of that part of him, though. He'd grown up in a different kind of family than mine, I guess. Churchgoing but not devout, with fewer expectations, fewer rules. And from what he did share about ballet, it sounded like a different world, too. I'm surprised he wanted to leave it.

That urge to make things better pulses through me again, and I wonder when I'll be able to tell him about the GSA. Not now. He's only barely started talking to me again. I'll need to ease into the GSA situation. Make sure he's ready. That we're both ready.

But after today in bio, I'm also wary about stressing him out. My fingers are itching to get my hands on my laptop and work on this project, but I tell myself I can start some of the steps tonight, on my own. Instead, I decide I'm going to impress Ben with just how "present" I can be.

"The air's so still right now," I say.

He doesn't say anything to this, and I try to think of something else to say that will seem calm and grounded and easy.

But then he says, "You ever see kids down in the creek anymore?"

Oh.

The creek is right in front of us, of course. Maybe it makes sense for him to bring it up. But I thought he'd want to avoid it, after what I did to him there.

I tread lightly. "Um, not as much. They fenced off the opening. And—" I stop myself from saying the next part out loud. *The creek feels different. Because of what I did.* Instead I say, "And kids these days. They're more interested in their screens." It's a pathetic attempt at a joke, and he rightfully ignores it.

"Can we still get down there?"

I'm still surprised he's asking about the creek, but I also feel a bump of excitement in my chest. *Like, the two of us? Like before? When we were friends?*

But then he says, "Makes sense for the project, right?"

Right. The project. Again, I'm not expecting this. I mean, of course the creek is an option, but there are other, less-fraught options. I'm also surprised that *he's* the one bringing up the project right now, based on our conversation in class. That he's already read through the material and knows we're supposed to choose an environment and take samples of the water there.

"Oh" is all I manage to say.

He looks over at me and says, "Right?"

"Yeah—yeah, totally." My brain is automatically filled with the pros and cons of this idea. Pros: (1) The creek is *right there*, and (2) maybe this could be a great way to reconnect with Ben—bring us back to all the good times we had there. Cons: (1) This could be a great way to remind Ben about everything that went down and what a terrible person I was and how much he actually hates me.

Ugh.

Even though I'm nervous about this, he's the one who contributed the idea, so it must be okay with him, right? And I don't want to shoot down his first contribution to this project.

"Okay, I'm game to use the creek if you are."

"I mean, why wouldn't we?" he asks.

I glance at him but still can't read his face. Is this a test? To see if I'll admit why we wouldn't? I decide to play it cool. There's no way he wants to get into all that heavy stuff, right? It couldn't possibly be good for his anxiety, I reason. "No—you're right. It's a great choice," I say.

"Cool."

"Yeah."

He leans his head back and closes his eyes.

I guess we're being quiet now. The type A part of me wants to suggest we get down to the creek immediately to take some samples, but I also don't want to ruin what almost seemed like a conversation. I try to stare off into the distance, but I'm not very good at it. I end up reviewing the project guidelines in my head and planning what I'll do later to get on top of things.

When I've done that, and Ben's eyes are still closed, and it's still very quiet save for Manika, who is now having a dream and letting out sporadic yips in her sleep, the silence gets the best of me. How patient am I expected to be?

"Are you thinking of joining any clubs or anything? Extra-curriculars?" I'm testing the waters. I need to know if he'd be interested in joining one club in particular.

He doesn't say anything at first and I wonder if he's fallen asleep, but then he says, with his eyes still closed, "Like what?"

"Like . . . I don't know. A sport? Or—there are lots of clubs to choose from?"

He finally opens his eyes, only to side-eye me. "I'm not really a clubs guy."

"But, like, there are so many different ones." I roll my eyes internally at myself, but it's like I can't stop saying more things. "There's even a comic book club." Ben used to love comics. "Or music—do you like music? There's a K-pop club, a rock band club, a world music club." I remind myself I'm supposed to be testing the waters. "Or—what about—um, the social justice club? Like diversity-and-inclusion stuff? What about that?"

I see his chest rise and fall and watch as he rubs his eyes, like he did in bio earlier, when I was stressing him out. But my mouth moves anyway.

"There's a mental health club, too. It's called something like the Breakfast Club, or maybe—"

Ben sits up and swings his legs around to the other side of his chair. At his movement, Manika jolts and scrambles to her feet, too. "No thanks. I gotta go."

"Oh, okay." *Cassie, you freak show.* "Um, should we figure out a time to collect samples?"

"Later."

"Okay. Let's plan in class on Thursday? Hopefully Mr. A gives us some time to work. But he can be annoying about that." I keep talking as Ben grabs his backpack, slings it over his shoulder, and pats Manika when she goes to him. "I can start to create some of the documents, though—get a head start."

"Yeah, cool. See ya."

He grabs one more cookie and is off the patio before I'm even out of my own chair. I watch as he unhooks the gate and walks up and out of the driveway. I notice his joint is already back in his mouth before he disappears down the sidewalk.

Another fail, Cassie. Manika noses into the back of my knee and whines, like she feels bad for me. She shouldn't. I don't deserve it.

CHAPTER ELEVEN

On Thursday after school, my stomach is going haywire with nervous anticipation. Our first Crosswalk meeting is tonight, and I have no idea what to expect, really. I mean, who's going to be there besides the four of us? And will I recognize anyone? Will they know *me* from something school related, like volleyball or debate or Model UN? My one comfort is that if they're there, then we both chose to support the GSA, so it's unlikely they'll judge me for it. And I'll make sure to clarify that I'm an ally as soon as I can.

"Hellllooooo?"

This is Kendra, who's beside me drying the dishes that I'm washing. It's actually her night to wash, but she never does it right, so I've taken over.

I guess I zoned out a little. "What?" I say, handing her a plate.

"Why are you just staring into the water like a weirdo?" Kendra has zero time for my general way of being. She excels in school, too, but she makes it look effortless, whereas I have to study my ass off. And she definitely doesn't work hard at making people like her. They just do. She's cheeky, spontaneous, funny, weird in that way that's quirky instead of awkward. I'm pretty sure she's on her way to atheism but goes through the motions for our parents. Sometimes it's just easier to pretend.

"I wasn't. I—"

"You *were*, and I even said your name twice already."

"Okay, whatever. I have lots on my mind. Eleventh grade is different than ninth grade, you know."

"Um, okay, nerd," she says.

She rolls her eyes at me like she does at least twenty times a day, both right in front of me and in my imagination. For some reason, Kendra's pretty, round face has become a measure for the way I gauge how acceptable my behavior is or is not to other people my age.

But some things I just have to accept as necessary sacrifices in service of other priorities, and I guess my sister's adoration (or even respect) is one of those sacrifices.

We wash quietly for another few seconds and then she says, "Why are you dressed up?"

"Dressed up" here means jeans and a sweater, but usually by this point in the evening, I'm in sweats.

"I have to go out soon."

Kendra places a hand against her chest in mock shock. "Out? On a school night? *Gasp.*"

"You're hilarious," I say, side-eyeing her. "It's for a course."

I told my parents that I signed up for an evening study prep course that's part of one of my classes. If it's about studying, I know my parents won't question it, as long as the hours are reasonable.

"Oh, gross. You really need a life, Cassie."

"And you really need to mind your own business, Kendra."

She throws some forks in a drawer. "But who will encourage you to be a cooler person if I mind my own business?"

I'm not interested in cooler. I just need to be better. "You're not *that* cool," I say, even though I know it's not true.

"Cooler than you."

Brat. But I can't disagree.

"Fine. You're the coolest. I have to go." I hand her the last plate, wipe my hands on a kitchen towel, and leave her in the kitchen, but her words stick with me and make me even more nervous than I was before. On top of all the other things I have to worry about with the GSA, now I'm also wondering if I'm cool enough to be a part of this group at all.

The "broom closet" is inside a smaller building on the Pinetree campus. Halle sent a message earlier that day to the group chat saying to "look for the secret sign" when we got there. I'd passed on the message to Nicky.

When I find the entrance, which is down a six-step staircase, the door is propped open with a little piece of wood and has a piece of paper taped to it. On the paper is an *X* with a stick figure in a walking stance after it. I take a deep breath, my heart racing, and push the door open.

Once inside, I walk down a semi-dark hallway to a doorway on the left, which has light spilling from it. When I round the corner, I find Halle moving things around. Another person is helping her. They look younger than Halle, with a stocky build and relaxed ponytail, and they're wearing a loose gray T-shirt and pink commando pants. I assume this is someone from Pinetree.

I'm one of the first to arrive. I am *always* early. It's a pathological need I have. Just another thing Kendra's face disapproves of in my head.

"Uh, hey, Halle." I really wish Sam and Nai were already here.

She looks up, and when she sees me, she doesn't look entirely unhappy about it, so that's an improvement.

"Are you always this early?" she says, instead of the more socially acceptable "Hello."

I sigh. *Kill her with kindness, Cassie.* "Yes. Do you need help?"

"Nah, that's what my brother is for. Jay, meet Cassie."

Jay smiles wide and waves at me. "Hi, Cassie! He/him pronouns over here." I can see the resemblance to Halle now—the full cheeks, long eyelashes, ski-slope nose—except I've yet to see a smile this wide on her.

I smile back. "Hey, Jay—I use she/her." Then I stand awkwardly for a few moments, looking around while they go back to arranging the room.

It's not a huge space, but much bigger than I thought a room called the "broom closet" would be—enough for fifteen people or so. A set of four lockers stands against one wall, a metal desk sits in a corner, and some sports equipment that looks like it's seen better days is piled in another corner. Halle's found a bunch of folding chairs and a few big cushions for the floor. An orange two-person couch from another decade rounds out the circle of seats.

To her credit, Halle has made this somewhat unfriendly space cozier by hanging some colorful twinkle lights along one wall and across the lockers, and by bringing in a bright red rug that is clearly not original to the place. A really cute rainbow lamp glows from the desk as well. I'm surprised that something so homey can come from someone so bristly. Maybe it's Jay's influence.

Eventually, I push a chair two inches to the right to be helpful and manage to ask, "Um, so how come you have the key to this place?"

Before Halle can answer, Jay says, "I'm friends with one of the custodians. She used to let me hang out here back when I'd get bullied for being trans. I don't really get bullied anymore, but I like hanging out here anyway."

Oh. "People at Pinetree bullied you?" I ask. I'm a little surprised to hear this, given the rainbow extravaganza plastered across the front entrance to the school.

Halle huffs. "Pinetree isn't *perfect*, Cassie. We still have people who are transphobes or racist or whatever. But it's a lot better now, right, bud?" She squeezes Jay's shoulder, and I notice her face softens significantly when she looks at him.

He nods. "A *lot* better. I don't think anyone would get away with being openly transphobic now, although that doesn't stop people from being terrible in private or online sometimes."

"How did things get better?" I ask, a small bubble of hope

floating around inside of me. I haven't witnessed any homophobic or transphobic language at St. Luke's, but I've heard it happens. And, of course, we don't have anything that actively addresses or works to prevent it, either.

"Well, the GSA, for one," Halle says. "And some better adults in the building, thank God."

I consider asking her if she's actually thanking God, but I decide against it.

"That's really cool," I say. "I hope St. Luke's can get there at some point, too."

"Maybe this joint GSA will help!" Jay says. "I think the idea is so awesome."

He grins at me, and I wonder how this utterly sweet, positive soul is related to Halle. But then she surprises me and says, "Yeah, this could be a good start, Cassie." One side of her lips lifts, and a small wave of pleasure runs through me.

"I hope so," I say, hoping as well that my pleasure isn't as obvious as it feels.

It's 7:15 and our Crosswalk meeting includes Jay, three other kids from Pinetree, and the four "founding members" (Sam really likes the sound of this and keeps saying it). Nicky hasn't shown up yet, but I'm praying that she's just artsy and late. I'm a little embarrassed I don't have anyone else here from St. Luke's and wonder if Halle and the others are second-guessing if this is worth their time.

I'm on the two-seater couch, next to Jay, who is snuggled in on the other side. He's petting Zoey, one of the two therapy bunnies that Sam brought with them—"To increase the cozy factor," they said. Jay looks about as Zen as can be, and I try to channel some of his calm. "So what now?" he asks.

Nai jumps into motion. First she goes over the confidentiality agreement we all settled on yesterday via our group chat. She stresses how essential it is that we "keep our members' identities and what's said here in the room, but take the learning outside of it."

Once everyone seems to understand that part, she says, "Let's go around and do names, pronouns, and . . . why we're here at Crosswalk? All optional, of course. I'll start."

I admire how in charge Nai is, but also how serene. I'm organized and on top of things, too, but I'm not sure anyone would describe me as calm or easygoing. Definitely not Ben, at least.

"I'm Nai, my pronouns are she/her, and I'm here because I'm queer *and* I think it's super cool that we've joined forces with St. Luke's. It's nice to meet new people who are also committed to safe spaces for queer folks!" She smiles at me. I smile shyly back.

Sam goes next, then Halle, then Jay. The three other Pinetree High kids go after that. Two are in ninth grade, one is in tenth.

The tenth grader, who's Black and has cropped hair and is fidgeting with their oversize cardigan, says, "I'm Lou, and today I'm they/them, but tomorrow I may be she/her—who knows?" They laugh, and we join them, though I'm still getting my head around how fluid some people seem to be in their identities.

Lou continues, "I'm here because my dad is hyper-religious and

I was raised to believe in God and stuff, but I'm not sure I really do. I thought it'd be cool to talk about that a bit?"

My eyebrows lift, and I glance at Halle. She never said anything about what would happen if Pinetree kids brought up religion. She glances at me, too, but her face gives nothing away.

Sam steps in. "That's really cool, Lou. I'm sure we can talk about that!"

The two ninth graders, Muriel and Quinn, are best friends, it appears, and Quinn is here to support Muriel as an ally.

Quinn, who is also Black and whose tight curls are dyed blond while their face and ears have more piercings than anyone I've ever seen, says, "He/him over here. Muriel's always been a Black Lives Matter supporter, and we tell each other everything. I wanted to support her in this, too."

I wonder just how long Muriel's been a BLM supporter, given she's only in ninth grade, but generally I'm just impressed.

Muriel adds with a big grin, "Yeah, I'm all about that activist life, you know? I use she/her pronouns, and I'm gay as hell and here because I just want to be in as many queer spaces as possible."

This kid, by all measures, looks like what some people might call a "nerdy Asian girl stereotype"—glasses, short bob, plain, practical outfit. But that seems to be where the stereotype ends. She reminds me a little of Kendra, actually, and I wonder if she's going to think I'm totally uncool, too.

By the time the intro circle gets around to me, I'm a little blown away by how open people are already. So far, by my mental note-keeping, Halle, Nai, Sam, Jay, Lou, and Muriel are all queer and out (to at least some people).

Sam, Jay, and Lou are all nonbinary, trans, or gender-nonconforming (terms I'm still sorting out for myself).

And Quinn is straight and cisgender.

That leaves me, who by all accounts is straight and cisgender as well.

I'm silently so thankful Quinn is here so I'm not the odd person out—even though I am in other ways, like being the only person here who started an underground GSA while also keeping queerness well away from herself.

"Um, I'm Cassie, she/her." Of course, I'd already planned out what I was going to say. "I'm here because I really think it would be great to have a GSA at my school, but it's a Catholic school and we have virtually no LGBTQ+-related programming. So this joint GSA with Pinetree seemed like a better way to go about it for now. Thankfully Pinetree's GSA heads are awesome." I smile at the three of them. "And I'm an ally." Can't forget that part.

"Do you really think a GSA could *ever* work at a Catholic school?" Lou asks, their face disbelieving.

"There *are* GSAs at some Catholic schools!" Muriel practically shouts. "So it's not *im*possible!"

Well, that's news to me. There are only three other Catholic high schools in the city, and I don't know if any of them have GSAs. I make a mental note to look into it. Or ask this ninth grader with superior knowledge on the topic.

Right now, though, I really just want to sound good to this group, so I say, "Yeah, like, queer people should be able to be themselves, regardless of their religion or background. You should be able to be religious and queer and still be happy. So I guess I *have* to believe it's possible for St. Luke's to help provide that, at some point."

When I'm finished speaking, I glance at Halle, since I've said the dreaded word "religion," but I feel like Lou opened the door, so it should be fine. Her face actually has something more like . . . contemplation on it, though. I could be wrong, but I think she even gives me a small head nod, maybe?

Lou very *clearly* nods their head and says, "That's cool. I hope it's possible, too."

Their affirmation is nice, but I cringe a little inwardly at the hypocrisy in my words. It's weird, I guess—like I could see the possibility of this for everyone but me. At least for now. When I'm older maybe, or at least out of high school. And living somewhere else. I could start fresh or something. But that part of me just feels too wrapped up in the kind of messiness I don't want to risk bringing out right now. It feels like something I can't control enough. But that doesn't mean I can't help bring that happiness to others for the time being. Like for Ben.

Right?

When we're through with introductions, Sam goes over some of the ideas we had for the group and opens it up to others' ideas. Just as Lou is about to suggest something, Nicky sweeps into the room, startling Rex the bunny, who's been sleeping beside Halle, who's sitting on a cushion on the floor. Halle picks up Rex and tries to soothe him. She's so gentle with the furry little ball that I'm momentarily mesmerized by her hands and fingers and the way she plants a series of soft kisses on the bunny's head.

She catches me looking, and I quickly turn my attention to Nicky instead.

"Sorry," Nicky says—to us, I think, not to the bunny. "My mom was being super annoying about having dinner with her before going out." She looks at me and gives a wave.

I wave back and say, "It's okay. We just did intros and now we're talking about possibilities for the club. Did you want to introduce yourself?"

"Oh, sure." She finds a seat on the floor next to Halle, looks at Rex, who's settled nicely into Halle's lap, and says, "Cute bunny. Can I?" She makes like she wants to pet Rex, and Halle half smiles and says, "Of course." It took Halle several interactions to finally smile at me that way, and my chest pinches at the sight.

Nicky scratches Rex behind the ears, and while she does, she says, "I'm Nicky. I go to St. Luke's." She looks up.

Halle says to her, "Oh, we're also doing pronouns and why we're here, if you're cool with that."

Halle's tone is so pleasant, and I wonder what makes Nicky so easy to like compared to me. The thing in my chest becomes more distinct. Like a screw tightening.

"Cool, cool," Nicky says. "My pronouns are she/her, and I'm here because that girl over there"—she points to me—"invited me and because I think stuff like this is super important. I'm also pretty fluid in my identities." She looks back at Halle and smiles. Halle smiles back.

I hate this whole interaction.

Nai reiterates the confidentiality agreement for Nicky, and then the rest of the meeting is filled with a mix of unrealistic ideas for the club (like holding a *Drag Race* event for both St. Luke's and Pinetree to "really shake things up" or throwing a "super-gay prom" between the two schools at the end of the year) and more reasonable ones (like trying to get in a guest speaker and having a movie night). Sam still holds out for their "club night" idea.

Throughout, I am preoccupied by precisely two lines of thought.

First, I'm assessing the vibe of the club, thinking about Ben and how he might fit in here. I'm trying to picture him with all these folks, wondering if they would overwhelm him or bring him out of the seriousness he seems to have adopted. I wonder if I can even get him here, given our exchanges so far.

And second, I am trying *not* to think about the hard, pointy thing in my chest when I see how close Nicky and Halle are, how their hands are both petting Rex at the same time, how uneasy and convoluted this makes me feel.

By the end of the night, I realize: One, I need more time to figure out when and how to bring Ben here. And two, I'm having feelings for Halle that terrify me and I have no idea what to do about it.

CHAPTER TWELVE

On most Monday mornings, I volunteer in the library, helping the librarian, Mr. Reyes, sort and reshelve books. I started doing this in the ninth grade after the librarian at the time, Ms. Taft, saw me reorganizing some books that were shelved incorrectly (because how could I ignore such a thing?) and put me to work.

But even before that, the library had been a small haven in the school for me—a bit of an escape from the rush-rush-rush I feel in most other places. I mean, I'm still efficient and productive and polite, because that's become too ingrained in me, but books, Mr. Reyes, the comfy chairs in the corner—they give me a brief respite from being quite so "on."

And I've been needing a respite after the Crosswalk meeting last week. It's been nearly impossible for my brain to settle since that night, the way it jumps around, replaying every part of the conversation. Everything I said that might have sounded dumb.

Every interaction between Halle and Nicky. Every emoji and message in the group chat ever since.

So the 7:30–8:30 a.m. shift in the library is welcome, even if it's early and I'm tired. But hardly anyone else is here at this time, which means it's nice and quiet. Peaceful. My mind can settle a little into familiar, simple tasks. And Mr. Reyes, who started working here last year, brings me tea from the staff room, so, bonus.

"Here you go, Ms. Perera," he says now, handing me a mug with a picture of an owl in glasses saying, "Whooo's the best teacher?" on it.

Mr. Reyes is older, maybe in his forties or fifties, with a mix of gray and black, neatly styled hair. He reminds me a little of my dad—Mr. Reyes is Filipino, not Sri Lankan, but they're both shorter with round bodies and loud laughter. Mr. Reyes also peers over his glasses at people, like my dad does. Not out of judgment, I don't think, but just out of nearsightedness. It makes him look curious and smart.

"Thank you," I say, and take a sip of the tea. Milky and sweet, just like we make it at home. This is like a breath, too.

"All right . . . sorting or late notices?" he asks.

I don't know how people can have late library books already. It's only the third week of school.

"Sorting?" I say.

"Great. I'll join you. There are a lot of books I just got in, so we need to organize, cover, and label them."

Organizing and labeling are my jam, so I'm very happy with this scenario.

We settle into an easy rhythm, applying Mylar covers and labels to the new hardcover books Mr. Reyes has ordered. Some people might consider this monotonous, but I like it. It's methodical and careful work, but doesn't tax my brain in the least. It also takes a certain amount of perfectionism, which I have in abundance.

"How have your first weeks of school been, Cassie? Junior year! That's a big one."

And I'm already feeling it. "Really good, so far," I say, despite the unsteadiness I've felt.

"Oh, good! What kinds of extracurriculars are you getting up to this year?"

Well, I helped start an underground GSA, and I'm strategizing a triumphant resurrection of a friendship I ruined . . .

"Volleyball and student government, but nothing else yet. Still weighing my options." I look up from the book I just perfectly covered and smile.

"Wow, I thought you'd already have six different clubs and teams going by now," he says, smiling back.

I know he's just teasing me, but this lighthearted comment sparks a little anxiety in me. "Oh, I will soon. I just want to also focus on my coursework—I need my grades this year to be top-notch for university apps, you know?"

He pulls out a length of Mylar and cuts it with scissors. "Right. But make sure there's some fun stuff in there, too." He winks at me.

What is it with teachers telling me I need to have more fun and relax? Aren't they supposed to be encouraging me to get good grades?

"Oh, yeah, don't worry. I'll find some fun. I mean, *this* is pure merriment, right?" I indicate our book-covering materials.

He giggles. I love his giggles. "Right, right."

We cover a few more books, and then Mr. Reyes pulls over a small stack of three novels. "I've heard really good things about these ones from the student survey."

Mr. Reyes put out an anonymous Google Form at the end of last school year, asking students and staff to suggest books for the library. I submitted sixteen titles, because who wouldn't?

He passes me the stack and starts to pull out more Mylar. I look at the covers as he does and my heart starts to race. All three covers show what appear to be "alternative lifestyles" (as one of my tenth-grade teachers put it when describing gay marriage). One has a boy dressed in feminine clothing. One has two girls gazing at each other with longing. And one has two non-gender-specific people holding hands.

My hands are instantly sweaty, but I try to play it cool. I just take one of the books and start taping the plastic to it. *Nothing to see here. Just a normal day at the library. No big deal.*

Some people may think this *isn't* a big deal. It's a library. Libraries have all kinds of books. But I've never heard about or seen anyone at St. Luke's taking out books from *our* library that have LGBTQ+ stories in them. I so badly want to ask Mr. Reyes if these kinds of books are allowed here. If people actually take them out. If there are more that I've just never noticed. If *he* approves of these books. I mean, he must, right? Approve? Or why would he order them?

My buzzing mind must show, because Mr. Reyes asks, "Cassie?"

I look up from the book I'm covering. "Mm?"

"Remember to tape to the hardcover, not the outside jacket." He points to the book, which I've taped incorrectly.

"Oh, duh. Sorry. I went into autopilot, I guess." I try to manage a smile, but I'm not sure it looks like one.

"That's okay. We'll just call it 'creative expression.'" He smiles an actual smile.

"Ha ha. Yeah." *Oof. Get it together, girl.*

But when the first bell goes, any breaths of fresh air the library has given me have been sucked up by all the questions swirling around me about those books.

CHAPTER THIRTEEN

"How many samples do we need?" Ben asks. I'm ankle-deep in the creek because I'm wearing boots, but Ben's still in his school shoes, so he's standing atop the creek bank, hanging on to the fence. I remember when we both would have just stripped off our shoes and socks, but things are different now.

"The project outline suggests at least six," I say, bending over the water and peering into it, "but I think we should take ten just in case."

Ben came over today after I was finished with volleyball, and I've been doing my best to keep things light and easy, even as we're immersed in the creek and I'm immersed in jittery thoughts of the past. But Ben was on time and brought his notebook, and now we're here, doing our project together, so I try to focus on the task at hand.

We collect a few more samples. We're quiet as we do this, and my body is finally beginning to settle.

As Ben and I walked down the pathway from my house to the creek, my anticipation turned into a full-scale twisting sensation in my stomach. To gain access to the creek, we'd have to use the same spot we always used as kids—the opening had a fence along it now, but it was easy enough to hop over. The closer we got, though, the more my whole body had tensed. The last time he and I were here, our friendship ended. Was it a mistake to go back? I'd had to push myself to keep walking and breathing.

But when we got to the opening, Ben didn't seem to be affected at all. He just folded his arms across the top of the chain-link fence, leaned his chin on them, and stared down into the creek. I watched him for a moment or two and then followed his lead, stepping up beside him and gripping the top of the fence with my hands. The metal was cold against my palms.

"Can't believe they put a fence here," he said.

I could. The banks had become overgrown, the water deeper, and everything got so slippery in the fall and winter. A little kid could easily fall in. But all I said was "Yeah. Liability, I guess."

Then he pulled himself up and hopped over the fence like it was nothing—graceful and athletic as ever. I, of course, was much less graceful about it.

I take a step toward the creek bank now, with two vials of water in my left hand and a bag of empty vials in my right. I tread very carefully, testing out each step for slippery rocks. But I'm not careful enough, because I suddenly feel my boot swipe sideways, and my stomach leaps up with the sudden sensation of losing my balance. I yelp and reach my arms out in front of me to try to stabilize myself, but it's no use—the water is fast, and in a matter of moments, my knees are at least a couple of inches deep in the muck between stones, and my hands have let go of their contents to brace myself. I'm on all fours, the cold water numbing my hands almost immediately, soaking through my jeans, and finding its way into my boots.

"Whoa," Ben says from the bank, but then he's right beside me, one hand gripping my arm and another on the opposite shoulder. "You good?"

Not in the least.

I'm still out of sorts and don't say anything at first, but when I look up at him, he's got the slightest smile on his lips.

The disgusting sludge on the creek bottom is squelching against my hands and knees. I can feel a bruise forming where my left hand landed on a rock before slipping off into the muck. My face is flushed from embarrassment and the cold. This is *not* where I want to be or how I want to feel.

"Do you seriously find this funny?" I say, frowning at him.

"I mean, it's not *not* funny." His smile grows a little.

I shrug off his hands and go to get up, but in my haste, I just push myself sideways and almost topple even farther into the water. It's Ben's hands that stop me, which is even more infuriating.

"Don't be a pest, Cassie," he says, tugging me up.

Ben probably used to call me a pest at least five times a day when we were younger. It's how he referred to his younger sisters, but then he started using it with me, too. Back then, I liked it. It made me feel like we were siblings, and the way he said it always sounded like a term of endearment.

I don't think I can hear anything like endearment in his voice now, and I'm not really in the mood to like it, given there's gross squishy stuff oozing between my fingers.

I let him help me up, but as he does, I grumble, "It's *not* funny."

"I guess it's all perspective, isn't it?" He says this like an afterthought—he's not even looking at me as he guides me toward the creek bank. His school shoes are soaked.

"Well, my *perspective* is this is gross and I hate it."

"So you're scared of a little muck now?"

I side-eye him as we grapple with the creek bank and climb to the top. His voice is laced with a taunt and challenge.

"I'm not *scared* of muck. I just don't particularly love the *feeling* of it. Do you?"

He shrugs. "There're worse feelings," he says, and climbs over the fence.

I wonder which feelings he's referring to, and if I've caused them. I'm not about to ask, though.

Once we're both standing on the other side of the fence, he shifts his feet and his waterlogged shoes make a very unsavory sound. Like two short farts. He looks at his shoes and then up at me. His face breaks out into a grin, and the sight takes me so by surprise, I grin back like a reflex.

"Speaking of disgusting," I say.

He shifts his weight a few more times to create more farting sounds, and I can't help but laugh.

I shift my weight a little, too, just to see what my boots will do, but all we hear is some sloshing.

"Here," Ben says, and offers a shoulder. "You should pour those out . . . unless you want to take some samples from them." He's still grinning, and I can't believe it took me falling into the creek to cause this response in him.

After I empty out both boots while gripping his shoulder for balance, I say, "Thanks. Sorry about your shoes, though."

"Whatever. They're just shoes."

"Won't your parents be mad?"

"Nah. They'll dry out."

Meanwhile, the knees of my jeans will probably hold the greenish-brown stains on them in perpetuity (SAT term). "Okay, well, I guess we have enough samples, even without those last two." The vials I dropped when I slipped are long gone down the creek by now. "Wanna call it quits?"

"Sure do."

We collect our things and head back up the path to my house, both sets of feet now a chorus of squelches and farts and burps—and both of us unable to stop our giggles.

CHAPTER FOURTEEN

I'm still thinking about Ben as our second GSA meeting starts the next day. I've been racking my brain to figure out how to get Ben to a place where I could actually bring him to one of these meetings. I feel like we made some progress yesterday—even if that progress came as an unexpected result of me embarrassing myself. But I definitely *don't* feel like we're at the stage where I could bring him to Crosswalk, and I wonder how to quicken the pace of the progress I make with him.

But since I've been put in charge of taking Crosswalk meeting minutes (because I am *excellent* at things like this), I have to shift my brainpower to really listening to everyone and recording the gist of our conversation. If I'm being honest, I love this role of record-keeper, even if a small part of me is worried the minutes could fall into the wrong hands.

We have the same group as last time, and the agreed-upon

topic for today's meeting is "Safe Spaces." I'm sitting on the couch again, cross-legged, with my computer on my lap.

I was surprised when Halle sat down next to me on the couch, and my body responded by instantly tensing and tightening into a smaller version of myself. Her "Hey" was relatively warm, though, and when a smile accompanied it, I let a small part of me believe she might like me a little. Then again, maybe she just wants to make sure I'm taking notes properly.

I start a new folder on Google Drive for our meeting minutes and create a new document. I write:

Crosswalk Meeting Minutes: September 23

**Minutes are strictly confidential to Crosswalk members. No sharing without agreement from all members.*

**Notetaker: Cassie P.*

- Check-ins and pronouns
- Nai: What makes a space "safe"?

Nai's question immediately sets off a series of other questions by a variety of people.

"And who is it safe for?"

"And can it be safe for *everyone*?"

"Are safe spaces always physical spaces?"

I try to write down as many of these questions as I can. Something in my busy brain tells me they might come in handy later.

"Such good questions, everyone!" Nai says. "Maybe we can

think about this in terms of queer folks and what makes space safe for them first? Noting, of course, that intersectionality exists, and queer safe spaces should also be safe for disabled folks and BIPOC folks and other marginalized groups."

It's become very apparent that Nai is a natural facilitator, and I envy her ease in situations like this.

"Personally," Muriel begins, "I love it when I walk into a space that I know has a lot of other queer people in it. So, like, the *people* in a space make me feel more or less safe, I think."

"Yeah, totally," Sam says. "But what makes queer people gravitate to that space in the first place?"

"Maybe if it's super transparent about what kind of space it is?" Jay says. "Like, if I see visible signs or messaging at the entrance of one place and not another, I tend to automatically choose the one with messaging, you know?"

Beside me, Halle nods and says, "Yeah, same. But sometimes those signs and messaging are just all talk, too, right? Like there's that restaurant downtown—Buds and Light or something—that's right next to a rainbow crosswalk and has rainbows and stuff up in their windows."

She's motioning with her hands a lot, and her arm keeps bumping into mine. I glance at her, and from the side, I'm struck by just how long her eyelashes are. I frown and look back at my screen.

"Looks great," she continues. "Looks like a cool place for queers to hang out, right? But remember when you and I went in there last year?" She looks at Jay, who nods with recognition. "The bathrooms were gendered male and female, and the sign on the 'men's room' looked like the traditional man symbol but with a beer bottle where the penis would be. And instead of the usual annoying skirt on the 'women's room' symbol, it had an upside-down martini glass. Super clever and funny, right? Maybe not the biggest deal? But, like, where would Sam go? Are you a beer bottle or a martini glass, Sam? Oh, I know—neither. So where's your safe space to pee?"

When I look at her again, I see that her face has grown red with indignation on Sam's behalf. Despite my body shrinking away from her the moment she sat down, her leg and arm are now pressed into mine, and I can feel her vibrating next to me.

The sensation is . . . troubling.

Sam winks at her and smiles. "Aw, babe, thanks for thinking of my washroom welfare. I mean, I'd probably be a martini in that situation, but yeah—I'd rather have a shot glass or champagne flute."

A few people giggle, but Halle continues, "Not to mention, *I* don't want to have to be a damn martini glass or skirt or whatever, either!"

"Okay, so I'm getting two important things here," Nai says. "One, that signage doesn't always ensure safety, and two, that in safe spaces for queers, basic human needs like washrooms should account for queerness."

I write down what Nai just said word for word on the minutes because she's summarized the conversation better than I could.

I look up and catch Halle examining my notes. We make eye contact, and her face remains neutral as she says, "You type fast."

"Uh, thanks." I'm not sure it was meant to be a compliment, but I'll take it.

"Question?" Quinn says, raising his hand tentatively by his cheek.

Nai smiles and says, "You don't need to raise your hand, Quinn."

He keeps his hand up anyway and says, "I just don't want to take up too much space as a straight, cis dude. *This* is supposed to be a safe space for queers, right?"

Muriel lets out a squeal and practically tackles him from the side. As she squeezes the crap out of him, she yells, "See? SEE? This is why I LOVE HIM."

"Um, yeah. That's pretty lovable," Sam says. "Thanks, Quinn! What's your question?"

"Okay, well, it makes sense to me that spaces that are mainly for queer folks can and should be safe for queer folks. But what about spaces that are still pretty straight and cis? How do we make *those* spaces safer for queer folks, even if they're not technically queer *spaces*?" He glances at Muriel, who still has her arms wrapped tightly around him. "Does that make sense?"

Muriel nods with vigor and says, "Perfect sense, platonic love of my life!"

"That's a great question," Halle responds. "Anyone have any ideas?" She considers me as she says this, an eyebrow cocked. I've been immersed in the adorable duo of Quinn and Muriel, and when Halle looks at me, I stare back down at my laptop and furiously write down Quinn's question. And then I add some random, unnecessary notes so I don't have to look up again. I have an important task. I don't have time to respond to questions, you see.

Nai saves my butt by saying, "Right, like is there a way to make a space like St. Luke's safer, even if it's not an entirely safe space?"

Nai's interpretation of Quinn's question strikes something deep in my chest. I write her question down and listen for possible answers, ready to type them down, too.

"Ooh . . . yeah!" Nicky says. "How cool would that be?"

She's been mostly quiet as well so far—probably too busy pushing her knee up against Halle's from where she's sitting way too close to Halle on the other side of this couch that is *clearly made for two*.

I'm startled out of my unjustified jealousy by Halle.

"What d'you think, Cassie?" she asks. "Is there a way to create safe space at St. Luke's, given it's Catholic and obviously not too far along yet?"

I'm trying to read her face and tone, but there doesn't seem to be the same bitterness or irritation in either as I've seen and heard at other times. Maybe a little sass, but mostly she just sounds . . . curious?

I try to hold her gaze, but she's looking so attentively at me that I let my eyes continue up toward the ceiling and pretend this is my thinking face. "Um, well . . ." *Come on, Cassie. Think. Look like you know what you're doing. Like you're an exceptional ally, just like Quinn.* But I'm supremely nervous now, and Halle's thigh is still touching mine, and I'm worried that I'll say something ridiculous. My mind goes blank. I employ a stalling tactic that I use in class when I'm caught off guard by a question. "I . . . can see possibilities, but . . . I might have to think a bit more on that question."

I glance at Halle, whose brow now holds a slight wrinkle, and then aim my eyes back at my laptop screen to punch on a few more keys.

"Okay, let's come back to that," Nai says, thankfully. "What about the original question—criteria for queer safe spaces in general?"

Even though I feel like I failed a small test, I also really want to hear more about what others have to say on this topic. It feels like one that might help me with Ben.

"Can you read back what we have so far, Cassie?" Nai asks.

Yes I can! Because I take amazing notes! I read back the points about having queer people in the space, signage (sometimes), and basic needs being met, like gender-neutral bathrooms.

"Anything else?" Nai asks.

"Something that also makes a space feel safer for me is if we're allowed to make mistakes. Like, there's less judgment about that, as long as people are open to also being called in about their mistakes?"

This is from Jay, and his comment lifts a little weight from my shoulders.

"And don't forget a good set of guidelines or norms," Sam says.

"And snacks! Can't have a really good safe space without snacks!" Muriel shouts.

"Including vegan and vegetarian and gluten-free, nut-free snacks, obviously," Jay says, and everyone laughs because the snacks Sam brought today are definitely none of those things, and Halle already criticized them about it, to which they responded, "Guess you're in charge of snacks now, Halle!"

The conversation continues, touching on things like accessibility, privacy, and more.

By the end of the meeting, I've taken pages of notes, and, on a separate Google Doc after the meeting, I also add some of my own thoughts. Because this conversation and Quinn's question about safe spaces within less safe spaces have tweaked something in my brain, and I think I know what my next move with Ben is going to be.

CHAPTER FIFTEEN

When I pick up my phone later that night, my heart is beating way too fast, and I have to take some deep breaths. I'm supposed to be typing a message to Halle, but my thumbs are hovering over my phone, *not* typing.

I squeeze my eyes shut. *Cassie, you have to do this. You have to do something.* I remind myself that I have a mission, and that mission, so far, is basically failing. Something different is in order. But I'll need help. I open my eyes and type:

Cassie: Hey.:)

I erase the happy face.

Cassie: Hey.

That sounds passive-aggressive, so I add an exclamation point.

Cassie: Hey!

I hit send and hope Halle doesn't read too much into the exclamation point. When she texts back a noncommittal sup a minute later, my heart does something between an annoying little twirl (she responded!) and a tight clenching (no exclamation point) in my chest. I try really hard to ignore it.

It was clear at our meeting tonight that Halle and Nicky are into each other from the fact that Nicky showed up *early*, sat next to Halle *again*, and kept leaning in to whisper side comments to Halle on the couch. *And* Halle seemed receptive to all of it.

So, since there's nothing I can do about this *thing* that I seem to have for Halle—given that I am committed to staying squarely in the straight zone, and, oh yeah, why would Halle be interested in me anyway—I've been trying very hard not to think about her as anything more than a coleader and new almost friend.

But. I also think she's the best person to help me with this idea I've come up with. I tell myself: She's super smart. She's a strong person. She seems to have so much knowledge about queer stuff and activism. Even more than Nai. More than Sam. Obviously more than me. So I have to turn to my excellent compartmentalizing skills and force my brain into thinking of Halle as a resource. An almost-friendly resource. That's all. I try to stay upbeat and casual.

Cassie: I have an idea inspired by Crosswalk and was hoping to run it by you! Would you have time tomorrow to meet up after school? Or before?

Cassie: No worries if not.

I'm shocked when Halle replies immediately, albeit with the same lack of enthusiasm.

Halle: sure

Halle: before school works

I'm a little surprised she opts for the morning—she doesn't really strike me as a morning person. Regardless, my heart is now breakdancing in my chest, and I'm trying to change the music to Enya. *Calm down, Cassie. Friendly resource. This is basically homework.*

Cassie: Great. When and where?

Halle: 7:45 at pinetree? I have an early ap start. Meet me at the front doors

Cassie: sounds good

It kills me to leave out the capital and period, but I have to make sacrifices for the greater good of perceived nonchalance (SAT word). At least meeting *before* school sets the right tone. There's nothing sexy or romantic about being at school before class starts.

Halle: Cool see u

I resist the urge to send one more text with a grateful emoji and instead throw my phone into the drawer of my side table and cover my face with my hands. *These feelings are* not *okay, Cassie. Get it together.*

I tell myself that my resolve will be better tomorrow.

I take my phone out a minute later to see if she texted anything else, just in case.

She hasn't.

It's fine.

I'm early, as always, but I force myself to loiter in the St. Luke's parking lot until it's 7:45 and *then* walk over to Pinetree. That way I'll be at *least* a minute late, and that's about as good as it gets when I'm trying to be cool and tardy.

Halle is already standing just inside the glass doors to the school, waiting, and I don't know why I'm surprised—she and Jay have arrived before me to both Crosswalk meetings so far.

When she sees me, her eyebrows lift and she swings open one of the doors, holding it for me as I walk inside.

We both say "Hey" at the exact same time. And then we both say "How's it going?" at the exact same time. And then we stand just inside, facing each other, and laugh awkwardly.

"Let's assume we're both good and move on, 'kay?" she says, a half smile on her lips.

"Let's," I say, and smile back. An involuntary urge to hug her overcomes me, but that feels impossible. Instead, I say, "Thanks so much for meeting me. I won't take too long, I promise. I mean, I guess we could've talked on the phone or whatever, but I figured our schools are so close, you know? So why not just meet? I prefer face-to-face anyway, don't you?"

I'm talking fast. I need to chill out.

She eyes me up, probably reconsidering meeting with me. "Yeah . . . totally," she says. "Come on." She walks us over to some couches around the corner from the entrance.

I've only ever been inside Pinetree for debate and athletic events. And I've never been here so early. This part of the school is definitely older than ours, and more impersonal, but I like that there are still Progress Pride flags adorning the halls even though Pinetree's Solidarity Week ended a week ago.

(I learned what Progress Pride flags are after I posted a photo of a regular Pride flag to our group chat to show my enthusiasm for gayness, and Halle very quickly corrected me with the updated version and a link to the Wikipedia page on it.)

Halle sits kind of in the middle of the couch, and I sit as far to one end as possible. Even so, we're only about a half foot apart. I hold my backpack on my lap and keep my feet firmly planted on the ground. It's an awkward way to sit, but I'm awkward, so here we are.

She sits facing me, one leg on the floor and one bent in front of her. She leans against the back of the couch, lays her hands in her lap, and says, "So . . . what's this idea of yours?"

Between her body language and tone, I can't quite get a handle on how she's feeling right now. Maybe some doubt mixed with curiosity?

I swallow and get my words out as best I can. "Um, okay, so I thought of a little side project that's related to Crosswalk, and I wanted your thoughts, because I could use your help . . . if you had the time, I mean."

She's looking at me very intently now, her lips pushed to one side and a slight wrinkle on her brow, and it is *very* hard not to stare at the perfect dimple that forms on her left cheek. I shift my eyes to her left ear instead.

"Okay . . ." she says. "I'm gonna need a bit more than that." Her eyes gleam, like she's teasing me.

The swirly, annoying feelings are back in my chest—from nerves and excitement, I tell myself. I keep my feet on the ground, even though I have to crank my neck to face Halle. I hold my right hand hard with my left against my backpack.

"But first," she says, before I can elaborate, "why don't you put this down for a sec?" She leans over and gently tugs the backpack out of my lap. I let her because it would be weird not to. She places the bag on the floor by my feet. I have no choice now but to face her, and when I shift my body, she's, like, *right there.*

I quickly launch into further explanation. "Right. Okay, so I've been thinking about our Crosswalk conversation last night—about safe spaces? About how, before, Jay used the broom closet as *his* safe space, when he needed somewhere to be."

I wrinkle my nose and squeeze my hands in my lap, feeling very *un*safe in my emotions right now—because of what bubbles up when I'm around Halle, but also because of how badly I need her help to make this work so I can stop anything worse bubbling up with Ben. I force myself to keep going.

"And then I started wondering what that space could look like in a school like St. Luke's—like what you were asking about—where things are . . . um, well, more *limited*, I guess?"

The more I thought about Halle's question after the meeting last night, the more disappointed I became as I realized just how *little* evidence of safe space for LGBTQ+ people there is at St. Luke's. Nothing to tell anyone who might be queer that it's okay. Could be okay. At some point.

My head is starting to hurt, and I blink a few times to clear my mind.

Three of Halle's fingers are suddenly on my knee, and I have to force my face to stay neutral, even though her touch sends a jolt of something between panic and thrill through me.

"You good?" she asks, the frown I've already come to know so well deepening.

Jesus. This is not how you recruit people to your cause, Cassie. I nod and force my own brow to smooth out. "Totally!" I say.

She doesn't look convinced, but lets her fingers slip away from my knee. I'm both relieved and devastated.

I start talking with gusto, so she knows I'm just fine.

"Okay, so *then* I was thinking, how cool might it be to create some *secret* safe spaces at St. Luke's? Like, we have the broom closet for Crosswalk, and that's awesome. But what about creating little pockets of queer spaces—however that might look—at my school?"

I glance at her to see how she's receiving this idea. Her eyes seem bright, but there's a bit of uncertainty in them, too, I think.

"You mean we have secret GSA meetings at St. Luke's or something?" she asks.

I remember how resistant she was to engaging with St. Luke's and religion early on, and I wonder if that's what she's thinking about now, too.

"No—not exactly," I say, hoping I can appeal to her sense of activism and rebellion. "I was thinking more along the lines of 'pop-up' moments of queerness to shake things up a bit at St. Luke's. Like, for instance, what if a rainbow display burst open somewhere overnight? Or some LGBTQ+ resources were posted in the bathroom? Or . . ." I look up, searching for another example, but she finishes my sentence for me.

"A rainbow pathway suddenly extends from the St. Luke's front entrance one morning?"

A playful smile appears on her lips, and I can't help but get excited. "Yes! Exactly! It's not the same as having a GSA, but maybe it could help make a few students feel *some* of what we get from being in *our* GSA, even if they can't or aren't ready to come to Crosswalk."

Like one student in particular. After our Crosswalk meeting last night, as I was going through my notes from the meeting and making them perfect, this idea was all I could think about. Maybe this is how I bring the GSA to Ben until he's ready to come to Crosswalk itself.

"I bet it'll piss off some people at your school, too." Her smile spreads into a grin. "Cool idea, Cassie," Halle says, knocking her knuckles against my leg.

My fingers ache from squeezing them, but her words turn my smile into a grin, too. "Yeah?" I say.

"Yeah. You're actually practicing what we talked about last night. Putting it into action." Her demeanor seems to shift to something more subdued. She crosses her arms. "That's really cool allyship."

Her words give me exactly what I want—to be seen as a good ally—and they also serve as a reminder that I'm just a straight girl in her eyes, which is what I need her to see. But knowing that's how she sees me still feels like crap.

I think, *This is a good time to look away, Cassie.* But I can't seem to. "Mm-hmm. Totally." *I'm a great ally. Yup.*

"You might be more badass than I thought you were," she says, and the pushy-lips/dimple combination is back.

"Badass" is definitely not a word used to describe me, like, ever, and I kind of wish Kendra was here to witness this exchange.

"Ha, well, I might need some guidance in that area," I say.

"Happy to," she says, and then just gazes at me for a moment.

The intensity of her focus makes me supremely nervous. My neck gets sweaty, my heart starts to thump.

I stand up, sweeping up my backpack as I do and clutching it to my chest like it's my newborn baby. "Okay!" I declare, facing her. "I should get going, but maybe we can meet up soon and start thinking through next steps. All right?"

"Yeah, good," she says, standing as well, a bemused (SAT word) expression on her face.

"Good" is nowhere close to the truth. My stomach is churning. My neck is on fire. I feel like my eyes are melting into my skin.

"Okay, well, bye!" I say in the cheeriest voice I can.

It's clear from her face now that she thinks I'm a complete weirdo. I pivot and walk away, unsure about how I'm going to manage my awkwardness or feelings while working with Halle, but also unable to see any other way to get to where I want to go.

CHAPTER SIXTEEN

Halle: Hey u free right now?

I'm deep into my usual Sunday homework session, finishing anything due in the next couple of days, and am actually in the middle of creating a *very* impressive virtual classroom for my AP French project, but obviously I can't say that.

After meeting with Halle on Friday, my stomach continued to twist inside of me all day—an unwanted tightening that I kept having to ignore. It didn't help that I wasn't as prepared as usual for most of my classes because I'd spent so much time on Crosswalk stuff . . . and on trying not to think about Halle but then thinking about Halle.

But I have to be able to manage all of this if I want to accomplish my various goals, so I set aside my French project and reply.

Cassie: Ya I'm free

Cassie: What's up?

Super casual. That's me.

Halle: been thinking about your project idea

A little bump of excitement thumps in my chest at this. She was thinking about me, too. Or at least, my project.

Halle: can I run some stuff by u? Wanna come over?

Over? Like, to her house? Just the two of us? The twisting in my stomach screws even tighter. *Bad idea, Cassie.* But my fingers have their own plans, because they type back:

Cassie: Sure. What time?

Halle: An hour?

Halle: should I ask Nicky too?

Halle: Might be helpful to have another st. Luke's pesron involved, but no pressure

I don't often swear out loud, but when I read this, an "Oh, fer fuck's sake" escapes my mouth, and I want to tuck and roll off my bed just to feel my body thump against the ground. Punishment for being so naive. Instead, I force a super-chill response, because I'll just look jealous or something if I say no to letting Nicky help.

Cassie: Great idea!

Halle: cool

A ridiculous vision of Nicky and Halle making out in the confessional appears, and I wonder where this overactive imagination is when I need ideas for creative writing in English class.

Cassie: Cool

Halle: see u in an hour

Cassie: Okay

Halle: 😎🙌

I hate both of these emojis. They scream friend zone. A "We're cool" followed by a hand gesture that involves zero contact with the other person.

But then, the friend zone is exactly where I need to be.

Cassie: 👍

Take that. Thumbs are the worst.

Halle's room is . . . not what I expected. I guess I was thinking there would be signs of insurrection and defiance everywhere—posters and books and flags screaming from every surface. But the first thing I notice is a small collection of colorful pillows in one corner that reminds me of the reading corner in my first-grade classroom—cozy and inviting. Then I notice her twin bed is made, and her books include everything from the expected texts—titles like *Gender Outlaw* and *Freedom Is a Constant Struggle*—but also a whole collection of very bright book spines with titles like *Let's Talk About Love* and *Felix Ever After* that suggest more romantic leanings, maybe? Three retro garden gnomes line the top of her shelf, while the expected posters of revolution and resistance cover the wall behind her desk, which, I note with delight, holds a very organized collection of stationery.

I guess in my mind, Halle was determined and focused, but also rough around the edges. Intense but unruly. Maybe a little dark. This room isn't rough or dark at all. Just unpredictable in a way I don't find scary.

I kind of just wish it *were* scary so my mind didn't instantly leap to spending more time here.

Nicky had arrived ahead of me (surprise, surprise) and is already nestled in the pile of pillows, her back against the wall. Halle sits beside her (*ugh*), and I sit across from them on an overfull cushion that makes me feel like I'm going to capsize at any moment. *Great choice, Cassie.*

Once we're all settled, Halle says, "This is a rad idea, Cassie. After we talked, I couldn't stop thinking about it."

"Yeah, and the fact that you're willing to help us is so cool, too,"

Nicky says to Halle, and I'd roll my eyes if I weren't directly in front of them.

Apparently, Nicky and I are an "us" now.

"I think it's worth it," Halle says, looking at me in a way that actually does make me feel like this could be worth at least some of the unpleasantness I feel.

I figure I should say something, since this was supposed to be my idea and all. "Yeah, thanks for helping, Halle. I'm hoping this'll be a cool, underground way to bring some of Crosswalk into St. Luke's."

"Right," Halle says. "Like, you bring students from St. Luke's to Crosswalk, but we bring queerness into St. Luke's in sneaky, feisty ways." She grins, and it changes her whole face. That dimple appears. Fine lines extend from her eyes.

I can see she's genuinely excited about this, and though I've been worried on a number of fronts and—now—irritated by the fact that Nicky is also a part of it, I can't help but absorb a bit of her excitement. And admire her face.

"Okay," she says. "What's the plan, Cassie?"

Right. The plan. Because I totally have one. Usually, I would. But I spent so much time playing catch-up on my homework this weekend, I hadn't really gotten that far. But I can fake it. I'm good at faking it when I need to.

"I thought we might make a list of ways we could infiltrate St. Luke's with safe queer spaces. There's no idea too ridiculous at this point." Mainly because I need as many ideas as possible.

"Wait," Nicky says. "How come we're not doing this with the Crosswalk group?"

They both look at me.

"Oh," I say, "we can involve more people if you want. I just thought we'd keep it small at first—in case. I guess I thought too many voices at once might get a little complicated?"

Halle and Nicky nod like this makes perfect sense, and in all honesty, this *is* one of the reasons I wanted to keep it to just Halle and me. More people equals more chances that the secret gets out.

I don't need to mention the part of me that craves more time alone with Halle. I don't really want to think about that part anyway.

We start to brainstorm, with me writing stuff down. Halle has some great ideas already, and I'm wholly enamored with her level of initiative. I can still admire her initiative, at least.

As she's talking, Nicky's leaning back against the pillows scrolling on her phone (which makes me think she's less interested in this project and more interested in the person sitting next to her), but I notice her other hand is resting across a pillow behind Halle. Halle is leaning forward, but the minute she leans back, Nicky's arm will be across her shoulders, and I'm suddenly obsessed with making sure that doesn't happen.

As Halle continues to point out on her iPad some rainbow displays she googled, I lean forward, too, hoping to encourage this mutual leaning action. At one point, though, I guess I lean a little too far and topple forward off my wobbly pillow. My hand lands on Halle's knee to steady myself, and my face ends up inches from Halle's face. Our eyes catch for a moment; Halle's eyebrows raising, her lips upturned ever so slightly.

"Sorry," I say, pushing off of Halle's knee to right myself again. "Precarious pillow."

"You're good," she says, the smile still there, a glance at my hand on her knee, which I've forgotten to bring with me, it appears.

I let my hand slip away and will my butt to stay steady on its perch but continue leaning as she resumes her explanations, because I kind of liked how our faces felt so close together. She smells like citrus, and I like that, too—so much so that when she seems almost about to finish showing me her ideas, I say, "Oh, but wait, can you show me that other photo of the stairwell again?" and she kindly does.

At one point, she even shuffles forward a little and lays the iPad onto my crisscrossed legs—so she can really zoom in and show me the photos on the screen, I assume. Her left hand is resting beneath the iPad on my legs, her forehead is practically touching mine, and I resist the urge to sit back to create a bit of space, because . . . I really don't want to.

Eventually, though, I run out of questions, she leans back against the wall, Nicky doesn't move her arm, and all is lost.

"These ideas sound so good, Halle," Nicky says, before I can.

Not that you were even listening, I think.

"They really do," I say.

"Thanks, y'all. But you know your school better than I do. Any other ideas?"

Nicky and I look at each other for a split second, and in that moment I can tell that I need to say something before she does so Halle knows I have a brain and that I'm serious about this idea.

"Books!" I almost shout.

"Books?" Halle says.

"Yeah . . . um, like, the library would be a great spot for some surprise safe spaces." I realize as I'm saying it that this is a legitimately good idea, and I try not to overthink it as I continue. "Like, what if we planted some queer books, or . . . maybe had some kind of system to let kids know where to *find* queer books?"

"Yeah, I like it, Cassie," Halle says.

Not to be outdone, Nicky adds, "But how would that work?"

I hesitate, because I'm actually not sure how it would work.

Luckily, Halle jumps in. "Well," she begins, "our school has queer books shelved with everything else, but I know some schools and libraries have specific displays for certain books."

"Right, but we probably wouldn't get away with that in our library," Nicky says. She's right, and I resent her for it.

"But," I say, my brain whirring into action, "I volunteer in the library, so maybe there's a way I can indicate books with queer content. Like . . . with a sticker or something? And the librarian, Mr. Reyes, is actually so kind, and I even saw some queer books that he ordered."

Nicky's eyebrows raise, but she has nothing to say, and it is very satisfying.

"Sweet," Halle says, "so you have insider positioning already." She's grinning again, and my chest fills with fireworks. "You could label the books and then somehow communicate to the student body what the labels mean."

I nod and can feel my excitement from before grow.

"But wait—what if someone tells the admin about the labels? Or, like, any of these rainbow displays and stuff?" Nicky says, apparently hell-bent on making my amazing idea seem less amazing with all of her *buts*.

I'm a little stumped, to be honest, until Halle says, "I think we just have to accept that as we create these little guerrilla safc spaces, they'll probably get taken down. But we just keep putting stuff back up. It'll be like Whac-A-Mole, but the moles are queer!"

The best thing about this response is that, in Halle's excitement, she leans forward again, and Nicky's arm is left empty and forlorn.

We continue to expand on our ideas, including resources we can use, the "how" and the "when" to create rainbow displays, and more. I feel like I come out on top of this conversation, because we agree that before school would be a great time to make things happen, and I'm always up early, whereas Nicky *isn't* a morning person, so she agrees to do stuff after her evening theater rehearsals instead. Which means I don't have to worry about Nicky's arm around Halle at seven o'clock in the morning.

"This is fucking cool, gang," Halle says as she adds a reminder to her phone to meet with me Tuesday outside St. Luke's.

I'm feeling good overall, if a little nervous, too, but then Halle looks up at me and says, "Cassie, this is awesome allyship—the queers thank you." She tips her head and her eyes rest on me for a few moments, as though waiting for something. When I don't say anything, because I don't know what *to* say, she turns to Nicky and they smile at each other . . . because they're "queers" and I'm not.

Ugh. Most of my good feelings wither away as I'm reminded of how my allyship and goodness are dependent on my straightness.

We say goodbye a little while later, and though I'm loath to leave Nicky and Halle to do whatever two cute queers do when they're alone, I am also somewhat relieved to be outside in fresh air.

As I cruise home at a safe and responsible speed in my dad's giant Mercury Sable, I convince myself that this side project is an essential part of my master plan to prove to Ben that I'm *not* an asshole, that I *am* a good ally, and that I can help him to feel safe being who he is.

And I ignore the part where who I really am still feels terrifying.

CHAPTER SEVENTEEN

I'm reshelving books in the library Monday morning, eyeing any that look like they may have queer content, writing these titles down, and planning to google them later to see if they might need a special label.

I'm examining a book with a bright blue cover and possibly queer characters dancing across it, when I hear an "Excuse me?"

I turn to find a very small brown boy who I recognize as one of the eighth-grade class presidents, but whose name I can't remember, standing at the end of the "Fiction G–L" shelf.

"Oh, hi. Yes?"

"Um, sorry. But could you help me check out some books, please? I've never done it myself before, and Mr. Reyes isn't here."

That's because he's making us tea. "Yeah, of course! Come on." The boy seems so nervous and unsure of himself, and I'm determined to put him at ease. I'm also a little mesmerized by his head of thick, curly, somewhat obstinate (SAT word) black hair as I follow him to the front desk.

I take the seat behind the desk and slide the mouse back and forth to wake up the computer. "Okay, sorry—I should know this—but tell me your name again?" I ask, giving him a big smile.

He scrunches up his nose and replies, "Oh, uh, Cameron Kumar."

"That's a movie-star name!" I say, hoping to get past his tentativeness, and I type it into the computer. His school profile comes up, confirming he's in the eighth grade and a new student. "Welcome to St. Luke's, by the way. So cool you're already a class president! I'm Cassie, in case you couldn't remember." I used to lead school tours as part of the admissions process for prospective families, so I'm very good at welcoming students and making them feel like St. Luke's is the right place for them. "How are you liking it here so far?"

He's fidgety—twitching his shoulders up and down and fiddling with the cover of one of the two books he's placed on the counter. "It's okay."

Not a glowing review. "What school did you come from?"

"Kingsford-Smith."

Kingsford-Smith is a public elementary school on the east side of the city. I always wonder how public-school kids find the transition to St. Luke's—from public to private, secular to religious. I knew from my interactions with the admissions team here that a lot of families come to St. Luke's because of its strong programs, not necessarily because they're religious or anything. "Was it a good school?" I ask.

His face lights up. "Oh, yeah! I loved it."

"Did a lot of your friends come to St. Luke's, too?"

His excitement dulls. "No. Most went to David Thompson."

"Oh, sorry." He looks kind of sad, so, whether it's true or not, I add, "You seem like the kind of guy who makes friends easily, though!"

He shrugs.

Hmm. Okay. "Here," I say, "let me scan your books." I hold out a hand over the counter.

He's looking at the books and still playing with the cover. He glances up at me, then to the side. No one else is in the library, since it's still early. He pushes one of the books toward me, and I take it, scan the bar code into the computer, then pass it back to him.

"Um, actually, I think I'll just take that one book out for now," he says. "I probably won't have time to read this one yet anyway." He slides the other book off the counter and holds it out of sight.

"Oh, don't worry—Mr. Reyes has a pretty chill policy about returns. As long as it's not a high-demand book and you ask for an extension, you can usually keep it as long as you need to." I smile again.

He doesn't smile back this time, though. "No, it's fine. I'll just take the one. I'll put this one back."

"I can do that—no worries. It's my job!" Okay, maybe I'm not reading the room here, but something's off about this exchange, and now I want to know what it is.

I hold my hand out again. Cameron swallows and looks a little like a trapped animal. I don't *want* him to feel trapped, but I also want to know what the deal is. Finally, he places the other book on the counter and slides it toward me.

I glance at the cover and see two boys holding hands. I keep my face as neutral as possible, but inside, my heart sinks at his nervousness to share this with me, then lifts again at what this could mean.

Coming on the heels of the conversation with Halle and Nicky, this feels like a sign. What's my play here? I need to buy some time while I figure this out, so I tap out extra clicks on the computer like I'm doing something very important and make some quick mental calculations.

I want Cameron to know this book choice is perfectly okay and maybe even let him know about the GSA, but I also don't want to overwhelm him. Maybe he doesn't want me to react at all. Maybe he just wants me to ignore everything. I definitely understand that impulse.

In the end, I decide on something in between overly enthusiastic and completely indifferent, but with the possibility of future contact.

"Mr. Reyes said he's heard so many great things about this book," I say, finally scanning the bar code. "You'll have to let me know how it is. I'll expect a full review so I know if I should read it or not myself." I hand the book back to Cameron with another smile.

Cameron's eyebrows raise a little, but still no smile. Instead, his lips squish to the side. "Um, okay." He takes both books and shoves them into his backpack. "Thanks," he says with a sweet little wave.

"See you in student government!" I yell after him, unable to contain some of my enthusiasm. He gives me a startled look and just keeps going.

Oops. But I'm glad we've made this connection anyway and hope he comes back. I'm also even more determined to get tiny rainbow labels on some of these books as soon as possible.

CHAPTER EIGHTEEN

"Father Davis said they need altar servers this Sunday," my dad says as he forks a pork chop onto my plate.

This, I know, is not just a random comment.

"Can't Kendra do it?" I say, not even looking at Kendra.

"Why can't you? We'll already be there," my mom says.

Right . . . with Kendra.

We're all seated around the kitchen table, because my parents insist we eat together if everyone is home. I don't mind it in general, but my homework load is already outrageous, and when I can, I just eat and work, so these dinners sometimes feel like lost time.

"I know, but I already serve twice a month." I narrow my eyes at Kendra, who isn't saying anything—just shoveling rice into her mouth because she knows she won't have to do this. My parents have a severe case of babying-the-youngest-child syndrome.

"I think they need someone older. You can do it," Amma says, with finality.

I stifle the sigh that wants to escape and force my exasperation into the act of cutting up my meat instead.

With that decided, my parents ask us about our days, we talk about the next food drive my mom and the Catholic Women's League are organizing for the Society of Saint Vincent de Paul, and then my mom continues the saga of the woman she works with—my mom's a nurse—who drives her bananas.

Then Amma says, "Marianne mentioned that you and Ben are working on some kind of project together?"

I pause mid-chew. Ben's mom and dad and my parents seem to have let bygones be bygones over the past four years. They all have to interact through various church-related activities, so I guess they just moved past what happened. Or ignored it. I'm not sure which.

I finish chewing and swallow, because my mother hates it when anyone speaks with their mouth full. "Um, yeah. We're working on a biology project together." I'm surprised Ben mentioned this to his mom at all. Maybe he's more open at home than he is with me.

Amma and Thatha glance at each other. Kendra keeps eating. She doesn't really know about all the stuff that happened. She was only nine back then.

"How's that?" my dad asks. He's trying to be low-key about it, but I know what he's really asking: *Does Ben hate you? Is it hard? Have you made things up to him?*

Or maybe I'm just projecting my own questions onto him.

"Fine."

Amma sighs in that way that says, *Not good enough.*

I tell them what they want to hear. "We've already made a really good start. We're using the creek water for the project and were down there last week. Ben's super smart." *The project is going really well. You don't have to worry. I have everything under control, and I won't embarrass or disappoint or worry you again. I promise.*

"The creek?" Amma says, her eyebrows raised. "It's safe?"

"Yeah, totally safe. Ben even suggested it." *See? It's fine. Everything's fine. Or at least it will be.*

"Well, good," my dad says, and smiles at me, then at my mom. His way of saying, *Let's move on.*

I'm more than happy to move on, so I say, "I already got a quiz back in English, and I aced it. That class is so hard, since it's an AP course, but I think Ms. Miller really appreciates how much reading I did over the summer."

I can see Kendra roll her eyes in my peripheral vision.

"That's wonderful, Cassie," my dad says. My mom, however, just nods and dishes more green beans onto my plate. I can see she's still thinking about the whole Ben thing—at least I think she must be, given the peak of her eyebrow, which almost always means she's skeptical of something.

Now that she knows I'm doing this project with Ben, I'm going to have to prove to her, too, that I'm making things better. That what happened before won't happen again and that she can be proud of how together I am instead of dismayed by any cracks.

After people found out about what Ben and I were doing at the creek that day, after those boys made everything sound so much worse than it was, I'd noticed a lot of skeptical eyebrows from my mom, uncertain glances from my dad—like they were trying to figure out where they'd gone wrong and what was happening to their well-raised daughter.

I remember hating every single look and working hard to clear my parents' faces of them, to earn back their trust and their pride in me. I even volunteered to go to confession, surprising my mom. Despite her attempts to make me and Kendra confess on a semi-regular basis, I hadn't gone to confession since receiving Communion for the first time in the second grade—when I had nothing more to confess than fighting with my sister and not eating all of my dinner the night before.

I remember Amma frowning when I asked about going again.

"Why?" she said, as though there might be even more things I wanted to confess that she didn't know about.

"Um, I thought it might be good to be absolved?" *And hope you'll absolve me, too, if I go? And stop looking at me like you don't know me?*

She'd taken me to confession the following week and prayed in a pew while I spoke to the priest.

I didn't say everything I could have said. Even though confession is private, even though the priest couldn't see me in the confessional, I was terrified he'd recognize my voice. It wasn't Father Davis, our regular parish priest, thankfully, but rather a visiting priest. But revealing those parts of me that only Ben knew—that only the creek and grass and trees had heard—seemed impossible if there was even the slightest chance that those parts might be connected with me and shared with others. That would just make everything so much worse.

I made up something vague. My mother would never know. I told the priest I was mean to my friend—which I was—but not that I broke his trust, or that I abandoned him at the first sign of threat, or that something inside of me was so terrifying that it made me into a terrible person.

He gave me a penance of ten Hail Marys and sent me on my way.

When I came out of the confessional and sat beside my mom, she contemplated me for a moment and then asked, "What did he say?"

I told her about my penance, and she indicated the pull-out bench for kneeling in front of us.

I lowered the bench and knelt. My mother knelt next to me, which wasn't surprising—she loved to pray—but I did find a small amount of comfort in her joining me instead of judging me from behind.

We both rested our elbows on the back of the pew ahead of us, bowed our heads, and said our prayers in silence. When I was done with my Hail Marys, I kept my head bowed and eyes closed for a few moments longer and said my own penance. *I'm sorry for all my secrets, too. I'm sorry I let those secrets eat away at my goodness. I won't do it again.*

Once done, we got up to leave, and Amma put a hand on my shoulder as we walked out of the church. She said, "I hope you feel better."

I didn't. But I was determined to.

CHAPTER NINETEEN

The following morning at 7 a.m., Halle and I meet at one of the back entrances to St. Luke's. I try not to think about how good she looks in a simple red hoodie, or the way that hoodie reveals a thin line of skin above her jeans.

"Hey," she whispers.

"Hey," I whisper back. We probably don't need to whisper, given how early it is, but it just feels right.

The only other people here at this time are usually some of the cafeteria staff, a maintenance worker or two, and *sometimes* Dr. Ida. But when I've been here this early before to set up for different events or leave on a bus for a field trip, the school has been pretty empty, so I'm not too worried as Halle and I slip down the hallway toward the eighth-grade lockers.

We'd decided that setting up a cute burst of rainbow colors and a sign that says "You are loved no matter who you love" where the eighth graders congregate would be a great place to start. We agreed that the youngest kids in the school should know as soon as possible that being queer is okay with at least *someone* at St. Luke's. And maybe I was also thinking about Cameron and hoping he'd appreciate it, too.

I'm *sure* Halle would have gone with something a bit more in-your-face and edgy, but as we passed ideas back and forth yesterday in our DMs, she seemed open to letting me take the lead, which I appreciated. She said it was a nice "soft start" to get the ball rolling, and besides, "everything about this project is badass anyway."

Every time she called me or what we were doing "badass," it sent unfamiliar thrills through me.

When we reach the lockers, Halle sets down the bag and backpack she's brought. I was in charge of bringing tape, string, and scissors and making the sign, which I did locked in my room last night after dinner. I actually enjoyed this bit of light work, even if I had to give up some study time to do it. Even if writing the words "You are loved no matter who you love" felt like a message meant for others, not for me.

"Okay," Halle says, looking around. "What do you think? Where's the perfect spot for a rainbow burst?"

I scan the area, too. The lockers line either wall of the hallway, and each set has a bench seat in front of it. On this side of the hallway, at the end of the lockers, a thick wall juts out at a right angle, the sole purpose of which seems to be to house a large alcove with a life-size statue of the Virgin Mary standing inside of it, her hands extended out in front of her, her eyes gazing over the area between the lockers, presumably to keep eighth graders in line.

Halle follows my eyes and her own light up. She says, "Oh my God . . . should we? I mean, how do you feel about it?" Her eyes are gleaming, and I can tell she's excited about the prospect of queering up Mary, Mother of God, and though I feel excitement at this, too, a resistance flares inside of me. I know what it is, because it's a familiar feeling—guilt. How *do* I feel about it? I know how my mother would feel about it. Would this be disrespectful?

My nose scrunches up. "Uh—I don't know." I feel like I'm losing "badass" points by hesitating, and it deflates me a little.

She gazes at me for a moment, hands on her hips. "Well, I mean, it's more or less just a statue, right?"

Is it? That's not really how it feels to me. "I just—I think . . ."

Halle puts a hand on my arm. "It's fine. You feel weird about it. It's cool."

I'm not sure how cool she actually is about it, or if "weird" captures what I'm feeling, but I'm still relieved to hear her say this. I'm about to suggest we just create the display on top of the lockers instead, when we hear voices coming down the hallway. Both of us look at each other, wide-eyed. I quickly move to the nearest classroom door and jiggle the handle, but it's locked. I doubt any classrooms are open, and the nearest bathroom is at the other end of the hall, where the voices are coming from.

We're shielded at the moment by the wall with the alcove in it, but as soon as those people walk past this area, we'll be visible. I'm panicky and look at Halle, whose eyes are still wide. She holds her hands up in a "What do we do?" gesture. Before I can overthink it, I grab her hand and yank her into the alcove, ducking beneath Mary's extended hands. There's just enough space for us both, but we have to tuck ourselves together behind the statue.

The voices get nearer, and I can hear that one of them is definitely Dr. Ida, while the other sounds like Mrs. Keenan.

"Honestly, I think the dress code is fine the way it is," Mrs. Keenan says.

"Well, we should at least consider the complaints," Dr. Ida replies.

She's close now, and I can hear that Dr. Ida's voice sounds a little exasperated, or maybe just tired. Halle and I press into each other instinctively as their footsteps get closer, our hands still gripping each other's. I'm too alarmed to even partially enjoy the contact. Or be freaked out by it.

"But, Janice, imagine if we had students walking around here with their hair dyed all manner of colors and boys with ponytails or shoulder-length hair. Students have plenty of ways to self-express through their uniform."

"Hmm. Yes, well, let's save this discussion for the board meeting, shall we?" Dr. Ida's voice is right beside us now, and I can see over Mary's robed shoulder as she and Mrs. Keenan walk past us.

Halle grips my arm with her free hand and then indicates the bags of decorations lying on the floor at the other end of the lockers. We look wide-eyed at each other, then quickly back to Dr. Ida and Mrs. Keenan. I will them to keep walking, to not notice the bags and supplies. As if to spite me, Mrs. Keenan's head turns sharply.

"What are these?" she says, pausing and indicating the bags.

Dr. Ida stops and turns as well, but seems irritated by having to do so. "Some eighth graders must have forgotten their things. It happens." She continues to walk, and I hold my breath as Mrs. Keenan keeps looking at the bags for a moment.

Finally, she shakes her head and follows after Dr. Ida.

Both Halle and I let out a quiet breath. But then I hear a stifled chuckle, and I look at Halle. She's covering her mouth, and I widen my eyes again to warn her to stay quiet. She leans into me and tucks her head into my shoulder, presumably to hide her laughter. I am simultaneously frozen by her closeness and the fact that I can still see Dr. Ida's and Mrs. Keenan's receding backs down the hallway.

Once I'm very sure they're both gone, I finally loosen my grip on Halle's hand, but her fingers stay laced through mine.

"I'm so sorry," Halle whispers, a smile on her face, which is only inches from my own face. "Hiding behind the Virgin Mary while we're trying to queer things up was too funny not to laugh."

It *is* funny, but my entire body is too alert and too overwhelmed by mixed emotions right now to fully engage in her amusement. I let out a big burst of air and try to calm my pounding chest.

"Oh, damn," Halle says, squeezing my arm again and holding my hand tight. "Sorry, I shouldn't be laughing." Her expression becomes more serious.

"No, no," I whisper. "It's okay. I'm fine. That was just . . ." I wave my free hand around to convey my overwhelm.

"Yeah, I get it. Should we abort our mission for today?"

The thought of *not* following through on this plan feels like the easiest, smartest idea. But it also feels wrong. Mrs. Keenan annoys me on the best of days, but her dress code comments irritate me even more right now. A little rainbow expression feels like the right move.

"No, I think we should go for it, but we'll have to be quick. That was the principal and vice principal, and it sounds like they were headed into a board meeting or something. That means we have some time, but let's get to it." I realize we're still squished behind Mary, and I inch my way out, ducking beneath her extended right arm again. Halle follows after me and finally lets loose my hand, which leaves it feeling very empty.

I walk quietly down the hall a little ways in the direction that Dr. Ida and Mrs. Keenan went. I listen for a few moments, and when I don't hear anything, I deem it safe to proceed.

I return to Halle and whisper, "Okay, let's do this!"

She grins. "Awesome. So where should we set up?"

I look past her to the Virgin Mary statue and my initial resistance withers away, replaced by resolve. I decide Mary is on our side. She just protected us from getting caught, after all. "I think Mary would want our eighth graders to know they're safe and loved, don't you?" I say, grinning.

Halle's face lights up. "Yeah, she does!" she says, placing her hands on my waist and giving me a little squeeze, which sends an achy pulse through my chest.

We get to work, and in no more than fifteen minutes, the Virgin Mary is a beacon of rainbow love and acceptance. The sign

"You are loved no matter who you love" extends above the alcove, her shoulders are wreathed in a rainbow-colored, tissue-paper boa Halle made, and there is a profusion (SAT word) of colorful sticky notes with encouraging messages stuck to the wall around her.

Knowing that the display would likely get taken down and we wouldn't get any of this stuff back, we kept things simple and inexpensive, but the overall effect is still eye-catching. We take a moment to appreciate our work, take a photo (without us in it), then quietly pack up and slip back out the way we came. It's not yet 7:30 a.m., but a couple of teachers' cars are in the parking lot already. I take note of that for any future guerrilla acts.

Outside, Halle holds up her hand for a high five and I reciprocate. "We did it," she says, grinning.

"We did," I say, also grinning.

"You know," she says, "I definitely don't trust all this religious stuff, but I gotta say, my limited understanding of Mary is that she was pretty kick-ass herself. I can get behind that."

I smile and nod. "Yeah, I think she's pretty cool." It takes me a couple of seconds to get the next words on my mind out. "And I think it's really cool you're helping me with this . . . given the distrust in religion part."

Her grin softens to a smile. "Hey, I know I can be hard on Catholicism—for good reason—but if we can help a few Catholic queers out, then I'm all for it. If what you say is true, and people can figure out how to be Catholic *and* queer, then those people deserve to be happy, too, right?"

Right. Because I said something like that, didn't I?

I just smile and nod like I'm not a complete impostor in so many ways right now.

"Anyway," she continues, "let me know what happens. I hope it stays up long enough for at least some kids to see it."

"Me too. I'll for sure update you."

"What're you gonna do now?" she asks.

"Hide out in the gym locker room. No one will be there until way later, and then I can slip out and blend in with the general public." I say this with a little eyebrow bob, like I'm a super-sneaky spy, and she laughs, which is everything right now.

"Good call. See you Thursday?"

"Yup."

There's a moment when we just stand there, facing each other. I hitch my backpack up my shoulder a little more. She glances at my shoulder as I do.

I guess it would make sense to initiate a hug. I want to. But instead, I say, "Okay, see you then."

She blinks. Smiles. "Yup. Bye."

Off she goes across the street, and I watch her, wishing things were simpler—that following through on these feelings I have for her wasn't so complicated—but also happy for now that we've done something cute and good together.

CHAPTER TWENTY

My first class that day is bio, and I'm on pinpoints in my anticipation at seeing Ben. As I hid out in one of the locker room bathroom stalls before classes, I scoured social media, hoping to see some evidence of Halle's and my rainbow burst. By 8 a.m., I hadn't seen anything and was worried that maybe Mrs. Keenan or someone saw the display and took it down before any students saw it.

But at 8:07, when I refreshed my Instagram feed, there, in full rainbow color, was Mary, Mother of God, blessing all her gay children. I had to stifle a squeal, just in case someone had slipped into the locker room without me noticing. As I continued to flip from one social media account to another, a few more photos popped up with captions like "My big gay mama" and "Holy gay Mary!" and "Love you too, babe!"

To say I was thrilled is an understatement. Even if the display gets taken down at this very moment, these posts will live on and plenty of other people will see them. The folks posting are in the tenth and eleventh grades—I only follow a couple of ninth graders and no eighth graders—which means there are likely even more posts from younger kids, given the display is in their neck of the woods.

And on top of that, the posts so far are positive. No barf emojis or rude comments whatsoever.

As I finally leave the locker room, a buzz of excitement zips through me, giving me at least a little more confidence to face Ben, who I've barely had a chance to speak to since my embarrassing fall into the creek last week.

I take the long way around to class so that I have to pass the statue of Mary. Coming upon the alcove, I see a bundle of younger students gathered around Mary and my excitement rises, thinking they're reading all the messages, but then I see that they're removing the sticky notes and other decor. I'm about to go over and casually ask "What's up?" when I see Mrs. Keenan overseeing the whole endeavor.

Pardon my vain use of the Lord's name, but *Jesus frickin' Christ.* Not only is she taking down the display, but she's making little kids do it? Cue my own barf emoji.

I quickly change directions and keep walking past the alcove and on to bio.

It's fine. The rainbow work has been done, so you can suck it, Mrs. Keenan.

It's not in my nature to tell teachers or administrators to suck it, even in my own head, but I'll admit, something about the inner thought feels good.

When I get to the bio lab, I walk in and sit down like a queen.

When Ben walks in, I don't cower and search for some sign he registers my existence, but instead smile at him and wave.

Even the suspicious expression he gives me as he nods in response doesn't spoil my mood. And as others enter the room, I overhear a few comments like "Who do you think did it?" and "I wish they'd just kept it up. Mary looked so cute in a boa"—which just increases my good vibes.

As class proceeds, I plan out what I'm going to say to Ben. I miss some of the lesson, but that's fine. I can catch up later. I need to cash in on this moment and feeling.

Mr. A gives us a decent amount of time at the end of class to work on our projects and begin studying our samples, which we've been caring for over the past few days. This is even better. Now I don't have to try to catch Ben after class.

I don't wait for Ben to come to me this time. I grab my laptop, binder, and backpack and stride to where he's starting to collect his things at the back of the room. I plunk my stuff on his desk.

"Hi!" I say instead of the usual "Hey."

He pauses what he's doing for a second and gives me another dubious look, but at least he says "Hi" back. Not "Hey," but "Hi."

Point for me!

I'm not wasting this on bio stuff. "Did you hear about the thing with the statue of Mary?" I ask, aiming for somewhere between eager and innocent until proven guilty. I'd already decided that I would wait to tell him it's me behind the pop-ups—gauge his reaction first.

"What thing?" he replies, the tiniest hint of interest in his tone.

Point two!

(Anything counts as a point at this stage.)

"Someone set up all this rainbow stuff around the statue—like, rainbow boas, cute sticky-note messages, and other stuff. Here, I'll show you a couple of posts."

He sniffs but doesn't seem averse to seeing the posts, so I glance over at Mr. A, who's feeding Sal the axolotl, and pull out my phone. "See? Cool, right?"

Ben looks at the photo, a small crinkle on his forehead, but I think it's just from concentration, not perturbation (SAT word).

"Huh. What's the deal?" he asks.

A curious question! Point three!

"It looks like the messages are around acceptance for LGBTQ+ people. Like, it's some kind of Pride display or something." *But that's all I know, honest.*

He glances up at me quickly and then back at the screen for one more look, then at his agenda. "Cool."

"Yeah, I've never seen anything like it at St. Luke's before. It's nice to see it here, though."

He doesn't say anything for a few seconds and a spike of worry pricks my chest. *Too much?*

But then he says, "Yeah" and "Should we figure out our next time to meet?" And even though he's moved on from the Pride display, he's also asking about meeting up again, and I feel like I just got fifty bonus points.

A few minutes later, I'm still buzzing with excitement as we observe our protists. "Here, you look," I say.

Ben is beside me, cheek flat against his arm, which is spread out across the lab table.

He drags himself up, and I shift to let him look into the microscope. We're supposed to be viewing our samples and recording our observations.

Through the lens, our protists appear like bright green leaves, their insides shifting around like little galaxies. We write down our observations. Ben doodles on the page, and I tell him (lightly) to stop it, and he draws a floating head that's supposed to be *my* head but looks like a Gorgon, and I roll my eyes at him, but secretly I love that he's teasing me, and it makes me think that telling him about the pop-up has had a greater impact than I could have even hoped for.

But this project is still important, so at the moment, I try to ease us into the upcoming stages without stressing him out like before.

"Is there some part of these next steps you prefer to take on? I mean, I'm happy to do whatever, but are you, like, especially passionate about graphs or slideshows or anything?" I try, keeping my tone light and a small smile on my face so he knows I'm joking around.

He stands and reaches his arms above his head to stretch. "Yeah, well, who isn't passionate about slideshows?"

"I mean, I don't know about you, but I dream about them—the colors, the transitions, the fonts, the animations."

He side-eyes me and lets his arms fall. "I bet you're not even joking."

"What kind of monster jokes about slideshows?" I say, and am impressed with how quickly the sarcasm forms on my lips.

Mr. A comes around at that moment to pass back some quizzes we did a week ago. "Here, you two. Nice work, overall!"

Ben barely looks at his paper. I look at mine and see I've received a B.

A what?

Mr. A taps my paper. "No haggling?" he says, his tone teasing, but in a way that is much less desirable than Ben's teasing.

"Huh?" I say, before I can align my response to the adult in front of me.

"Huh?" he echoes, an eyebrow raised.

"Sorry, I mean, pardon?" I struggle to keep the irritation out of my tone.

"Remember when you used to haggle with me over one percent? Slacking off, aren't ya, Cass-o-lass?" he says to me. Then to Ben he adds, "I thought I was in fight club!" He laughs. A few kids beside us laugh, too, which seems to encourage him, because he adds, "Better watch out with this one, Ben. One wrong move and it's—" He makes a throat-slitting motion with his finger.

Ben's eyebrows raise, but he looks to me, uncertain. I'm not sure it's uncertainty about if I'd actually murder him over schoolwork, or uncertainty about how he should respond to this situation.

I'm not sure what to say or do, either, to be honest. I'm embarrassed—by the grade and by Mr. A's comments. The last time I needed to process a B was probably in seventh grade, when I hadn't yet figured out how to study properly. And I must look like such a loser to Ben right now—someone who's so uptight they haggle over grades. (But let's be clear, I still haggle over grades when it's necessary.)

I blink, trying to gather myself. Aimlessly shuffle some papers on the desk. I shift my jaw, which suddenly feels tight.

This is not a big deal, Cassie. Get it together.

I plaster a grin on my face. "I'll hunt you down later, don't worry," I say to Mr. A.

Mr. A continues to address Ben. "Uh-oh. If I'm not here next class, Ben, send a search party."

His jokes are dumb and he's dumb, but my chest is tight and I feel dumb, too.

When Mr. A leaves, I snap open the rings on my binder and place the quiz inside, then snap the rings shut. I close my binder, trying to breathe out the tightness in my chest as I do.

When I'm finally done, Ben says, "You good?"

"Yup" is all I say, shoving stuff into my backpack. Ben doesn't say anything for a few seconds, and I hate the silence but also don't know how to speak through this tightness.

Thankfully, he finally says, "I'm good with graphs. When do we need them?"

I appreciate that he's just bypassed the whole conversation with Mr. A, but he's looking at me like he's worried I'm going to freak out. I'm embarrassed about the whole thing. About how much it bugged me. About Ben *seeing* how much it bugged me. *This* is not the me I want him to see. I have my shit together. I'm not someone who freaks out and makes things worse.

"Oh, um, I think they're due in four weeks."

I know exactly when they're due, but I hope this makes me sound less intense. Like he has nothing to worry about. Because I'm totally chill and together, just like he needs me to be.

"Cool. I'm on it," he says.

I nod, say "Thanks," and leave before he sees anything else I don't want him to.

CHAPTER TWENTY-ONE

I'm sitting in the student government meeting on Wednesday after school wishing I had this time for other things—namely, figuring out how to make up for that B in bio.

But the group is very animated right now about planning our booth for the fall fair that happens next month, which is an annual fundraiser for St. Luke's Parish. I put on my game face and zero in on the conversation.

"So the theme Natasha and I decided on is 'Falling in Love'—because, get it? It's fall?" James, one of our twelfth-grade class presidents, says as though he's very clever. "And we thought it'd be cool to decorate in a whole autumn theme with colored leaves and such, and all our games can be cute, matchy things that give people silly love horoscopes and predictions, or pair them with someone of the opposite gender in the school, or a celebrity or something, just for fun. We'll also have candygrams people can purchase and send to other students."

James, I've noticed, takes up a lot of talk time in our meetings. I'm getting so used to how considerate everyone is of each other at Crosswalk that James is starting to annoy me.

Some of his ideas wouldn't pass by the Crosswalk crew, either. And I know I should say something—point out that the gendered stuff is problematic. But talking about those things at Crosswalk is a lot different than talking about them here, where James will probably just gaslight me (Crosswalk word) or worse—interrogate me about why I care if the activities are gendered or not.

So I don't say anything.

But Yumi in ninth grade does. "Can people send candygrams to just friends, too?" she asks, and I notice Cameron is sitting beside her again. I wonder if he has a little crush on her. And then I wonder again about those books he was taking out of the library. Maybe he likes boys *and* girls? Or just . . . anyone?

I give my head a little shake. *Maybe you should just tone down your speculations, Cassie.*

Natasha is about to say something, but of course James gets there first. "I mean, I guess so. But it'll be more fun if we get people sending them to their crushes, don't you think?" He looks away from Yumi before she has a chance to respond.

I notice that Yumi is frowning at James but doesn't say anything more, either. And Cameron is staring intently at the doodles he's creating in his notebook.

I feel shitty about not saying anything, either, but I need to choose my battles right now. And James is not a battle I want to bother with.

"Okay! So we need people to sign up for jobs," James announces.

We spend the next few minutes sorting out who's doing what—from candygrams to games to decorating to supervising to cleanup. I sign up to decorate, because it's something I can do ahead of time and that hopefully won't take too much work.

Once that's done, James says, "Okay, the other thing Dr. Ida and Mrs. Keenan wanted us to be aware of is that there's going to be a special ceremony at the end of the fair this year—to reveal a new statue and gazebo that was donated by one of our alumni. We've been asked to help set up for this, too, so make sure you're free in the morning, at recess, and at lunch that day. We'll need all hands on deck."

I roll my eyes at James's self-importance but then wonder if this is what I sound like when I'm taking charge. The thought makes me frown at myself.

The fair takes place during last period on a Friday and extends to just after school. It's really fun, usually. The whole school gets the last period off from classes, and parents and alumni are invited to attend, and the whole building is filled with food, games, and entertainment.

But it's also a lot.

By the end of the meeting, I now have yet another thing added to my plate, and my stomach feels jittery at the thought of everything I need to get done. But I'll just do what I always do—make a list, prioritize it, and get to work.

CHAPTER TWENTY-TWO

"HOLD UP!" This is Halle, who is incensed by the story Lou is telling right now. "He did *what now*?"

We'd started our Crosswalk meeting tonight with check-ins—each of us sharing a highlight, lowlight, or "weird-light" from our past week (this is Nai's idea, and I swear she must have been a camp counselor or something). Two new people show up—juniors from Pinetree whose names are Jesse (she/her) and Tansi (she/her/they/them). They're holding hands and are way too attractive for me to even look at them for too long.

It's still just me and Nicky from St. Luke's, and I really hope I'll be able to get a few more people here soon—one in particular, of course. I'd been feeling optimistic about that possibility for a minute or two on Tuesday, but after that weird situation with Mr. A, I'm not sure where Ben and I are at. Why would he want to hang out with someone who's so uptight when he's clearly trying to stay calm?

Anyway, I'm hoping tonight's meeting will reinspire me, but so far, the discussion is mostly frustrating.

Lou—who's using she/her pronouns tonight—has just shared a lowlight about how one of her cousins just came out to his parents, and how his parents had their family minister write a letter to him about the "impurity of homosexual acts," which prompted Halle's indignant response.

(Halle, by the way, is sitting cross-legged on the couch, and one of her knees is overlapping Nicky's thigh, and I have never wanted to be a thigh so badly in my life.)

"Yeah, my cousin read me the whole thing over the phone. It's really awful—like legit 'fire and brimstone' stuff. He was in tears, and I feel so sad for him." Lou's voice gets choked at the end of her sentence and she goes quiet.

Gently, Nai says, "Did it worry you? About how your own parents might react?"

Lou nods but doesn't say anything. Her chin is wobbly, and I wish I knew what to say, but my own throat tightens wondering if this kind of response would be part of my own future, too. I'm afraid if I try to say anything, I'll choke up as well.

Quinn hands Zoey the bunny to Lou, who gladly accepts the little bundle of comfort.

"That is some straight-up bullshit," Halle says, some fire and brimstone in her own voice. "This is what I'm saying—religion really fucks people up." She folds her arms and looks over at me where I'm sitting on the floor and trying to take notes. Any understanding or concession she's given religion is out the window, apparently. I mean, I get it, but it still hurts a little. It's like she's mad at *me* personally. Like everything we did together on Tuesday around the statue of Mary is forgotten.

"Okay, whoa"—this is Jay, who's squished in on the other side of Halle—"we can probably chill on the massive generalizations, sis."

"Oh, so we're just gonna pretend that religion *doesn't* cause more problems than it solves?" Halle replies, confrontation all over her face.

"Well, I think we can probably discuss it in a bit more depth before we start denouncing the whole thing," Jay replies. This kid is fourteen going on forty, and I'm obsessed with him.

Halle scoffs.

Again, I feel like I should say something, but my throat is still constricted. I think of how my parents responded after what happened with Ben. Maybe they didn't have our priest write a fiery letter, but they'd definitely made it clear that Ben's and my actions were "not normal," and they *had* made me speak to Father Baird, who urged me toward goodness. Our act had seemed so simple as we were doing it, but so complicated once people found out. I can't imagine how my parents would respond to anything more.

Nai pipes up now and says, "I totally agree. I think there's lots to talk about here. But, Lou, do you want to talk about this now, or maybe another time?"

Lou lets out a breath and just says, "Yeah . . . 'nother time, I think."

"Cool. Done." Nai shoots Halle a warning look, and Halle huffs in response.

We continue around the circle with check-ins, and when it's my turn, I've been so absorbed with running through all the things I *should* have said in response to Halle earlier that I'm taken a little by surprise. "Oh, um. My week's been fine." My highlight was setting up the Virgin Mary rainbow burst with Halle and holding her hand for several minutes, but I'm obviously not going to say any of that right now, and I'm not about to share any of my low-lights, and I'm not really a weird-light kind of person.

So I do what I do best—I fake it to make it and say what I think will sound good. "Honestly, this meeting is the highlight of my week." As soon as I say it, I realize that it's not *not* true, even with Halle's fury and my jealousy over Nicky's thigh.

"Cute!" Sam says, and moves on to the next person, to my relief.

But as Muriel describes a really sweet highlight about how the girl she likes helped her with her homework, and Quinn tells an entertaining weird-light about his massive crush on an anime character, I start to wish I could share something more with this group. And then Halle reveals how she's worried about her mom, who's a single parent, works two jobs, and seems to barely sleep these days. I wonder if this is also part of why she seems so tightly wound tonight. As she and Jay give each other a little side-hug, my heart pinches and I feel a bit guilty about sharing the bare minimum.

"Wait!" I say, in the pause after Halle shares. "Can I share one more thing?"

"Of course!" Sam says.

I look at Halle. "I was going to share about our project . . . ?"

Halle's eyebrows rise ever so slightly. But the tiniest lift of her lips and a nod are enough to encourage me.

"Okay, well, I guess this is another highlight, but also something we just wanted to share with you at some point anyway," I say. "Halle and I . . . and Nicky . . . started a little GSA side project on Tuesday."

"Oooh!" Muriel says, clasping her hands in front of her. "What's the project?"

"We're creating these surprise pop-up safe spaces at St. Luke's," I continue. I pause to see if Halle wants to jump in, but she just looks back at me, that half smile on her face.

"We—Halle and I—started by creating a rainbow display near the eighth-grade lockers on Tuesday morning."

Nicky inserts herself, always trying to get in on the action. "It sounded really cool," she says. "Unfortunately it was taken down pretty quick, but lots of kids saw it."

Halle must be unable to contain her enthusiasm for our pop-up, even with her remaining umbrage (SAT word), because she finally speaks up. "We have a photo, though," she says, and pulls out her phone. She has to shift to get it from her back pocket, and I'm pleased to see her knee separate from Nicky's thigh. Halle finds the photo we took and passes her phone around.

Lou's eyes go wide when she sees it. "Oh my God! You queered the *Virgin Mary*? This is amazing."

"What? I gotta see this," Muriel says, and practically swipes the phone from Lou.

While the photo makes its way around the circle, I keep talking, heartened by everyone's reactions. "So far, there've been no repercussions, except that our vice principal made an announcement during chapel service on Wednesday morning asking anyone who knew anything about the display to come forward."

I feel kind of rebellious telling everyone this, and I like it.

"This is so amazing, guys—" Quinn begins, and after we've made him do his required push-ups to rowdy cheers and clapping, he continues. "What's the next pop-up?"

We spend the next few minutes talking about the ideas we already have and brainstorming new ones with the help of this small but amazing hive mind. Halle and I catch each other's eyes a few times throughout the conversation, and—even though I'm sure I'll need to address Halle's ire at some point—we're both beaming over the excitement that's filled the room.

CHAPTER TWENTY-THREE

Friday is its usual long slog. It's only the first day of October, and I feel like we've been in school for ten years already. By the end of the day, I'm ready for a nap, but we have an exhibition volleyball game, so rest will have to wait.

I am more than a little surprised when Ben shows up at our game after school—partly because no one comes to watch our volleyball games, and partly because it's the first time Ben has collided with the rest of my world outside of biology-related things, which doesn't count, because we're too busy awkwardly working on our project, or dealing with Mr. A's annoying jokes and my annoying responses to them.

Since the embarrassing situation with Mr. Asmaro, Ben and I haven't really had much contact, since Mr. A hasn't given us any more class time this week to work on our project. I'm also trying my damnedest to give Ben some space and just trust that he's doing the graphs like he said he would without poking my nose in and proving Mr. A right. So I'm both boggled and nervous when I see him in the gym.

He's sitting on the lowest bleacher and still wearing his backpack, his elbows on his knees. He's looking my way, and when he sees me notice him during warm-up, he lifts his chin in what I guess is a physical version of his usual "Hey."

He stays for the whole game, and even after we've shaken hands with the other team and had a postgame team chat, Ben is still sitting on the bleachers.

I walk over to him, tentative, and say, "Hey. Surprised to see you here."

He stands and stretches. "Guess I was bored."

You must be, I think.

He looks across the court at the other team as they pack up their things. "You like this?"

It sounds like an insult, and I'm mildly offended but let it slide. "It's fun," I say.

He looks at me when I say this like he's surprised.

"I do like having fun, you know."

He smirks. "If you say so."

"I do say so."

"What else do you do for fun?"

I think about this for a moment. It's true that "fun" is not typically high up on my priority list. It's usually on the same line as "going to the beach." But when I think about the past few weeks, I realize that my time with the Crosswalk crew has been fun. I mean, it's also felt complicated at times because of the wonderful-terrifying-confusing moments with Halle, and my main focus is still to bring Ben to a meeting sometime soon, but there's also been a lot of exhilaration and laughter.

We've only had three meetings so far, but last night's meeting left me and the others with sore abs from laughing. After we talked about possible pop-ups, the last half hour of the meeting was basically Sam doing his impressions of his dads arguing, which made their fights sound like a cross between *High School Musical* and *The Terminator*.

And then there's poor little Rex, the American fuzzy lop, who likes to hump Halle's foot so much that Halle has to sit cross-legged on a chair or the couch at all times so he can't get near her.

And Muriel continues to be very *loud* and *very* gay and *quite* proud of it. She cracks us all up.

I'm not always at ease in these meetings—I still feel like a newbie, and sometimes I get a panicky sensation in my chest when I think I might be revealing too much. It can be confusing—trying to be an ally while also trying to keep my own messy identity at bay. But despite all that, I'm also starting to feel like I really belong there. I wonder if Ben will feel the same way when I bring him into the group. I hope that he does.

"Can't think of anything, huh?" Ben says, and I realize I've been pondering a little too long.

"What do *you* do for fun?" I ask him, genuinely wondering. He doesn't seem so great at "fun," either.

"Hang out with you, obviously."

So cheeky. I roll my eyes, but it's wasted since he's not looking at me. "Okay, *besides* our blowout, two-person protist parties, what do you do?"

He tips back and forth on his heels for a few seconds, eyeing me up. His gaze feels like an analysis of some kind.

Then he says, "Come on," and turns to leave the gym.

I'm sweaty and have homework, but I follow him, feeling like I need to latch on to any chance I have of connecting with him.

We exit the gym, and he starts walking in the opposite direction of my house, but not really in the direction of his house, either.

It's dark already and fall leaves crunch beneath our feet. I love this time of year, minus the school workload. The heavy rains haven't begun yet, but the air is so fresh, like it's been washed clean.

We walk to the end of the block, and then he turns and walks through the narrow opening in the chain-link fence that surrounds Sir Leopold Scott School (always with the colonizer names). Scott is the only elementary school of the four in this area. The playground is more compact and older than the one by my house. A swing set, a slide, a small jungle gym.

I can't imagine what fun there is to be had here.

I follow Ben to the swing set, where he sits on one of the two swings and starts pumping his legs. The last time I was on one of these was probably in elementary school. I sit on the other seat and push off.

We swing for a while, Ben really going for it, while I keep my movement steady and small. I realize I don't love the feeling in my stomach when I'm falling backward—like I'm leaving my stomach in the air while my body retreats—not like I used to love it as a kid, when swinging high and wild was the only option. So I swing low and slow and try to keep my stomach inside of me.

"So this is your fun? Is that what you're trying to tell me?" I say, watching his legs reach forward, almost as high as the top of the swing set.

He swings back and forward a couple more times, then suddenly he's in the air, sailing forward, and then landing in a crouch on the wood chips. I almost think he's as graceful as an Olympic gymnast and expect him to rise to standing and fling out his arms in a V like they do, but then he stays in the crouch, leans forward in slow motion, and does three somersaults. Except they're not normal somersaults. They're crooked and his long limbs are all over the place, and I have no idea what I'm looking at.

He comes to a stop and flops onto his back. He emits what sounds like a happy sigh.

Laughter puffs out of my mouth, partly out of amusement and partly out of surprise.

I've stopped swinging. I stopped as soon as he hit the ground. I ask, "Are you . . . okay?" but in that way that says, "What the hell is wrong with you?"

He tips his head back to look at me so that he's seeing me upside down. "Just letting go a little."

Huh.

"Okay . . ." I walk over and sit cross-legged next to him. He somersaulted off of the wood-chip area, so we're on grass that's the kind of cold that feels damp. My sweat from volleyball has cooled, and all of this together sends a shiver through me.

I want to ask if he ever has fun like a normal person, hoping to get some insight into whether he'd enjoy Crosswalk with all its jokes and impressions and general teenage nonsense, but instead, I ask, "Why'd you come to the game?" because I'm still wondering.

He glances at me from the ground and shrugs. "You seemed kind of stressed out in bio the other day. Just thought I'd check in."

My body stiffens, but my response is quick. Maybe too quick. "It was fine. Mr. A is just annoying sometimes."

"You didn't really seem fine."

He says it like a fact, not a judgment, but it still creates a nauseous sensation in my stomach. I hate that he's seen a crack. That he feels the need to check in. I'm supposed to be making things better for *him*. I look down into my crossed legs, and my body is vague and indistinct in the dimming light. I have to really focus to see my hands balled up together in my lap. I have to blink to keep them from disappearing.

I blink hard, feel my fists, and repeat, "Well, it was fine."

There's a pause before he says, "Okay."

I hope that's the end of that, but then he says, "I put up with a lot of bullshit at ballet school, too. Just kept plowing ahead, even when it was getting under my skin."

My brain splits in two. On the one hand, he's sharing with me, and I want him to keep sharing. On the other hand, this topic is not one I want to have to talk about with him or anyone. I aim to keep the focus on him. "What kind of garbage?"

"Nothing shocking—high expectations, harsh instruction, big egos."

"Those programs must be pretty intense. But . . . isn't that kind of what it takes to be the best?"

He scoffs. "Yeah. Guess I just didn't have what it takes."

Oh. This feels like a misstep. "Sorry, that's not what I meant."

"It's fine . . . now. I'm good with my decision. My brain feels better away from all that. It was worth it for me to walk away."

We're quiet for a while. I wonder if he's giving me advice, or if he's just trying to relate, or what. I'm not about to continue this part of the conversation, though.

I guess he takes the hint, because a minute later, he says, "You never answered my question—what d'you do for fun?"

I jump at the opportunity to shift topics and energy. "Well, it's Friday night and that means takeout and movies." And then I surprise us both. "Wanna join?"

After a moment, his voice rises from beside me, where he's still on his back. "Really?"

I shrug, worried now that I'm being overeager and that I might scare him away. "Yeah. We always order too much food," I say, trying to sound indifferent.

He sits up and says, "Okay. Sure."

I'm thrilled and ill at the same time but tell myself this is exactly what I need to get him to Crosswalk.

On the way back to my house, Ben calls his mom to let her

know he's having dinner with my family. I'm a little nervous as he talks to her, wondering how she'll respond to this news. Working on a project together is one thing, but how will she feel about us hanging out again? When he gets off the phone, though, he says, "My mom says hi."

I'm surprised and relieved by this. "Oh, that's nice of her."

"She's a nice person."

I glance at him to see if there's any subtext to his comment, but his face is as neutral as ever.

I'm suddenly tired of trying to guess what he's thinking and of second-guessing my own words. I decide this evening is going to be *fun*. I will make it so. I will loosen up and show Ben that I am *fine* and that I can have fun and that we can be friends again. That he should *want* to be friends again. A genius idea pops into my head, and before I can question if it will make me look good or weird or something else, I spit it out.

"Should we watch *Dirty Dancing* tonight? I still have my VHS copy, and the VCR is somewhere in the rec room, too."

This might not sound so genius, but we watched *Dirty Dancing* easily over a hundred times as kids. Sometimes just me and Ben, sometimes with other friends, sometimes with my sister and parents, but it was mostly our movie. I always thought Ben loved Patrick Swayze as much as I did, if not more. Maybe it will bring us back to those times, when things were simpler, sillier.

"You still have the *tape*?"

He's behind me on the stairs up to the deck, and I look to him now—his face is in disbelief, but there's a half smile on his lips. I grin, genuinely excited by the prospect of this whole evening now, and that *he* seems a little excited, too.

"Yup. I mean—how could I throw it out? That tape has seen things, you know?" Like the time I had a sleepover with some of the girls from school, and we made a rap song to the beat of Patrick Swayze's "*ga-gong ga-gongs*." Or when Ben and I spent an hour trying to replicate the lift at the end until he gave up because I had no sense of balance or timing, nor did we have water to practice in—just the brown shag carpet in our rec room with a concrete floor beneath it that was waiting to shatter my face.

He shakes his head, and I finally hear the sound I've been waiting for—a laugh at something I've said. Almost a laugh, at least—more like a small huff. "I'd be up for that, actually."

I'm thrilled.

When we walk into the house, my dad and Kendra are in the kitchen, making brownies. We always have Chinese takeout and homemade desserts on Friday nights. It's a habit we rarely break from, even if Amma has a shift at the hospital, which she does tonight.

"Well, well, well!" my dad bellows, and I worry he's going to overwhelm Ben right away. "Ben Yang. Is that you?" Thatha glances at me, but I can tell he's going to go with the flow, unlike my mom, who would probably question what I'm doing with Ben here.

Kendra scrunches up her nose, which means that she's either feeling shy because this tall, good-looking boy has just walked in or wondering why he's here on Friday family night. She probably doesn't remember him much, though she played with his sisters after church sometimes. I cross my eyes at her, and she sticks her tongue out at me.

Ben smiles fully for the first time, and it warms his whole face. "Yup, it's me. How are you, Mr. Perera?" His entire persona has shifted into one I know well—it's "Please the Parents" time. But he was always respectful to adults, so maybe it's not a persona at all.

"Good, good, my friend! It's nice to see you here again. It's been too long!" My dad begins to pepper Ben with questions about his parents and what he's been up to, but I put a stop to that as quickly as possible.

"Dad, give him a break. He just got here."

My dad makes a fake offended face and says, "Okay, Ms. Bossy." He nudges Kendra with his elbow like they're commiserating (SAT word) over how bossy I am, and I roll my eyes. "Well, I hope you've invited him to stay for dinner at least," he adds.

"Actually, I did. *And* we're going to watch *Dirty Dancing* tonight, too. So dibs on the TV." I say this specifically to Kendra, who I always have to fight with over the TV, because she loves watching sports, and I think watching sports on TV is a giant waste of time.

But she lights up at this news. "Yes! I *love* that movie! I'll make kettle corn!"

A part of me is actually relieved she wants to watch with us. It will take a bit of the pressure off—she's better than I am at keeping things light.

While Thatha and Kendra make brownies, I'm put in charge of ordering food, and Ben says he's just going to "step out" for a minute. I have a moment of panic. Does "step out" mean he's going for a smoke? Is he really going to get high before spending the evening with my family? That's not cool, right?

But then I also think about what he said about his anxiety. Maybe he's nervous about being here but still wants to be here. Maybe this is a good thing? I really have no idea.

Chill out, Cassie. Tonight is about fun.

CHAPTER TWENTY-FOUR

We are full of Chinese food, Thatha has told us to "go watch your filthy dancing movie" while he washes the dishes, and Ben has managed to get through dinner without letting on if he smoked up or not. At least I can't tell. Maybe he's into those gummies, too. Thanks to my dad and Kendra asking him a million questions despite my attempts to divert them, however, he actually spoke more over dinner than he's said with me since we've been hanging out.

I learn that he "kind of likes school" (I am shocked by this). He does not know how to use chopsticks, which makes us laugh, to which he responds with actual humor, "Just 'cause I'm Chinese doesn't mean I know how to use chopsticks, guys. Don't be racist." And when he's embarrassed (like when he tries to use chopsticks and fails catastrophically), his cheeks still turn a fierce scarlet color.

I also learn that he *is* capable of real laughter, thanks to Kendra and her antics. This inspires both gratitude and jealousy in me.

Now Ben and Kendra are sitting on opposite ends of the couch, Kendra in her usual spot and Ben in *my* usual spot (I don't say anything, obviously), and I'm hooking up the VCR, which takes a few minutes because I can't remember which wire goes where.

Finally, we are watching the tape crinkle into action and the first few notes of "Be My Baby" begin and all those sexy, slow-moving bodies in black and white start shifting across the screen. The sounds and sights instantly bring me back to a million moments in this same rec room, watching this same movie with Ben. I feel a small pinch in my chest, but force myself to just be here, in the present, and enjoy what's happening now.

As the movie continues, Kendra sings along to some of the songs, and Ben and I laugh at her. When she decides it's time for kettle corn, she asks us to pause the movie.

"Really? Like you haven't got all the songs and lines memorized?" I ask.

"I don't want to miss a *thing*, you hear me, Cassie Perera?" she retorts. Ben laughs at this, too.

"Jeez. Fine." I get up to press pause, since the VCR remote disappeared long ago.

When Kendra has twirled herself out of the room, I feel her absence immediately. Instead of just sitting back down, I do a quick scan of the rec room to find something I can use to distract me and Ben until Kendra gets back.

My eyes land on the board games and card decks that are stacked beneath the coffee table in front of Ben.

Perfect.

"Quick game of Speed? If you dare?" I ask, an eyebrow peaked. I used to whip Ben at Speed when we were kids. It's one of the only things I'm actually pretty fast at.

He scoffs. "Way to pick a game I suck at."

"Okay, then—you choose. I'd say we have about ten minutes before Kendra comes bouncing back in."

He contemplates for a moment, then says, "Nah, I'm good with Speed. I might have learned a few things since we last played."

"Oh, really?"

He shrugs and moves to the floor right in front of the coffee table. This is where he'd sit when we played down here as kids, too—whether it was board games or cards or Legos, we'd always set up this way.

I remember how, on days that were too cold or rainy to play in the creek, Ben would come back to my house after school and we'd play *Degrassi* reruns in the background while we romped around the rec room, play-fighting or being ridiculous.

He'd even tried to teach me ballet moves down here, to utter failure. I didn't mind failing as much back then, though, I guess, because my disastrous attempts at a plié or a pirouette ended in a fit of giggles instead of stress and tears. He would show me his perfect form, I would create a pathetic imitation, and he would try to make an adjustment to my leg or arm or hips, which would usually prompt ticklishness and laughter—but never embarrassment or awkwardness. I loved that we could have that physical closeness without it being weird, maybe because we both knew there was zero attraction between us. Or maybe just because we were such good friends.

We were.

I wonder, as I sit on the other side of the coffee table from him, what he'd do if I brought those moments up now, but I'm too self-conscious to say anything. He'd probably think I was a nerd for mentioning it. So I sit, quiet instead, as that ache tries to pinch at my heart again, and I quash it quickly, this time by turning my attention to the game.

As I shuffle the cards, Ben asks, "What was that guy's name you were obsessed with at Our Lady?"

I do a double take. Is Ben seriously asking about my fake elementary-school boy crush?

"Gavin Berry?" I say, wondering where the heck this is going.

"Yeah, Gavin. Where's he now, do you know?" He's watching my hands deal, not looking at my face.

"No idea. I think he went to Holy Cross or something."

"You mean you don't stalk him?"

I check Ben's face. Neutral. "Um, no, I don't *stalk* my elementary-school crush, dude."

"You were *really* obsessed."

If you looked at my diary from those days, his words would appear to be true. The whole thing is basically Gavin's name (sprinkled through with "Patrick Swayze," obviously), or my first name with Gavin's last name, or cartoon caricatures of me and Gavin going on romantic dates or getting married. The *true* truth was different, but on paper, being obsessed with Gavin Berry seemed like my only choice. Ben knew the off-paper truth, though, so I don't know why he's asking about it now.

And I certainly don't want to let that truth into this room.

"Okay, okay. So I was a little obsessed. Gavin was cute." Then, because I want him to have a chance to share *his* truth, I ask, "Who were *you* obsessed with back then?" He'd never really told me about any crushes on the boys in our grade. But maybe he had crushes on boys he danced with.

He doesn't say anything at first, and I think maybe he won't say anything at all, but then he replies, "I wasn't obsessed with anyone. All those people at Our Lady were assholes."

I study his face but it's still not giving much away. "Yeah, that's true." I wonder if he includes me in that group of assholes, but there's no way I'm going to ask. I don't really want to know.

We play a quick game in silence—I let him win. And I thank God when Kendra comes breezing back with her arms circling two big bowls of popcorn. I clear the cards, and she hands the smaller of the two bowls to me. "That's yours. Ben, you and I can share, 'kay?"

God. Speaking of crushes.

"Sounds good to me," Ben says, and his voice is almost jovial. Whether or not the tone is real, I don't really care at this moment. I'm just glad Kendra is here and there's popcorn and we're not talking about obsessions and assholes anymore.

We watch the rest of the movie in silence, except for our munching, and I let myself get caught up in celebration as Baby is brought out of the corner and then lifted into the air, finally.

CHAPTER TWENTY-FIVE

On Saturday morning, I'm neck-deep in homework when I get a notification on my phone. I started using a focus app when I'm studying so I don't get too bogged down in my new social life (between the Crosswalk founding members group chat and the Crosswalk club group chat, my phone has become very distracting), so I have to wait another twenty minutes before checking my messages or my poor virtual tree will die. I am way too invested in a perfect forest of "homework trees" to let a decrepit, lifeless stump into the mix.

I'm really hoping the message is from Ben, though. I'm hoping that last night, even with its talk of crushes and assholes, moved us into new territory.

When I do check my phone, it's not Ben who's messaged, but I am both surprised and delighted to see a DM from Cameron the eighth grader.

Cameron: Hello there. I hope you're well and that it's okay to message you here. But I just thought I'd let you know that the book I checked out last week is very good, since you asked for a review. I would give it 4.5/5 stars for great characterization, a good dose of humor, and some inventive plot twists. The romance between the two main characters is also very believable and heartwarming. I can bring the book back this week so you can read it if you want to. See you later!

Okay. This is worth being distracted from my homework for. The fact that this eighth grader had the guts to not only check out that book, but then *also* message an eleventh grader (albeit, not the most intimidating eleventh grader) about it is enough to leave me in a melted mess of all my soft bits. But that his message is also so formal and polite makes the melted mess seep into the floor. What the heck.

I guess a cooler eleventh grader wouldn't message him back so soon. But I'm not that cool, and I'm way too touched by his courage to wait.

Cassie: Aw! I'm so glad you liked the book. It sounds wonderful. I'd love to read it. I only volunteer in the library on Monday mornings, so maybe come by then? But feel free to say hi in the halls, too! ☺

When I hit send, I see that he sees it right away but doesn't respond. I try not to let it bother me that an eighth grader has more chill than I do and instead let myself enjoy a little of the excitement I feel over the fact that I might have met another St. Luke's student for Crosswalk.

I finally get the ping on my phone I was hoping for when Ben messages me that afternoon.

Ben: Sara asked me 2 some party tonight. U going?

I'm not surprised Sara is making her move. She's been eyeing up Ben all month. But I *am* surprised that Ben is interested in going and is asking *me* if *I'm* interested in going.

Cassie: Oh. Wasn't sure yet.

More to the point—I didn't even know there was a party because I have way too many other things to think about.

Ben: want 2?

Oh, man. I definitely do *not* want to. I have so much homework and was planning on a nice, quiet night in with my AP French dialogues. But I can't possibly say no if Ben is inviting me to hang out, right? Like, this must mean our movie night really did swing the pendulum if he wants to go to a party. With *me*.

Cassie: Sure. Why not?

So many reasons why not!

Ben: cool see u there

Oh. So I guess we're not going together. That's fine. He still asked me. He still wants to see me there. And to be honest, I'm a little curious to see what he's like at a party.

I stare at the pile of textbooks on my desk and the cue cards with macro terms next to them. Color-coded stickies poke out of my physics workbook at perfectly spaced intervals. My cursor is blinking on the screen where I was trying to type out the outline for my English essay.

I have so much to do.

I also need to make things right with Ben.

But I have so much to do.

But.

I'm already worried about the lost study time, but I tell myself I can just get up a couple of hours earlier tomorrow and stay up a little later tomorrow night. And it's only 1:17 p.m. now, so I can get in a good seven or eight hours straight before the party.

No problem. I got this.

CHAPTER TWENTY-SIX

The party is at Remi's, who's in my grade. Her house isn't huge, but at present, it is very loud and very full. It looks like our whole grade is here, plus some. I'm nervous as I scan the living room. It's not like I've never been to a party before, but it's rare, and though I know a lot of people in our grade, I don't know anyone well enough to really party with.

I really wish I'd come with someone.

I had no idea what time was cool to arrive, so I aimed for nine thirty, hoping that was late enough. I have to be home by midnight anyway, or my mom will kill me. It was hard enough to convince her that going out tonight was a good idea in the first place.

I head to the kitchen, where I often hang out at parties since they're generally well-lit and where the snacks are. I make small talk, put up with a few predictable jokes about "Class President

Cassie Perera making an appearance," and keep an eye out for Ben.

I finally see him talking to a group of people in the corner of the living room as I make a loop a little while later. Sara's in the group, and she definitely seems especially attentive to Ben. He and I make eye contact, and he gives me one of those chin nods, then saunters over, leaving Sara looking a little despondent.

"Hey," he says.

His eyes are a little red, but I resist the urge to comment on his extracurriculars. Instead, I say, "Hey. Fancy meeting you here." *Oh, that's much better, nerd.*

"Shocked you actually left the house."

"Hey! I leave the house!"

"On a Saturday night? For a party?" The slightest of smirks appears on his face.

I shake my head. "Whatever."

I start to feel awkward standing there, unsure about what to say next, when I hear, "Nicky, you came!" and there are drunk greetings and squeals. I look toward the front door and see Nicky . . . with Halle and Sam next to her. Someone from St. Luke's is hugging Nicky, and she sees me over their shoulder. She waves and I wave back. Sam and Halle see me now, too. Both of their faces brighten, and they wave at me as well.

Of course Halle is here. And of course she came with Nicky.

I turn back to look at Ben. He's eyeing up Nicky and the others, and I can't read his expression. I wonder about this sudden collision of Crosswalk and Ben. Maybe this is meant to be. Or maybe this is a disaster waiting to happen.

I forge ahead. It will be good for him, I decide—to meet these folks. Just like it's been for me. "You should meet my friends," I say. I also like that he knows *I have friends*. People like me. "They're really great."

"Huh" is all I get for my enthusiasm and good intentions.

The other three have slipped through the crowd and are suddenly next to us. Nicky gives me an off-balanced hug. She is definitely drunk. Halle gives me an amazing hug. She smells like peaches. Sam is checking out Ben but then turns their attention to me as well to give me a hug.

Nicky squeezes between Halle and Sam and puts her arms around both their waists. I try not to look at her hand on Halle's hip. "Welcome to your first St. Luke's extravaganza, friends! You should feel very hashtag blessed to be in the presence of so many *angels*!" She cackles at herself.

I cringe internally but smile like she's saying something original and hilarious.

"Oh, I can *feel* the blessedness," Sam says, but they're back to checking out Ben. I'm a little anxious about the vibes coming off of Sam right now, but am more interested in bringing Ben together with the Crosswalk crew. I attempt to introduce them.

"Um, Ben, this is Halle and Sam. They go to Pinetree. And you probably know Nicky already?" The three of them smile at Ben.

He says, unsurprisingly, "Hey."

"Hey, Ben! I've seen you around, lookin' all mysterious and such," Nicky says, her words stumbling over one another.

"Y'all are besties, then?" Sam asks, their curiosity about Ben obvious.

"We went to elementary school together, and Ben just joined

St. Luke's this year!" I say, hoping to control the narrative a little. No one here needs to know about the pieces in between, or that we are definitely not "besties." At least not yet.

"Oh, nice!" Sam says, their enthusiasm full and bright. "So you're right across the street from us!" They grin at Ben, whose eyebrows pop up. He seems more amused at Sam's excitement than anything else.

Nicky takes Sam's enthusiasm and dials it up. "Oh my gosh—you kept in touch from elementary school all this time?! That's so cuuuute!"

"Yeah, and why haven't you mentioned Ben before, Cassie?" Sam adds, making eyes at me like I'm nuts for ever keeping them apart.

Ugh. I do not like this line of questioning, nor drunk Nicky, nor amorous Sam, but I need to suck it up and act like I know what I'm doing here.

"Oh, well—we kind of lost touch. Ben's been in a seriously intense ballet program for the past four years."

"Ballet?" Sam says, his eyes brightening further.

"That's really cool, Ben," Halle says, genuine admiration on her face. "My uncle was in the ballet for a long time."

"I actually tried ballet for a while," Sam pipes up. "But I have terrible balance. Come, Ben, let's go drown our sorrows for our lost ballet careers." Sam indicates the kitchen and, to my surprise, Ben smirks and says, "Sure."

"Ooh . . . I'll come, too!" Nicky says, and inserts herself between them as they head to the kitchen.

Halle and I watch them retreat for a moment, and then Halle

says, "Nicky may have had a few."

When I face her, she's smiling. "Yeah. Got that," I say.

"So, are you and Ben . . . ?" Her tone is casual, but the look she gives me isn't.

Oh. "No, no—just friends." Although I'm not sure even "friends" accurately describes what we are at this stage.

Her expression lightens. "Well, that's good, 'cause I was about to say that Sam is probably about to hit on your boyfriend." She grins.

"Ha ha . . . oh God. I hope Sam goes easy on him. Ben can be a little . . . reserved." It's possible Ben's reservations are mostly for me, though.

"Sam's good about respecting people's boundaries, don't worry," she says.

"Glad to hear it," I respond, and then instantly run out of things to say as she gazes at me. We're standing next to the fireplace—one with a thick wooden mantel along the top that has statues of Mary and Jesus standing piously in the center. We have very similar statues in our house, too, except our Jesus and Mary are a little more old-school—from the eighties, yellowed with age and sunlight. This Jesus and Mary duo looks like they just had a spa day, and I swear Jesus is wearing eye shadow. Could Jesus be getting gayer? Could the holy family be getting more glamorous?

"So, are Pinetree parties like this?" I finally get out.

Halle takes a sweep of the room. "Mm . . . mostly. I mean, barring this Jesus and Mary over here, and that crucified Jesus, and the Last Supper wood carving over there . . ." She points to each item with a sly smile on her face.

I smile back, because this feels less like criticism and more like playfulness. "No Jesus paraphernalia in the homes of Pinetree students?" I ask. "There are definitely *some* religious kids at your school, though, right?"

"Yeah, of course. I'm just not sure they're the ones hosting the ragers." She nudges me, teasing.

I love the nudge and the teasing. "Well, that's because parties are for Satan's enterprise, you see," I say, keeping my face very serious, hoping to make her laugh.

She does, and the sound fills my chest.

"Yeah, well, hell sounds amazing to me—all those queers and partyers and nonbelievers."

My chest tightens a little at her words—worried that someone around us might hear her say "queers," but no one seems to be paying any attention to us.

"Ha ha . . . yeah" is all I can get out until my chest eases again.

Halle leans a shoulder against the wall, which brings her closer to me because I have my back against it. My skin tingles at her proximity.

"So—how are you figuring all this out?" she starts. "Like, how do you do all the religious stuff and then still do all the Crosswalk stuff? Does it feel weird at all?" A slight frown lines her brow, but her expression doesn't feel judgy . . . yet.

Weird is an understatement. And I'm not sure I'm prepared to have this conversation with her right now . . . here . . . like this. *Can we please just get back to casual banter instead?*

"Uh . . . I mean . . . it doesn't *not* feel weird. I guess . . . I'm trying to sort things out for myself as I go? I mean, I'm learning a lot from Crosswalk and you all—but I also get a lot of comfort out of church, too."

"Like how?"

I think I detect the slightest edge to her tone, but I could be making it up. "Like . . ." I want to share with her about the grace and ease I find in church—in the routines and people—but now I'm second-guessing myself, hearing her responses before she's made them: *But aren't the people the ones who've interpreted the Bible in ways that hurt other people? Don't the routines encourage a kind of mindlessness?*

I realize I'm not saying anything and just blinking at the floor in front of me. My shoulders and neck feel stiff.

"Cassie?" Halle says, her fingers wrapping lightly around my arm, which is hanging, limp, by my side. Her thumb strokes my skin a couple of times. Her touch brings me back to the room, not in an unpleasant way.

"Sorry—like I said, I'm still figuring things out. I've grown up with the church my whole life. I guess I just need more time to sort out which parts of it can continue to be in my life while also not hurting the people I care about." I glance up at her as I say this, because, I realize, *she's* a person I care about, as are the rest of the Crosswalk crew.

That half smile appears on her lips. Her hand squeezes my arm and stays right where it is. She nods slightly. "Got it. I might keep asking questions, if that's okay. I'm trying to understand how the whole religion and queerness thing can possibly work, too. So much of it still seems really harmful and limiting to me. I hate that religion—or at least the way people choose to practice it—hurts people *I* care about, like Lou, for example. You know?"

I gaze back at her for a moment, taking in her words—the doubting *and* care in them. "Yeah, I get that. And you can ask. I just might not always have an answer for you."

She scoffs and rolls her eyes in an exaggerated manner. Her hand moves from my arm to punch me playfully. "*Jeez, Cassie.* I expect answers *every time*, you hear me?" She's grinning now, and my neck and shoulders ease instantly.

"So pushy . . ." I say, smiling.

She actually does push me with her shoulder and says, "Come on, we should probably check up on those hooligans."

"Oh, okay." In truth, I was kind of enjoying a bit more one-on-one time with Halle, even if it wasn't completely comfortable. But I guess she wants to get back to Nicky, as well. Of course.

She puts a hand on my hip (*Lord help me*) and moves us forward to find the others, who we eventually discover on the back porch, sitting on the steps that go down to the yard. It's a bit chilly out here, but the fresh air is welcome after the sweaty atmosphere inside.

"Hey, team," Halle says. "What's up?"

Nicky is slouched against the banister on one side of the steps, while Ben and Sam sit next to each other on the other side. I wonder if Sam and Ben *will* hit it off, and the thought is kind of nice.

"Hey, babes!" Sam says when they turn and see us. "We were *just* talking about you! Well, not you specifically, but Crosswalk."

Oh. That happened faster than I had planned for.

"Yeah, Cassie . . . how come you didn't tell Ben about Crosswalk already?" Nicky blabbers as Halle and I take a seat on the upper steps. Halle's knee is nudged up against my knee, and I'm not mad about it.

"Oh. I . . . just hadn't quite got there yet," I say, glancing between Ben and the others.

"Well, get there, girl!" Nicky yells at me, and then cackles again.

I'm feeling a little out of sorts here. Of course, this is what I wanted—to invite Ben to Crosswalk. To get him there and show him what I created . . . for *him*. But I'm not sure where he's at with me right now—whether this is something that he's ready for, or if I'm just going to scare him away.

But I guess my hand is being forced.

I try to play things lightly. I'm not great at it. "Ha ha . . . right." I look to Ben, whose lips, if I'm not mistaken, have a tiny smirk on them. Probably relishing my discomfort. "Well, um, you're totally invited, obviously. If it's something you'd be into." *Please be into it.*

"What is it exactly?" he asks, cocking an eyebrow and glancing at the others.

The others are looking to me for this, though, so I take a breath and say, "It's a group—a club, really—that a few of us formed. To make some kind of safe space for people at St. Luke's who identify as . . . um . . . LGBTQ+ . . . but also as allies. It's kind of an underground thing for now, because St. Luke's isn't really ready for something like this yet."

A slight crinkle appears on his brow. "You all started it?" He says "You all," but he's looking squarely at me.

"Yeah!" Sam says. "Cassie, Halle, me, and another girl, Nai. We have, like, ten people or so right now, I think?"

Ben folds his arms and leans into his knees. "Wait . . . does this have anything to do with the statue of Mary getting decorated or whatever?" Ben asks.

I still can't quite read his tone. He's asking questions, though, which feels like a good sign.

"Yup," Halle replies, smiling at me and squeezing my shoulder. "Cassie and I nailed that one."

I can't help but smile back at her, thinking about those moments behind Mary. Her hand in mine. Her face laughing into my shoulder. I take another deep breath and switch my attention back to Ben, though.

"I just think it's important," I say, "for kids at St. Luke's to have some kind of affirmation, too, you know?" *Like you. I want* you *to feel that way.*

"So you coming, or what?" Nicky suddenly inserts, having been absorbed in her phone for the past couple of minutes.

Ben stares back at me for a moment, then shrugs. "Yeah. Sure. I could check it out."

I try to control the excitement and nerves that immediately surge through me. "Oh, cool" is all I say.

Sam is less concerned with playing it cool. They thrust their arms up in the air like they just won a marathon and shout, "Boom!"

This makes everyone laugh, including Ben, and though nerves still wriggle through my stomach, my excitement outweighs them.

CHAPTER TWENTY-SEVEN

The rest of the weekend is a blur of altar serving, studying, and having moments of anxiety at the thought of Ben coming to Crosswalk. I almost sleep through my alarm on Monday morning but manage to drag myself out of bed with enough time to finish my physics homework.

When I arrive to school early for my library shift, I have to walk past the eighth-grade lockers. Last night, Nicky updated the group on her plan to create a drag display in the theater dressing rooms Tuesday night after her rehearsal. We all agreed that if any Pride pop-up was going to prevail a little longer, it would be somewhere the theater crowd hangs out.

As I pass the alcove where our rainbow display was, I glance at the statue of Mary and see a small splash of color on the palm of her left hand. I slow and look around to see if anyone else is nearby, but it's 7:25 in the morning, so it's quiet in the school.

As I peer closer, I see the thing on Mary's hand is a purple sticky note. It says "I love you as you are."

My chest clenches and my face instantly crumples. I glance around again, irrationally worried that someone will appear out of nowhere to see me crying like a fool in front of this statue. Even though I know it's silly, I make sure all of the nonexistent people can't see me by tucking myself behind the statue again. I press my fingers into my eyes like I can push back the tears and try to calm myself.

But seeing that someone took it upon themselves to place that message there . . . it means *someone* else at St. Luke's knows or wants that sentence to be true, too. And I guess—even though I know it's a student or staff member who wrote it—thinking about it as a message from Mary herself fills me with something like longing . . . for some kind of sign that it's okay—with her—that . . .

But I need to get a hold of myself. I can't hide behind this statue forever. Leaning my forehead against Mary's back, I take quiet, tight breaths until my chest unclenches and the tears stop. I use my sweater sleeves to wipe away the wet from my eyes and cheeks. Mr. Reyes will be arriving soon, and I don't need him seeing whatever this is.

I slip back out from behind the statue and take out my phone, then snap a photo of the sticky note and send it to the Crosswalk group chat.

Cassie: Look! Someone left a cute sticky note on Mary!

I follow my message with an abundance of hearts and rainbows and flowers, not annoying crying emojis. I let myself be bolstered by the quick replies from Halle, Nai, Sam, and the others and hope the puffiness around my eyes disappears by the time I get to the library.

As I organize and shelve books that morning, Mr. Reyes brings me a Tim Tam cookie on a napkin from his private stash to accompany my cup of tea, as though he knows I've just had a ridiculous, emotional outburst, which I really hope he doesn't. But I appreciate the tea and treat anyway.

Librarians really are our saving grace.

I'm organizing books at a corner table when I feel someone approach. I turn and it's Cameron.

"Hey, Cameron!" I say.

"Hi," he says. "I came to give you the book, like you said to."

"Oh, yeah—totally. Here, I can just take it." I extend my hand, and he gives me the book. "I'll check it back in and then check it out for myself. Can't wait to read it." In reality, the chance of me reading a book for pleasure before winter break is implausible (SAT word). An eighth grader wouldn't understand this, though.

"Let me know what you think." He glances around, and seeing only Mr. Reyes through the glass walls of his office, he adds, "Do you, um, know of any other good books along these same lines?"

Little waves ripple through my stomach—from equal parts nervousness and excitement. I know what he's asking but want to confirm. "Like, romance, or young adult, or . . . ?"

"Um, yeah. Like stories with, uh . . . diverse characters and stuff."

"I get it. Like not the same old boy-girl stuff, you mean." I smile to let him know that *I* know what he's asking and also that I'm okay with it . . . for him anyway.

He shrugs. Very noncommittal, but I get that, too.

"There are a couple of other new ones Mr. Reyes just brought in that looked good. Let me see if I can find them for you."

I know exactly what the titles of both books are because how could I forget them? I can't remember the author names, though, and I haven't had a chance to add my queer labeling system yet, so I look the books up in the library database and, once found, lead Cameron to the shelves. He follows me silently like a little shadow.

"Here's one, and"—I run my hand along the shelves—"here's the other." I hand the books to him. "Want to have a look before I check them out for you, or . . . ?"

He takes a quick glance at both covers and says, "Nope. Yup. I'll just check them out, I think."

I am *awww*ing and grinning internally. "Great. Let's do that, then."

As I'm adding the books to the computer, I notice him glancing around again. "Something my old school did was they had a whole section in the library for diverse books. It was pretty cool," he says.

"Oh, that *is* cool," I say, both impressed and jealous that this elementary school was more gay-friendly than our high school. I make a firm commitment to have those labels sorted out as soon as possible.

"Yes, it just made it easy to, you know, find what you're looking for."

He says this, and I suddenly feel like I'm in a spy movie. Like he's a detective looking for clues or connections and dropping hints for me to see if I take the bait.

I do.

"Well, if you're looking for more diverse content, I know of something a little 'off the books' that might be of interest." I am pleased with my pun, and it gives me the confidence to say, "Did your old school have a GSA or anything like that?"

His face is a bloom of fireworks. "Yes! It was amazing! We did a little Pride parade and everything!"

Oh my God. What? Okay. I try to tamp down my disbelief and envy. "Well, that sounds amazing, and we're not quite there yet, but we have a kind of"—I glance back at Mr. Reyes in his office, but he looks immersed in his computer—"underground GSA with the school across the street. Would you want to come to that?"

He nods so hard his lush curls bounce around his head. "When is it? Where?"

I write down the details on a tiny piece of paper, because this *is* a spy movie, after all, and hand it to him. He reads it over quickly, and I think he's about to swallow it or something, but then he just tucks it into his pocket like a normal person. "Thank you!"

"No problem. I'll see you Thursday. If you have any trouble finding us, just message me. I'm an *ally* and you can totally trust me," I add, just to keep things very clear.

"Okay, I will!" he says, and practically skips away.

I walk back to my stack of books to organize, but I'm practically skipping inside, too. That's *two* possible new people for Crosswalk from St. Luke's. And one of them is Ben. And I'm honestly not sure how I'm supposed to focus on anything else until Thursday.

CHAPTER TWENTY-EIGHT

So I don't focus on much else, really. As much as I try, I can't seem to concentrate very long on schoolwork. On Tuesday, I'm on my way back to the library at the start of lunch, determined to get my rainbow-labeling system up and running, especially after my interaction with Cameron the previous day.

As I'm headed up the stairs, Mrs. Keenan is coming down and she stops me.

"Cassie, I need you to do something for me."

No request or "please" or even "hello," I notice. I pause and hitch my backpack farther up my shoulders. "Okay," I say, not really wanting to do anything for her.

"I'm still trying to track down whoever put up that ridiculous display around our blessed Mary, and I wonder if you could ask around? See if anyone knows anything?"

What? I mean, sure, I guess I've been a go-to person at the school for certain things—like speaking to new parents, or covering at reception if needed—but now she's outright asking me to be a snitch? Is that really the vibe I'm giving off?

"Oh, um, I don't think anyone would really tell me anything . . ."

She frowns like she just expected me to say "Sure! No problem! Of course I'll do your dirty work!"

"Well, ask around anyway, please. Someone must know something."

I realize the only way to get out of this is to say, "Okay. Sure. I'll let you know if I hear anything."

A look of satisfaction comes over her face. Smug lips. Gleeful blue eyes. "Wonderful. I look forward to your findings."

Findings? Really?

I make what I hope passes as a smile as she walks past me.

My conversation with Mrs. Keenan irritates the heck out of me, but I'm also relieved to find that she doesn't seem to have a clue who's behind the pop-up. And I'm not about to let her get in the way of my next pop-up plan, either. If anything, she just motivates me even more. I set up camp in the corner of the library and lay out my textbooks like I'm about to study my ass off.

Mr. Reyes isn't here for the first half of the lunch hour. He takes his lunch break and the checkout desk is closed during this time. Right now, the library is filled with the usual mix of studious students and those looking for a cozy place to take a nap.

I spend a few minutes pretending to pore over my books, then glance around. No one's paying me any attention, which is perfect. I grab my phone and the package of small rainbow stickers I stole from my sister, who has way too many stickers haphazardly pasted to all of her binders and laptop.

Casually, I make my way around the fiction shelves, glancing at the list on my phone and then finding the books whose titles I've been slowly collecting over the past two weeks—all of which have queer content, according to my research. When I find one, I paste a rainbow on the spine and keep moving.

It takes me only about seven minutes, and it's only about twelve books, but I feel like a nerdy superhero after I'm done. Now I can tell Cameron to look for the books with rainbows on them, and he can tell the friends he trusts with the knowledge, and so on. Another pop-up safe space created, this time with books and stickers.

Sucks to you, Mrs. Keenan.

I sit down with my own textbooks as Mr. Reyes comes back into the library, cup of tea in hand. He sees me and waves with vigor, then makes an "oops" face as some of his tea sloshes over onto his hand. He grins at me, and I grin and wave back.

I did consider telling Mr. Reyes about this plan but then realized that if the signs or labels were discovered, Mr. Reyes might be the one to take the heat, unlike our other pop-ups, which aren't really in the "realm" of any one person at St. Luke's . . . except for me. This way, if anyone tattles or discovers the labeling system, Mr. Reyes can legitimately say he has no idea where the stickers came from.

After trying to get some actual studying done for about three minutes, I can't help but pull out my phone again.

Cassie: Hey! If you're looking for more diverse books in the library, follow the rainbows . . .

Cameron: ?

Cassie: I'm trying out a new system for finding certain books. Look for the little rainbow stickers. Tell anyone you trust who might be interested.

Cameron: Okay, I will! Thanks!

Cassie:

I don't even worry about this information getting into the wrong hands. I trust Cameron, even though I just met him. Maybe this is another part of queer safe spaces—an immediate kind of connection with the people in them.

By the end of lunch, I've gotten zero homework or studying done, but I feel like I've accomplished something even better.

CHAPTER TWENTY-NINE

By Thursday, I'm exhausted from trying to focus enough to catch up on homework and assignments so I don't get any more unacceptable marks, but also from volleyball and volunteering and trying to sort out decorations for the fall fair, now that James has very explicitly told me "the decorations should be tasteful but fun, in order to attract as many students and adults as possible." *Ugh, James.*

After volleyball practice, I head straight home, shower, scarf down some leftovers while cramming in an hour of homework, and then get ready for our Crosswalk meeting. I practically have to drag myself there, I'm so worn out, but I need to get my shit together. If Ben shows up to this meeting, I need to be on top of my game. He has to see that I know what I'm doing. That I'm an integral member of Crosswalk and an ally.

I text him half an hour before Crosswalk starts.

Cassie: Hey. Want to meet up before the meeting tonight?

He takes a good three minutes to get back to me.

Ben: sure

Yes!

Cassie: Great. Corner of Maple and Cypress?

Ben: 👍

Ugh. The dreaded thumb. But better than nothing, I guess.

When I get to our meeting spot, Ben is already there. I think I will always be shocked that he is an early arrival person.

He has a lollipop in his mouth, and I wonder if it's the special kind, because his eyes are a little hazy. I wonder if he's nervous and using weed to ease his nerves. I can't imagine that helping me—I've never smoked pot, but I bet I'd be the paranoid, anxious smoker rather than the chill kind.

He pulls the lollipop from his mouth to say, "Hey."

"Hey," I say back.

And then I have no idea what to say next. I am suddenly very, very aware that if Ben isn't impressed by this meeting, by Crosswalk, I have zero plans beyond that. Which is so unlike me. I usually have a B and a C plan. And sometimes even a D.

The thought makes me a little unsteady.

Thankfully, he asks, "So where's this thing happening?"

Okay, this is an easy one. I go into automatic mode. "It's in this semi-secret room on the bottom floor of Pinetree. One of our members has a key to it so we can get in there after hours. It's pretty cool." I glance sideways as we start walking to see if he thinks it's cool, too. But he just frowns and eyes me up.

"Huh. Okay, then."

We walk the rest of the way with only a few brief comments about volleyball and his siblings. I expect him to ask me more about the group, but he doesn't. I use the time to think about how I'm going to introduce him to the group instead. How I'm going to impress him with my amazing allyship.

When we enter the basement room at Pinetree, most of the regular Crosswalk crew is there and the room is filled with chatter. My eyes light up when I see Cameron nestled in beside Nai and looking right at home here. He waves and says, "Hi, Cassie."

I grin wide and say, "Cameron—hey! So glad you made it!"

"Ben!" This is Sam, who's on the couch, squeezed in next to Jay and Lou. They've got Rex in their lap, and the bunny hops over to Jay, startled by Sam's exuberant wave.

Ben raises a hand to Sam and gives them a half smile. I take the moment to introduce Ben to the rest of the group. "This is Ben, everyone. He goes to St. Luke's, too. And so does Cameron." *See? I'm doing it! I'm making things happen!*

"Welcome!" Nai says, her expression as welcoming as her tone.

I scan the circle for a place to sit. Halle is seated on the floor next to the couch—*not* beside Nicky—and there are two empty pillows beside her. She smiles at me and pats the pillow next to her.

Anticipating—maybe even hoping for—some overlapping knee action, I swallow, smile, and move to the spot, beckoning Ben to follow.

Once seated, Halle says, "It's awesome you're both here, Cameron and Ben. Should we do a round of intros?"

Our pillows are *close* and are knees are *even closer.*

Sam says, "For our newbies, this is where we just introduce ourselves with names, pronouns if you want, and how your day has been. I'll start."

We make our way around the circle, and when it's my turn, I say what I'd very carefully planned out already.

"Hey. I'm Cassie. She/her. And I'm your friendly neighborhood ally. I was super tired before I got here, but now I'm excited to have new folks in the mix. I think it's a good start to changing things for queer folks at St. Luke's, along with our pop-ups."

I've been practicing my use of the word "queer," and it rolls off my tongue, no problem.

I take a quick glance around the room, and most people are smiling at me. Ben's side-eyeing me, but that's nothing new. Halle's eyeing me up, too, her expression . . . scrutinizing?

I don't have time to decipher her look, though, because Ben's up next, and I am oh so curious as to what he's going to say.

He's finished his lollipop and pulls the bare stick out of his mouth. His lips are bright red, which makes him seem kind of childlike. "Uh, my name is Ben. He/him. I'm here 'cause some of you invited me."

He jabs the lollipop stick back in his mouth, signaling that he's done.

I'm not sure what I was expecting, but I guess I hoped he'd share a little more about why he actually *came.* Like, maybe even say something about being queer? But maybe he's just taking stock of the group first. I can understand that, even if impatience is needling away at my stomach.

When the intros get to Cameron, he says, "I'm Cameron. I use he/him/his pronouns. I'm new to St. Luke's, but was really involved with the GSA at my last school and am so excited this one exists. I'm still figuring some things out, but I think I might be bi or pan? Thank you for listening." Then he swipes a swath of hair away from his face before it bounces right back.

When he finishes, I can *feel* the collective sigh of adoration. Halle seems past whatever that previous look was, because she even reaches over to squeeze my thigh at this cuteness. What I feel when she does is definitely something other than cuteness.

Once intros are done, most of the meeting is dedicated to planning our first GSA field trip. I kind of wish we were having some kind of discussion that would let me show Ben how much I've learned these past few weeks, but it's hard not to get excited about a field trip when everyone else seems so thrilled about it, too. Especially Muriel.

"I found something we can do!" she shouts now. She shouts a lot. It would be annoying except that she continues to shout hilarious things, and her exuberance is too endearing to be irritating. "Can I say it?" Her eyes are wide and she's holding Zoey the bunny up to her cheek like she's part of Muriel's show.

"Go for it!" Sam yells, matching her enthusiasm.

I glance at Cameron, who now has Rex and is petting the bunny in long, slow strokes. He looks perfectly comfortable here, and I can tell by his quiet listening that he's biding his time, taking everything in to see what we're all about.

Beside me, Ben seems to be doing the same thing. His long legs are stretched out in front of him and crossed at the ankles, his posture is upright but somehow also relaxed, and his hands are folded in his lap. It's taking all of my willpower to *not* look at him every ten seconds to see what his face is doing.

"Okay, there's a coffee shop downtown that does a drag story hour, but, like, for grown-ups. But, like, it's also all ages so not just for grown-ups. So we could go! And it's not just drag queens, but all kinds of drag people. And they tell stories they wrote themselves!"

We all catch the buzz in her words, and there are lots of affirming comments.

"When is it?" Halle asks.

"Oh, that's the best part! Well, not the best part, but, like, an added *bonus* part! It's on every second Thursday, so we could go on our regular Crosswalk night next week!" She looks like she's about to explode, and it's super cute.

But.

I know it's nerdy, but I immediately start to worry that it's on a school night *and* next week, which is the week before midterms. Crosswalk meetings are one thing—at least they end at a decent time, but from what I gather, gay things always seem to start late and end late.

"What time does it start?" I ask, before I can stop myself. I know instantly I look like a huge loser for asking. I'm sure Ben is rolling his eyes. "I mean, sorry—I just—it's a school night . . ." I say, making things even worse. I avoid looking at Halle in case her face is telling me how absurd I am. I am one hundred percent sure she doesn't care what time it starts or ends.

Muriel replies, "Oh, it starts at eight."

"Which probably means eight thirty," Sam adds.

"Yeah, probably," Muriel says, "but I don't think the show's that long. Or, like, you can leave whenever, right?" She—this fourteen-year-old—looks at me like I'm the oldest person on the planet.

"Oh, that's totally cool," I say, like the least cool person on the planet. I wish I could take back the last two minutes. "Nerd who can't stay out past 8 p.m. even for a cool, queer event" is not the look I was going for with Ben here.

"This sounds amazing—did anyone else have any ideas? Or should we go with drag story hour?" Nai asks.

Everyone in the room appears enthusiastic about Muriel's idea, so it's decided. I feel a mixture of hesitation, trepidation, and excitement. I've never been to a gay thing before, besides Crosswalk. I've never seen any kind of drag live. And this is a very public thing. But it's a queer event, so it should be a safe, public thing, right?

And I wonder if Ben is at all interested in coming? And if he does come, I'd definitely need to be there, too. And be a lot cooler about it than I'm being right now.

My body is a bundle of nerves for the rest of the meeting, but in the end, I've convinced myself that (a) I will get Ben to this event with me; and (b) I will have an amazing time there, no matter how late it goes.

I'll just need to figure out what to tell my parents. And remember to take a nap.

When the meeting is finished, I make sure to walk out with Ben. He mostly stayed quiet the whole time, except when Nai asked him and Cameron if there was anything in particular they wanted out of the group. Cameron had lots of ideas, which he articulated clearly and concisely like a little boss, and Ben's response was "Not really. Whatever you all do is fine with me."

At least his answer suggested he might come back, though.

"So what'd you think?" I ask, as we start to walk toward our houses.

"Yeah, it was all right. Seems like a good group of people, at least."

From anyone else, this answer might feel subpar, but for Ben, this was a lot of words and a lot of positivity, so it gives me a bump of hope.

"Yeah, they're really cool. I'm learning a lot about allyship from them." *Know what I mean?*

He's quiet for a bit and then he says, "So, like, you started this club for . . . other people?"

For you, actually. "Yeah! I just saw the need for it, you know? Like, St. Luke's has literally nothing for queer folks, as I'm sure you've noticed, and I thought it was important." *Because* you're *important.*

"You're still, like, religious and stuff, though?" he asks.

I wonder if he's struggling with this part of things himself and that's why he's really asking. "Are *you* still practicing?" I ask, refocusing on him, just as a good ally should.

He shakes his head. "Not really. I mean, I'll probably still do the twice-a-year thing—you know, Christmas and Easter—but it's not really something I need."

I guess he'd decided that his queerness is more important than his relationship with the church. I guess that works for some people. But his mix of queerness and faith had never led him to be a shitty person. He'd never seemed scared of it.

Anyway.

"I get that" is all I offer. Wanting to change the subject and the pinching feeling in my chest, I say, "Want to come to drag story time with me?"

He shrugs at first. Then, after a few more steps, he says, "Not sure. It's past my bedtime."

My head whips toward him. He's smirking, and instead of feeling like a loser like I did before, I let out a scoff and shove his arm. "You're a jackass!"

"Little old ladies shouldn't use that kind of language." Something like a laugh comes out of his mouth. He's clearly pleased with himself.

I let him have it. Because him teasing me is better than him hating me. "Okay, so provided I can stay up past my bedtime, would you come?"

We come to the juncture where I need to go straight and he turns left. "Yeah, I'll go. But you'll need to pick me up. I don't have a car."

I'll have to figure that out with my parents and the whole staying-out-late thing, but I'm not about to say that now. "Yeah, no problem. But I drive like a granny, too, just FYI."

"Shocker."

"Yeah."

He sniffs and looks down the street. "'Kay. See you in class."

"When those graphs are due." *Ugh. Cassie.*

He rolls his eyes. "Couldn't help it, could you?"

"Sorry."

"They're already done. So you can sleep well tonight."

That actually *will* help me sleep better tonight. "I never doubted you for a second," I fib.

"You're full of shit, but okay. Bye." He lifts a hand and turns to walk away.

"Bye," I say, hoping he doesn't *actually* think I'm full of shit.

CHAPTER THIRTY

"I'm not sure where they came from, Kelly," I hear Mr. Reyes say as I walk into the library on Friday morning to study. He's in his office with Mrs. Keenan, and she's standing over him while he sits at his desk.

I pause by the front entrance where they can't notice me yet. Mrs. Keenan never comes in here. And from the way she's standing—arms folded, rigid back—she seems pissed.

"How is it you don't know what's happening in your own library, Gerald?"

"I mean, I can't control what everyone does while they're here, right?"

Mrs. Keenan's back is to me, but I can picture her haughty face as she says, "Well, I want those stickers off the books, and I'd like to see every book that has a sticker as well."

My stomach drops.

"Because . . . ?" Mr. Reyes says. I can just see him past Mrs. Keenan's figure, and his face has a look I'm not used to seeing on him. Irritated. Angry.

"Because some books are not age appropriate for a high school library."

"Which books are not appropriate?" His voice has a waver to it that I'm also not used to hearing.

Mrs. Keenan sighs. "Gerald, you know exactly what I'm talking about, so don't pretend you don't."

Even with my stomach flopping all over the place, I am seriously offended on Mr. Reyes's behalf at her tone. Like she's a parent and he's just a little kid and not a grown-ass man who is way smarter and more interesting than she is, as far as I'm concerned.

As they go back and forth over what Mrs. Keenan refers to as "next steps," I try to figure out my next step. Should I intervene here? Take responsibility for the stickers? But then would that put other pop-ups at risk? And what kind of trouble would I get into? Suspension? I can*not* risk missing school right now, or having that kind of thing put in my file or whatever the school does.

My heart is racing. I have to do *some*thing. I start walking before I can decide against it, as though I just entered, and say, "Good morning, Mr. Reyes!" as cheerfully and loudly as possible. When I come into full view, I stop, and add, "Oh, hi, Mrs. Keenan," with decidedly less enthusiasm.

Mrs. Keenan looks very unimpressed that she's been interrupted, but Mr. Reyes looks relieved. I'm happy about both responses.

"Good morning, Cassie," Mr. Reyes says, giving me a little wave and smiling.

I come around the front desk toward his office, bolstered by his smile and ignoring Mrs. Keenan's impatient body language. "Sorry to interrupt, but I was hoping I could get your help on a project I'm researching?"

"Oh, yes, of course!" Mr. Reyes says. "That's what I'm here for, after all."

I don't miss the testy glance he gives Mrs. Keenan. She doesn't miss it, either, because she literally huffs and places her knuckles on her hips like a petulant (SAT word) child. "Mr. Reyes, we'll continue this conversation later. Please come by when you have a chance."

As she's passing me, she says, "Ms. Perera, I hope to see you soon, too."

She's referring to all the intel I'm supposed to be passing on to her, of course. But she sure as heck won't be seeing me anytime soon for that.

Once she's gone, I look at Mr. Reyes, my eyebrows raised. "Do you . . . need help with anything?"

He eyes me up for a moment, and the look in his eyes makes me wonder if he knows the stickers are my doing. I'm a logical choice, after all, given how much time I spend here. But then, I've also never given him any reason to believe I'm some kind of rebel for the gay cause.

But whatever he does or doesn't know, he just says, "Nope! But you said you needed *my* help?"

Right. I did say that. "Oh, um, to be honest, I just thought . . . you maybe needed . . . an escape."

The grin that takes over his face makes me grin, too. "Well, my professionalism keeps me from saying anything to that, but . . . thank you." He winks at me and then flicks his hand my way, shooing me off.

I'm still grinning as I go to my usual spot to study, but once I settle in and have my books open in front of me, I spend most of the time trying to figure out how to stop Mrs. Keenan from removing all the queer books from the library.

CHAPTER THIRTY-ONE

"Welcome, Perera family!" Father Davis smiles at us as we enter the hall after church, shaking my parents' hands and giving me and Kendra a squeeze on our shoulders.

After Mass, we always come here for tea and snacks. This is one of my favorite parts of going to church. When Kendra and I were younger, we'd run around with the rest of the kids our age while the adults talked about adult things. We'd eat too-crunchy store-bought cookies and drink Tang. At our church, people still bring homemade snacks, too, and now I bypass the cookies and Tang for Nanaimo bars, lemon squares, and tea. Instead of running around, Kendra usually finds her friends and I hang by my parents' side, nodding and smiling at whatever they're discussing with other churchgoers.

The time here feels predictable and comforting. Nothing about it has really changed—the same hall, the same white-haired ladies volunteering in the kitchen to help serve and clean, the same tables and chairs and banners on the wall with "Faith" and "Love" on them.

I'm munching on a cookie now as Father Davis chats with my mom and me. He's been the parish priest at St. Luke's for eight years. My parents know him well through their work with the church, and both have the utmost respect for him.

I've always liked him, too. He's got a good sense of humor, which makes his homilies way more interesting than some I've heard, and even though he's probably in his sixties and has been a priest for most of his life, he seems like a fair kind of guy—progressive, even. Some of his views seem to veer from the more traditional views of the Catholic Church—references to "resisting the easy path of what has always existed" for "what is more in line with love," or "shifting with the times to include *all* those marginalized."

It's not groundbreaking stuff. I'm sure Halle would say, "That's the bare minimum." And I guess she's right. But I also just like that when I talk to Father Davis, I never feel like he's judging me. Which is more than I can say for some people—Halle included, at times.

"How are you today, Father?" my mom asks. I swear, the way she looks at him, I think she has a (very chaste) crush on him.

"Wonderful. The sun is shining. We're here together." His smile is warm and open. "And how is my favorite altar server?" he asks, looking at me.

I'm fairly sure he doesn't have favorites, but then, I *am* an excellent altar server, so who knows? "I'm well, thank you." I return his smile.

"Things must be getting quite busy for you, yes?" he asks me.

But before I can answer, my mom says, "She works very hard, Father. Always stuck in her room, homework over dinner, you know." Her words suggest I'm working *too* hard, but her beaming face tells me how hard I work makes her proud, as do her next words. "She's a good girl."

I think my mom is most proud of me when she's talking to Father Davis. Or maybe this is just when she shows her pride the most. Maybe she thinks it will keep me in good stead with God.

"Of course she is. She's always been so dedicated to the things she does," Father says.

I wonder what he'd think if he knew about some of the things I'm dedicated to now. The thought makes my stomach flip. I hope he'd maybe see it all as precisely in line "with love" and a way to "include all those marginalized," but I also wonder sometimes about the limitations of those words when it comes to certain groups. Is he even thinking about queer people when he says them? I can't imagine he is.

I keep smiling like I always do. "What's the point in doing something if you're not wholly dedicated to it?"

Gross, I hear Kendra's voice say in my head. If she were here, she'd say it to my face. Thankfully, she's across the hall with her friends, stuffing her face with Nanaimo bars.

But my words have the intended effect on my mom and Father Davis, which is smiles and head nods, and then they start talking about the upcoming food drive. As they do, I wonder if my goodness here will ever line up with the kinds of things I feel when I'm around the Crosswalk crew. If I could ever feel "good" in my mother's eyes and Father Davis's eyes, while also being good in the eyes of Halle, or Cameron, or Ben. Or if I'd just need to be a different person for different people forever.

CHAPTER THIRTY-TWO

It's Thanksgiving on Monday, so we all have a day off to eat turkey and pretend this holiday isn't a complete colonizer sham, as Halle pointed out in the group chat. My family doesn't really do the whole turkey thing, so for me, it's just an extended weekend to get prepared for midterms, which start next week.

But Halle and I also decided that this would be the perfect day for another pop-up, and even though I'm nervous about Mrs. Keenan's increasing ire over our rainbow actions, the chance to spend time with Halle and annoy Mrs. Keenan even more is too good to pass up.

I guess I'm also motivated by the success of the first couple of pop-ups. Though the library stickers might be removed this week, photos of Nicky's drag display in the theater changing rooms were posted as well. So far, that pop-up has remained and the admin hasn't caught wind of it yet.

Though we *had* seen a few negative comments on the posts about Rainbow Mary over the past week—stuff about how disrespectful it is to "graffiti" Mary and ignorant comments about "throwing gayness in people's faces"—most reactions were still positive.

So after getting up extra early to do enough homework that I won't feel as stressed, I tell my parents I'm taking Manika for a long walk, which isn't a complete lie, and make my way to St. Luke's, where Halle is waiting for me with the buckets of chalk that brought us together just a few weeks ago.

"Hey!" she says, standing at the entrance to the school. Her eyes light up when she sees Manika, who is hard to miss—lumbering, slobbery beast that she is. "Is this your dog?"

"Yup."

"What's their name?"

"Manika."

"Cool. Does it mean anything?"

"I think it's something like 'darling' or 'sweetheart' in Sinhala." I lean down to squish Manika's face. "Because you're just such a little darling, aren't you?" I say, with some measure of sarcasm, because she's not little at all and she chewed up one of my socks this morning. I give her ears a scratch, though, which makes her groan in contentment.

We spend the next minute crouched beside Manika, scratching and petting and smooshing so that she's in doggy heaven. I'm certainly not hating this, either—Halle so close, her hands brushing against mine every so often.

No, Cassie.

My conversation with Father Davis and my mom about how good I am makes an unwanted arrival and I stand up.

"Okay! Let's make the magic happen!" I say, swallowing the quick pulses emanating from my chest.

Halle gives Manika one final squish and stands as well. "Magic, it is."

Both St. Luke's and Pinetree are deserted, of course, since it's a holiday, so we have ample time and space to carry out our simple plan.

I loop Manika's leash around a bike rack close by, where she immediately flops to the ground, and we set to work. The original rainbow crosswalk from Pinetree's side of the street to ours has long since been washed away, but Pinetree's new painted rainbow entryway is there for good.

St. Luke's entrance has a covered walkway leading up to it, so it's a perfect spot for us to add a chalk rainbow. Maybe the school will remove it first thing tomorrow, but Halle and I just hope some kids will see it and post pictures of it like before.

"Stoked for drag story time?" Halle asks as we start in on the white triangle of the Progress Pride flag. We're crouched on our hands and knees, and our heads are only inches away from each other's. I try to keep Father Davis's face in my mind, which is a bit jarring as I craft this very gay flag.

"Definitely. It sounds really fun," I say, because it's true, even if I'm still a little nervous about staying out late and being in a public queer space. And how Ben will receive it all.

"Have you been in a lot of queer spaces before?" Halle asks, and I'm reminded that I'm supposed to have the experiences of a straight person. Luckily, that's exactly what I *have* had.

"Oh, uh, no—not really. I mean, besides Crosswalk."

"I fucking love queer spaces. I feel completely different in them than in other places."

"You mean, more welcome and stuff?" I ask, because I really want to know what that feels like.

"More welcome, more safe, more myself."

I'm a little surprised by this. "You seem so yourself all the time," I say.

Halle leans back on her knees. I glance at her but then keep coloring, because her face has a tinge of red to it from the cold air, and it makes her seem so fresh and lovely.

"Mostly, I am, I think," she says after pondering for a few moments. "But there's something about having queer spaces that's freeing in a different way, you know? Like, when I know the people in a space share that particular experience—even though obviously not every queer person's experience is the same—I just feel like I can be more honest, say things I might not say around straight people—that kind of stuff."

Oh. This feels weird. *I'm* supposed to be a straight person, so is she not saying certain things around me? Is she trying to tell me she's less comfortable around me than the others? I think about our Crosswalk discussion about safe spaces and wonder if I don't qualify as one for Halle.

Maybe she anticipates my worries, because she says, "*But* some straight folks are a bit easier to be around than others, too."

I look at her now and she's gazing at me, her head tilted in that way that seems to be inquisitive. *Ugh.* I love that she's looking at me, but I hate that she's referring to me as "straight folks," even if that's exactly how I need things to be. I smile at her, though, of course.

"Anyway," she says, leaning back down to continue coloring, "it's kind of like the GSA, right? A way to carve out some space that's distinctly, intentionally safe for people who need to feel that safety more so than some other people. I just don't get how anyone *wouldn't* want that if they care about human beings in any way—Catholic schools included."

This resonates on so many levels, I don't even know how to respond at first. A safe space for me. A safe space for Ben. A safe space for other students at St. Luke's. For other queer Catholic kids.

"I wish we—you—could have that kind of space everywhere," I say, my heart thumping at my almost misstep.

"Yeah. That'd be nice, wouldn't it? But in the meantime, we have our GSA, and these pop-ups, and drag story time." She grins at me and puts the final touches on the white triangle. "On to pink!"

Once we've finished the white, pink, blue, brown, and black sections, we draw out the straight lines of the rainbow, which will extend all the way to the door of St. Luke's, directly beneath a cross with Jesus Christ on it.

"I love this," Halle says. "It's like Jesus is saying, 'Come on down this rainbow path to me, my queer kiddos!'"

I like that she's bringing Jesus into the gay mix, instead of just pointing out how bad he is.

"Jesus *and* Mary, on Team Rainbow," I say, grinning now, too. "The big man himself, joining our crew!"

"Or . . . big woman? Maybe?" Halle says, holding her palms up by her shoulders in a "Who knows?" gesture. "I mean, I don't really believe in that stuff, but if there *is* a God, why does she have to be a 'he'?"

Kendra always refers to God as a "she," even around our parents. They tend to just scoff at her, but it always makes me smile a little. "Yeah . . . God could totally be a 'she,'" I say.

"Or a 'they'?"

"Right . . . I mean, shouldn't an omnipotent being be as well-rounded as possible?"

"Exactly. Gender and sexual binaries are so *limited*. Any *true* supreme being would encompass *all* genders and sexualities, obviously," she says.

We're grinning and laughing as we color, but what we're saying actually makes sense to me. Why *wouldn't* God be everything and all things and maybe even *beyond* the things we know? Maybe I'll ask Father Davis about this sometime. Like, in ten years.

By the time we complete the rainbow, it's noon. We take a photo of our work to show the Crosswalk crew.

As we pause to admire our pathway, Halle swings her arm around my shoulders. "Nice work, Cassie." The half smile she's giving me is too cute and too much. My arm wants so badly to wrap itself around her waist, but I force it to stay at my side.

"You, too," I say, staring down at the triangles pointing away from our feet.

"TBH—I wasn't sure you had this kind of thing in you at first, but maybe there's some serious rainbow warrior in there, after all."

I can feel her looking at me. And I can feel my heart racing. *Ugh. Stop it. Both of you.*

I don't move, though. Because I don't want to. "Well, I'm a total badass, remember?" I say, trying to tiptoe the line between too much and too little.

"That you are. What should our next project be?" she asks, her arm slipping away from my shoulders.

I picture her and me planting rainbow glitter bombs beneath Mrs. Keenan's desk and in other small, silent spaces.

Jesus, Cassie. Cool it.

I lean over to start collecting the chalk pieces still strewn on the ground, trying as I do to swallow the heartbeats pounding up my throat. "Not sure."

"Ooh, what if we did something in your gymnasium? Like to the boys' and girls' locker rooms?" She makes air quotes when she says "boys'" and "girls'."

I feel a little unsteady on my feet, so I get down onto my knees to collect the rest of the chalk. "Yeah. That'd be cool" is all I can get out.

After a few moments of silence, Halle asks, "What's up?"

I look up at her and her brow is crinkled, her eyes considering me with a mixture of kindness and concern.

Instead of her worry making me feel wrong, the expression makes me wish I could tell her what happens inside of me whenever I'm around her, or when she touches me, or now, as her gaze holds me like this.

What would that feel like? I wonder.

But instead, I say, "I actually need to figure out how to stop my vice principal from taking all the queer books out of the library."

"*Pardon me?* She's going to do *what*?"

The sudden fury on Halle's face would be amusing, if the reason for it wasn't so crappy.

"I know. It sucks. But I guess she found out somehow about these rainbow stickers I put on all the queer books—to make them easier to find, you know? And now she seems intent on analyzing and removing them."

"First, nice job with the stickers. Second, that's bullshit about your VP. I will *definitely* help you figure out how to keep those books there, even if we have to build some kind of hidden closet in the back of the library that only opens when you pull out a copy of the Bible," she says, holding out the bucket for me to drop my handfuls of chalk into.

The thought makes me smile as I stand up. "That sounds amazing. I vote for that option."

She smirks back. "Seriously, though," she says, placing the bucket on the ground and then a hand on my arm to give it a squeeze. "We'll figure something out. We're a good team."

Her eyes flick to my lips and her hand is still on my arm, and she's right here in front of me, saying we're a good team with that soft smile on her face.

And all of it makes me feel so completely off-balance again that I do the only thing that might keep me upright. I hug her. Right there in front of Jesus and our gay walkway. And she hugs me back, her arms tight around my waist. And her embrace steadies me for a few moments. I feel my chest move into hers with each breath. We stay like that for what feels like several minutes but might only be thirty seconds, I don't know. And when we finally pull back, our cheeks brush each other's, and our mouths remain so close that we must be breathing the same air.

Her eyes are on mine, searching, and this is a moment that could change so many things, I know, but what if it changes *too many* things? What if the changes are rips and ruptures and cracks?

I tug myself away and say, with much effort and a wavering voice, "We *are* a good team!" And then I laugh like all this is just friendly and normal, and my insides haven't turned into a complete mess, and Halle's eyes haven't turned into confusion and hurt.

"I should get home," I say, disappointment at myself edging my voice. "My parents are going to wonder where I went. So is my giant stack of homework."

I lean down to unwind Manika's leash to avoid having to look into Halle's eyes.

"Yeah, sure," Halle says, and I can hear disappointment in her voice, too. "At least we have drag story time, I guess?" The uncertainty in her question is so unlike her usual tone that it makes my heart ache, knowing I caused this.

At least we have that, I think, trying to convince myself that it's enough.

CHAPTER THIRTY-THREE

On Tuesday, I wake up with wavy feelings in my stomach about the previous day and my time with Halle. The ebb and flow is a result of both wanting more of those moments of closeness and steadiness with her but also feeling so uncertain about how to get past the terror they bring up.

When I arrive at school on Tuesday morning, though, and the rainbow walkway to Jesus is still there, excitement slips past the unease. It's eight o'clock, and I'm a little surprised, actually. I wonder if the school is worried about the optics of washing away the Pride flag as students enter in the morning. Or if they're just waiting until we're all inside before getting rid of it. Either way, a few other students are arriving and checking out the display alongside me, and their comments continue to cheer me up.

"Whoa. Cool!"

"Are we doing a Pride week or something? What's the deal?"

"Bless me, Gay Jesus!" one guy yells as he walks into the school and makes a peace sign at the statue of Jesus.

People are snapping photos, so I take out my phone and snap a couple of shots as well, to blend in, but also to show Ben, in case he doesn't see it himself. But as I view the rainbow through my phone and listen to the positive comments around me, I suddenly want Ben to see the real thing. I want to celebrate this with him. Without overthinking it, I text him.

Cassie: You here yet? Come to the front entrance!

I linger to the side of the entrance as I wait for his response. I'm supposed to be getting to my AP Macro class for our early start, but it will have to wait. This is too important. A couple of minutes later, he replies.

Ben: What's up?

Cassie: Just come see already. 😜

Ben: 🙄

Despite the eye roll, Ben arrives a few minutes later, hands in pockets, loose toque over his head, but no jacket—just his school blazer. He's looking at the rainbow, but his face remains neutral.

I decide to bring his face out of neutrality and into something much better.

"What d'ya think?" I say, grinning. "Halle and I did it yesterday." I keep my voice low.

"Wow. You're really going for it, huh?"

"Like it?"

He looks at the chalk rainbow, then at me, then back at the rainbow. He finally says, "Yeah . . . it's cool."

I leap on this tiny bit of affirmation and lean in. "Hopefully this makes a few people feel more welcome." I grin.

"Totally . . ."

My excitement boils up inside of me. The fact that Ben is here, seeing this display, and likes it, and that he's been to a Crosswalk meeting and is coming again this week, *and* that he seems to be warming to me just the way I wanted him to—it all makes my body buzz with possibility. The buzz comes through in my voice, which maybe gets a little louder than it should.

"We really need more of this at St. Luke's." I think about the books in the library. "It's kind of ridiculous how far behind we are."

Just as I'm saying this, I hear, "Oh really, Ms. Perera?"

Mrs. Keenan appears, walking over from her prime parking spot in front of the school.

My stomach does an abrupt flip. I glance at Ben, who's looking at me with raised eyebrows, as if daring me to prove what a great ally I am in this moment.

Even though it feels like my heart is being whacked back and forth like a tennis ball in my chest, I can't back down now, not if I want Ben to believe *I've got this*.

"Well, yes, actually." Hearing the slight sass in my voice makes me ill. I never talk to teachers like this, let alone to admin.

Mrs. Keenan's eyebrows raise now, too. "You think St. Luke's needs more graffiti? We support vandalizing now?"

"Um, well, this isn't really *vandalizing* . . ." I can feel my sass retreating in the face of Mrs. Keenan's reproval. I also need to make sure she doesn't think it was *me* who did this.

"No? So whoever did this went through the proper channels, then? Had permission?"

"Uh . . . I don't know. Did they?" I ask, trying to sound innocent, not cheeky.

She folds her arms and frowns at me. I try to *look* innocent, too, but also don't want to back down in front of Ben, or in front of the other kids who are still standing around. But being dressed down by an adult so publicly is also a very new experience—and I hate it. That wavy feeling is creeping up from my feet, and I try to push it back down by squeezing my toes.

"I suggest you refrain from publicly supporting this kind of defacement, Cassie."

This kind? Like, gay defacement? I swallow hard and blink back the burning sensation in my eyes. "Is there a kind of defacement I *should* support?"

Holy crap. The sass is back, apparently.

"I *beg* your pardon? You're bordering on disrespectful, Ms. Perera."

I'm freaking out but also angry but also worried about what Ben is thinking. I channel my inner Halle, if one even exists. "I'm not trying to be disrespectful, Mrs. Keenan, but maybe this particular display is helping some people feel safe here, you know? Like, there are people here who might really appreciate this?" I try hard not to look at Ben while I'm saying this, but I fail. Mrs. Keenan glances at Ben, too, who looks away, rubbing his nose.

"I just mean, people in general. Not anyone in particular," I babble on. "You know what I mean."

"No, I'm not sure I do, actually," Mrs. Keenan says. "It almost sounds like *you're* behind this."

Shit. I can't risk going down this path with her. I don't want to jeopardize Crosswalk . . . or put myself in jeopardy, for that matter.

I put on my most surprised face. "Me? No—not at all. I think this is cool, but I didn't do it." My jaw stiffens. "I *wish* I had, though."

Mrs. Keenan lets out a disbelieving noise that sounds like something between a cough and a laugh. "Ms. Perera, I'm not sure what's gotten into you, but even if you didn't do this, your attitude right now is unacceptable. Meet me in my office at break today so we can discuss a fitting way to address your lack of respect."

What? "Oh, but I have to meet with Mrs. Hansen at break to go over an assignment." *That I'm behind on.*

"That's too bad. You'll need to reschedule. See you then," she says as she's walking away, up the rainbow to Jesus, which, I'll admit, takes a tiny bit of the edge off of what she's just said. But mostly, I'm panicky and my body is jittery. I have to keep it together, though.

"Oops," I say to Ben, who's looking at me with an expression

I can't quite read. I'm hoping he's maybe impressed by both my creation of this display and now with my willingness to stand up to Mrs. Keenan. Maybe?

"Yeah, that was . . . messed up."

I really hope he means Mrs. Keenan's nonsense and not something about me.

"Right? But I mean, gotta do what's right, right?" I note the triple use of "right" and cringe inwardly at myself.

"Sure. I'm late. Good luck with all that."

I don't have a chance to say anything else to him because he's gone in an instant. Watching him walk beneath gay Jesus isn't even enough to make me feel better.

When I arrive to Mrs. Keenan's office at break, having just spent the entirety of first period growing more and more anxious, Mrs. Keenan sits at her desk, hammering away at her laptop.

"Hello?" I say, my voice coming out with a creak.

She glances up and then back at her computer screen. "Come. Sit."

A flash of anger sparks in my chest. *Sorry, am I a dog now?* But I do as I'm told. I can't get in any more trouble than I'm already in. I need to keep the pop-ups and Crosswalk safe. I can't risk Mrs. Keenan calling my mom, either.

Once I'm seated, she finally looks up but keeps her laptop open in front of her. "Cassie, I am *very* disappointed in you and the way you spoke to me earlier. What on earth has gotten into you?"

Just a bit of the Holy Gay Spirit, Kelly. "I'm not sure what you mean, Mrs. Keenan. I just thought the display was kind of neat, is all."

"Neat? You think treating the Mother Mary and Jesus Christ as some kind of joke is neat? You don't think it's disrespectful of this institution and of *God*?"

God? Really? The drama. "Maybe it's not a joke. Maybe someone is just trying to . . ." I pause. I can feel my heart beat faster, and I need to calm down. If I defend the pop-ups too much, it'll make me look way too guilty. I try to tamp down the anger and defensiveness rising inside of me and say, "I'm sorry I was disrespectful. I think I'm just really tired." I decide to play the stressed-out-kid card. "I think I took on a bit too much this term, and I haven't been sleeping much. I promise it won't happen again."

The self-satisfaction that comes over her face is almost enough to make me take back everything I said, but I literally bite my tongue.

"Well. I certainly hope it doesn't. And please refrain from supporting such acts of disrespect to our blessed family as well. We don't need people thinking our class president champions such things. Remember, you're meant to be helping me *stop* these acts."

Ugh. I need to get out of here, ASAP. "Yes, of course," I say, hating every word coming out of my mouth.

CHAPTER THIRTY-FOUR

By the time my meeting with Mrs. Keenan is over, the chalk rainbow is already washed away. That, added to Ben's apparent irritation with me and Mrs. Keenan's annoying face, leaves me with a mix of disappointment, worry, and anger.

I message Halle with a photo of the newly washed entryway and several sad emojis. She texts back with #NoRegrets and a raised fist emoji.

This only makes me feel mildly better.

I try to shrug off my disappointment and get on with my classes, but it isn't easy. Luckily, our volleyball game was canceled, so to make up for my many brain lapses throughout the day, I stay after school to get some work done in the library.

After checking to see if the rainbow stickers are still on the books I labeled (they are!), I find a table away from the gaggle of eighth and ninth graders staring at their phones in the middle of the room and pull out my homework.

I'm a few minutes into getting a head start on a very large history project proposal when Mr. Reyes comes around and starts placing books onto a shelf close by. I must look like I'm thinking really hard, because he glances at me and says, "Penny for your thoughts, Cassie?"

I don't even know what I was thinking about. I know what I was trying *not* to think about, but I'm not about to tell Mr. Reyes about any of my many issues, so I look down at the homework I was supposed to be doing and say, "The impacts of colonization on Indigenous peoples in the Americas." I mean, this *is* what I was *trying* to focus on anyway.

"Wow. That's a lot to think about on a Tuesday afternoon. How's it going?"

Not well. "Seems like a pretty shitty deal if you ask me." My eyes go wide. I just said "shitty" to a teacher. I've never done that before. Apparently I'm on the fast track to hooliganism as of today.

Mr. Reyes's eyebrows bounce up, and his lips turn downward in what looks like amusement. He lets out a small laugh.

"Sorry—I didn't mean to say that," I say.

"Didn't you? I mean, you're right, after all. And sometimes curse words are the only way to describe something so awful." He winks at me and puts another book on the shelf.

I'm surprised by this response, but since he makes nothing more of it, neither do I. I'm about to go back to my homework when he adds, "We have a pretty good selection of books on residential schools and the Indian Act here—have you looked?"

"We do?" Another surprise in the book stock department.

"Yup."

"But . . ." I hesitate, because I've noticed people get defensive around here when residential schools come up.

"But what?" He turns to me now, pausing his task.

"Um. Are the books . . . biased at all? I mean—do they really depict the reality of residential schools and stuff? Or . . ."

"Or do they make it sound like the 'schools'"—he makes air quotes—"were well-intentioned, yada yada yada?"

"Yeah. Yes."

"Don't worry, I made sure to include a variety of sources, and they're all accurate. Most are written by Indigenous people themselves."

"Oh." *Cool.* "I'll have to check those out. Thanks." I don't want to take up any more of his time, so I look back at my laptop screen.

But then he's suddenly seated at the table across from me.

"Did you know," he says, "that a lot of Indigenous groups are matriarchal? And that they acknowledged and honored gender fluidity?"

"They did?" I don't know why he's telling me this, but he's definitely got my attention.

"Mm-hmm. Yup. And then colonization went and ruined it all. Well, not all. Lots of Indigenous folks are reclaiming that part of their culture. Many groups are more open-minded than all our strict versions of gender and sexuality."

This makes me think about my conversation with Halle the previous day—about how God could be more than one gender, or even beyond gender—but I also wonder why he's saying these things to me. My heart starts to beat faster. Is it because I overheard his conversation with Mrs. Keenan last week? Or does he know something about Crosswalk? About *my* conversation with Mrs. Keenan? About the pop-ups? About *me*?

I have to force back my rising apprehension to be able to say, "Oh. That's cool. I mean, not the colonization-ruining-everything part, but the rest. Um."

"Yeah, and there's a term—two-spirit—do you know it?"

Before I can reply if I do know it or not—which I only vaguely do from Halle's breakdown of the 2SLGBTQIA+ acronym during our first Crosswalk meeting—he keeps talking. He's getting more and more excited with each word. "It's for Indigenous folks who kind of encompass more than one gender, and it's a really honored identity, you know?"

He's almost getting wistful, and I don't know if I'm supposed to say anything or not, so I don't, which is fine, because he just keeps talking.

"We have a similar term in the Philippines for a kind of fluid gender. It's called bakla. If you're interested in any of this, I could bring in some books for you."

He turns his wistful look across the room into an expectant look at me now, and I guess it's my turn to say something.

"Uh—well, I've been focusing more on the way colonization has impacted certain aspects of the environment, but thanks anyway."

"Oh." He almost looks disappointed. "Okay, well, if you ever want to talk about any of this stuff, let me know—I think it's so exciting and important."

Watching him now, I think about that rainbow on his office door. That small stack of queer books already making it into the hands of kids like Cameron and me.

"Are you . . . allowed? To, like, bring in those kinds of books?" I'm careful with my tone, because I don't want him to think I'm threatening him or judging the topics of the books. "It just sounded like . . . from what Mrs. Keenan was saying . . ."

He eyes me up for a moment. "Well, I mean, they're real things, right? People's real lives and identities? And we're a school, so . . ."

"But some people seem to get antsy about that kind of stuff, don't they?"

"You mean, stuff that suggests there might be many genders and many sexualities?"

"Yeah, I mean—are we even allowed to have this *conversation*?"

He laughs a little, but then his face becomes serious. "You're right that we don't have a lot of conversations like this here. And that some people at the school might have a problem with a conversation like this. Or books like that." He leans in. "But those books aren't going anywhere, okay? And *I'm* not one of those people, all right?"

The way he says this makes my heart rate pick up again—like he really wants *me* to know he's not one of those people. Like that rainbow on his door is more than just a bright bit of color. Like maybe he's a safe person here in a sea of unknowns.

"Okay" is all I can say.

He smiles at me now and taps the table with a finger. "Well. I should let you get back to your homework. And *I* should get back to my books. But"—and he cocks an eyebrow at me—"my door is always open for a good chat, got it?"

"Got it," I say, trying really hard to keep a neutral expression on my face.

Mr. Reyes goes back to his books and I try my damnedest to go back to my homework, but instead I end up googling some of the terms Mr. Reyes mentioned and start to rethink the focus of my history assignment, welcoming the distraction from my own issues.

CHAPTER THIRTY-FIVE

The conversation with Mr. Reyes came at the right time, as did the photos of the rainbow entrance Halle and I created that some students caught before it was washed away. These were circulating on social media on Tuesday with mostly positive comments like Oh snap! Come thru gay Jesus! and The rainbow fairy strikes again! 😍

I need all the good vibes I can get after my chat with Mrs. Keenan *and* after getting back an assignment for AP French with a "79%" staring at me from the top of the page. My teacher, Monsieur Leeds, even kept me behind after class to see if everything was okay. I told him I was fine and promised I'd make it up on the midterm.

And I would. I needed to. I'd have to really buckle down this weekend and kill it on *all* my midterms. This was getting out of hand.

But right now, I had to pick up Ben and spend the evening trying to act like I wasn't nervous at all to be at an openly queer event with both him and Halle there.

I was already nervous when I left the house. I'd had to tell my parents my prep course was going later tonight so I could hopefully see the whole show, but my mom wasn't happy about it.

"What kind of course goes until ten p.m.?"

"It's just a one-off thing, I promise. I have an easy day tomorrow—don't worry." False. I had two quizzes and a practice test the next day.

Eventually, my mom let me go with a very clear warning to be home by 10:30 at the latest, and my dad let me borrow the Sable. My parents are stricter than most, but, truthfully, I like being in bed by ten anyway, seeing as my alarm usually goes off at 6 a.m. most days, including weekends. Prime study time, you know?

But I also really don't want to be nerdy, safe Cassie tonight—not in front of Ben or Halle.

So my nerves are already frazzled with all of these competing needs when Ben gets into the car with the usual "Hey," and the tension in my body makes me overtalk. "So have you ever been to one of these before? I haven't. But Muriel was so excited about it, and some of the others said it should be really good, so I'm excited. Are you excited?"

God in heaven, Cassie.

"Why are you acting weird?" he asks.

Fair. I blow out a breath. "Sorry. I'm overtired, I think." *Or something.*

"What happened with Mrs. Keenan?"

Oh. How do I tell him I totally caved? "Well, I had to protect the pop-ups and Crosswalk, so I just kind of denied and apologized, you know?"

I can see him nodding in my peripheral vision. "Makes sense."

"I'm glad you're coming tonight," I blurt. I want him to know this.

"Okay" is all he says.

"So . . . *have* you been to one of these?" I repeat.

"Nope. I mean, I've seen drag before. But not drag story time."

Oh. Right. Of course he's "in the know" about gay things.

"Have you?" he asks.

I laugh. "What? No. When would I have gone to a drag show?"

He shrugs. "There're tons of drag shows around, all the time. It wouldn't be that strange for you to have gone to one."

Yes it would. But I don't want him to think *I* think it's strange to go to drag shows, so I say, "No, I guess not. But as you've probably gathered, I'm not exactly a 'nightlife' kind of gal."

"Right. Well, maybe you should change that."

I scoff. "Oh yeah? With all my extra time, I should start hitting up all the drag shows in town, too?"

He shrugs again. "Maybe. It could be good for you."

I glance over at him while we're stopped at a light, but he's looking out his window. His words make me think I'm right—I need to play my cards carefully tonight. I need to get out of my safe shell and show him that I can be fun and cool and supportive. I need to show Halle I'm not a complete confused mess. Maybe I need to show myself this, too.

“Yeee! This is the bomb, y’all!” Muriel is practically falling out of her seat, her head on a swivel, taking in the scene at the café. Everyone joins in her excitement, chattering around the table.

At Muriel’s request, we’re all crowded together near the front of the large room, as close to the stage as possible. Drag story hour is about to start, and all the regulars from Crosswalk are here, except Tansi and Jesse, who have some other cool gay thing to go to, apparently.

That makes for eleven people who *did* come, and a very squishy situation at this table meant for six.

So far, though, the squish factor is mostly pleasurable—what with Halle’s thigh pushed up against mine on one side. I’d sat down beside her, urging myself to regain a little of the closeness I probably spoiled on Monday at our pop-up. She seemed a little surprised when I slid onto the bench seat next to her, but her smile was warm, and it gave me enough of a boost to think I hadn’t completely ruined everything between us.

Now, I’m trying to tap into the energy around me. I remind myself that I’m here to have *fun* tonight. I force myself to shift a little closer to Halle instead of away. I take in the mix of cozy and vibrant atmosphere in the café. Every table is full, and laughter emanates from around us.

And some of that laughter is from Ben, who’s on the other side of me, and I may be imagining it, but he seems looser here, rowdy, even. Sam’s next to him (of course), and they’ve been cracking jokes since we arrived. I allow myself a little pat on the back—for helping to create this group that is genuinely fun and helpful, and for getting Ben here (even if I had help doing it).

I'm drawn out of my thoughts by Lou, who's craning their neck to watch the drag queen who is currently meandering through the café, engaging in playful banter with the crowd. Lou asks, "Has anyone ever been to one of these before?"

"My mom and I took my younger brother to the little kids' version over the summer," Nicky says. "It was suuuper cute. My brother got right up onto the lap of one of the drag kings and didn't move until the story was finished. My mom took, like, a thousand photos." She rolls her eyes, but it's obvious she loves this.

"That's awesome your mom is down about that stuff. Does she know you're not straight?" Jay asks. He's sitting cross-legged on a stool with a mug of tea in his hands, like a little Zen statue.

"Nah. I don't feel the need to share that with her yet."

"That's cool," Jay says, nodding.

I've been pretty quiet so far, so I decide to add my two cents here, because maybe I can use this topic of conversation to impress Ben and really solidify my status as ally extraordinaire.

"Yeah, you should be able to come out when you're ready. It's every individual's choice," I say.

Halle nods beside me and says, "Yeah, for sure. But also, 'coming out' is a cis- and heteronormative concept. It assumes straightness and puts the onus on queer folks to have to assert their identities over and over again." She says this like it's the most obvious thing in the world, and I hope Ben doesn't think I'm a dummy for not saying this instead. I notice he's silent beside me but listening.

"It is," Lou says, "but it's helpful to have language to describe something we have to do all the time, right?"

Bless them.

Halle replies, "Yeah, that's true. But wouldn't it be cool if we didn't even need a term because no one has to do it because all genders and sexualities are just accepted?" She's looking straight at me when she says this, and my stomach flips. "Wouldn't it be great if people could just be whoever they are, no matter what their religion, background, ethnicity, or whatever?"

Everyone at the table nods or murmurs in agreement, including Ben, and I nod as well, hoping the chaotic feelings her words and look are causing in me don't show.

Our conversation is interrupted in the next moment by a short, round Asian drag queen who is standing onstage and tapping at the mic with her lengthy lime-green nails. A pair of matching green antlers rise out of her yellow wig.

"Welcome, welcome, my babies! My name is Sheela Sheen, and I'll be your host for the night." Everyone claps and cheers. She goes on to give a land acknowledgment, explain the evening, thank their sponsors and the café, and tell a few jokes that hover around a PG-13 rating.

The first storytelling queen gets up onstage and shares a story about a haunted pair of high heels she once owned. The stories that follow shift between hilarious, heartwarming, cheeky, and more, and help to ease some of the chaos in my chest.

As we listen, though, I am still very aware of Halle's thigh (as always) and her reactions to each story. I find myself responding more to her reactions than to the performances, which I guess is kind of weird. She looks at me a few times, smiling or sharing a sympathetic look if the story is touching.

I am also very conscious of Ben—on the other side of me—whose energy reminds me of how he used to be, when he would practically bounce off the walls, or talk nonstop, or show his doodles to a perfect stranger on the first day of fourth grade. He and Sam provide a running commentary in between performers, offering their alternative endings to the stories or connections to pop culture. Sam does their rendition of Michelle Visage from *Drag Race* judging each performer, and Ben laughs louder than I've heard him laugh since he got back.

My entire body seems overstimulated with what feels like pure positivity. The warmth from Halle's arm against mine, the odd bump from Ben when he thumps his hands together to show his appreciation for a performer. Their laughter vibrates through me. My excitement about being here with them, about getting Ben here, about the newness of it all, bubbles up through my chest.

The time doesn't even occur to me until it's intermission, and I check my phone. I had to get over my initial apprehension at going out on a school night, but that apprehension is back when I see it's 9:30 and there's still a twenty-minute intermission and half the show to go.

I haven't told Ben yet that I need to be home by 10:30. He's having such a good time. *I'm* having such a good time.

Now I have to figure out if I'm going to be a total loser and leave early, or stay longer and risk getting in trouble with my parents. As a few folks rise from the table to get more drinks and use the bathroom, Halle turns to me to ask, "Want another drink?"

"Oh, um . . . I think I have to go." *Ugh.*

She gazes at me for a moment, and I have to look away. But then she says, "You should definitely stay."

I look back at her, and she's smiling. It is *very* hard to not look at her lips. "I want to . . . I just . . . my parents are a little strict."

"Yeah, I get it. But, like, you're here, right? And it's your first queer event, you said?"

Right. And you're supposed to be a supportive ally, supporting queer events and queer people, Cassie.

"Right . . ."

"Can't help but overhear"—this is Nicky from the other side of Halle, who "can't help but overhear" because she was probably listening in—"you're *leaving*, Cassie? But why?"

I roll my eyes internally.

"I just . . . my parents—"

"Why don't you try texting your dad to ask him if you can stay a little longer?" Ben inserts. I turn to him and his face seems neutral, but I can tell he's got a challenge in his eyes.

My dad is the more easygoing of the two, but I reply, "He'll say no, guaranteed."

Ben narrows his eyes at me, and I know this means trouble. "What if . . . you *didn't* tell your parents you're staying out later, and you *snuck into* your house? I mean, would they ever *expect* you to break curfew?"

I can hear the subtext without him needing to say it. *Loosen up, nerd. You brought me here, and now you're leaving? What kind of friend is that?*

Nicky pipes up with "Yeah, will your parents really be that mad if you get caught?"

Yes. "Um, I don't really know. Maybe."

"Well, then, I guess you can't get caught, right?" Halle says, grinning at Nicky like they're on the same team or something, which I obviously hate. "We can help you—what's the best way to sneak into your house?"

For the next few minutes, I'm bombarded by Halle and Nicky, Ben and Sam, plotting my delinquency. By the time they're done, I'm apparently sneaking in through my bedroom window—a contribution from Ben, who reminded me that he climbed through my bedroom window when we were kids and I'd locked him out of my house as a joke. Then I'm going straight to bed without brushing my teeth (*ugh*) so as not to wake anyone.

My parents are usually in bed by ten, so this plan might actually work. Although that doesn't stop worry from invading my stomach.

"Okay! So it's settled. You're staying, you're sneaking, you're winning at life, bro!" Halle practically shouts. She grins at me and gives me a side-hug. I notice her hand remains on my hip for longer than it needs to, and I don't mind it. Ben even holds out his fist for a fist bump, and I like that, too.

My stomach continues to feel a little woozy, but a tiny flicker of excitement sparks in my chest again. The thought of sitting here next to Halle for another hour, of enjoying this night with Ben, makes me giddy. And being a little bad also spurs some unfamiliar excitement, too.

By the time everyone refills their drinks and gets back to the table, I'm trying to just sit with that excitement. Cameron settles in across from me, and I smile at him. He doesn't seem the least bit worried about being out this late on a school night, so . . . that's cool for me.

"I checked out two new books with the rainbows on them," he says above the chatter around us.

"Wow—that was fast!" I say, impressed, given that I only added the labels last week. I'm also thrilled to hear the books and labels are still there. Mr. Reyes said they would be, but I wonder what kind of magic he conjured to avoid Mrs. Keenan's attempts at censorship.

"I'm a voracious reader," Cameron replies, and my heart melts.

"You must be."

"Yeah." He sips his second hot cocoa. "How are your decorations coming for the fall fair?"

In truth, I've barely thought about the fall fair and the decorations I'm supposed to be making. "Oh, fine. How about you? You're in charge of advertising, right?"

"Yes, I am. But I'm not really sure how to advertise for our booth."

"What booth—what are y'all talking about? I love a good booth!" This is Sam.

"Oh, St. Luke's has this fall fair every year, and Cameron and

I are class presidents. So we have to help with a booth and some other stuff," I say.

"But it's a weird theme," Cameron adds.

"What do you mean?" Nai asks.

"Yeah, maybe we can help?" Halle asks from beside me, and others turn to listen, too.

"Oh, well . . . the theme is 'Falling in Love,' and it all just feels a little . . . um . . . heteronormative?" Cameron explains.

Of course this kid is already using language I'm just starting to get used to.

"Is there a way to make this booth a little more inclusive?" Nai asks.

Cameron and I glance at each other but don't say anything. The MC announces the show will start again in five minutes. And then the table shakes with the force of Halle's hand slapping against it.

"Y'all! What if we do a super-gay pop-up at your fall fair?" she says.

My stomach dips at the suggestion. The fair is only a week away, and I hadn't planned to add yet another thing to my plate, since midterms are next week.

But I obviously can't say any of this, since I'm supposed to be an ally and all.

Everyone else, though, seems super excited about the idea.

Cameron grins, Nicky shouts, "Hell yeah!" and Sam asks, "OMG . . . can I help, please?"

Ben doesn't say anything—just looks intently at me.

"What do you think, Cassie?" Halle asks.

What could I possibly say? "Oh, um, yeah, that could work" is all I come up with.

She grins and her eyes fall to my lips for a moment, again. I feel her hand give my leg a little squeeze. "Awesome," she says. "You're awesome."

I'm momentarily elated by her response and that squeeze, but as the group gets giddy about possibilities around me, I can't help the nerves that creep back in.

Holding a pop-up at the fall fair feels like a much bigger risk than the other pop-ups. More public. I'm already on thin ice with Mrs. Keenan, so we'll have to be extra careful, and now my involvement in the fall fair will go beyond just creating some decorations. So much for making my next week all about midterms. For the rest of the night, I can feel "fun Cassie" starting to slip away even as I try hard to hang on to her.

CHAPTER THIRTY-SIX

It's 11:30 by the time I'm sneaking up the stairs to the deck. I hope to hell I didn't wake my parents while parking the car in the driveway.

The whole drive to Ben's house to drop him off, I had to stifle the ripples of anxiety moving through me—from the new plan developing for this fall fair pop-up *and* from the realization that I would now have to climb through my bedroom window. I had to tell myself this was all in the service of being a good friend and ally . . . of doing the right thing for Ben and Crosswalk and all those kids at St. Luke's who needed *something* to tell them they're okay the way they are.

I can't see any lights on in the house, so that's a good sign. I tiptoe across the deck to my window, which is almost never locked because I like to leave it open a crack while I sleep. I slide it open, remove my shoes, and throw them onto my bed, thinking this will be even more stealthy. I haul myself through the open window as silently as I can.

But when I step onto my desk, my sock slides against a sheet of paper and I feel my foot skating off the surface, my other leg buckling, and my entire body tilting sideways.

Of course an overdue physics assignment would be my downfall.

My foot kicks over my desk chair, and I fall hard onto my bed and bang my head against the wall. The thumps and bumps are so loud, I'm not surprised when I see the hallway light go on and seep under my door, which flings open a few seconds later.

I scramble to my feet and try to think up some excuses for why I'd be climbing through my bedroom window after curfew, but before I get past my first thought, Amma appears in the doorway, backlit in her nightdress. I can only just make out her face, but I can see enough to know that it's full of fury.

She comes right up to me, stealthy and quick like a ninja, and grabs my face. I have no idea what she's doing until she pulls me close and sniffs at my mouth. She thinks I've been drinking. Well, at least this is in my favor, since I haven't had any alcohol whatsoever.

When she's sufficiently satisfied that I'm not sauced, she steps back and points to the bed, stabbing the air with her finger. I follow her finger and sit down, bracing myself. At least she can't yell at me right now. If my dad's still sleeping, she won't want to wake him.

After shutting thc window and picking up my chair, she stands over me and lays in, her voice a harsh whisper-shout. "It's eleven thirty! I tried calling you—why didn't you answer?"

Oh, shit. I was so wrapped up in the people beside me and the feelings overtaking my body tonight that I hadn't even looked at my phone after intermission.

"I'm sorry. I forgot to check my phone—"

"You forgot? You missed curfew and didn't think it would be a problem?"

Ugh. I should have known she'd stay up waiting for me. I hardly ever stay out late. She was probably sitting here worrying the whole night. I start to feel a little bad, but as soon as I feel it, I resent it. I never break her rules. Why should I feel bad about being a normal teenager, doing normal things? Why should I feel bad about something that actually felt good, even if it was a little scary?

"I'm only an hour late!" I say, immediately hearing how ridiculous that sounds.

"Only? You have school tomorrow! And I *only* have to be up in a few hours for work."

"No one asked you to stay up!" *Shit. Not a good move.*

"I beg your pardon?" she says.

"Nothing," I barely say.

"What?"

"Nothing," I say a little louder. Then: "I'm sorry."

"Where were you?"

"At . . . my course, like I said."

"Cassie."

"Afterward a couple of us went to this girl's house to keep studying." *Liar, liar.*

"*Cassie*," she harsh-whispers.

It's no use. I'm a bad liar, and she's a good lie detector. "*Okay.* I went to a café with friends. We went to see an open mic." Not exactly a lie. "I lost track of time."

"I don't know what's gotten into you, Cassandra. Since when do you lie to me? Make terrible choices like this? Stay out late on a school night and break your word?"

I'm sorry that I've kept her up, but I'm also annoyed by this extra lecture. Nothing's "gotten into me." I've done everything my parents have asked of me and more these past few years.

"I said I'm sorry!" My voice comes out louder than I mean it to, and my eyes immediately go wide at my mom, who gives me the look of doom.

In a low, even, and terrifying voice, she says, "Get to bed right now. We're going to talk about this more. You're not going anywhere except to school tomorrow and then church on Sunday, do you understand me?"

I nod and say yes. She leaves my room. Even though I could brush my teeth now that my mom's seen me, I don't. I strip off my clothes, pull on my pj's, and crawl under my covers. I get a message from Halle a few minutes later.

Halle: hope u did the thing, badass! 😈💖

I don't bother replying. What would I say? Instead, I spend the next two hours staring up at the ceiling, trying to calm the anger and irritation in my chest and failing.

As ordered, I come straight home after school on Friday, which, to be honest, I probably would have done anyway. I hate to admit it, but my mom was right. I was exhausted all day today. I got up at the same time as always, even though I usually go to bed hours earlier than I did last night. But I had stuff to get done this morning, and I wasn't going to be irresponsible *twice.*

Classes were a struggle, though. Some kids take naps in secret spots around the school, but (a) I am not a fan of sleeping at school where someone could see me and think I'm being lazy, and (b) every second of the day was filled with something—meeting with Ms. Miller at break to go over my essay, peer tutoring at lunch, no spares. I tried to fake my way through bio, just to show Ben I could stay out late and it was all fine, but I'm sure he could tell how tired I was because he just gave me an awkward pat on the back and left me alone.

When I get home, Amma is back from her shift, too, but I'm relieved to find she's napping. Thatha won't be home for another couple of hours. Kendra is watching TV in the rec room.

I plunk down beside her on the couch.

"What're you watching?" I ask, trying to make sense of the tangle of preteen characters on the screen.

"*Horror High.*"

"What's it about?"

"Watch it and find out," she replies, her eyes still on the screen. So sassy.

I fold my arms and try to let myself get lost in the show, even though it's mostly just irritating. I need a brain break. I can feel my eyes are heavy, but I don't want to fall asleep now. I'm determined to stay up until at least nine tonight and be as perky as possible so Amma can see that one late night isn't that big a deal.

The show continues to be boring and nonsensical, so I pull out my phone. I stare at the messages Halle has sent me over the past several hours.

Halle: so?? How'd it go last night?

Halle: oh no . . . did u get caught? R u ok?

Halle: updates plzzzz

I don't have the energy to respond and relive last night's failure, so I don't.

I check the Crosswalk chat instead, but that's just become a running log of everyone's ideas for the fall fair pop-up, which stresses me out. I start scrolling through Halle's Instagram page like some kind of self-punishment, even though I've done so half a dozen times already.

"Why're you so obsessed with your phone all of a sudden?" Kendra asks, still not looking at me.

"*You* should talk."

"I *should* talk. You have a boyfriend or something?" She giggles like that would be wildly impossible, even if I were into boys.

"Maybe I was messaging *your* boyfriend . . . you know . . . *Ben*?" I extend my leg and poke her in the thigh with my toe.

"Cassie, dooooon't!" she whines. "I'm trying to watch my show!"

"Oh my God. You're incorrigible." (SAT word.)

"Ew. You sound like you're a hundred years old."

"Well, *you* sound like you're three years old, so I guess we're both aging inappropriately." I can *feel* her eyes roll without even seeing them, but she's smiling, and it *almost* makes me feel less irritable and pathetic.

Just then Amma appears at the door to the rec room, her arms crossed. She looks sleepy. And grumpy. *Great.*

"Cassie, I want to talk to you. Kendra, only another thirty minutes of TV, okay? You'll need to make the cookies on your own tonight. Dad won't be home until six."

"Okay," Kendra says, as I lift myself from the couch and follow Amma out of the room.

Amma and I go up the stairs in silence, but when we enter the kitchen, she says, "Sit down," and points to the kitchen table. The kettle is boiling and clicks off as I sit.

Amma takes out the teapot and three teacups. "Did you have any tests today?" she asks.

"Yes," I answer, staring at the cups.

"And?"

"And I was ready," I say, holding back a sigh. "I studied all day yesterday and have been preparing for weeks." This is only half true. I barely studied at all yesterday, and the past few weeks have been so full of other things, I've prepared way less than I normally would have, nor have I had time to work on the bio project as much as I would have liked.

"Anything else due?"

"Just one small assignment." Well, it was an entire essay, but I got it done.

"And?"

"And I finished it two days ago!" My voice betrays my irritation at this line of questioning, given that I have never, before this year, fallen behind in my work. And she doesn't know how behind I am right now, so she has no reason to question me.

Her voice is equally irritated. "So you think because you didn't have too much to do today, you could lie to me and come home late?" She spoons sugar into each cup. Adds tea bags to the pot.

"What? No. I just really wanted to hang out with my friends because for the first time in a long time I was having *fun* and laughing for *real*! And people were acting like I was just one of the gang, and I hardly ever feel that way. Like I belong. I just felt silly and loose and connected and, yes, maybe even a little rebellious. But then I knew you'd be mad if I was late because of something as *impractical* as spending time with friends, so I gave you an excuse I thought you'd accept!"

Except I don't say any of this, of course, because these are not the kinds of things we talk about in my family. My mom would never understand how I felt last night, or why I felt it. I'm still getting my head around it, too.

What I actually say is "I'm sorry." Because she looks tired, and it's my fault she looks that way. And because I just want this conversation to be over.

But of course, it's not over quite yet. The hot water gurgles and hisses as she pours it into the teapot. "You're not like all these children who run around on weeknights and stay out late and lie to their parents, Cassie. We didn't raise you that way, and we're not sending you to private school so you can waste your time with all that nonsense. You know better, so do better."

Yes. I know.

"Your father and I have worked too hard, and *you* have worked too hard to start messing around now. You'd better focus on your studies this weekend, and nothing else, okay?"

Okay.

I know I'm not really expected to reply, just to do the things being asked of me, so I just nod. My throat feels too tight to say anything anyway. The swirls in my stomach become hot and angry. This is *bullshit*. I do so much that's *right*, and she's acting like I'm a problem child or something.

Amma gives the pot a little swirl and then pours an equal amount of tea into each cup. As she turns to get the milk from the fridge, she says, "Go tell your sister her tea is ready." As I move to leave the kitchen and do as I'm told, my mother puts a hand on my arm. "Okay?" she says again, accompanied by raised eyebrows and a head wobble.

"Yes, okay," I say, feeling the quiver of anger beneath my words . . . and yet knowing I'd do everything Amma has asked me to do and more.

CHAPTER THIRTY-SEVEN

And there is so much more to do.

On Saturday, when I start to take stock of everything I need to accomplish in order to ace my midterms and upcoming assignments, and now plan for this pop-up, I realize how far behind I am in some classes and that I should have already started to prepare for the fall fair.

This realization sets alight some measure of panic—I'm supposed to be handling everything. I can't let my mission with Ben or my time with Crosswalk and Halle get in the way of everything else I have on the go. Drag story time was fun. Dealing with my mom was not. Dealing with her if I fail my midterms (and by "fail," I mean get anything less than an A on any of them) will be even worse. She'll probably ground me for the rest of the year, knowing her.

So right now, it's back to regularly scheduled business. It has to be, or I can kiss my A+ average goodbye. Not good enough for my parents, not good enough for university apps, not good enough for me.

Not good, period.

I've given up on my focus app because I was getting too obsessed about whether my forest of trees was full enough by the end of the day, and instead I've turned off my alerts for my social media entirely—because the Crosswalk chats are always blowing up with ridiculous memes and such and because I'm trying to mitigate (SAT word) how much I let Halle draw my attention.

I only check the group chat once a day to catch up on plans for the fair pop-up. Halle has really taken the reins there, but obviously she needs me, Cameron, and Nicky to help pull things off. The more we plan the pop-up, the more nervous I get—it's the most ambitious one we've done so far, and it's going to be so public.

By Sunday morning I'm almost caught up in two classes, but I had to stay up until 3 a.m. to do it and am even more exhausted.

Today is my altar-serving day, so I'm supposed to be at the church earlier than my family. I've crammed in a few more minutes of studying, though, and arrive a little later than usual. When I do enter the sacristy at the back of the church, Father Davis is already dressed in his vestments and preparing the wine, which is my job.

"Good morning, Father. I'm so sorry I'm late."

"Good morning, Cassie! It's no problem."

But it *is* a problem. "Here, let me finish," I say, and move toward him.

He glances at me, at my clothing, and says, "Maybe you should get dressed, right?"

"Oh, okay. I'll be quick, I promise."

I rush to get my robes on and back to my regular duties.

Altar serving has always been a little like meditation to me. I know the rhythms and responsibilities so well now that I can kind of sink into the motions without overthinking them, like I used to do when I first started serving in fifth grade. Unlike almost everything else I do, this feels fluid and not mechanical, comfortable rather than tense. I guess that's a little strange—to find a kind of looseness in something that's supposed to be so devout, but that's just how it is for me.

Today, though, everything feels a little more rushed, a bit haphazard. Maybe because I'm exhausted and know how much I still have to do when I get home.

We get ready for Mass in silence for the rest of the time, as the congregation arrives and the murmurs grow from the church pews out front.

When it's time to start Mass, I allow myself to move through the motions and try to just be present, here, as I walk the cross down the aisle, hold the book for Father Davis, gather and replace each item needed for Mass. As I sit through his homily, however, I can feel my eyes drooping. I fight to keep them open wide, though—my mother would kill me if I looked like I was sleeping through Mass, especially if I'm altar serving.

But when it comes time to get the wine from the credence table and bring it to Father at the altar, my feet feel so heavy and I can't wait until Mass is over. I carry the cruet with wine in it from the back of the sanctuary and move toward Father.

I feel like I'm falling before I'm actually falling, I think. Or maybe it's just that moment before you fall that makes your tummy flip. Or maybe I'm just in a constant state of falling at this point.

Whatever it is, my elbows are on the soft carpet of the sanctuary, the wine is splashed across the carpet in front of me like a child's painting, and the cruet is tipped on its side—empty.

A collective "Oh" comes from the parishioners in the pews, and then Father Davis and Mr. Garfield, the head usher, are on either side of me, their hands crooked under my armpits and lifting me up.

It takes me a second to process what's just happened. I have never once, in six years, made a mistake while altar serving. And this is beyond a "mistake." This is an embarrassment. I glance over to where my parents and Kendra are sitting and see Amma's and Thatha's mouths open, Kendra's fingers pressed against her own mouth. Amma is gripping the back of the pew in front of her, poised at the edge of her seat.

I'm back on my feet, but I don't feel at all balanced. Even Father seems at a loss as to what to do—probably because he's never had to deal with something like this before.

"I'm so sorry, Father," I whisper, my voice threatening to crack.

"You're fine, Cassie," he says, also in a whisper.

Fine, but not good.

There are murmurs from the crowd as we muddle through

the next minute. Mr. Garfield has taken me to the sacristy while Father continues Mass.

"I can get more wine," I say, almost on autopilot now.

"No, no—you stay here. We'll manage." He pats my hand and leaves me sitting on a chair next to the row of altar-serving robes, hovering over me in judgment.

I feel nauseous. I look down and see some wine has splattered across my robe. Great. I've not only ruined a robe, the carpet, and Mass, but I'm *wearing* what was meant to be the blood of Christ.

By the time Mass has ended, I haven't been able to bring myself to move from this spot. I'm supposed to help clean up. I should stand and start helping.

"Cassie? Are you all right?" Father Davis asks as he comes into the sacristy from the sanctuary.

I can't even look at him as I reply, "Yes. I don't know. . . . I'm so sorry, Father."

He sits beside me. "These things just happen."

Do they? To who?

"But the carpet . . ."

He chuckles. "Don't worry about that. Mrs. Perusi will get it out. She's a miracle."

This only makes me feel mildly better. I've made a fool of myself. Someone else has to clean up my mess. I still have to face my mother.

"Why don't you get out of this robe—we'll get that cleaned, too—and then head out to your parents."

"I should clean up . . ."

"Mr. Garfield is doing it. You just focus on having a better day, okay?"

I'm not sure what that looks like, now that everyone in our parish has seen me spill Christ's blood.

"Okay. Thank you, Father. I promise it won't happen again."

"No need to promise—mistakes will always happen again."

I know this is meant to make me feel better, but it really doesn't.

When I walk around to the front of the church, my family is huddled on the front steps, waiting for me, instead of in the hall like they usually would be. I guess even they don't want to face all the eyes that will be on us after this.

My dad extends his arm as I approach. I avoid my mother's eyes as I walk to him, and he puts his arm around my shoulders. "My dear, are you okay?" he asks.

"Yes. I just lost my footing."

Amma humphs. "You must be exhausted. You've never done that before."

I make the mistake of glancing up at her and see the frown and expectations on her face. The expectation to be better than this. To keep it together.

"Nothing's wrong. I just stumbled. I told Father it would never happen again."

"Maybe you need some sleep!" Kendra says, eyeing me up. "You look all ragged."

"Thanks."

"It's true! Your eyes are all baggy and stuff."

"Thanks." My voice is laced with anger this time.

She shrugs. "Just saying."

We head home without going to the hall for snacks. I'm fine with that, but I know my mom and dad probably aren't.

We're all quiet as we enter the house, save for Manika, who wags her whole body in welcome and then huffs and grumbles at being left alone, like she always does. I can feel Amma's eyes on me as we walk in, but she mercifully refrains from giving me another lecture. She must be at a loss with me at this point. I ask to miss our usual post-church brunch and get back to my homework. Amma allows it but not without adding, "You should take a little nap as well. There's no point in studying with your brain only half working."

Right. Like I have time to nap. I go straight to my room, determined to get myself sorted out so no more mistakes happen.

I leave my bedroom only for bathroom breaks until my dad makes me come down for Sunday dinner.

"Working hard or hardly working?" he asks as I sit down for his famous meat loaf and mashed potatoes.

I don't say anything at first because I'm anxious and stressed and not interested in his dad jokes tonight. After a few moments of silence, Kendra jumps in with "Thatha, that joke is so *old*."

"Well, *I'm* old, so what?" He winks at me.

I half lift one corner of my mouth to satisfy him, then reach for the potatoes.

"What's happening with you now?" my mom asks, suspicion in her voice as well as on her face.

So many things, apparently. "Nothing. I've just been studying all day."

"Well, eat, eat, my daughter," Thatha says. "Feed your brain, you know?" He digs into his own plate.

I'm hungry but also nauseous. Drained but wired. This all makes it very difficult to sit still at a table with my family and act like all is fine.

But I do, because the last thing I need right now is for my parents to get all up in my business. That would just lead to more talking, which would take up more time, which would cut into my homework time and force me to think about where I'm falling apart.

I serve myself a smaller-than-usual portion of food and eat it as quickly as possible while Kendra thankfully goes on and on about the movie she watched last night with friends. I can feel my mom eyeing me up still, but I keep my own eyes on my plate and try to plan out my next steps in our bio project.

"Cassie!"

I must have really zoned out, because when I look up, my mom has that face that says she's been trying to get my attention for a while.

"What?" I say, without thinking. Then, at her raised eyebrows, "Sorry. Yes?"

"Your sister asked you a question," Amma says.

"Oh." I turn to Kendra. "Sorry. What'd you say?"

"I *said*, 'How come Ben hasn't come over again?'"

Oh my God. Get a grip.

"Must be busy, I guess," I mumble.

"Are you dating? Did you have a fight? What'd you do?"

"What? No. Stop being so annoying."

"Oooh . . . defensive! You're dating, you're dating!" she sings in the most annoying younger-sister voice possible.

"Ugh! You're such an annoying little brat! You wonder why I can't stand being around you!"

I don't mean this. I *can* stand to be around her. I even like it, sometimes. But I can't stop the words from falling out of my mouth, and once they're out, I don't know how to take them back.

"Cassie Perera!" my dad says, his voice as stern as it gets. Quiet but firm. "Apologize."

"What? What about *her*? She's the one who's being a jerk, even though I'm tired and don't even want to be at this table right now!"

"Cassie!" This is Amma now. Her voice is *not* quiet, and mixed in with her sternness is disbelief. Her overachieving, obedient daughter turned rogue.

"What!" I shout, not even caring anymore what the outcome is.

"What is the matter with you?" she says. "Why are you acting like this all of a sudden?"

"I'm not acting like anything! I'm just stressed and *she's* annoying, and *you* act like I'm such a mess just because I missed *one* curfew and made *one* mistake in church and then got annoyed with my annoying sister!"

The table is silent. I realize my dad didn't know about the curfew part, but he doesn't say anything. I hear Kendra sniff next to me. I frown into my meat loaf. I'm *not* going to cry, and I'm *not* going to apologize. I'm ready for my mom's wrath and bite down hard to feel the ache in my jaw.

But Amma sighs and leans back in her chair with a thump. "Okay. That's enough. You can leave the table, Cassie."

There's no wrath, only disappointment. This is so much worse.

I drop my fork, which I've been gripping so hard, my fingers have turned white, and push my chair back. I don't say anything as I leave, nor do I look at anyone. I know what I'll see there and the last thing I need is to face my own failure in their eyes.

CHAPTER THIRTY-EIGHT

Mr. Reyes lets me do homework on Monday morning instead of my usual library duties. He also leaves me alone—after four hours of sleep and with eyeballs full of stress, I must look like I need to be left alone.

I'm hunkered over my books at my usual corner table when I sense some movement in front of me and look up.

It's Cameron, and beside him is Yumi, the ninth-grade class president who likes to give James a hard time in our student government meetings.

"Hi," Cameron says, holding up a hand in hello.

"Hi." Normally, the sight of Cameron and this spicy little ninth-grader Yumi together here would have me both elated and curious. Today, though, I just hope whatever he needs won't take long, and I feel instantly bad about thinking this. But I really just want to focus on school and nothing else right now. I don't want to think about the fall fair or Ben or Crosswalk.

"Um, you remember Yumi from our student government? She was wondering how to bring in some books to the library."

"Okay . . ." I say, frowning and unsure about why Cameron is bringing this to me and not to Mr. Reyes.

"For the rainbow sticker collection, I mean."

Oh. That. I glance at Yumi, who's scrunching her nose, which pushes up her glasses.

I know I should be happy on a number of fronts: That, as I found out from Mr. Reyes, he ordered extra copies of a few of our rainbow books and gave them to Mrs. Keenan so that the original copies could stay put without her knowing. That Cameron is spreading the word about the rainbow sticker books. That this is another person at St. Luke's who wants to read queer books. That he's coming to *me* about this.

But I'm not happy. I'm embarrassed about church. I'm irritated with my family and with myself. And I'm tired. I'm just trying to make it through this week, and I don't have the energy for this.

"Oh. Um. I'm not sure I can help with that right now. Maybe just . . . write them down or something? Or wait till Mr. Reyes puts out his annual survey in June? Or something?"

Cameron frowns at me. Good. He should.

Yumi folds her arms like a little product-line supervisor and says, "June?"

I just stare at her.

She looks at Cameron. "I thought you said she could help?"

Cameron keeps frowning at me. "Yeah . . . I thought she could."

I try to ignore the oozy, sticky sensation in my chest—the one that makes me feel like I'm sinking deep into mud.

"I really need to get back to this—sorry." I don't wait for them to say anything and just stare back at my computer, even though the numbers and words are blurry.

"Come on, Yumi. We'll figure it out." They leave, and I concentrate on bringing the figures on my screen into focus.

I'm almost able to when Mr. Reyes arrives at the table. So much for leaving me alone. My heartbeat begins to quicken. I'm getting sick of being interrupted. Can't people see I have shit to do?

"Cassie? Sorry to interrupt—I know you're very busy—but I have something I thought you'd want to see sooner rather than later. Come with me for just a second?"

Ugh. If you know *I'm busy, it* should *be later.*

I follow him to his office but don't sit down. He practically leaps over to the small book cart in the corner of the room.

"Look! These are all new books that I ordered specially for you. They just came in. I think you'll find them very useful for your history project."

I'd told him that I switched over to researching the way colonization impacted gender roles. I *wanted* to look more into how it impacted gender *identity*, based on what Mr. Reyes had said about the terms "two-spirit" and "bakla," but the thought scared me a little at the time. I wasn't sure how my history teacher would react or what my classmates might think. I figured the topic of gender roles was a bit more mainstream. Now I was glad I stayed safe. I didn't need to create any more problems for myself.

"Oh, thanks," I say, unable to muster the kind of enthusiasm he's showing. His face falls a little. I feel bad, but it's not my fault his timing sucks.

He brings his smile back, though, and says, "Come take a look and if there's something that interests you, we can quickly label it so you can check it out!"

I. Don't. Have. Time. For. This. I sigh and slump over to the cart. I give the spines a quick glance. I humor Mr. Reyes by opening up a couple of the books and pretending to read the book flaps. His Mylar covers are perfect, but I can't even take pleasure in that right now.

I choose a couple randomly. "These look good," I say, and hand the two books to him.

He's looking at me with a crinkle on his forehead. He takes the books and asks, "Everything okay?"

This is honestly the last question I want to be asked right now. Well, this and maybe "What's it like to be a complete mess?"

"Yes, I'm fine," I say, through gritted teeth.

"Are you sure? You seem a little—"

"I just have a lot to do."

"Oh, right. Of course. And here I am, interrupting your prime study time!"

In reality, this is my volunteering time that he's *letting* me use for studying, but I don't feel generous enough to correct him.

"Okay, well, let me get these checked out for you, and I'll bring them over. You get back to studying!"

"Okay, thanks," I mumble, and turn to go.

"Remember, I'm always available for help, okay?" he says to my back.

"Okay" is all I say, without turning to look at him. I don't even feel bad about it.

My first two midterms are a struggle. No matter how much I studied over the weekend, my eyes feel like pinpricks and my brain is in a fog. I have a terrible tightness in my stomach as I write the bio test, and by the end, I legitimately have no idea how I did, which is never the case.

On Tuesday, Cameron, Nicky, and I meet with Halle, Sam, and Nai after school to talk about the pop-up, even though I have volleyball practice, which will make yet another person angry at me—this time Coach Sylvan. But it's the only time I could meet with them, since my mom won't let me go out in the evenings this week. The pop-up plan has already been set via conversations over our group chat, but Halle wanted to see the physical space we'd be maneuvering around, just to be on the safe side.

As I show them where the donated gazebo is being built and where they can probably enter school grounds without being seen by too many people on Friday, I can feel Halle watching me closely, examining me the way she does. I guess she's wondering why I've been so unresponsive over the past few days. I guess she's wondering what the hell my problem is. But I'm in no shape to address any of that with her, so I just go through the motions like a robot and avoid her gaze.

Once we finalize everyone's roles over the next few days, we say goodbye. I'm about to turn and rush to my volleyball practice when Halle touches my wrist. I stop and glance down at her hand, then back up at her with a questioning look.

"Hey—sorry, I know you have to go, but can we talk for a second?"

"Like, a literal second?" I say, and immediately feel bad when her brow crinkles. But I'm late and tired and irritated that Halle is trying to talk to me now, when she *just* said she knows I have to go. I sigh. "Sorry. Yes. Sure." What's a few more minutes of missed volleyball practice and the disappointment of yet another person?

She shakes her head. "Never mind. If you need to go—"

"No, it's fine. What's up?" I fold my arms across my chest.

She glances at my arms and bites her lip. Her hands fidget by her sides, which I'm not used to seeing. Finally, she takes a breath and says, staring somewhere at my chin, "I've been trying to figure out how to say this, and I'm still not completely sure. But"—her eyes lift to mine—"I'm confused about us. About how you feel about me."

Oh no.

"Sometimes it feels like . . . maybe . . . you like me? Like, as more than friends?"

I'm about to protest—because I'm not prepared for this. I can't deal with this right now. I don't know how. But she heads me off.

"I know—you said you're straight. And I'd never want to . . . pressure you or anything like that. Or second-guess you. I just . . ." She shakes her head and sighs. Rubs her forehead. "I told you I wasn't sure how to say this." She pushes her fidgety fingers out, holding them taut, and she says her next sentences firmly. "I like you. Sometimes it feels like you like me, too. But then it doesn't. And I'm not someone who likes uncertainty. So I'm asking. I'm just asking. Am I wrong? About this?" She points between me and her.

No, you're not wrong. I'm *the one who's wrong.*

"I . . . really can't do this right now," I say, staring somewhere near her knees. My voice is brittle and low, like I can barely control it.

"Okay . . . is there another time we can talk, then? Please?"

"I really can't . . ."

"Why not?"

"It's too much," I say, barely audible.

"What?"

"It's too much." This time, my voice comes out hard and sharp. I can feel her body flinch. "I have to go," I say, already walking away.

I don't know who decided that the fall fair would be the same week as midterms, but I'm guessing they weren't in the eleventh grade at the time. Or on the student government, because Cameron and I have to gather with the other class presidents for an extra meeting on Wednesday after school, and I have to miss it because I have a volleyball game and Coach Sylvan is already mad at me.

James makes sure to send me a text letting me know it's "too bad" I'm too busy to attend this important meeting, though, so that's cool. And our volleyball game is a disaster. We get hammered. My setting is atrocious because the lights in the gym make my eyes even smaller than they are from lack of sleep and the sharp pain that lives right behind my pupils now.

Cameron catches me up on the student government meeting that night, though.

Cameron: Our booth will be on the main floor and James said you should start decorating in the morning the day of the fair so people see the booth during the school day and get excited.

Yeah, great idea, James, I think. But I try to show a little enthusiasm when I respond, even if I don't feel it, because I feel bad about the other day with Cameron in the library.

Cassie: Okay, thanks, Cameron!

Cameron: So I guess you'll need to do that first, and then you and I can meet Halle and the others to work on the pop-up?

Cassie: Yup. Right.

Even though I have every intention of avoiding Halle as much as possible that day.

Cameron: Is there anything else I can do to help you?

Bless his little heart. But there's no way I'm letting this eighth grader think I need his help.

Cassie: Nope! But thank you. I'll just get to the school extra early on Friday so I'm ready for you all at 7:30.

Cameron: Okay. See you then!

I wish I could generate *actual* excitement, but I barely have energy to get myself up from my desk to go pee. I do, though, finally, and while I'm washing my hands, I get a message from Ben.

Ben: Hey just wondering about the slideshow 4 our presentation? Wanted to add our graphs

Shit. Here I was worried about Ben completing the graphs on time, and I haven't even started on the slideshow.

Cassie: Oh, yes—just tightening a few things up. Will share it with you in a bit, okay?

Ben: Yup. Cool.

Ben: I can also do that part if you need me to.

Absolutely not.

Cassie: Thanks, but it's all good.

Ben: 👍

There go the next couple of hours.

That I was supposed to be using to study for my AP Macro exam.

And finishing my AP Lit paper.

And cutting out leaves for the stupid student government booth.

CHAPTER THIRTY-NINE

By the time I get to school on Thursday, I'm starting to feel that blur again, and I move in a daze through the school day. I tell myself it's only a lack of sleep and I just have to get through this week. I try to snap myself out of it—try to bring myself into focus, but my macro exam looks like it's swimming around on the desk in front of me. It's like I'm stabbing at the Scantron sheet, just trying to pin down the answers. By the time I'm heading to bio for last period, I still feel like I'm floundering, unable to get a firm grip on anything.

Instead of being early, as usual, I walk into class right at the second bell—having almost fallen asleep over lunch while studying in the library. Mr. Reyes had to poke me. Embarrassing.

When I do walk into the bio lab, Mr. Asmaro seems a little surprised and says, "Cassie Perera? Arriving at second bell? *Gasp.*" He puts his hand to his chest in mock astonishment.

I'm not in the mood for his crap and want to roll my eyes so badly but refrain. Instead I say, "Ha ha, good one, Mr. A," and head to my seat, waving a limp hand at Ben.

When Mr. A only gives us ten minutes at the end of class to meet with our partners about our projects, Ben plunks his stool in front of my desk, folds his arms on the table, and yawns so wide I can see his tonsils for at least a full two seconds.

After he's done, he looks at me and says, "Now what, boss?"

Boss? Is he being sarcastic? I try to blink myself into focus, which only gets me so far.

"What's wrong with you?" he asks.

"What?"

"Why are you blinking like that?"

Shit. Was it that noticeable? I shake my head and say, "I'm not. I'm just blinking like a normal person."

"No, you're not."

Jesus, Cassie. Get it together. "Maybe I'm just tired or whatever. Um . . . you got the slideshow, right?"

"Yup. But, um—"

"But what?" I don't have time or energy for *buts*.

"Nothing . . . it was just a little . . . underdone? For you, I mean?"

"For me?"

"It's no big deal. I just think we should probably look it over a bit before submitting."

Okay, maybe I didn't have a chance to look it over six times like I normally would have, but I spent hours on it last night. "Sure. You feel free to do that."

A small frown appears on his face. Concern.

Nope.

I straighten up and open my laptop. "Okay, here's what's next." I pull up my master to-do list. It's a Google spreadsheet, and it's my color-coded pride and joy, usually. When I'm feeling overwhelmed with everything I need to do, this list grounds me and keeps me breathing. But as I stare at the number of things BOLDED and RED and in ALL CAPS right now, I can't seem to find the ground. My eyes start to water, and I am instantly embarrassed on top of being a murky mess.

I keep my eyes on the screen. I want to blink to keep the tears back, but if I do, Ben will just comment again. "Um. I'll be right back," I say, and swing off my stool. As I start to leave to make my way to the bathroom across the hall and wait out whatever this is, Mr. A says, "What's up, Cass-o-lass? Can't wait till last bell? We only have a couple more minutes of class."

No, it can't wait. And stop calling me that! Not wanting to face him, I do this awkward half-turn thing, and to the whiteboard I say, "I really need to go."

"Trying to dump all the work on Ben again, huh?" Mr. A says.

I know he's joking. I know he's trying to be funny and chummy with me, trying to tease Ben. But I'm mad that all his social-emotional leanings don't help him see that I just really need to leave this classroom right now. I'm mad he's making me engage with him. This makes me say things I usually wouldn't to a teacher.

I turn to him, not caring now if he can see my teary eyes and flushed face. *Wanting* him to see them. "Actually, if you must know, Mr. Asmaro, I'm bleeding in that way girls do, and I really need to deal with it. But thanks for making me say it in front of everyone."

His face drops. A couple of kids titter. A couple of other kids outright laugh. My stomach plummets, but I ignore it all, turn, and leave.

I lock myself in the single-stall staff washroom instead of the multi-stall, very gender-specific student bathroom because why should only adults get privacy just because they're adults?

I run some water. I splash my face. I don't look into the mirror because I know exactly what I look like, and I know everything will be blurry anyway. I press paper towels into my face and hold them there. I scrunch them up against my stupid, blurry, wet face and press even harder. My whole body tenses with the effort. If I could scream, I would, but I don't need anyone to hear me. So I just clench my jaw as hard as I can, feel the grind of teeth against teeth, the tightness of my skin, the lock of my jaw. I do this until I'm exhausted with the effort.

Only when I remove the towels and drop them into the bin do I look at myself in the mirror. I still feel like a streaky mess, but I scrape my persistent flyaways into my ponytail and rub my eyes. I move my jaw around a little to loosen it up. I straighten the collar of my dress shirt and stare hard at myself until my face sharpens in the mirror.

The bell goes and I wait another minute before leaving the bathroom, hoping Mr. A and the others have left class so I can grab my stuff. But when I open the door, Mr. A is standing in front of it. His eyebrows bounce up.

"Cassie? Why are you in the staff bathroom?"

I see Ben off to the side, my backpack slung over one shoulder, his own bag over the other. I am a mixture of embarrassed and irritated. *Can't you just let me have this one? Let me deal with my fake period and leave it be?*

"Things were messy, Mr. A. You know? I needed some privacy. Is that okay with you?" I say this last part like a challenge, not a question, and his expression shows his surprise.

"Beg yer pardon, Cass? Listen, I get you're dealing with girl stuff, but that doesn't warrant disrespect."

Girl stuff? Jesus. All this talk of the blood of Christ, and people around here still can't talk about the blood of girls without using vague euphemisms.

Usually, I am a genius at making teachers feel like I respect the hell out of them, even the ones I think are way too old-school, or completely disorganized, or trying too hard to be best pals with their students. But I don't have it in me right now. I want to get out of here, shut myself up in my room, and slow things down so I don't feel like I'm dissolving.

I'm about to say something I'll probably regret when Ben steps up next to Mr. A. "Uh, I don't think Cassie's trying to be disrespectful, Mr. A. I just don't think she's feeling great. When my sisters get their periods, it can really hit them hard. Like, way beyond anything us guys could ever deal with."

I am momentarily very grateful that Ben hasn't pulled one of those "Hey, you know how chicks are when they're on the rag" moments with Mr. A, that he's stepping in to help me, but that gratitude is quickly replaced once again by my embarrassment that he *has* to step up to help me.

Mr. A's face shifts into "I hear you" mode, and he says to Ben, "Oof. Yeah. I totally get it. Thanks for sharing that, Ben."

Even in my messy, all-over-the-place emotions, I can't help the sarcasm that enters my brain. *Yeah, thanks, cisgender man who doesn't experience menstruation for explaining to other cisgender man how awful menstruation can be so he can "totally get it."*

Clearly uncomfortable with how to handle me, Mr. Asmaro fake smiles and adds, "Good thing women are having the babies, am I right?" He huffs out a laugh that's as forced as his smile, and we all stand there in painful silence for a few moments.

Finally, Mr. A says, "All right—bye, folks! Feel better, Cass-o-lass!" and retreats into his classroom.

Jesus fucking— I rub my face with my hands and want to scream again, but obviously can't do that in the middle of the hallway like this, with Ben standing in front of me. I move my hands to my ponytail and tighten it some more, which sends a sting across my scalp.

"Here," Ben says, and holds out my backpack.

I take a big breath and accept the bag from him. "Thank you." My voice comes out more wobbly than I want it to.

"Not a problem." He eyes me up. I hate that his attention right now is out of pity. I've finally got him talking to me again, he seems to even maybe *like* me, and now he's just going to think I'm a mess. "You're doing that thing again."

"What thing?"

"That blinking thing."

Damn. Really? I didn't even realize it that time. "I think I just have a bit of a headache, is all. Annoying teachers will do that to you."

"Whoa . . . Cassie Perera disparaging a teacher. Makes you some kind of sinner, doesn't it?" he says. His voice is serious, but there's a hint of joking in it that I am desperate to get back to—the lightness and playfulness. Not this pathetic state I'm in.

"Very funny."

We gravitate in silence toward my locker. Ben's isn't next to mine, but I guess he doesn't need anything from it, because he just stands next to me as I open mine and add my three-pound AP Macro textbook to the four-pound bio textbook in my backpack.

As I dig around in my locker, he just stands there, like he's waiting for me to say something.

So I do. I whip myself back into shape and infuse my voice with some energy. *I've got this I've got this I've got this.* "Wait till you see the pop-up tomorrow! St. Luke's isn't going to know what hit 'em."

Ben hasn't really been a part of the planning, except that initial conversation at drag story time. I didn't really expect him to be. The fact that he's hanging out with the Crosswalk crew at all is more than enough for me. But I still hope he's impressed with tomorrow's pop-up.

"You're not worried after your little run-in with Mrs. Keenan?"

I sure am. "A little, I guess. But this is important." He has to know by now what I mean by this.

"Right. Well, I hope it works out."

Me too. "Thanks." I shut my locker, maybe a little harder than I mean to. "Okay, I should go study. I have one more test tomorrow, plus a bunch of stuff I have to do for the fall fair. You're going to Crosswalk tonight?" I wouldn't be there, since my mom still has me under lockdown this week for everything except school, volleyball, and church, but I still hope Ben goes.

"Yeah, probably. You still grounded?"

"Yeah. Sucks." *On the other hand, at least I'll have time to study for this test.*

"Don't worry, I'll take some super-nerdy notes for you or something."

"Ha ha."

"You good?" he asks. His eyes are so intent on me that I have to look away.

"Yup! Thanks! Bye!" I say, and start walking away before he can ask me anything more.

CHAPTER FORTY

For the whole day on Friday, the school is abuzz with preparations for the fair. The event takes place during last period and goes a little past the school day, to maximize the number of students who attend (because attendance is mandatory until the final bell).

I somehow managed to get to school at 7 a.m. today, as I'd planned, even though last night was another long-haul study session. I set up the decorations for our student government booth, which were an assortment of construction paper leaves in fall colors (as per James's directive) scattered around our booth and pinned behind the table on a bulletin board. They're subpar, but they'll have to do.

Instead of meeting Halle and the others before classes to help them set up the pop-up as planned, I sent Cameron on his own, using my midterms as an excuse. The truth is, I couldn't face Halle. We haven't seen or spoken to each other since Tuesday, and

I don't even know where to begin repairing the damage I'd done there.

Then I took my final midterm first period, which, for all the cramming I did, felt like a giant disaster.

Throughout the day, after a lot of lurking and false starts and near fails, all communicated via our group chat, Cameron, Nicky, Halle, Nai, and Sam had successfully enacted our planned pop-up, despite it being broad daylight and busy with people. They'd even skipped classes to help. Luckily, our "target" is in a small yard beside the chapel, which is mostly out of the way of the fair preparations.

By the time lunch is over, the new gazebo with a statue of Saint Thérèse of Lisieux inside is all set with our pop-up. It's currently covered up by a large green sheet, waiting to be revealed as part of the fair.

I'm in the middle of adding cheesy love messages to my paper leaves because James said they were "kind of bland"—which, okay, they were, but, like, kiss my butt, James—when I hear my name being called. In my mom's voice.

That can't be right.

But when I turn to face the entrance of the school, that's exactly who's coming toward me.

"Mom?"

"Yes? Who does it look like?"

"But what are you doing here?"

"What do you mean? I'm helping with the fair. You knew that. The Women's League always helps. What's the matter with you?"

A couple of kids walk by, glancing at us and smirking.

Ugh. Honestly, my mother could have told me she was my new biology teacher over this past week, and it probably wouldn't have registered. My brain is basically a melted mass of goop at this point.

"Oh. Sorry. I forgot."

She sighs. "You look tired. You better get some sleep tonight."

"Yes, I will."

She surveys the booth and my handiwork and says, "Looks pretty good."

"Thanks." I scratch my nose. "Um . . . are you . . . staying?"

She looks at me like I've lost it, which isn't totally inaccurate. "Of course I'm staying. I have to help with the used clothing sale. And I want to see the unveiling of Saint Thérèse."

Oh, good. My mom will be here for the unveiling. And the pop-up. That's just great. Perfect, even. Any latent anxiety in my body about this pop-up shoots right up. I'd been dampening it with my busyness, but the thought of my mom being here for this . . . my entire body goes tense.

"Cassie?" Amma puts a hand on my back and rubs hard, like she does. I hear a snicker as more kids pass us. "Are you sick or something?"

Snap out of it, dummy.

I turn away from her and back toward the table. "I'm fine. I just need to finish this."

I know exactly the look on her face right now—eyebrow cocked, deep frown, pursed lips—but she must be feeling busy herself, because she says, "Hmm. Okay. But we'll go home right after everything is done. I think you need to rest."

"Okay," I say, without looking at her.

"See you at the unveiling."

"Yup. Bye."

When I'm sure she's gone, I squeeze my eyes shut for a long moment and then reopen them to finish my job here. The stakes for pulling off this pop-up, without anyone finding out I'm part of it, just got a lot higher.

Once lunch is over, the school opens up to families and alumni, and the atmosphere is even more "buzzy." My stomach feels like it's filled with bees, too—teeming with hectic energy. And my brain is so tired, I'm practically delirious.

Luckily, I don't see my mom for the most part—the used clothing sale is in the gym. But I do have the pleasure of running into Mrs. Keenan, who gives me the kind of disdainful expression that I have never received from a teacher or staff member at St. Luke's before. The last time I received a look like that was in elementary school. And even though I can't stand Mrs. Keenan, and I don't even know what the look is for (it could be for so many things at this point), her expression guts me.

I feel ill as Cameron tracks me down.

"Cassie, we should, you know . . ." He flicks his head toward the main entrance like a little man of mystery, and if I weren't so freaked out and nauseous, I'd think it was adorable.

"Yeah, okay . . ."

To James and Natasha, who are behind our booth, I say, "Cameron and I are just going to . . . help my mom with something." At least she's providing me with an excuse to leave our station right now.

"That's fine. Just don't be too long," James says, and I want to paper cut him with a leaf so badly.

Cameron and I make our escape and meet up with the others around the side of the building. Nicky arrives at the same time and asks, "How'd it go?"

"Good, we think," Halle says.

"You think?" I can't stop myself from saying. *There can be no room for error here, people.*

Halle cocks her head to the side, a small frown forming. "I mean, we did our best," she says.

"Right, great," I say, avoiding her eyes and not really feeling anything like right or great.

Halle continues, her next words robotic and cold. "So, Cassie, you'll be over there and will set off the confetti when it's time. The banner should just fall open when they remove the cover. The statue is all set."

When she lays out the elements of our pop-up like this, all I see is my mom's face, watching them unfold, and the storm in my stomach grows.

"Maybe," I blurt out, "we shouldn't do this."

The others look at me.

"What?" Halle says.

"But why?" Cameron adds.

"I just—I wonder if it might be too much? Like the statue and unveiling really mean something to some people here?"

I know as I say the words that it's way too late in the game to pull out. But my nerves are in control now.

"Cassie. Relax. I'm sure the Catholics will survive a little rainbow inspiration," Halle says.

"Relaxing" is not an option right now, but thanks for that, Halle.

"It's just—my mom's here . . ."

"But no one will even know you've got anything to do with it," Nicky says.

"And think of all the gaybies who will love this!" Nai adds.

"And think of how pissed your vice principal will be," Sam says, grinning.

Thinking of these things doesn't wipe away the image of my mother's face. But these folks won't understand that.

"Sometimes allyship is hard, Cassie," Halle says, her voice also hard.

This feels like a dig, and I want to reply with something sharp and harsh in return, but the others are already eyeing us up. I try to sidestep my anger by saying, "Right. Totally. Sorry. I'm just nervous. Sorry." Something painful and tight thrums in my chest.

"I think that's understandable," Nai says.

"But I also think we're kind of in the thick of it, now," Sam adds.

Halle's gone silent, her jaw clenched. I've made her angry. Or disappointed. *Because of course I have.*

"Yup—it's all good. Just a momentary panic. I'm fine."

I'm not.

CHAPTER FORTY-ONE

It's 2:45 p.m. and Mrs. Keenan has just announced over the PA system that the unveiling will take place in five minutes outside. People are moving to the front entrance and out the doors toward the chapel.

An overwhelming urge to run inside and hide behind Mary again takes over my body, but I harden myself against it and plant my feet where Cameron, Nicky, and I are standing off to the side, about fifteen feet from the statue—close enough to set off the confetti cannon remotely.

Nicky was able to "borrow" the confetti cannon from our theater, and apparently I get to push the button because I'm the ally and didn't really do much else for this pop-up since I was busy with the student government booth and avoiding Halle and missed the Crosswalk meeting yesterday because my mother doesn't want me to have a life.

The cannon is just behind the statue and is currently hidden beneath the sheet that's covering the statue, which is all inside the gazebo. And the whole gazebo is *also* covered by a green sheet, given that it's an addition to the school, too. Halle said the extra layer of concealment really helped her and the others stay hidden as they set things up.

The sequence of events, which I am obsessively playing over in my mind right now, is (1) the presenters (Dr. Ida, Mrs. Keenan, our school chaplain, and the president of the alumni association) will make some comments and then remove the sheet from the gazebo; (2) they'll then remove the sheet from the statue, which is attached to the banner Halle created, which will unveil itself as the sheet is pulled off; and (3) I will set off the confetti cannon.

The air is crisp and cold, but I'm sweating through my school shirt. I have the remote behind my back in my hands, and my back is to Nicky, who's standing behind me for extra secrecy. Cameron is leaning into me so close, he's practically on top of me—from nervousness or excitement, I'm not sure.

Halle, Sam, and Nai are way in the back, able to see but inconspicuous among the crowd.

"Welcome, everyone," Dr. Ida starts. "On behalf of St. Luke's, we want to thank you all for coming to our annual fall fair. And we want to thank all the students, staff, and parents who have helped to put this event on."

People clap politely. I try to keep a smile on my face, since I can't clap.

"We are very excited this year to also share a new addition to our campus—one that will serve as a constant reminder to continually perform the little deeds that serve a higher purpose. Saint Thérèse once wrote, 'Love proves itself by deeds, so how am I to show my love? Great deeds are forbidden me. The only way I can prove my love is by scattering flowers and these flowers are every little sacrifice, every glance and word, and the doing of the least actions for love.' We invite that spirit into our school now with her presence."

Do you, though? I can't help but think. *Is love really the goal here? And if so, whose love?*

The chaplain and alumni association president say a few more words, and then Mrs. Keenan invites the two tenth-grade class presidents to pull the sheet off the gazebo. They grab fistfuls of the fabric and start to walk away from the structure as people in the front of the crowd make space for them.

I only realize now how big this crowd is. Most have uniforms on, since the whole high school has been forced to come, but teachers, guests, and a smattering of parents—including my mother, who is, of course, front and center with Kendra beside her—are packed in around the chapel for the unveiling. I spot Ben about six feet away from me, off to the side, hands in pockets, bored gaze on his face.

The crowd *ooh*s and applauds the gazebo, which is white and, to be honest, not that special. The statue inside has a purple sheet over it, and James and Natasha are now asked to pull that cover off. As they do, my stomach is in tight knots; my fingers are sweaty and twitching around the remote behind my back.

The sheet finally travels up and over the top of Saint Thérèse, slipping down over her face, but instead of revealing that face, another sheet is pulled down over it, having been attached to the end of the first one. It covers Saint Thérèse all over again, like one of those old-timey sheet ghosts, except this is one heck of a gay ghost, because Halle, Sam, and Nai painted the sheet with a very full-figured drag queen.

The words "This Saint loves her LGBTQ+ children" appear over the drag queen's dress. The words are a little hard to see because of the folds in the sheet, and to be honest, the drag queen's face is a little scary because of how the sheet is hanging. Nonetheless, the effect on the crowd is instant. Gasps and laughter occur simultaneously. Mrs. Keenan looks like she's just seen a puppy being murdered, and Dr. Ida is frowning hard.

But my eyes find my mom, whose mouth has dropped open. I guess I'm searching for something in her face—something that maybe shows understanding instead of dismay, but I realize how utterly ridiculous that is.

"Cassie!" Nicky harsh-whispers behind me. I've had my hand on the button I need to push this entire time, but got so wrapped up in everyone's responses to our drag queen that I'm late to hit it. I try to push it now, but it's like the joints in my thumb are stiff. When I remain frozen, Cameron reaches behind me, takes the remote, and pushes the button himself.

The confetti cannon goes off, as planned, but *un*planned is the force of the confetti as it lets loose behind the statue. One would think a statue of that size would be pretty solid, standing there like it is. Or that it could withstand a little confetti explosion. But one would be wrong.

The statue tips forward, our drag queen taking a reverse death drop, face first. My stomach tips as well, and I feel like I might face-plant, too.

Natasha rushes to catch the statue and is joined by the chaplain and Dr. Ida. They're able to stop it from tipping all the way forward, but the statue is cumbersome, and all three of them struggle to keep it up. Mrs. Keenan flutters about unhelpfully while two parents rush forward to help from the front of the crowd. Everyone is covered in confetti, which would be hilarious, if it wasn't mortifying.

This pop-up was meant to be cheeky and celebratory. Now it's something else. To make matters worse, James is beside me all of a sudden, pointing at the remote in Cameron's hand and saying, "What's that?"

Cameron looks at the remote, then at me, his face utterly stricken. I don't say or do anything, because I'm still frozen, and I can feel so many eyes on me now, including Ben's. He's watching everything very closely, and it makes me want to speak up, but my mouth won't move. When I stay silent, Nicky, of all people, steps forward and says, "It's mine. So what?"

"Looks like a remote or something to me," James says, because James is just so damn brilliant.

"Yes, James. You caught us. Congratulations" is all Nicky says. She's putting on a brave front, but I can hear a tremor in her voice. I glance over to my mom and see that she's looking directly at me.

Dr. Ida and the others have managed to right the statue of Saint Thérèse, and apparently Mrs. Keenan has ripped off the drag queen sheet, because it's twisted and scrunched in her hands. Her eyes are on us, too.

Shit, shit, shit.

Without even really thinking, my feet shuffle sideways, away from Cameron and Nicky, as Mrs. Keenan makes her way over to us. Meanwhile, Dr. Ida takes the mic again and says, "Well. I'm not quite sure what to say, I'll be honest. I'm sorry our special ceremony has been interrupted by this . . . surprising display. But, on the bright side, we have just witnessed the rescuing of a saint today!" That gets a few titters and applause from the crowd, like everyone is just desperate for release from the tension we've caused.

Dr. Ida continues to speak, but Mrs. Keenan is now standing in front of Cameron and Nicky. Her voice comes out hushed but furious.

"*What* is going on here?"

Nicky and Cameron glance at each other.

My entire body goes ice-cold.

Nicky is about to say something again when Cameron speaks up. "We didn't mean to knock the statue over, but we *did* mean to send a message," he says, like a fearless little warrior.

"Oh, really? And what message is that?" Mrs. Keenan says, her voice raising.

"We're just trying to make the school safer for people," Nicky says.

"I assume you're behind these . . . these *displays*, then?"

To their credit, neither of them even glances at me. That makes me feel a thousand times worse, though. Like dirt. But even that feeling doesn't make me step up.

"Guess so," Cameron says, with more sass than I ever thought him capable of.

Nicky shrugs. "Yeah."

Mrs. Keenan frowns and folds her arms, eyeing them up for a moment. "Fine, come with me, then."

My heart couldn't be beating any harder as she leads them away, back into the school, to do what, I'm not sure. I don't even know where to look. Some of the crowd is still watching Dr. Ida, but the people around me just saw the whole interaction with Mrs. Keenan go down, including Ben. And including my mom, who has made her way over as well, dragging Kendra along with her.

"Cassie? What was that all about?"

Well, I just let my friends take the fall for something I started. I just proved what a shitty person I am in front of the person I was trying to prove the opposite to. I just let down a whole bunch of people who were trying to help me. I'm a liar and a coward and a complete mess. What more would you like to know?

"I—I'm not sure," I say.

Her frown is deeper than I've ever seen. I can barely look at her face. "Come. Let's go."

She tugs me away. I keep my eyes squarely on the ground as we pass Ben. I don't look at the crowd, where Halle and the others have finally realized I'm not a good ally or person at all.

CHAPTER FORTY-TWO

On the short car ride home after the fair, my mom prattles on about "what a disgrace" and "some people's kids" and "who could do such a thing" and "do you know those students or why they would do such a thing?"

I deny, deny, deny with head shakes and shrugs and *no*s. Kendra is mostly silent in the back seat, which is unusual. But she and I have barely spoken this week after I blew up at her at dinner. She probably just doesn't want anything to do with me.

I head straight to my room under the guise of needing to do homework. It's not a complete lie. Midterms are over, but I still have the bio project and the normal heap of items to check off my to-do list.

But when I get to my room, I just crawl under my covers and lie there in a ball. I feel muddy—like an indistinct mass of something dark and wet and earthy, and all I want to do is sleep and forget what I did today for a little while.

But I see my phone light up from where it's tucked into the mesh side pocket of my backpack. Like I have no will of my own, I lug myself out of bed and cross my room to get it. I know it's a bad idea. I do it anyway. Since when do I make good decisions?

It's the Crosswalk group chat. There are a couple of messages from twenty minutes ago, which must have been when my mom and I left—Nai and Sam asking us to send updates. Then a new set of messages coming in right now.

Nai: Hey all. Nicky, Cameron, Cassie? You folks okay?

Sam: ya, shit got a little bananas yall

Nicky: just got out of keenan's office. Parents called. 2 day in-school suspension next week. 🫠

Nai: Nooo!

Sam: omg that sucks I'm so sorry

Cameron: Crosswalk is safe, though! ✊

Sam: nice cameron!

Lou: wait . . . what all happened??

The next slew of messages is a play-by-play of the failed pop-up, complete with color commentary from Sam of what it looked like from where they were standing near the back. It was confetti mayhem! The catholics were aghast!

No one mentions my name or what I did . . . or didn't do. I also notice that Halle's name doesn't appear at all. Not even in solidarity with Cameron's little brown fist.

I put my phone in my desk drawer. I crawl back under the covers. I hope sleep comes, but it doesn't.

Sometime later, a forceful knock that can only belong to Amma bangs against my door. Before I can say "Come in," she comes in.

I sit up immediately. The only light in my room is from a lamp on my desk.

"Cassie? What are you doing? Sleeping? It's dinnertime."

"I know. I was really tired. I just needed a nap."

She folds her arms and stands over me, contemplating my face, my room, then my face again.

"Are you sick?" She pushes the back of her hand against my forehead.

In a way. "I don't think so. Just . . . this week was a lot. Midterms and all."

Her frown is so deep again, I don't know how it doesn't hurt. When I was little and made a sour face, she would tell me my face would stay that way if I wasn't careful. Maybe she should take her own advice.

"Well, come and eat something, and then maybe you should

take it easy this weekend. Church and rest and nothing else."

I have no interest in doing much else, so that works for me.

I don't check my phone until the following morning when I read through the rest of the Crosswalk messages, like some kind of self-punishment. There's a personal text from Nai, checking in. I ignore her. Her kindness knows no bounds, and I don't deserve it. I'm surprised to see there's also a text from Ben. He doesn't mention the debacle from yesterday, though.

Ben: we should probably get this presentation sorted, right?

I try to dissect his words, to see if there's disappointment or hatred or frustration in them. Does he avoid the mess from yesterday because he doesn't really care? Or because he thinks I'm terrible but needs to just get this project done? Is this a test? Does he want *me* to say something first? He saw the whole thing. He knew I was part of the pop-up. I was so proud of it. And then I was so useless when it mattered.

I have no idea how to respond, so I don't. Our presentation isn't until next Thursday. I can't—and don't want to—think about that right now.

I fake sick on Saturday night to get out of church on Sunday morning. How the hell am I supposed to sit there and listen to Father Davis go on about goodness or faith or generosity or love when I haven't shown any of those things?

It is *very* difficult to fool my mother, but I must actually look terrible—and, technically, I *do* feel sick (nauseous, disgusting, pathetic)—because she lets me stay home. She even lets me stay home from school on Monday, which I almost never do. It's too much work to miss school. But I can't stand the thought of walking in on Monday and possibly seeing Nicky or Cameron serving out their in-school suspensions in the library or outside of Mrs. Keenan's office, or wherever people who are suspended are stuck all day.

And I can't imagine seeing Ben, either.

Whereas I'd usually use a sick day at home to get on top of some homework, I use this one to ignore the world and all the shit I've caused. I throw my phone into a desk drawer. I watch the worst TV shows I can find. I eat my sister's stash of Cheezies and gummy bears. I play mindless free games on my laptop. But by noon, I'm already tired of all of these things and the house is too silent, so I take Manika for a walk, avoiding the creek and park and instead going on a route designed to avoid as many familiar people and places as possible.

When I get home, I finally look at my phone—not for any other reason than I happen to be addicted to my phone.

The Crosswalk chat has been popping off for the past two days, but I haven't opened it, knowing people will see I've checked the messages once I do.

But there are two other messages that I can't resist opening, even though I know it's a terrible idea. The first is from Ben.

Ben: sooo . . . i guess I'm doing the presentation by myself??

The second is from Halle.

> **Halle:** not sure you were planning on coming to the mtg thursday, but pls don't. people might not feel safe with you there

A distinct sinking sensation comes over me as I read Halle's message. Like something is pushing me down, away from the air and oxygen. But I can't sink. I don't know what's down there.

Panic takes over. I become frantic to stay afloat.

Not knowing how to deal with all of the messes I've created, I revert back to what I know best. I know to-do lists. I know physics. I know essay structure and graphs and slideshows. These are things I can understand—that I can do properly with some effort.

I throw my phone back in my desk drawer, turn on my desk lamp, and go into homework mode.

When I look at my master to-do list, I decide that the bio presentation is something that I can focus on and control and get right. So many other things on the list—the Crosswalk group, the pop-ups, Halle, my mom—all have too many moving parts, too many complications, too much room for even more risk and failure.

I will kill it with this bio presentation. Ben will not do this alone. I will take the reins with days left to go and make sure everything is as it should be. This is easy. Besides, getting a good grade on this presentation has to be a priority, I tell myself. It just does.

When I see Ben in bio on Tuesday (I can only fool my mom for so long), I have reviewed the project guidelines and made myself a master to-do list *specifically* for this project and this project only. I have gone over all of the data Ben and I collected. I've revamped most of the charts and graphs and visuals and slides we've already done. I've written out the script for the presentation. I've divided this into parts for me and for Ben. I've added video clips and funny GIFs and an "engagement opportunity" so that the class isn't bored to death just listening to us speak. I've written an adroit (SAT word) reflection—one that proves I am a Very Thoughtful Biology Student who values process over product. I've made sure I've completed everything on the list and then some.

I am ready to do this.

"Hey," I say to Ben, aiming for clear, concise, and confident. "Sorry I didn't get back to you—busy weekend—but I have everything we need for the presentation. Want to see?"

It's the end of the class, and we have two minutes until the bell. He eyes me up.

"What?"

"The presentation. I've done it. We just need to practice."

"Why didn't you just message me back so we could work on it together?"

I sigh, like the answer should be obvious. "I had a ton to do this weekend, and then I got sick. I just needed to do it so it got done, all right?"

He cocks an eyebrow. "So, we're just doing this now?"

I almost frown but manage to maintain the calm on my face. "Doing what?"

His head shakes, almost imperceptibly. "Whatever this fake bullshit is that you do when you're freaking out?"

I blink. *What? Nope. Uh-uh. We're not doing this. Here. Ever.* "Cool, thanks for your input. The slides and materials are in our shared folder. Just look over the script before Thursday, okay?"

I turn and go to leave the classroom before the bell has even gone, daring Mr. A to say something as I do.

He doesn't.

CHAPTER FORTY-THREE

After school on Tuesday, I sit in the computer lab, hammering out an assignment that was due yesterday, and by the time I leave, it's raining hard. I speed walk home, only a hoodie over my polo shirt and my umbrella doing little to keep the rain off me. All I want is to lock myself up in my room where it's warm and dry and where I can shut out the rest of the world to get some work done.

But when I get to the entrance of our driveway, Kendra is out in the rain. She's upset.

"Cassie!" she screams at me. "Where *were* you? I texted and texted!"

I had my volume off. Because I'm ignoring my phone. And all the messages I don't want to see.

I pull it out now. Six missed texts, three voicemails.

"What's wrong with you?" I ask. My words feel mushy in my mouth. I don't have energy for whatever this is.

"You left the back gate open this morning! Manika got out, and it's *your fault* so don't act like *I* have a problem. It's *your* problem! When I couldn't reach you, I called Amma and Thatha at work and they are *not happy*."

My eyes fall closed for a moment. *Yup. Perfect.* Another screw-up. I'm the only one who uses the back gate in the mornings.

Something inside of me shuts down, and I go on autopilot. *This is punishment. I deserve this.*

Without saying anything more to Kendra, I hand her my backpack and the umbrella, which won't do me any good at this point. I head down the path toward Our Lady of Mercy.

I cross the bridge and walk toward the opening to the creek, past the parking lot. I'm not really dressed for the water that's slipping down my neck or soaking into my school shoes or pelting my face, but I don't really care. Better this than tears.

Manika almost always heads straight for the creek. She loves throwing herself into the water and turning herself from a yellow lab into a chocolate lab. I don't let myself think about her outside all day, or that she could be anywhere by now, or if anything's happened to her.

She's in the creek, I tell myself. *She's fine. Everything's fine.*

When I get to the spot where you can climb down into the creek, it's muddy and the creek water is running higher and faster than usual. I call for Manika and wait, but hear and see nothing.

I don't think about how cold the water is. I take off my school shoes and tights—my off-kilter brain telling me I can't get my shoes wet or Amma will be mad—climb over the gate, and slide down the embankment on my butt, my kilt riding up as I do. I feel the wet mud against my thighs and seeping instantly into my underwear.

It used to be possible to stand at the bottom of the bank and contemplate which rocks to step onto in order to cross, but the mud is too slippery and carries my feet right into the water, ankle-deep. The rush of icy water is immediate.

It's fine. I already feel numb anyway.

I look down the creek toward the wood bridge. No Manika. I look the other way, where the creek disappears beneath the road. Nothing. I call again. Nothing.

The water is so rapid, I can feel it pushing and shoving at the backs of my ankles, my lower calves, trying to topple me over.

I take four large steps through the water to the other side, only to find that this embankment is even muddier and slicker than the other one. I'm able to grip handfuls of grass to haul myself up to where the bank evens out a little, and I continue to use the long grasses to guide my way into the brush. My feet squelch into the wet earth with each step.

Sometimes, once she's muddy enough, Manika will tromp through the grass, eating it and rubbing her fur against the thicket. It will be tricky to see her, camouflaged as she surely is with mud.

I prod my way through the overgrown brush, listening for Manika splashing around in the creek or crashing through the vegetation. I lose my footing and slip into a dip in the land.

Here, overgrown but still a small opening in the weeds, is the hiding hole Ben and I used to crouch in to take our secret notes. There is nowhere to sit anymore—the sides of the hole have washed out somewhat, and clumps of grass poke out like little spears. But some people must still use it from time to time because there are cigarette butts and potato chip bags strewn throughout, drowning in brown, mucky water.

Instead of thinking about how disgusting it is that my feet are bare in this garbage water, I think, *You deserve this.*

So I just stand in the middle of this empty, muddy space, my feet engulfed in filthy water, and my body drenched from head to toe.

Halle's words creep into my brain.

People might not feel safe with you there.

Because I'm not a safe person. I'm not a *good* person. A good person doesn't leave their friends to fend for themselves. They don't let their fears outweigh their decency. They don't lie. They don't hate themselves.

I climb back out of the hole and slide down to the creek again, the cold water cleansing my dirty feet and ankles.

Standing in the middle of the rushing flow, I stare up and down the creek again, searching for an out-of-place movement. I stare and stare, my feet burning with cold. When I try to take a step, my foot is stuck in the sucking mud. I try again but feel myself sink in a little more.

My heartbeat quickens with panic. My face crumples. *Perfect. Now I'm going to die in six inches of water.*

The thought makes me choke out a laugh. I look up at the sky and let out a breath against the falling raindrops. I let my feet sink. I feel the stickiness, the slow pull, the muck oozing between my toes. The water continues to rush around me, but I let myself be still.

I close my eyes. Water is everywhere. I feel it dripping from my nose, from my fingertips. My kilt is heavy with it. The rain keeps falling, the creek swirls and pushes and flows.

But inside, my heart beats, my breath circulates, my stomach settles.

I'm not sure how long it is before I hear a crash and a high-pitched bark. I open my eyes to see Manika bounding toward me. Only her snout is clear of mud from where she's probably been sticking it into the creek to drink.

I am simultaneously furious with her and overjoyed to see her. "Come here, *now*!" I yell, my voice betraying both feelings.

She stops short at my words and lowers her head, eyes on me the whole time. Sniffs the air for some hint of how much trouble she's in.

"*Now*, I said!" Gentle won't work with her. She'll just think we're playing.

She shakes her coat and slowly makes her way to me, knowing that she better come or else. As soon as she's close enough, I grab her collar and pull her across the creek and up the embankment, which isn't easy, given how wet and muddy we and the embankment are. I have to guide her under the fence through a small opening she must have used to get in. I tell her to "Stay." She barks back at me, indignant, but stays.

Once I've climbed over the gate, I collect my shoes and tights.

I grip Manika's collar all the way back up the path to our house, hose her off in the driveway, hose my feet off, and bring her into the basement.

Amma and Thatha are at work, so I text them with fingers I can barely feel to let them know I found Manika and am at home now. Kendra comes down and, seeing us both drenched, her eyes widen. But she doesn't say anything—maybe my vibes are telling her I can't really speak right now—she just gets us some old towels.

Once I've used the towels to dry off Manika as much as I can, I use the baby gate we have, just in case, to confine her to the basement while she dries completely. Then I strip down, throw all my sopping wet clothes into the washer (even my kilt, which is supposed to be hand-washed but who really cares), and turn it on.

After a hot shower, I'm finally in my room, where I wanted to be. I'm warm and dry.

I lean back on my bed and stare at the ceiling.

I think, *Maybe I can be still, like this, for a moment.*

I think, *Maybe the muck is where I need to be.*

CHAPTER FORTY-FOUR

I lie on my bed for hours—not sleeping, just being still. Just allowing myself to be with the past few days and all of my mistakes.

When I finally leave my room just before nine o'clock to pee, Kendra and I run into each other in the hallway on my way out of the bathroom.

We do that annoying thing where we try to sidestep around each other but then keep moving to the same side a few times.

She laughs, but it's nervous laughter, and I feel a pang of guilt for making her nervous around me. She's rarely nervous. But I was terrible to her at the dinner table, and the sloppy mess I was in after finding Manika must have been off-putting, I'm sure.

"Thanks for letting me know about Manika. Sorry I took so long to respond," I say, the words like grit in my mouth.

"Oh." She looks surprised that I'm even talking to her, and I feel even worse. "Yeah. No problem. You found her in the creek?"

"As usual," I say, trying to bring some lightness to my voice.

We stand there for a second before she says, "Um."

I wait.

"Are you okay?" she asks, and I'm both surprised she's asking this and concerned about what she knows that's making her ask. She's only in the ninth grade, but the St. Luke's grapevine knows no limits.

"What? Why?"

"Um," she says again. "You just seem . . . kind of . . . off? I mean, you're always kind of weird, but this is . . . different?" She scrunches up her nose, a tiny smile starting.

Little shit. I narrow my eyes at her for a moment, but then, "Yeah. I guess I am a little off. I messed up. Big-time." I'm not sure why I'm saying anything at all right now. Maybe it just feels easier with someone who's fourteen. Maybe I'm just ready to say something.

I lean back against one side of the hallway. She leans back against the other.

"What's the mess-up about?"

I think about this. What *is* it about? How I tried to fix my mistakes but made everything worse? How I let my friends down? How everything inside of me feels messy and I let that mess get out? Or is it that I kept the mess in for too long in the first place?

"Um. I think it's about . . . me being scared." I only know this as I say it.

"Oh. What of?"

"I don't know. Like, a lot of things, I guess. I'm scared I might not be the person everyone wants me to be. That *I* want me to be. Or something. I think I might be . . . like, a bad person?" My eyes start to water. I shrug and wipe at them.

"Oh." She seems to think about this while she stares down at her feet, pushing them into the floor. Then she looks up and scrunches her nose again.

"Does it have to do with that confetti thing at school?"

My heart catches. "What?"

"Um . . . I think . . . well, I think I saw you? With the remote thingy before that other kid took it? I just thought, maybe . . ."

"Oh." *Fuck.* My heart pounds now. "Uh . . ."

She shrugs and grins. "I think it's cool if you *were* a part of it. Did you do the other things, too? The Mary statue and stuff?"

She looks so excited by the prospect, and for once in my life, I just want her to think I *am* cool. I nod. "Yeah. Yes. I did those, with some other people."

"So awesome," she says. But then her grin falters. "But you let the others take the heat? Is that the bad part?"

Yup. Exactly. One of many bad parts. "Yeah."

"Why did you?"

Her face is so open and curious. I let out a wavering breath. Try honesty. "I don't want people to see . . . something . . . about me."

"Something bad?"

"I think so? Maybe?"

"Can you tell me? I won't judge, I promise."

I stare at her for a moment. Can I actually do this? Should I? "I think . . ." I can barely get my words out past the thud of my heartbeat. I take a painful breath and swallow. "I think I might be . . . that way. I mean, the pop-ups . . . the rainbows and stuff . . ." All that practice and I can't get the word out when it really matters.

"Queer?"

My eyes go wide at her. My mouth is frozen open.

"But that's not bad."

She says it so matter-of-factly, I instantly think I might be the dumbest person on earth for ever thinking it was. But that's how it *feels*. Or at least, felt. Or still feels? I'm not sure.

"It just—doesn't feel like I can be that and everything else, you know?"

"Oh. Like Catholic and stuff." She barely hides an eye roll.

"And a good daughter and well-liked and yeah . . . a good Catholic."

I slide down to the floor, legs bent in front of me.

Kendra comes to sit beside me, and it feels very unnatural and also very comforting at the same time.

"Perhaps all is not lost, child," she says, in the most unidentifiable accent.

I give her a "what in God's name" look.

She grins. Then drops the grin and says very seriously, "That's my God voice."

I laugh out loud at this, and it makes her smile so fully and genuinely that I feel a surge of warmth. She actually looks like she's happy to have made me laugh. Like she cares if I laugh or not.

What the hell have I been doing, acting like her laughter doesn't matter to me, too?

"Oh my jeezus, you're such a weirdo," I say, shaking my head but still laughing. "I wasn't sure you even believed in God, given all the zoning out you do in church."

She shrugs. "I'm still figuring it out. But if I *do* have a God, it's not some kinda white, hipster-looking dude. She's a sexy brown drag queen with that cool voice I just did who wears stilettos and bowler hats and struts with a bedazzled gold cane. And she definitely doesn't care if you're queer."

My eyes widen again. I nod slowly. "Okay, then." Something tells me I need to take Kendra to a drag story time soon. Something tells me I might have my own little ally here—when I'm ready to have allies, that is.

"Anyway, I think you can fix it. Just think about what'll really matter to your friends," she says. "Focusing on others for a hot minute might help."

What the hell? "Maybe *you're* God, oh wise one," I say, knowing full well this is blasphemy and not really caring at all.

"I mean, it's not *un*likely," she says, without any hesitation whatsoever.

I can't help but laugh again, shaking my head into my knees. But after a second or two, I stop laughing. "I'm sorry I acted like you're *not* awesome. You definitely are."

She looks at me, and her bravado falls away. Her eyes glisten. "Oh" is all she says.

I push into her with my shoulder and say, "Thanks for the pep talk, Your Royal Godness."

"Actually, it's Angel Singh, if you must know. 'Singh' spelled the brown way. Duh."

CHAPTER FORTY-FIVE

I do exactly what my sister, Angel Singh, suggests: I think about what my friends would want. And then I start to work on giving them those things.

My new to-do list looks much different than my school one, and a lot scarier, too. But it also feels right. I message Ben that night.

> **Cassie:** Hey. I know I've been a jerk and I get it if you don't want to hear from me. But I'd love to explain, in person, if you're willing to give me your time. I'll be at the swings at Our Lady tomorrow morning at 7:30. (Sorry for the early start)

Predictably, I don't hear anything back from him. If he doesn't come to the playground, I'll try to talk to him tomorrow at school, but doing this at school feels wrong to me, so I really hope he comes.

By the time I'm walking Manika down the pathway to Our Lady, the morning is cold and a little misty. I give Manika a long leash from a pole so she can just sniff around and pee when she's ready. I sit on one of the swings with the creek at my back and start a slow back-and-forth. I can see my breath in the dim light.

I don't want to think right now. I just want to swing forward and back, forward and back. I want to stare at my feet as they kick out in front of me, then at the ground as my legs kick back. I want to suck in the cold air and feel it burn my lungs. My swings get higher and higher—I both hate and embrace the awful feeling in my stomach when my body drops backward.

As I reach the peak of my forward swing, I let go and let my body fly out of the seat. I land off-balance and topple over to the side onto the grass. Unlike Ben, who kept rolling, I just lie on my side, breathing hard and letting the white clouds of my breath evaporate around me.

"Are you dead?"

I sit up and look behind me.

It's Ben. He's wearing his uniform with just a hoodie over it. He must be freezing.

I rise and wipe at my sweatpants, which I'm wearing because my kilt is still wet, and which now have grass stains on them.

"Not quite," I say.

We stand there in silence for a few moments.

He takes a seat at the swings and starts to move.

I want to just say what I have to say, but instead I follow his lead and start to swing, too.

We move back and forth for a while. His legs are much longer than mine so we're almost never in sync. I slow myself down and drag my feet against the wood chips to a complete stop. Eventually, he slows to a stop as well.

"I'm so sorry, Ben." It comes out as a whisper, and I'm instantly mad at myself. I turn to him and say, more clearly, "I'm so sorry."

For a few moments, he stares at his feet as they flex against the ground. Then he looks at me and says, "For?"

What am I not *sorry for?*

"For what I did. Back then. For all the things I *didn't* do since then. For acting like such a freak since you've been back." *Take your pick.*

He nods, looks back down, and asks, "Why'd you do it?"

"Do . . . ?" There're so many shitty things he could be asking about right now.

He glances back at the opening to the creek and points his chin at it.

The pang this creates in my chest is painful. I take a long, deep breath and let all of it out before speaking. I should have thought this through more. Or maybe I shouldn't have. Either way, I didn't, so I guess I'll just have to do my best.

"I was scared. Terrified, actually."

"Of?"

I have to swallow back the fear that's rising now. My stomach is trying to leave my body the way it does when I reach the height of my swing and fall backward.

"Of people finding out about me."

"That you're queer?"

When I don't say anything at first, because my throat has closed up, he glances at me and tilts his head a little. "You know I knew."

"But I tried so hard to hide it."

"Yeah. I know you did. But people don't just stop being queer, Cassie."

"I did."

"You just stopped expressing it."

I'm quiet for a moment, knowing this is true.

"But you never said anything. All this time?" I ask.

"It was up to you to say something, not me."

That makes my heart pinch. He gave me so much space.

"What about you?" I ask.

He starts swinging a little. "What about me?"

"Aren't you ever scared? It's like you don't even care what people think."

"I *don't* care what people think, for the most part. But also . . . I'm not queer, Cassie."

My eyes shoot up at him. My lips fall open. "What?"

He shakes his head, stares into his lap. "You assumed I was. Everyone did. I have a lisp. I dance ballet. I'm not some macho dude. So I must be gay, right?" His eyes find mine now, and he gives a small shrug. "And I mean, who knows down the line? But so far, I like girls. I always have. I just . . . don't act on it that often."

Oh. OH. Shit.

"But you . . . you always seemed to want something more with boys," I say.

"I *do* want more with boys. I want more than boys are allowed to have with each other anyway."

Oh. His eyes are glistening, and maybe it's just the cold morning, but it breaks my heart a little anyway.

"But—why have you never said anything? Why'd you just let everyone think you were queer?"

He shrugs again. "I guess I convinced myself I shouldn't have to prove I'm *not* queer. I mean, why should I? I think it would've felt weird anyway—to point out my straightness. If people want to assume stuff about me, that's their thing."

I was one of those people making assumptions. Instead of just getting to know my friend.

"But you came today. To hear me out. You didn't have to do that."

"No. I didn't."

"So why . . . ?"

"I was thinking about you and Mr. Asmaro. All that blinking you were doing. Your face when you came out of the bathroom last week."

"My face?"

"Yeah, man. You looked like you'd just bullied yourself into submission or something."

Oh.

"And I guess I just kind of understood—what it's like to try so hard to be perfect. I did that for a long time, too. Ballet has given me a lot, but it also cost me something. That's why I stopped."

I'm surprised to find that even though he's bringing up the

messy parts of me, of himself, these moments with Ben actually feel okay. Like there's some kind of understanding between us that I haven't really had with anyone else before, and that I'm not even sure I fully understand right now. I try to articulate it anyway.

"Yeah," I say. "I guess sometimes I just feel . . . off-balance. Like everything's moving around me so fast, and I can't quite keep up. But I need to keep up."

I scrunch up my nose, mostly to myself, because I'm not sure I'm making any sense, but I also feel like I'm starting to figure it out.

"Yeah. That sounds . . . hard. I used to feel like that sometimes, too. And sometimes it just felt like *I* was the one who was moving too fast, and I couldn't quite get a footing, you know?" he says.

I smile at him and nod. I think I do know.

"Anyway," he continues, "I just figured you were probably beating yourself up more than I ever could. I wouldn't have gotten anything out of refusing your apology or whatever."

After a few moments of silence, I say, "Thank you."

He shrugs. Pushes himself a little more on the swing.

After a while, I say, "I started the GSA for you." I don't say it to make myself look good. It wouldn't make sense to anyway, now that I know Ben's not even queer. I say it because now it seems funny. Silly. Ridiculous. I smile to show what I'm thinking.

He smirks. "That seems like something nerdy you'd do. So 'extra,' as the kids say."

Even though he's basically insulting me, I can't help but smile even more. "I know. I *am* extra. I'm trying to tone 'er down a bit."

"Yeah, it's pretty cringey sometimes."

"Okay, I get it, thanks."

He smirks. But then the smirk is gone. "But for real, Cassie. Making things right doesn't have to involve creating a whole club, being some kind of super-ally, or whatever. I would have just accepted some truth and an apology."

Easier than it sounds. But also, not complicated at all. I'm silent for a while. I'm trying hard to process everything, to formulate something substantial in response, but I've never been good at doing that in the moment. Instead, I just say the obvious. Truth and an apology.

"I'm queer and terrified. And I'm so sorry for everything."

"So now what?" Ben asks as we walk to school after dropping Manika off at home.

I swallow. I can't decide if the next item on my to-do list is more or less scary than the conversation I just had with Ben. "I need to clean up my mess with the Crosswalk crew."

"The fall fair thing?"

"Yeah."

"Will you be okay if it doesn't go well?"

Ugh. Clearly he thinks it won't go well. "What I did was pretty shitty, huh?"

"It was. I get it. You were scared. But, like, it's not just what you did at the fair."

I look at him. He's looking at me. I guess we're just letting it all out now. "What do you mean?" I ask, knowing I won't want this answer.

"You've been lying to them, haven't you? About being straight?"

Right. "Well, yes. I mean, I've been lying to *myself,* too, though. I really did think I could push it away if I tried hard enough."

He nods, his eyes on the ground. "Yeah. It's so fucked that you felt like you had to do that."

"You're being way too nice to me. It's disturbing," I say, with a small smile.

He smirks back at me. "Not everyone's a full-blown asshole like you."

I'm so shocked, I let out a bark of laughter. "Wow. Cool. Thanks."

We come to the entrance of the school and stand there for a moment. I wish Jesus was still beckoning us down the walkway with a rainbow. It would make this next part a little easier.

"Good luck," Ben says. He shoves me in the arm. "Just say the real thing, asshole."

Honestly, it's exactly what I need to hear.

CHAPTER FORTY-SIX

When Dr. Ida's assistant, Ms. Nita, leads me into Dr. Ida's office at lunch that day, I feel like I did four years ago walking into the chaplain's office at Our Lady of Mercy. Like I'd disappointed everyone. Like whatever good inside of me had crumbled away, revealing something else that was very, very wrong.

But I force my feet forward anyway.

This is different. It's a good thing. I'm not wrong about this.

Dr. Ida and Mrs. Keenan have squeezed me in for a meeting, because I'd emailed them last night, telling them I had more information about the pop-ups that I thought they would want to know. I knew Mrs. Keenan would take the bait, given how much she loves informants.

As I'd expected, Mrs. Keenan is accompanied by her laptop, which is perched on her knees, ready to record anything and everything.

"Hi, Cassie. Come in and have a seat," Dr. Ida says.

When I do, Mrs. Keenan starts with "What is it you know? Is there someone else—"

"Cassie," Dr. Ida interrupts, and a spark of glee bursts in my chest at the look on Mrs. Keenan's face. "How are you?"

"Oh, um . . . I'm . . ." *The truth.* "Not great."

Dr. Ida gazes at me for a moment. "I'm sorry to hear that. What can we do to help?"

I fold my hands in my lap to keep them still.

"Uh . . . I just needed you to know that . . . it was me. Behind the pop-ups. They were my idea, and I carried them out. All of them. And I know I should have come forward sooner—I know I shouldn't have let Cameron and Nicky take responsibility. But I was scared, and I acted like a coward." My heart feels like it's in my throat.

Dr. Ida nods slowly, taking in my words, but Mrs. Keenan speaks immediately. "There should be an apology attached to that confession, don't you think?"

I almost apologize out of habit, but I catch myself. Because while I need to come clean, I'm also not going to lie to make her happy. "I'm not sorry I did what I did, though. I still think it was the right thing to do."

"The right thing to do?" Mrs. Keenan asks in that way that isn't really a question. "The right thing to do was to sneak around the school and expose people to—"

"Expose people to what?" I say, not caring that I've just cut her off. "To *true* acceptance? To some joy and awareness?"

"Cassie—" Dr. Ida starts.

"I wasn't doing anything wrong—except in letting my friends take the blame," I say, my voice firm. "St. Luke's doesn't have safe spaces for LGBTQ+ kids. We don't have a Gender and Sexuality Alliance, we don't acknowledge that kind of diversity in any part of school life, we don't even want those stories in the library." I make sure to say this last part directly to Mrs. Keenan. She opens her mouth to say something annoying, but I continue before she can. "Shouldn't the school teach us to stand up for what we believe in? To promote acceptance and love and belonging for all kinds of people?"

As I talk, Mrs. Keenan is typing the entire time, and I have such an urge to side kick her laptop off her lap. I can feel myself spending too much energy on her and not enough on what I really came here to share.

Nervous but defiant, I ask, "Dr. Ida, can I speak with you alone, please?"

Her eyebrows raise. Mrs. Keenan frowns.

"Why is that, Cassie?" Dr. Ida says.

"I need to tell you something . . . personal . . . and I think I just need to say it to you first. Please." I keep my eyes on her and ignore Mrs. Keenan's scoff.

Dr. Ida gazes at me for a moment. Folds her hands in her lap. "Yes. Okay. Mrs. Keenan, we'll catch up later."

The look on Mrs. Keenan's face and the way she slaps shut her abominable laptop communicate her indignation, but I couldn't care less.

Now that it's just Dr. Ida and me, my irritation falls away a little. I try to refocus on what I came here to say. I try to find some stillness.

"Okay, Cassie. I'm listening."

I pull my chair a little closer to her desk. From my blazer pocket, I take out the cue cards I'd prepared. I stare at them but then just start talking.

"I know you and Mrs. Keenan probably think that the pop-ups were meant to disrespect the school and church somehow."

Her face is neutral, as it often is, but she's listening—not taking notes, not trying to interrupt me, not even glancing at her phone, which is lighting up with a constant cascade of notifications—and I take that as an encouraging sign.

"But I need you to know why the pop-ups are so important . . . from . . . a personal stance."

Dr. Ida shifts a little in her chair, and I think she's going to cut me off, but she doesn't.

"I've spent so much of the past few years hiding parts of me that I thought were terrible. Things that felt messy and awful and wrong. But the only reason I thought they were terrible is because I wasn't taught anything different. I never saw anything around me to show me those parts were normal or okay."

I'm skirting around certain words, I know. I can't really tell how Dr. Ida will respond. My gut says it will be okay, but my brain only knows uncertainty. And I've never been great at trusting my gut.

But I try to now. "Dr. Ida, I'm . . . figuring some things out, but I know I'm not straight." I have an entire tornado in my chest and can't quite look Dr. Ida in the eyes, but I force myself to continue. "I've been trying really hard *not* to know that. And my fear of *other* people knowing that has made me do things that actually *are* terrible. Like abandoning my friends when they needed me most. But once I spent time around people who showed me it could be okay to be . . . um . . . queer"—*holy crap*—"it was like I could maybe see it as a possibility."

I can feel tears forming, and I let them. "But I shouldn't have to search so hard for those kinds of people and places. My school should be that for me."

Tears are flowing now, and Dr. Ida hands me a tissue over her desk. I take it, murmur "thank you," and blot my cheeks. I'm rambling but she's still not stopping me, so I keep going.

"I need to know that there's a place for me here, Dr. Ida. And it's not enough that teachers aren't homophobic or that we talk about kindness and stuff. I need something here that tells me my school thinks I'm normal and okay and that I belong here. That I can have a good life just as I am. And I *know* I'm not the only one who needs this." I think about Cameron, about Nicky, about that lone sticky note inside Mary's hand.

I'm silent for several moments and mash the tissue up against my nose, which is runny and gross. I must look atrocious, but I don't really care. Things are messy. I'm messy.

Dr. Ida must take my silence and nose-blotting as a sign that I might actually be done, because she finally speaks.

"Oh, Cassie. I'm sorry. This must all be so hard." She leans back and lets out a breath. "I can see how important this is to you—and I can understand that need to feel seen here. To have people actually acknowledge your existence and honor it. I truly understand that."

She's silent for a few moments herself, and I wonder if she really does get it.

"This is a hard situation. It's not something we can push through quickly without taking the necessary steps, Cassie. It's so—"

"Difficult, I know. And tricky. And some people will be angry, and parents will complain. But—isn't this worth all that? Isn't this the right thing?"

She's looking at me intently. One finger taps the arm of her chair. "Cassie, let me see what I can do."

I start to object at what feels like empty words, but she heads me off.

"I know that sounds like a stalling tactic—but you have my *word* that it's not. I just need to do a little soul-searching here—as it looks like you've been doing." She smiles at me, and I can see that she means everything she's saying.

"In the meantime, I need you to do something as well."

I wait for the ball to drop—is she going to ask me to keep our conversation to myself? To stop trying to bring queerness into the school?

But instead, she says, "If you're comfortable doing so, I'd love for you—and anyone else you think might be willing to—to write a letter. It can be anonymous. But I'd love them to share why a GSA or something like it is important to them. What they would get out of it. Ask them to imagine their audience to be parents and teachers. I suspect students *aren't* the ones who'll need convincing." She winks at me. I don't think I've ever seen Dr. Ida wink.

"Oh—okay. Yes. I can do that."

"Thank you." She leans forward on her desk. "Now. I'm sorry, but we do need to talk about these pop-ups. Whether you're sorry or not, what happened at the fall fair was dangerous and almost disastrous, and two students have just been undeservedly suspended for it."

We spend the next few minutes sorting out consequences, and while I'm scared shitless about the part where my mother will find out I was behind it, I can't say Dr. Ida is unfair in her treatment of me.

"Now, my dear—if I don't get going, Ms. Nita will come in here and chastise us both." She smiles again and I smile back.

"Thank you for listening," I say.

"Thank you for being honest. And brave. I'll try my best to do the same."

CHAPTER FORTY-SEVEN

I'm on my way downstairs to where my mom and Kendra are folding laundry. I want to come clean about the fall fair pop-up before she hears from the school, but then I hear my mom on the phone.

"You're saying she damaged school property?"

I stop on the third-to-last stair. *Shit.*

I'm too late. I hope to God it's Dr. Ida on the phone and not Mrs. Keenan. I stay where I am and listen.

"Why would she do such things?" my mom asks, her voice somewhere between irritable and genuinely confused with a touch of panic. She's quiet for a while and then responds, "Yes, I know. She's not been quite herself. But stress is no excuse." More silence. "That sounds fair to me. And yes, I will make *sure* she understands the consequences of her actions."

Like I don't already.

Once Amma gets off the phone, it takes everything I have to not just turn back and head straight to my room—as though I could actually escape any of this—but I take the last couple of steps and enter the laundry room instead. When Kendra sees me, her eyes go wide and questioning. I give her a little shrug and head shake.

"Mom?"

Amma is pairing socks and stuffing them forcefully inside of each other. She looks up at me. "That was Dr. Ida." She has that face that says she's seething but trying very hard to keep it together.

"Right. I—"

"Cassie, I am *livid*."

"I know, I—"

"But Dr. Ida said I should let you explain."

I let out a breath.

This was something Dr. Ida and I talked about. She understood I wasn't ready to tell my parents everything I told her, so she promised to let me handle the details around *why* I set up the pop-ups. It was a blessing I appreciated more than she could know.

I fiddle with a shirt yet to be folded on the table between us. "Uh . . . well, I was trying to . . ." I had a whole plan here. But my mom's frown is formidable (SAT word). My words get jumbled in my mouth. "I was—"

"Mom," Kendra blurts, "those displays are so necessary. There're so many people at St. Luke's who never have their whole selves acknowledged. They're like . . . gay, or just not straight, or trying to figure things out, but there's nothing at the school to support them. I think Cassie was just trying to let them know it was okay to be who they are." She looks at me. "Right?"

My words still won't come . . . but now more because my little sister is a fucking miracle. I just nod, my mouth falling open a bit.

Amma is still frowning and folding socks and considering me. "Why you?"

"Why me?"

"Why are you making this your cause?"

"Um . . . I have friends who need this. People at the school who need someone to do this for them. Why not me? I just—I think it's important." I hope she can't see through my half-truths.

"There aren't better ways to show your support? You don't think it was a little disrespectful?"

I'm a little surprised that she doesn't make more of an issue out of me supporting queer people, and it takes me a second to respond. "Disrespectful to . . . ?" I finally get out.

"To the school? To the Virgin Mary? To Saint Thérèse? You almost caused some serious damage. What if that statue had fallen and broken? And those other children . . ."

"I know. I definitely hadn't planned on all of that. I made a mistake. I'm trying to fix it." My fingers are bound up in the shirt. I let them loose and meet my mom's eyes. "Um, but, I guess I thought . . . the religion we've always practiced as a family—the kind you've taught us—has been kind and welcoming and compassionate. I think our version of Mary and Jesus would want everyone to know they're loved and that they belong. I wasn't trying to be disrespectful. I was trying to make *everyone* feel respected."

I see a small shift in one of her eyebrows. It rises—just a touch—out of the frown.

"I love that!" my sister practically shouts, which startles my mother out of her frown completely. I shoot Kendra a grateful look. She grins back at me, then at my mom.

My mother definitely isn't grinning, but her demeanor seems to have shifted as well. "Hmm. I still don't like all this sneaking around. It's not like you. You need to refocus on what matters." She pauses and tilts her head a little. "Understood?"

I know she wants me to just agree and move on, but I can't. "But this *is* something that matters. To me, anyway. I've been letting other things slip—I know that—and obviously I'm not going to sneak around anymore. But I'm not going to stop working on this, either." Amma's eyebrows pop up at my defiance. I quickly add, "Dr. Ida said she would even try to help!"

"And what are you going to do about your behavior and mood?"

Oh boy. "What do you mean?" I keep my voice calm—I'm tired of fighting.

"Staying out later, faltering in church, exploding at the dinner table?"

I take a breath. "I guess I've been a little stressed lately. And tired."

"And staying out late helps with your stress and exhaustion?"

I can see Kendra roll her eyes as she folds, and it actually helps me stay calm.

"I think—I think I just need to let loose a little and have fun sometimes. I'm trying to figure out how to be all the things you want me to be and also be all the things *I* want myself to be. But . . . it's hard. And things have felt a bit . . . messy for me lately.

I promise to balance things out a bit more, though. School is still important to me. So is church. I promise."

It's going to take me some time to figure all that out, but I already feel so much lighter after being honest with Ben and Dr. Ida. I know things won't be *easy*, but I don't think they'll be as hard, either.

"I see," she says. Her folding hands grow still, and she gazes at me. "Your father and I just want you to be happy, you know that?" Her voice is serious, but her eyes are soft.

"Yes, I know."

"Maybe it will help to talk to Father Davis? Or we could go to confession tomorrow?"

"Um . . . maybe. I'm not sure yet." I decide now's not the time to tell her that if I were going to talk to anyone right now, it would probably be a counselor, not God or one of his disciples. Not that I'm done talking to God—I think I just need some coping strategies and professional guidance more than I need scripture or Hail Marys at this stage. But one thing at a time with my mom.

She nods slowly. "Okay. But . . . you'll let me know if things get too . . . messy again?" She looks at Kendra. "Both of you?"

Kendra nods. I say, "Yes."

"Okay." She nods once like that's that and goes back to folding. "You're still grounded. Now start folding."

Kendra and I share incredulous looks with each other as I pick up a sweater.

CHAPTER FORTY-EIGHT

That evening, I write a message to the Crosswalk group chat.

> **Cassie:** Hey everyone. I really messed up. I don't know how to explain why I did what I did, but there's no excuse for everything I've done anyway. I'm just really sorry for letting things go so wrong. And for hurting people. I promise to do better. I really am sorry.

I don't tell them about talking to Dr. Ida. Taking responsibility for the pop-ups was the least I could do. A bare minimum.

The chat remains silent, save for a few typing dots from Sam that eventually subside. The silence brings back some of that rotten, mucky feeling. I guess it will be hard to tease apart that feeling and the parts of me I thought were wrapped up with it. I have to be patient with myself, I know, but I'm not great at that. Yet.

I stare at my phone for a few more minutes, hoping to see something from someone. But there's nothing. I throw it in my side table and refocus. Ben's coming over to prepare for our presentation tomorrow. At least I have that and him.

When he arrives, we hunker down in my room and go over our material. He doesn't ask me about the other stuff, which I appreciate at the moment. He makes suggestions for our presentation that I hadn't even thought of, and we make the changes. After the past few days, the bio project feels like a relatively insignificant blip on my radar, but after my chat with Amma, I also don't want to blow it entirely.

Once we've figured out as much as we can, it's almost eight o'clock.

"Do you need to go to bed now?" Ben asks, a smirk on his cheeky face.

"What if I do?"

"Yeah, you look like you need it."

I roll my eyes. "Ass."

He gets up from the floor where he's been sitting for the past hour and strolls over to my desk, then casually begins rearranging my very carefully organized stationery and books. I'm on my bed, watching. Loving and hating that he's doing this.

"What's going on with the group and pop-ups and stuff?" he asks now, as he mixes my highlighters with my ballpoint pens like a monster. Ben's not in the group chat yet. He said he's "not really into that."

The brief reprieve from thinking about the unresponsive group chat ends with his question. "Not much," I say. "I apologized."

He looks up at me but starts shifting papers around with his hand. "And?"

"And . . . nothing. No response. I didn't really expect one, though."

"Yeah. But you said what you needed to say."

"Yeah."

"Time and all."

"Yeah."

"So . . . I guess you're not going to the meeting tomorrow, then?"

"No. Halle said not to anyway. I get it."

He nods, looks back at the desk, and starts flicking an eraser around its surface.

"Are you going?" I ask, trying very hard to ignore his obvious attempts to rile me up.

"I might. That cool with you?"

"Oh my God—of course. Why wouldn't it be?"

"It was kind of your thing."

"It's not. It's supposed to be a thing for everyone. If you like it, you should go. I want you to. But you should let Sam know you're into girls, maybe?" I say, teasing.

He flicks the eraser again. Smiles. "They know. We already covered that. We're friends."

"Oh. That's awesome. Sam's awesome."

"So is Halle."

I frown a little, but try not to react too much. "Okay . . ."

"Just saying."

"What're you just saying?" My heartbeat quickens.

"You're not ready for all that, huh?"

"Not ready for . . . ?"

He looks up again and stares me dead in the eyes. "Cassie."

Right. Just say the thing. I sigh. "I don't know. Sometimes I get excited about the idea of being with someone . . . like, romantically, even if I was trying really hard to *not* think about it. And I like Halle. A lot. Even if she kind of pushes my buttons. But other times the thought of expressing that side of me freaks me the hell out. Like, before, it just felt impossible. Now . . . it feels more possible, but still fucking scary."

"Whoa, Perera with an f-bomb for the win!" Ben says, grinning at me, which makes me smile again. His grin softens. "I'm sorry. That must suck."

I shrug. Then I want to take the shrug back. "It *does* suck. I want to kiss a girl so bad!" Even though the words make my gut ache with the yearning of them, I'm also laughing at how good it feels to say them out loud to someone.

Ben laughs, too. "I don't blame you. Kissing girls is fun."

We make plans to get to class the next day a little early to set up, Ben promises to fill me in on the meeting tomorrow, and then he pulls out all of my desk drawers to varying degrees like a jerk and leaves.

But at least he leaves me smiling.

After he's gone, and after I've placed everything back to its correct position on my desk, I open the drawer to my side table—tentative, like my phone might actually just scream, "They hate you now! Give up!"

But when I check my messages, there's at least a small hint that this isn't true—a separate message from Cameron.

Cameron: Dr. Ida called my parents today. She said you took full responsibility for all the pop-ups? She said all our teachers would be notified and we'd get extra time to make up anything we missed during our suspension. Thank you for doing that, Cassie.

Cassie: You don't have to thank me, Cameron. I owed it to you. I'm so sorry for getting you in trouble.

Cameron: I forgive you.

And then a few seconds later:

Cameron: But is it wrong that I kind of liked being bad?

Crosswalk Meeting Minutes: Oct. 28

**Minutes are strictly confidential to Crosswalk members. No sharing without agreement from all members.*

**Notetaker: Cameron K (in lieu of Cassie P)*

- Check-ins and pronouns
- Topic: Pronouns & Neopronouns
- Halle gives us a "Pronouns 101" overview (see slideshow linked below for more info).
- Definition of neopronouns: words that are created or repurposed to use as pronouns but that don't express gender (e.g., ze, zir, vamp, vampself)
- Possibly originated on Tumblr?
- Questions: Are there limits as to how "creative" or alternative pronouns can be? Should society be expected to accommodate every kind of pronoun? Could this be a way for people to break out of the "gender box"?
- Key points:
  - Respect a person's pronouns!
  - A person's pronouns can change over time or even from one moment to the next.
  - Only a small percent of people intentionally misuse pronouns (e.g., to make fun of pronouns).
  - If you make a mistake: say sorry, do better.
  - Offering your own pronouns can sometimes help others to offer theirs. **No one should be

pressured to give theirs, though.**

- Any other business?
  - Nai: "Pop-up safe spaces" at St. Luke's still happening?
    - » Halle: Suggests we take a break.
  - Halloween fun?
    - » Bonfire at Tansi's on Saturday night! All are welcome. Tansi will message the group chat with more info.

Reading the meeting minutes on Thursday night gives me major FOMO. Ben makes good on his promise to give me his own update, though. He actually *calls me.*

"You were a hot topic tonight," he says.

"What? Why?"

"Nicky and Cameron told us what you did, taking all the blame for the pop-ups. Why didn't you tell me that yesterday?"

I shrug, even though he can't see me. "Didn't feel the need to broadcast it, I guess."

"Well, that's a switch."

I deserve that. "Jerk."

"Takes one to know one."

We're silent for a few seconds.

"Um, so . . ." I start.

"Oh, right! I guess you want to know how people reacted to the news?"

Jackass.

"Ben."

I can practically hear him grinning over the phone.

"Rest assured, the news was well received. People thought it was pretty cool you took full responsibility, even though you weren't the only one involved, obviously. I think it's somewhat sort of cool, too, I guess."

A small amount of relief settles into my chest. "What about . . . ?"

"She was a little harder to read. Sorry."

"Right," I say, knowing this makes sense, but still feeling shitty about it.

"But the general sentiment seemed to be good old-fashioned forgiveness with a side of 'We hope she comes back,'" Ben says, trying to cheer me up.

And it does, at least a little.

Crosswalk Group Chat:

Tansi: Bonfire at my place! 🎃🔥🔥🔥

Tansi: 2892 alexandra st anytime after 8

Tansi: COSTUMES

Tansi: the gayer the better 🧚

Sam: sweeeeet

Cameron: Are grade 8s allowed?

Sam: 😳

Tansi: OF COURSE Cameron! ur one of us, silly

Cameron: 🙋

Nai: Can we bring anything?

Tansi: byob (or not). I'll have snacks and pop

Halle: Dibs on gay dracula

Jay: newsflash sis - dracula's already gay

Sam: 🤭

Halle: gay-ER Dracula then

Jay: 🧛+💅👠👑

Halle: 🤘

Lou: can't wait! See u all there!

CHAPTER FORTY-NINE

Crosswalk Founding Members Group Chat:

Nai: Hey team. Maybe we should all get together and talk about stuff?

Halle: like?

Nai: I think we need some kind of open conversation about how to move forward after everything with the last pop-up.

Sam: I'm game! I miss our Cassie!

Halle: not ready sorry

Halle: but u all go ahead if u want

Nai: That's fair.

Sam: Cassie? Can u meet up tomorrow?

I'm ecstatic that Nai is reaching out, but I don't know how to respond to the chat with Halle there and clearly not ready to hear from me. So I message Nai and Sam separately.

Cassie: I can meet up tomorrow after school. Do you want to come to our library?

Cassie: Also, thanks for being willing to talk to me.

Sam: OBVS

Nai: Sounds good, Cassie. See you then.

The consequences for my part in the pop-ups included an in-school suspension on Thursday and Friday, except that Dr. Ida gave me permission to attend bio class for the presentation, which had gone well overall. We kind of fumbled through the engagement activity I'd planned, because I was a little out of sorts from the suspension and didn't set up the prompts properly, but Ben and I both really knew our stuff and answered the class's questions like pros.

I'd spent the rest of Thursday and Friday in the library, which was basically a gift, not a punishment, but admin didn't need to know that. It even gave me and Mr. Reyes a chance to search out and order more queer books.

Though Mrs. Keenan had continued to poke her nose into the library to see if any more rainbow stickers managed to find their way back onto the books there, her quest fell apart after I told Dr. Ida I was behind the stickers and then explained to her how important those stories are for the kids here—especially since we don't have much else that acknowledges the existence of those experiences and identities. Dr. Ida spoke with Mr. Reyes and put him in charge of deciding on the "developmental accessibility" of the texts in the library. I *wish* I'd seen the look on Mrs. Keenan's face when Dr. Ida told her this.

Dr. Ida said we should be ready for some pushback, but if Mr. Reyes and I were willing to do some research and put together some arguments for diverse books, she would be willing to use those arguments if it came to that.

By Friday afternoon, we had a list of about thirty books that Mr. Reyes promised to buy over the course of the year, and I would keep adding the rainbow stickers to them.

So by the time Sam and Nai showed up, I was in a pretty good mood for someone who'd just spent the last two days suspended and who could probably have used the time in the library better to catch up on homework.

Once I'd met them at the entrance, brought them back to the library, and introduced them to Mr. Reyes, we settled into the cozy chairs and couch near the back. I'd been nervous, but both

Sam and Nai gave me big hugs when they saw me, which made me feel a lot better.

"This library is adorable," Sam says, settling in beside me on the couch.

I kick my school shoes off and bring my feet up on the cushion. "I know, I love it."

"How are you?" Nai asks from the chair across from me, her eyes as kind as ever.

"Okay. Better. It's been a week, that's for sure," I say. "Thanks again for being so open to talking with me."

"Of course, babe! We all fuck up," Sam says, and then covers their mouth and glances around. "Oops."

"It's fine. The librarian here is amazing." I add, "And this *was* a pretty big fuckup. Several, actually."

"True," Nai says, "and some folks are probably going to take a little time to get past it"—we both know who she's talking about—"but I think that's because she just really cares about you." She gives me a little smile.

"Or *cared*, at least," I say, giving her a sad smile back.

Sam puts a hand on my knee. "Still cares. You know how protective she is about her safe spaces."

I wonder if Nai and Sam know the whole reason behind whatever Halle's feeling about me right now. If Halle told them about liking me. Or about thinking—knowing—that I like her. All I say at the moment, though, is "I get it."

"But," Sam continues, "my new bestie Ben might have helped you out last night!"

"What do you mean?"

"He stayed for a bit after the meeting and said some really awesome things about you. I think it helped give a bit more context."

Oh God. "Like what?"

"Just a bit about the expectations you've grown up with. How important it is for you to make your parents proud. But also that you've been trying really hard to make things right," Nai says. "It's one of the reasons I reached out to you yesterday. That and just because we love you." She winks at me.

Her wink and words make me blush. I struggle against the urge to tell myself I don't deserve either and win in the end. "Thank you" is all I say.

"So! What next?" Sam asks.

They look at me for the answer. "I mean, I'd love to come back to Crosswalk, when everyone's okay with it. And when I'm not grounded anymore," I say, smiling.

"We'd like that, too," Nai says.

Sam suddenly sits up and grabs my arm. "In the meantime, you should come to Tansi's party!"

"Oh. I mean, that would be cool. But . . . there's that whole grounded thing . . . and won't Halle be there?" But in my mind, I'm already thinking of how I could convince my mom to let me do this one thing.

"Well, I can't help you with the grounding part, but I officially invite you! The party isn't a Crosswalk event, technically, and Tansi said to invite whomever. And I'll talk to Halle, don't worry," Sam assures me.

I *do* worry, but I'm also full of excitement. After this week, I'd love to go to a party with this group of people and just have some fun.

"Um, okay. But I'll need to figure my mom out. Can I let you know?"

Sam squeals semi-quietly because of where we are. "Obviously!"

I spend the rest of the evening when I get home convincing Amma over Chinese food that this party is essential for my mental health. She's not really convinced by that part, but like some kind of saintly miracle, she lets me go after I promise to clean both bathrooms, take my sister to her soccer game on Saturday, be wide awake for church, and spend all of Sunday afternoon in my room studying. And be home on time, of course.

"No sneaking in through windows ever again, Cassie."

And with this reasonable request, I'm good to go.

CHAPTER FIFTY

Ben agrees to go to the party with me, which makes things a thousand times easier. Most of the Crosswalk crew is there by the time we arrive. Tansi's backyard is essentially a wide-open field with several derelict cars sitting around the edge, a large brick building in one corner, and all manner of machinery parked in various spots. The bonfire is raging just in front of a small house at the edge of the field, which must be where Tansi lives.

All kinds of seating surround the fire, and strings of outdoor lights travel from one structure to the next. Some Halloween decorations—bats and witches and spiders—hang from the bare branches of a tree next to the house, punctuated by red lights.

As Ben and I appear around an ancient truck, a few people turn to look at who it is.

I wave a little hello, still nervous about approaching this group of people who saw me throw two of them under the bus and who

I've also been lying to about my own identity—even if they don't know about that part yet.

But then Sam squeals and flings the plastic spider they're holding behind them as they rush toward me, a long black wig flowing behind them. "Babe! I'm so glad you're here." When they gather me up in a huge hug, I feel it right down to my toes. Then they lean back and glance behind me at Ben. In a quasi-whisper, they say, "And you brought Ben—ooh la la!"

"Sam, he's—"

"Into girls—I know, I know. But I can still appreciate, can't I?" They wink at me and go to greet Ben with a warm hug, leaving me shaking my head but smiling.

I walk over to the rest of the group standing next to the bonfire. Muriel flings herself into me to give me a tight hug and yells, "Forgiveness is super Catholic, right? Well, we forgive you and love you!" She's dressed as the Corpse Bride and I see Quinn is Bonejangles (I only know this because Kendra made me watch the movie with her two Halloweens ago).

I notice Nicky over her shoulder, sipping on a drink. We make eye contact, and she gives me a small chin lift. She doesn't seem entirely happy with me, but I get it. She came through when I couldn't, and then got in trouble for it. I'd have to re-earn her trust. I give her a small smile back.

Muriel releases me, and I am subsequently greeted by everyone else there—including Cameron, who gives me the most awkward side-hug, but seems in his element as Tickle Me Elmo. The whole gang's here now, except Halle, I realize, which causes my heart to sink a little. I still have no idea how she feels, beyond what Sam and Nai told me. I take a deep breath and try to get back to the people who *are* here, though.

"Tansi, this is a perfect place for a bonfire," I say. Tansi and Jesse are snuggling on a log, lit by the glow of flames, and appearing very adorable in their Bert and Ernie costumes.

"Yeah, spooky, right? Like all these cars might come alive and attack us or something." They're both grinning, but that sounds terrifying to me.

Over the next half hour, more people arrive—strangers to me, but all seem to know Tansi and some of the others from Pinetree. I know enough now not to assume anything about anyone's sexuality, but based on Tansi's "the gayer the better" costume instructions, and the general "vibe" of the folks who arrive, I'm guessing they're all either queer or queer-friendly. The whole crowd feels very safe and fun, especially when Sam and Lou start up with some Halloween-themed games. I'm quickly immersed in playful renditions of *Fear Factor* and *Truth or Scare.*

We're all losing our minds as Lou tries to do her best impression of Winifred from *Hocus Pocus* when I see Halle. She's just arrived and is standing next to some kind of digger machine. As mentioned in the group chat, she's dressed in a Dracula costume—but gay. Purple cape over a burgundy velour suit and ruffly shirt. Hair slicked back but also dyed purple. Sparkly Doc Martens. I imagine there are fangs in her mouth, but immediately try to stop thinking about her mouth.

She catches me looking at her and smushes her lips to one side.

I'm not sure what the smush means, but at least it's not a glare.

I want so badly to talk to her, even if I'm scared to, but I also want to give her space. I swallow back my yearning (for now) and watch as she greets everyone with hugs and waves. After more rounds of *Truth or Scare*, the circle starts to break up into smaller clusters.

Halle takes a seat a little ways from the bonfire and the commotion, on what looks like a back seat that's been removed from a car. She's staring up at all the Halloween decorations in the tree above her.

Ben is in my cluster of people and sees me looking. "You could just test the waters. See if she's open to talking. And then awkwardly slink away if she's not." He's smirking.

"You make it sound so easy and pleasant."

He gives me a little nudge.

I rub my face, gather up some courage, and walk over to her.

"Hey," I say, standing in front of her.

She turns her face to mine and responds with a very neutral "Hey."

"Can I sit with you for a minute?"

She gives me nothing for a full five seconds, then shrugs.

I hesitate, but then sit down beside her. Not too close. Not too far.

I lean my shoulder against the back of the seat and face her. She shifts so she's facing me, too, which feels like a win.

"I just"—I look away for a second because she's watching me so intently like she does, but I force myself to look back—"I owe you an apology. And an explanation, if you're willing to hear me out? I'd understand if you're not."

She shrugs again. "It's fine."

I swallow. "I'm really sorry, Halle—for giving you such confusing signals and then just shutting you out when you tried to talk to me about it."

Halle's eyes water, which surprises me, but she doesn't say anything.

"I've been such a mess . . . trying to do the right thing but not even knowing what that really means. The thing is, I only started the GSA and pop-ups to impress Ben—because I messed up my friendship with him a while back, too. I was just trying to make myself feel better—to prove I wasn't a shitty person. But then—you all made me excited to be a part of the group, and working on the pop-ups with *you* made me genuinely want those safe spaces for kids at St. Luke's—and for me."

Her eyebrows lift ever so slightly at this last part. I adjust my school tie—a last-minute attempt at a costume—and continue.

"You're so fierce and strong in your beliefs. And so *you*. You . . . pushed me in a way that felt scary as hell but also necessary. I didn't like it all the time—sometimes it felt like too much for where I was at, for how I was feeling about myself. But other times, I *did* like it. I wanted to give in so badly to the feelings I was having. But it felt impossible."

My heart is thudding against my chest. *Whew. You got this, girl.*

"What I'm *saying* is, I *do* like you. Like, *like* you. But I had no idea what to do with that because I've been lying to myself for so long. I was too scared to face up to my feelings about you."

I want to reach out and take her hand, but instead I place my hand flat on the small space between us.

"I just wanted to say I'm sorry in person. For lying to you. And for hurting you. I know I broke your trust."

She's quiet for a moment, her eyes set in a soft gaze at my chin. My hand retreats back into my lap, but I keep my own gaze on her.

"That must've been hard to say out loud," she finally responds. "I'm not going to lie—feeling like I got you so wrong really pissed me off—I was mad at you *and* at myself."

My chest tightens.

"But," she continues, "it's also been really easy for me to be myself. People didn't judge me the way they judged Jay, my mom has always accepted us, and I don't have a whole religion to contend with. So I get it. Or I'm trying to. Sometimes we do shitty things when we can't be ourselves. Or when we don't let ourselves be ourselves."

"But that still doesn't make what I did right—and I'm sorry. I really am."

She nods.

We continue to meet each other's eyes for a few moments.

Then, because I'm the queen of interrupting nice moments, I say, "I also thought that maybe . . . you and Nicky . . . ?"

"Nicky! No—we aren't—she's just a friend. I think she wanted more, but I liked *you*. But you were . . . straight." She rolls her eyes.

I shake my head at myself. "What a mess."

We listen to Hayley Kiyoko sing about demons for a bit. I know it's Hayley Kiyoko because I know gay things now.

After a while, I say, "So—do you think we could try . . . um, hanging out? I'm not sure what I'm ready for yet. I might just need to go reaaalllyyyy slow."

She smiles again. "Yeah, we can try that."

She lays her open hand out in front of her and tilts her head at me, and I find it so easy to place my hand on hers for a few moments.

Our hands still together, she asks, "So, do you think you'll tell the rest of the group? About you?"

"You mean, will I tell the group that I've been faking straight while starting a GSA because I've been too scared of God and my parents and the universe to be gay?"

We grin at each other. "Yeah, that," she says.

"I want to. I wanted to tonight, actually. But there are so many other people here . . ." I glance over to the bonfire and the crowd around it.

"You don't have to rush it."

"Yeah . . . but I really want them to know. They're a big reason I'm even able to tell *anyone* now."

She squeezes my hand. "If you really want to, let's make it happen. But only if you *really* want to. Do you?"

Her hand in mine feels so, so good.

"I do." *I really do.*

She grins again and looks around her. After a moment, she says, "Wait over there in the back of that truck." She points toward a truck with no wheels that's a few feet away from us. The flat part at the back is decorated with a string of pumpkin-shaped lights. Her hand leaves mine and she's off, fast walking toward the crowd.

I climb into the truck and sit with my back against the cab. Tansi's tucked an old rug into the truck bed, and the lights make this derelict vehicle less scary. I watch as Halle casually whispers to the Crosswalk crew and indicates where I am. As she does, I try to breathe through the jitters forming in my stomach.

I hadn't exactly pictured myself coming out to the group in the back of a rusty, Halloween-themed truck, but in a few minutes, that's exactly what's happening. Everyone's here, including Ben, even though he already knows.

Once we're all squeezed in next to each other—Halle right beside me—Muriel announces, "Impromptu Crosswalk meeting! I love it!"

"What's up, Cassie? Halle said you have something to tell us?" Nai asks.

"You're not leaving the group, are you?" Sam asks. "I won't allow it!"

Everyone's looking at me now, but it's fine. I can do this. I want to do this.

I clear my throat. "I wanted to tell you that . . . I'm not straight. I'm queer, too. I've just been too scared to face it. And say it. I'm not ready to share beyond this group, but I'm sorry for lying to you all. And for letting my fear make me act like such a coward."

"OH. MY. GOD." This is Sam.

Muriel lets out a squeal that I'm sure causes permanent ear damage to Quinn, who's sitting beside her.

Nai grins so widely at me I can't help but grin back.

Ben is just smirking at me like a brat.

And I can feel Halle beside me, leaning in just the right amount.

"Thanks for telling us, Cassie," Nai says.

"Yeah, girl, that must've been hard," Sam adds.

"I knew it!" Cameron says, and everyone bursts out laughing.

There's a flurry of questions that I try to answer as best I can, but eventually, Halle tells everyone to chill out, and Tansi has to go back to hosting her party, and we all climb out of the truck and wander back to the bonfire.

I feel different, though. Lighter. My stomach is still wobbly, but Halle is holding my hand and that steadies me a little. I spend the rest of the night relieved and laughing and warm by the fire.

CHAPTER FIFTY-ONE

Ben: wanna meet up before crosswalk tonight?

Cassie: Sounds good. 6:40 at our corner?

Ben: sure. Sam'll be with me

Cassie: Well aren't you two cozy.

Ben: besties, actually. they don't abandon me at creeks.

I freeze for a second. This is one of his many playful digs, I know, but despite all my progress over the past week, my mistakes are still very real for me, and this reminder still makes my heart skip. I calm myself down enough to respond:

Cassie: They might if they get to know you better

Ben: lolllllll

His "lol" makes me happier than it probably should.

Ben: see u there jerkface

Cassie: For sure, dum dum!

This banter hasn't gotten old for me yet. It's been almost a week since the party, and my mom has eased up enough on my restrictions that I'm allowed to go to my "evening class," as long as I don't "dawdle" afterward. I'm still lying to her about where I actually am, of course, but I feel like this is one of those necessary lies. The kind whose benefits outweigh the negatives.

When Ben saunters up with Sam, it's 6:50 and I give him heck for it. He and Sam smirk at each other, and I have to refrain from making it mean anything terrible about me.

Sam keeps us entertained as we walk over, and as we head into the building, Ben asks, "You think you'll ever get a room aboveground or something?"

"Yeah, our big goal is to have a window," Sam says, laughing.

"But in the meantime, this is kind of cool, no?" I say. Though I'm feeling hopeful about the situation with Dr. Ida and the school, I'm also grateful for this little group and our secret, but safe space.

"Yeah. I mean, it's no hidey-hole in the creek bank, but it's fine," Ben says, and the fact that he invoked our hidey-hole gives me a superfluous (SAT word) amount of glee.

So I'm already grinning when I walk into the room. But then my grin falls into surprise. Everyone is already there, and Lady Gaga is playing, and rainbow balloons adorn the lockers, and there's an array of gaz and toot and other treats on a table against the wall.

What the . . . ?

Sam yells, "Surprise! It's your secret coming-out party!"

"We had to make sure you didn't get here too early, like the nerd you are," Ben adds.

My eyes widen and my mouth opens.

"Uh . . ." I really don't know what to say. My feelings are all over the place. Warmth. Nervousness. Shock. Overwhelm.

Luckily, Muriel always has words. "You're queer! And my crush asked me out! And we're together! So much to celebrate, right?" She clasps her hands at her chest and looks about ready to combust.

"Um . . . right," I say, because it's hard not to agree with her.

"Get in here, already!" Nai says, turning down the music. "Let's do check-ins first—I want to hear about what's going on at St. Luke's!"

I'd shared a little with Ben, Sam, Nai, and Halle about my discussion with Dr. Ida, but I give everyone the full version now.

"You think she'll really follow through?" Halle says. She's sitting beside me, her knee finally overlapping *my* thigh. Since the party on Saturday night, she and I have hung out almost every day, even if it's just a few minutes at lunch to walk through the neighborhood around St. Luke's and Pinetree. I'm still not quite ready to hold her hand in public, but just being around her with this new truth between us feels more intimate than holding hands anyway.

"I don't know," I say. "I hope so. But I think I got through to her—with honesty. She seemed to get it."

Halle considers me closely, then nods and smiles. My whole body tingles. "That's cool, Cass. I'm proud of you."

I'm proud of me, too, to be honest.

A lot has happened in the past few days, and I am definitely not perfectly at ease with how many people know I'm queer, or how the consequence of all my emoting over these last weeks has been a clear, slippery slope to low As and probably even some B and C work, but I'm in this safe space with a bunch of people who actually know more of me than most, and who don't seem to mind my messiness. And though things still feel fast and uncertain, I've been able to find some stillness in the rush. My feet feel firmly planted.

"Yeah, that's amazing, Cassie," Jay says. "And what about the pop-ups? Are you going to keep doing them?"

I glance at Cameron, who grins at me. He's sitting next to Yumi, who he's brought to Crosswalk for the first time. "Yup!" he says. "Cassie and I are still going to make sure there are queer books with rainbow stickers in the library!"

"Yeah, and Mr. Reyes, our librarian, is going to bring in a bunch more queer books. There'll be rainbow stickers all over the place,"

I add, grinning back at Cameron. I'd already reached out to him about the books, hoping to make up for my poor showing with him and Yumi that day in the library. Cleaning up after myself was taking a lot of time and effort, but every bit seemed worth it.

"Yeah, *and*," Nicky pipes up, "the 'Wall of Fabulousness' is still up in the theater—no one wants to take it down, and our drama teacher thinks it's 'glorious.'" Nicky's still a little cool around me, but her recent run-in with admin seems to have lit a fire under her butt.

"*And*," I add, "if you peek behind Mary, Mother of God, she's hiding a whole bunch of cute messages on the back of her robe."

Muriel lets out a frenzied scream, and we all stop to look at her.

"Are you . . . okay?" Nai asks, genuine concern on her face.

"I JUST CAN'T HANDLE ALL THIS CUTE GAY-NESSSSSS!" she continues to scream, and the rest of us dissolve into laughter.

"This is the perfect time to get our party on, people!" Sam yells.

Like she's time-jumped or something, Muriel appears in front of me and throws a rainbow boa around my neck. Sam hits play on their phone and launches into a high-pitched rendition of "I'm Coming Out," which booms out of a speaker in the corner. Everyone sings along.

The old Cassie worries that someone will hear us, that we'll get busted and shut down. The new(ish) Cassie is thrilled that everyone here knows I'm queer and is celebrating it loudly.

When the sing-along ends, Sam continues to play super-gay music, and people even start dancing. Sam's finally getting their night at "the club," I realize, and smile to myself.

After a couple of songs, Halle takes my hand and leads me out into the hallway.

"I have something for you," she says. She hands me a little box wrapped in tissue paper that has tiny unicorns all over it. "It's nothing fancy." Her cheeks grow pink and it's so endearing, and I can't wait until I'm comfortable enough to do something about it.

For now, I open the gift to find a necklace—a small cross beaded with rainbow colors, attached to a chain.

"I picked out the materials and whatnot, but Jay made it. I don't know the first thing about beading. I thought you could wear it without anyone really seeing it if you don't want them to."

My eyes well up. "This is really special, Halle."

"I wasn't sure where you were at—with things." I know she means being queer and Catholic. "I still think the Catholic Church has a lot of work to do, and I'm sure we're gonna fight about it at least a couple times a week . . . but I hope you're able to find a way through that works for you. I was hoping this necklace might help."

Lord. This girl. My chest swells. "I'm still figuring things out, but I think you're right—this will help. And all of that, of course," I add, indicating the room filled with our friends. "Can you?" I hold up the necklace.

She grins and takes it. I turn and let the good shivers run across my skin as she clasps the chain at the base of my neck.

When I turn, I start to say, "Um, could I—"

But before I can finish asking, her arms wrap around my waist and my arms are around her shoulders. The feelings in my chest and head and stomach are proof to me that this thing I've been hiding for far too long belongs inside of me. For the first time, it doesn't terrify me. And I realize, I *am* ready to do something about it.

I pull back but stay close. I let my hands rest at Halle's neck. Her hands are still around my waist. Neither of us is going anywhere.

I lick my lips and look at hers, then back to her eyes, which are waiting for me to make the call.

It's not a perfect kiss. I'm nervous and tentative and maybe a little fumbly. But we giggle and smile into the space between us after and that feels perfect enough.

When Halle and I come back into the room, the party is in full force, and I see, with an enormous amount of shock, that Ben is in the middle of the group, performing several break-dancing moves as everyone cheers him on. Watching him so loose and laughing as he dances, I wonder if these people are still his people, even if he's not queer.

Muriel soon joins in, because of course she knows how to breakdance.

I notice Cameron and Yumi getting cozy on the couch, and my heart squeezes so tight I think I might die right then and there.

Nai is rearranging the gaz and toot and grinning at the dancers.

Jesse and Tansi are slow dancing in a corner even though it's a fast song, and Lou and Quinn have their arms across each other's shoulders, cheering Muriel and Ben on.

Sam looks like they were trying to find the next song on their phone, but they've frozen mid-search, mouth open and eyes transfixed on Ben.

I don't know what will happen at St. Luke's with the GSA. Maybe Dr. Ida will come through, maybe she won't. Maybe a GSA won't happen until after I've graduated. Maybe a secret GSA isn't ideal—we shouldn't have to hide out in a basement room to do and be all the things I'm seeing in front of me right now.

But I'm not mad about the scene before me. Everything about this feels good. *I* feel good. Maybe not perfect, or together, or even right. But if it weren't for these folks, this room, these Thursday nights, I wouldn't be standing here, still and sure and ready to be more myself than I've ever been.

EPILOGUE

Dear Dr. Ida,

High school is the perfect place to feel alone. No matter how hard you try to fit in, or how well you actually fit in, there will always be something different about you. Something messy. When you're a kid, more often than not, you think that different really means "less than." Growing up means embracing these differences—seeing them as a beautiful part of you and not some detached parasite that you can't shake. But this is no easy process, especially when others tell you the same things that run wild in your head: that you are innately *wrong* because you are you. Besides, even when you come to the conclusion that you are perfect in all your messiness, whether at the start of high school or fifty years down the road, you will always need a support system that embraces you. That celebrates you. That reminds you how beautiful you really are.

That's what GSAs are all about. They are about pushing people toward acceptance and love, encouraging them to explore and celebrate their unique identities. They bring together communities of people with shared experiences, spreading queer joy. So many people, students and adults alike, need this space. I sure do.

Thanks for listening,

A St. Luke's Student

To whoever needs to hear this:

The GSA at my old school provided me with excellent treats and snacks to steal during my many AP Euro prison breaks. More than anything, though, it was a warm, caring, and overall comforting environment. It was a promise that we queer folk have a place in this world and that we have each other; that we are a cemented group that cannot simply disappear. For many years I have been a proud representative of the plus in our lovely "LGBTQIA+" abbreviation. I'd be honored to be a part of a GSA at St. Luke's, to hear the voices of others, and to be able to openly love. The GSA is a constant reminder that one is loved.

Anonymous

To whom it may concern:

That Christianity condemns queerness is a theory at best. Where the 1946 Revised Standard Version of the Bible translates Leviticus 18:22 to "you shall not lie with a male as with a woman; it is an abomination," German Bibles of the nineteenth century translate the passage to "man shall not lie with young boys as he does with a woman, for it is an abomination." Where the 1946 RSV translates the Greek word "arsenokoitai" to "homosexuality" in 1 Corinthians 6:9, saying homosexuals will not "inherit the kingdom of God," Martin Luther's 1534 German version translates "arsenokoitai" to "knabenschander," boy molesters, meant to condemn pederasty, not homosexuality.[1]

The argument that the Bible forbids queerness is so young, yet persecution of queerness on the basis of the text is so widespread it's as if homophobia has been with Christianity since its founding. We may not know the precise meaning of Christianity's tenets at some places, but isn't that a chance for us to decide how we carry the religion forward? By denying St. Luke's a Gender and Sexuality Alliance, you choose an interpretation of Christianity charged with hatred over interpretations that advocate love and acceptance that this gap in knowledge offers.

I have thought for so long about what to put in this letter. I want to tell you that I considered opening with an apology: I am sorry to bring to your attention another queer person lurking in your school. I am sorry for intruding with what is certainly an unwelcome proposal. I even considered "I would say I'm sorry to ask of you a GSA, except I'm not sorry," yet in that attempt at irreverence, I have somehow apologized twice. And I suppose the fact that an apology came to me first when I thought of asking a Catholic school for a Gender and Sexuality Alliance is evidence enough for the necessity of its existence.

QPL (Queer Person Lurking)

---

1 www.forgeonline.org/blog/2019/3/8/what-about-romans-124-27

Dear Dr. Ida,

There is freedom in the lilting laughter that echoes down our hallways—into classrooms and cubicles and out into open air. I suppose laughter travels quickly because love always finds a way to evade the fickle facets of life: time and age, schedules and schooling. But where love is pursued, love is challenged. In the same hallways and classrooms that hair is braided and laughter echoes, there are slurs and degradations. It's then that the spaces we dedicate to inclusivity become havens. Because beyond the politicized presence and projected polarities, a GSA is not only a place where one can truly *be*—it is a place where one can *become.* Not "become" in the way that might suggest one might suddenly turn gay or trans or queer by the sprinkle of some mother-made home remedy. But rather "become" in the sense that a person might find comfort in who they are, find pride in what they stand for, and feel freer in how they love. Freedom fosters love, and love fosters communities of vibrancy and color. We are in a process of becoming, and the GSA is the site of this genesis. A place where hair is braided, laughter travels, and love is celebrated in all its forms: however messy, complicated, and imperfect it might be.

Sincerely,

A messy student

ACKNOWLEDGMENTS

I realized I write long acknowledgments, but writing books is a culmination of a lot of relationships, support, and learning, and I believe in gratitude!

As always, I am grateful for the land I live on—the unceded territories of the Musqueam, Squamish, and Tsleil-Waututh First Nations—as well as for the continued stewardship of these lands by Indigenous communities. I learn so much from the Indigenous storytellers around me, too, and I hope I do justice to their words and experiences in how I write, teach, and live here.

I'm also immensely grateful to my editor, Jennifer Ung, who saw something in my writing from the get-go and has made me feel like I have something to offer to readers ever since. Jen, I value your guidance and enthusiasm so much and was thrilled to place another book in your skilled, supportive hands.

To my agent, Jim McCarthy—I still can't believe I landed with you. Thank you for sticking with me through my hits and misses and continuing to provide key insight into books and the business!

Thank you to the incredible folks at HarperCollins / Quill Tree who made this book happen: from copy editors to the publicity team and beyond, and to Isabel Ngo, who offered such helpful advice around Catholicism and queerness. And of course, to David DeWitt and Jeff Östberg, who created this delightful cover, which captures the precarious balancing act that Cassie and so many young people undertake in order to please others.

So much of my teaching life is wrapped up in this book, and so I owe an avalanche of thanks to some of my past and present colleagues and students.

My most valued counselor friends and GSA coconspirators, Joanne Darrell Herbert and Ly Hoang—you've provided me with both wisdom and support since the beginning, and I adore you. Our GSA wouldn't be where it is without you both. I wouldn't be where I am, either.

Anaheed Saatchi, thank you for talking me through some sticky (and tasty!) bits in the plot, but more importantly, for being the first kid who trusted me with parts of yourself that were still scary at the time. That lunchtime conversation when you were in the ninth grade and those adorable cue cards remain one of my most cherished moments as a teacher, and I continue to be so proud of you.

Because I teach brilliant humans, I asked four previous students to beta read this book for me—Sheba Duan, Ruby Harris, Isabella Demianczuk, and Sophie Abbott. Thank you for your incredible attention to detail and your honesty. All of your feedback—from your comments on social media, boys' haircuts, and kissing, to your sensitive thoughts on identity, to your attempts to correct my punctuation (!)—was both amusing and appreciated. I feel so lucky to have taught you and read your own incredible writing . . . including the four letters at the end of this book. I cry every time I read them, and I know they'll touch other readers, too. What important messages each one holds.

Thanks to my "biology consultants," Julia Fasseske and Becky Fellows, for making sure I didn't look like an ignorant English teacher who said farewell to science class after the tenth grade!

Thank you to the York House colleagues who have shown their consistent, dedicated commitment to creating safe and beautiful spaces for our kids.

And big shout-out to my SOGI (Sexual Orientation and Gender Identity) Lead team from other schools. You all have been a constant source of inspiration and support over the years as we try to build schools where kids can be their full selves. I'm so grateful for you.

A number of educators and students from Catholic schools gifted me with their time and experiences, as well—thank you to Paul Fraser, Maureen Wicken, Hailey Krueger, Mika Hamanishi, Pam, Sydney, and others who helped me gain some insight into what it's like for *some* students and staff at *some* Catholic schools. I appreciate your openness in speaking with me.

Shout-out, as well, to *all* educators, students, and parents doing that work, especially those in places where they're facing so much resistance, ignorance, and hate. I hope this book makes your work a little easier, somehow.

I learn so much about writing and life from my students, and so much inspiration from their courage. So, thanks to them, and to all the kids who helped our own GSA grow over the years. Your impact is bigger than any of us know.

Beyond teaching life, I have to shout out my favorite café writing spot for this book—Livia! When I lost Cafe Deux Soleils as my go-to writing nook, I was nothing short of forlorn. But thank goodness for this cozy, gluten-y space that fuels my writing with the best sourdough in town.

I also need to say a huge thank-you to Elana K. Arnold and her fabulous course, Vision Season, which led me to realize that two separate ideas about a childhood friendship and an underground GSA belonged in the same book. Elana, I value your insight and generosity so much.

And huge thanks to Elana (again), Katherena Vermette, and Robin Stevenson for being willing to read my book and say nice things about it. I am truly lucky to have such talented, generous writing friends like you.

Readers! Bless you for reading and listening to books. I value you.

And then there's family. Thank you, as always, for making me who I am. Growing up Catholic and queer was not all that fun. But, like Cassie, I also have joyful memories of our church community, and I'm especially grateful to my mum, Pamela Boteju, who moved her own personal mountains to prove that you can be

Catholic and still fully embrace queer people, including your own kid. Amma, you're a model I hope more people will follow, and I love you.

Finally and always, to my Jennifer, who's doing her own hard work of creating beautiful spaces for kids to be themselves in her classroom and school. Those kiddos are lucky to have you, just as I am. It's possible I could do this whole writing and teaching and living thing without you, but am I ever glad I don't have to.